Praise for *The Not Yet*

"This fully realized and expertly rendered vision of the future has much to show us about the here and now. *The Not Yet* is a provocative contemplation of what it means to live in a world of haves and have-nots, in which the desire for longevity and beauty has overtaken good sense and human longing matters even as it is thwarted. It is also a great story—the kind that keeps you up late because you want to know what happens."

—Elise Blackwell

"A vivid, suspenseful, and (literally) layered imagining of what's to become of New Orleans and humanity (a new kind of love?) in the Twenty-Second Century."

—Roy Blount Jr.

"New Orleans has always been an island, and in Moira Crone's new novel, *The Not Yet*, the island is literal and the city is flooded for eternity. New Orleans has always been a crossing of worlds visible and invisible, and in Crone's lyrical prose the intersection includes the future and aliens and transformations beyond our dreams. New Orleans has always signified decadence and death for our gothic region of the South, and Crone's story begins with a boatman ferrying something very much like a dead man into a place very much like the land of the dead. New Orleans has always created monsters, so why not Crone's race of Heirs, superbeings who hold Creoles and Cajuns as pets. To classify this novel in any way would detract from its ability to resonate on many levels, as myth, as high literature, as science fiction, as fantasy, with the hints of a graphic novel in the rich imagery and finely honed writing. Malcolm's odyssey, like a good gumbo, cannot be described but begs to be tasted. I have not read a more compelling novel in a very long time."

—Jim Grimsley

© Rodger Kamenetz

About the Author

*M*oira Crone is a fiction writer living in New Orleans. The author of three previous collections including *What Gets Into Us*, and a novel, *A Period of Confinement*, her works have appeared in *Oxford American*, *The New Yorker*, *Image*, *Mademoiselle*, and over forty other journals and twelve anthologies. She has won prizes for her stories and novellas, and in 2009, she was given the Robert Penn Warren Award from the Fellowship of Southern Writers for the entire body of her work.

Dear Kathy —
Hope you enjoy, with all my
love — M

The Not Yet

MOIRA CRONE

UNOPRESS

Printed in the United States of America

Moira Crone

The Not Yet

ISBN: 978-1-60801-072-1

Library of Congress Control Number: 2012931179

(Electronic Edition ISBN: 978-1-60801-077-6)

Copyright © 2012 by Moira Crone

Cover photo by the author
Cover design by Bill Lavender
Book Design: Allison Reu

unopress.org

University of New Orleans Press

Managing Editor: Bill Lavender

This book is dedicated to
Dr. Anna Lisa Crone, 1946-2009,
brilliant, engaged, very brave,
my big sister—always close, even now.

Eternity is in love with the productions of time.

—William Blake

"What are you, one of them, a Bonesnake?" she asked from the stage.

I was about to say, "I am Malcolm, a Not-Yet, one day I'll—"

But just at that moment, another fate rose up and sang to me.

First and Last

"*M*alcolm, I've called you in to tell you how things are," my guardian began in that voice they all had—full of sizzle, like a rattle. His eyes didn't blink, I noticed. I sat in front of him on a bench with a thick cushion and fat legs, my feet not touching the floor. It was his office in the old Audubon Foundling House, on the Islands of New Orleans. The lit sconces with half shades above our heads were giant fireflies to me. I asked them for help, maybe for strength. Could I be strong? I didn't know. This was the first time Lazarus had ever summoned me. I was only five, and I was shivering.

At dawn, the cook Marilee had awakened me with news of this meeting, said I needed to get ready. Instead of breakfast, she had made me drink a tumbler full of something foamy and yellow, which tasted like chalk. Half an hour later, my stomach exploded—fifteen runs to the bucket. She said that got rid of the worms. In the garden she poured kerosene on my head, then, a strange green oil. After, in the sunlight on the banks of the Old River, she combed out my nits. Finally, she led me to a room with a large stainless steel tub on a pedestal. It was a shock: I was used to being hosed down. She scrubbed me with stinky pine soap, washed my hair and rinsed it twice, lifted me out in a fluffy towel. She gave me new clothes which made me very proud: a collarless shirt and thin pants that fell past my knees. She'd sent me down the hall to my guardian's office, with my head still wet.

Lazarus noticed my teeth chattering. "I trust your ablutions were not too taxing?"

I didn't know how to answer.

"That Marilee was gentle?" He leaned back, and the slow, thick features of his padded face closed in. He was round-shouldered with a big head, his hands small. I stared at him, failed to speak.

"She praised you, said you were quite the little stoic, the silent type." He took a very long pause. My friend Ariel had told me, *you always have to wait when you talk to them. They are slow on purpose to drive us crazy.* "So, to begin. There are two kinds in this world, the lucky and the unlucky. The lucky have a Trust. If you don't build one you will have a hard, hard life—and it will end, like—" He tried to snap his fingers, but he couldn't, his overskin was too slick for that. For some reason he looked surprised. "Do you know what I mean when I say, *end*? Do you know about the unlucky? What happens to them?"

You were supposed to say, "The unlucky do the so-long goodbye." But the rough boys in the play yard chanted, *they dribble down the drain. They suck the black.* It was the most dirty, awful thing that could happen. "I know," was the first phrase I uttered. "It will never happen to me."

Lazarus was pleased. "Now, we can dream, the wise men say, but we can't observe eternity, so we shouldn't say *never*, but we can say, 'not for a very long time, a very long—'"

"Never!" I tossed my head, which somehow I knew he'd like.

"That's the spirit. That's the Promise of the Reveal, which is so far, being kept. We aren't supposed to tell our counts, but I'll do it: I'm approaching two hundred—do you realize how long that is?" He smiled, showed bluish teeth. "And this is all you have to know, for now: there are two kinds in this world, those who are certain they will not last, and those with wonderful lives, and every reason to hope for eternity, like me: we are Heirs, or for slang, 'T's,' for Treated. Now, we don't insult the unfortunates by calling them dirty Low Naturals, or Nats, or Lowns. We use their enclave names. *Free Wheelers, Chef Menteurians, Port Gramercerians,* and so on. Why add to their misery with cruel epithets?" (I didn't know what epithets were.) "And those with hope like me are the Treated ones who don't have to do that dirty awful thing, at least, not any time soon." (His laugh, a gush.) "We prefer to be called Heirs. The only difference between Nats and Heirs is the Trust. To be an Heir, you must be Treated, and to be Treated, you need a Trust. Money. And it's best to start building one as soon as you can." His face widened. "I've brought you in to say that you can begin today. The scouts from Celebration Sims picked you out. You have a role already! That's why we've cleaned you up. A marvelous opportunity. Don't let us down. Most of all, don't let yourself down!"

Just outside—footsteps. Lazarus looked up. "Come in."

When the door opened, a large man was standing there in a pale green cloud of a suit. He was fair skinned, with a black mustache. I wasn't sure if he were an Heir or not. I'd only seen a few. But when he came in and squatted down and touched my shoulder, I knew.

"Malcolm!" this stranger said, his voice deep. "I'm Jeremy. How are you?"

He was at my level and a little hilarious—besides the mustache, two very thick eyebrows made a big 'M' at the top of his face. His dark hair was thick and short. He looked up at Lazarus. "Oh, my, where do you get these gems? So fresh, still wet from his bath. Delightful. Look at the bones, the little pretty lip." Returning to me, he added, "Ready for adventure?"

I nodded yes, though I wasn't sure.

"You have to speak," he said.

"Speak boy—" Lazarus commanded.

"Yes," I said, in my normal tone. But I saw they wanted more, so I took a deep breath and shouted, "*Yes, adventure.*" I was eager to please.

"Oh my," Jeremy said, with a grin that straightened his mustache. "Lungs. Very useful."

Lazarus finally came out in front of his desk and stood quite close to me. I was thrilled to be so near him. He was a sort of father, in my dreams, though I knew in truth that I was fatherless. He leaned in for a moment, cleared his throat. I was about to get what my mate Ariel had called *the Speech.*

"Now, dear boy, so far, you have been very brave. But there is more to endure. At times, the contrast between this place and the world of Heirs will make you consider your life here one of suffering. The things you have to do to add to your Trust may seem very hard. You will struggle. But the good news is you will have years, decades, and centuries, to iron out any wrinkles, to unbend any kinks. We have marvelous therapies for you once you are one of us: intricate, sublime. Implants. Extracts. Reprogramming. Re-description. Everything that happens to you out there can be cured. I've done it. You can too. This is all Prologue. This is all just your Prologue!"

Prologue, I eventually decided, meant you weren't supposed to live now, so you could live later, when you deserved to.

"I have it here, hope it's the right size," Jeremy said, bringing out a thin silver ring with a figure eight lying on its side in the middle. "This is your Not-Yet collar. Some people say 'Nyet.' It's short for *not yet treated.* It says you have a chance. So you are ahead of the rabble." He opened the clamp, put it round my neck, and closed it again. Then he threw back his head so I saw his, a black-greenish line with a squiggle in the middle, digging into his Adam's apple. "See, the same! When you are twenty, you get a new one, at your Boundarytime. You dedicate, become confirmed. Then you are on your way, just like me!"

Lazarus hovered a few inches away. "First day on the job!" He stepped back, so Jeremy could take my hand.

As I was marched off, I distinctly remember wanting Lazarus to hug me.

And, I already knew how wrong it was to want such things.

*

The last time I went to see my guardian, it was my idea, not his.

I had worked all my life in the Sims. I was lucky, I had a great Trust, and was getting ready for the Boundarytime, the first ceremony.

But then I received word my money was "in escrow." Someone else had first claim on it, a lien. My money. The WELLFI Bank would only answer my queries by saying, "*Ask your Trust Executor.*"

I tried contacting Lazarus, over and over—no word. No explanation. I had to go, get an answer.

I was living and working on the shore of the Sea of Pontchartrain then. Soon as I could, I hitched a ride to Audubon Island with a young fisherman named Serio from Chef Menteur Enclave. He had a single stop to make, in Port Gramercy, and then we were headed across to the New Orleans Islands. Eight hours' journey, I thought.

I stood on the prow as we pulled away from the dock, touching my Not-Yet collar. It was now as tarnished and tight as Jeremy's had been when I first met him. I was planning to get a new one, my last, very soon. There were transgressions I'd confess then, things I'd promise to give up—in fact, in preparation I was fasting, toting up my sins. I tried to tell myself I'd get the answers from Lazarus, that all would be put right.

I managed until we came to our first stop. There, I was thrown into jail for a single conversation.

And, almost as soon as they let me go—

The men came to kill me.

Part One:
Serpenthead's Find

I

4:50 AM October 12, 2121
Port Gramercy Enclave Docks
Northeast Gulf De-Accessioned Territory, U.A. Protectorate

"You dead?" the Yeared was yelling that filthy word. That was what I woke to. I opened one eye to see his squat silhouette against the blue broth of the sky.

"Well, you live. I saved you. Call me Serpenthead, how do you? Saw it all. Port G. trash came after you. Plus one cop—"

Why was he so loud? I turned my head and saw the puddle of blood, and realized the clanging pain was coming from my ear. He was assuming I'd be deaf.

"Oh, let me see that. Bullet just grazed you. Lucky," he said. "Ahhh—I know who you are." His pitch, rising. "I was behind you in line day before yesterday, at the Customs house? Remember me? You named Malcolm, right?"

I recalled coming in with Serio, being in the queue at Customs— but—he slid his huge, soft-fingered hand over my features. I was too groggy to protest. I was a Not-Yet, couldn't he see? How could he touch me, not ask, break that rule? At that, my heart started to pound. I felt my awful news, stored in a part of my brain still aching. The whole world was a wall right next to me, with a crack in it. What caused it?

"Last night, I was trying to curl up on this tub?" He banged the side of the boat. We rocked. "Then I saw you, then I saw the hooligans coming. Boom. Boom. Want me to speak louder?"

He was plenty loud already. I brought him into focus. He had on a full tunic, long and dirty, with lots of pockets. His pants were light, and blotchy. Big belly, huge boots. He was stooped, bow-legged, and bald. Jeremy must have told me a million times to avoid such types. But this old man had saved my life—so he claimed.

"Three inches of water on this deck," he still yelled. "Rained a while back. Can drown in a teacup—you ever hear that? Isn't it good I was stealing this place to sleep? You lucky or what? I grabbed you and rolled you to the side. Just as the shot came." He had a fine generous smile, caramel skin—those that still named race, not enclave, would call him yellow, some would call him Creole. He waved his arms about to show me what had happened. Then, without asking, he touched me again, grabbed me under the arms, dragged me over, and propped me up against the rail of the deck. "I was you, I'd leave this place. They don't like you. They were yelling. You tell them some dirty thing? You *do* some dirty thing?"

I recalled this much: I had been trying to flee and had gotten to the docks, to the boat, but—no way to start it. Oh. I realized I was going to have to talk, no matter how my jaw felt. I got up the courage. "K-K-Kee," I managed, without opening my teeth, just my lips. The vibration of the word going through my head was hell.

"What say?" he said.

"Kee-ee," I tried again, in the gullet. I meant I had no key. Because my companion, this boat's pilot, Serio, had it. He was locked inside a jail, inside the walls of Port Gramercy.

"I can start anything," the Yeared said. "You still going? Where?"

I remembered, just at that moment—the where, not the why. I nodded, and looked at him, with faint hope. "N'orlns."

"Outer Orleans Islands or Museum City? Or Sunken Quarter—that's where I'm headed. You?"

I nodded, my spirits rising slightly, trying not to rattle anything. I wasn't going to the Quarter, I steered clear—mixing of strats there. I was headed to Audubon Island. The Foundling House. To see my guardian, Lazarus. Of course. I tried, front teeth touching. "Aubahn."

"No problem. Five miles up the Old River from the Quarter. I'll help you if you promise to drop me off. Just slink on up." He climbed over me into the little wheelhouse, eyed the dials. I had no idea how to drive the thing. "This engine takes compos fuel? They got that on the Basin side in the Quarter. I know where. Off the 'Lysiana Canal. There's enough to get across. Why don't I start you? Steer this tub for you? You drop me off? We get the fuel cheap cheap so you can go back up to Audubon?"

I trusted him, though I knew it was wrong to. Couldn't help it.

"I've got to get to a gig there? You know, I sing? You sing?"

I said "uh-unh," for no.

"Pity. How about this?" Now he was holding up something stringy and beige. Old cooked chicken, it looked like. I hummed "no," again. I wasn't eating meat, or much of anything.

"Oh, tapering off, eh?" he said. "Thin soups, miso, little shredded things? Swearing off the hard stuff, land meats, pastes, fruits of flour?" He smacked his lips. "Can you open at all? Wanna drink?" From one of the many pockets in his tunic, he produced a small vial and a straw, said, "Sip? It's just GeeTea."

I allowed it. I was weak.

The liquid offered me clarity. When he took out the straw, I formed my first sentence. "Where you from?" The words clanged in my head, after.

"Convergence is all, I say," he said. "Coincidence is convergence without the cause. I am who I am. Come behind you other day in line. Took a look. Liked your face." He touched his own cheek and crossed his upper lip with his index finger then rested on the opposite jaw, formed an "L" with his hand to frame his face. "Serpenthead the Singer."

I touched the side of my jowl where the injury was, with trepidation. I found the slot in my ear—gooey, sticky, stinging, but I was okay with pain. High tolerance. Among my gifts.

Serpenthead reached across to my forehead. "Ringing? Dizzy?" he asked. "Pain killer? Try this in your trap."

He offered gum. I couldn't chew. Jancy gum.

"Suit yourself." He shrugged, momentarily dejected, but he recovered. "How about we get this thing started?"

I watched him climb up and slide under the wheel. He reached in one of his pockets and produced a huge folded knife, multi-armed as a crab. All kinds of implements fanned out of it—screwdrivers, serrated knives, can opener, clippers, and a wriggly flat wire no thicker than a fork's tine that he slid into the key slot. He tricked the starter to turn over. "Good. Juice," he said. "Can you get up? Open the throttle?"

When I moved, I heard a faint roar. Was it from inside my ear or outside, I couldn't tell. It took my balance. I staggered. I didn't know what the throttle was. He showed me, explained the dials.

"Lever other here," he said, his hand pointing, his head staying down. "Press it up."

How did he know where the lever was? I got up and did what he said. The engine, to my amazement, coughed to life. Soon he'd undone the rope that tied us to the dock, and we chugged out into the open water in the indigo-before-dawn.

*

In fifteen minutes, we were far enough away from Port Gramercy to see it whole—it was a line town on the rise between the Old River and the Sea of Pontchartrain, a meandering scarf of twinkling lights, docks, syrup refineries, cranes and sluices for cargo that went to foreign ports, the fugue countries with no Heirs. By six in the morning, the sky had gone from dark blue to candlelight-through-muddy water, to full-blown pink. October, late in the storm season. I finally turned away from the complicated shore, and looked into the cold wind, the open sea. The chill almost distracted me from the ache on the left side of my head. I kept sane with the thought of how close I was to Lazarus, to home, but then I remembered that crack in the wall, that doom was seeping through. What? I could only make out the sense of it, not the fact—it was like the effort of trying to recall the details of a nightmare in the morning. I had almost been killed, a few hours before, apparently—no recollection of that, either, just the bloody ear. It was so awful I resisted to protect myself, perhaps. So many blows at once. I had been in jail, too, but not for long. Exactly why? Had I committed a crime?

The pain bit down hard. I sat, holding my throbbing skull, next to this huge-headed Serpent who was beginning to sing.

He cupped his ear, and began, "*When the black Kat slithered across the East at dusk—*". Then he asked, "You heard any of the Great Storm songs? Last century songs?"

I hadn't.

Eventually, he went through that whole ballad inventory. He had a beautiful voice. I applauded, despite myself.

"You know, you will lose your pipes if they make you over, treat you. They all got those awful reptile voices. Really."

I shrugged. I'd never thought about the loss before, or even concluded their voices were ugly. They were very low, and airy, and—dry—I considered their sound the sign of the luckiest.

"You steer for a while."

I had to learn. I assented, my balance slightly better. He scurried to the stern where the poles that held Serio's fishing nets stuck out, but there weren't any there right then. He found a thin white cord I think was used for mending. I saw him take a piece of the chicken he'd offered for breakfast and tie it to one end. Watching him, I turned the wheel by mistake. He noticed. "Hey, look out. She's listing. Due East."

Next thing I knew, he was back at the helm holding a living silver thing in his chubby yellow hand. Water dripped over the seat beside me. He offered me some, saying the words, "Drum, delicioso!" He produced the complicated knife again from one of his pockets. With its sharp paring blade, he tore the skin off the fish while it was still alive. With another, he separated the meat from the bones, dug out the intestines and lungs, and sliced it in cubes which he put on the board above the dials. Then he tossed down the bloody head and spine, which landed on his boot, and said, "Take your choice."

I had been watching with great interest, I was ashamed to note. But at the last minute, I managed, "No."

"Can't hear you," he said.

"Naa hungry," I said. The tendons of my neck vibrated.

"How can you not be hungry?" he asked.

I knew the fish was cold from the water. Its sharp circle eye looked at me now from the wet deck. Those little dices of pink flesh. Places under my tongue started to sting. But I couldn't sink like that. Bad enough the new friend I'd made. What would my Heir benefactors say?

"Really?"

"YESH A FASHT," I said through my teeth, wishing it was easy.

"So-kay, I see." Then he sat, a little sad, and ate the fish himself, raw. He chewed each morsel for a very long time, made grand work of it. I would have left, but it was the only place on the boat that had any roof. If I went below deck, I might have been sick—the cabin stank, and there was a chop.

"You been readying all your life, huh?" he said when he was finished.

I nodded. "Boun'ry ti— "

"Boundarytime? You old enough? When you start out? What age?"

I held up five fingers.

"What you do?"

"Sims."

"You earned enough at those? I don't believe it. You some kind of star?"

I nodded, proud, remembering those years of applause, the thick faces of my Heir fans, their marvelous feathered headjobs, their braids and jewels. *Bravo*, they used to say, *Encore. He doesn't stink!*

He turned to me full face as if something startled him, though he kept the wheel steady. "I hear those cops in the Customs House say there was a problem? With your Trust?"

Finally, my awful news flowed like dark ink into my brain. My Trust. "No," I lied. What was he doing, following me? Reading my mind? But that was the thing—it all came back—day before yesterday, at Port Gramercy Customs, the officers pulled up my records to harass me. I begged them not to—I pleaded, got them mad. The humiliation.

"It's okay?" Pressing was Serpent's mode.

I nodded. But it wasn't okay.

"Well, well. Glad to hear it." He looked ahead again, changed the subject. "See that land? New Orleans Islands. Beautiful, still, don't you think? Bella, like Venezia, hah?"

Far on the horizon, I could make out the outline of the old Sky Rail Station, the marvelously high wall of the Museum City. It would only be hours now, and I'd be home. But what would I find there? And who or what, exactly, had claimed my future?

We sailed on.

*

5:30 PM October 12, 2121
New Orleans Islands, Northeast Gulf De-Accessioned Territory,
U.A. Protectorate

PONTCHARTRAIN SEA-RIM SKY RAIL
CLOSED UNTIL FURTHER NOTICE
BOATS: DETOUR BAYOU ST. JOHN LINK TO
NAPOLEON TRENCH /PROCEED AT YOUR OWN RISK
ENTERING NORTHEAST GULF DE-ACCESSIONED
TERRITORY. U.A. PROTECTORATE. SUBJECT TO
SECURITAS PATROLS.
HAVE VISAS, ID'S, ENCLAVE CARDS READY FOR
INSPECTION

*I*t had been two and a half years since I'd seen the city and at that time, the Sky Rail system had still been working reasonably well.

Now it was half-submerged. The Y-shaped supports for the cables were poking up from the waters like deformed, yellow trees. Seagulls and brown pelicans were perched on every artificial branch. We passed what was left of the station platform and saw two bulb-shaped gondolas lying on their sides on it—humongous, rusted onions, the gray blue sea slapping at their hulls.

Serpenthead maneuvered our tub with some skill, into the Trench. He knew his way, even with so many landmarks under water. In a little while, we passed a few hipped roofs peeking out, what was left of the old shore homes. Not long ago, they'd been handsome, on their high stilts, and the Sea of Pontchartrain could wash underneath in tidal surges. Water birds—egrets I guessed—flew in a low V formation over our heads. It was clear they thought of this place as their exclusive territory now. Once, it had been for people, only.

A mile or so inside, we came upon our first occupied house, and then our second, then a row of five. These were really just the tops of old two-and three-story houses—Outliar compounds. No enclaves here. I made out the rotting, fan-shaped attic windows of the tall Victorians, the humps of the camelbacks. It looked as if the occupants had moved into the upper rooms, and turned eaves into living space, former upper balconies into front porches, abandoned the flooded lower floors, and managed to seal them off. Ringed by rails and gates, which served as the lounging spaces, docks, and security perimeters, these rickety homesteads could be taken for stationary houseboats. On the gatepost of one, the sign: *"Leave a Wake, You Won't Wake."* And the skull and bones.

When I had been through here last, those houses stood on muddy patties of land, still fending off the sea most of the time. Now they had succumbed. Yet the occupants had not fled. Their very existence was illegal, in a sense—here, no one persecuted them exactly, but no one helped them either.

Lazarus had always complained the problem was the territory had been let go by the United Authority years back, but they never allowed it the freedom they'd promised. "Always some limbo," he'd say. True independence was not the fact.

I was totally depressed about the question about my Trust. Why had Lazarus not answered? This landscape didn't help. When we came to a wide expanse of water, the Broad Marsh, Serpenthead stopped, pushed in the throttle, and said, "We are almost on empty, and we'll use the current here."

The motor stopped chugging so we drifted. Suddenly everything was quiet. A little past the open water there were houses again—rougher, more fortified. Outliar camps surrounded by high fences, guarded by bigger dogs. No water birds here. On a few of the houses, the balcony columns were wrapped in barbed wire mesh forming the cages for fuel tanks.

I could hear things from inside now—human shouts, guitars, the rough harmony of semi-wild dogs, the rattle-roar of generators—a cacophony, almost pleasing over water. I was sorry when we had to accelerate to veer into the Tchoupitoulas Canal. From there we cut into the Old River at the Napoleon Segue.

"Bandits this way," he shrugged. "Different neighborhood."

We glided past the great floodwall of the Museum City. It was guarded by sentries, Securitas. I'd never gotten inside, but I had heard of the wonders there. In my heyday as an actor, many of my fans lived in those mansions, but they never actually invited me in.

The light was getting low. I was tired. Of course, I had not eaten. The pain in my jaw, my ear, and my neck was a little worse. I went to the cot below decks for a few minutes, put up with the stench.

I must have dozed, for I startled when Serpenthead said, "The Quay, Malcolm. Coming up."

I climbed the stairs. The setting sun bit at my eyes.

It took me a while to realize what I was seeing, for the water reflected the lowering sun, flashing orange and blue and gold. But then something sorted itself out. It was wet and shining as the water, but smooth. It might have been the flat back of a sea monster for it had something like scales. Then I saw the "scales" were paving slates—it was a curving road at the edge of the Old River. Big thick poles the size of children poked up from it. When we were close enough, Serpent threw a rope over the head of one the pylons, and called it "a bollard."

This was a busy place. Around us were other craft—boats with bigger wheelhouses, several with multiple swivel seats for fishing. Along the slate road were stalls and stands selling provisions.

"But where is the Quarter?" I asked. Surely it had to be nearby.

"Sunken Quarter," Serpenthead called out. "Over there."

But I looked and saw nothing, save for a pointed narrow tower, which stuck up out of nowhere. For a second I thought this "Quarter" might be made up. There were so many stories about it, it might as well be. "I don't see anything," I said.

"Over there, and *down*," Serpenthead said, excited.

I looked.

The paved road I discerned wasn't a road at all, or a proper bank. It was the wide top of a huge, encircling barrier. We had pulled up to the top of an amphitheater, a bowl, the irregular perimeter that held back the Old River.

Below, the wonder.

What I saw first were bronze roofs with steep dormers. Next, the crowns of palms, which I'd never seen from above before— lush, green blooms. Underneath, buildings with bright shutters. The old cathedral, an ancient edifice, in the middle. Its spire pierced the horizon, the one structure taller than the level of the Quay. It alone caught natural light. Everything below in that valley set into the water had already descended into an almost garish, electrified night. All of it gleamed, for it was coated in glazes. The city itself seemed to be made of porcelain, like something kept in a cabinet for a giant's delight. I felt I was breaking a law, coming to visit this place everyone in my boyhood talked about in whispers.

"Now, you know how to start this without me?" Serpenthead took out the spiral wire he fashioned from a scrap he'd picked up on the boat, to be the "key," and offered it to me. "You have the controls down?" He pointed. "Throttle, clutch, compass, tachometer, fuel? Got it?"

I wasn't listening. I was distracted by the creatures on the stairs. Throngs out for a promenade at early dusk. Very strange.

"Malcolm, pay attention," he said, the back of his hand patting under my chin. I didn't even object.

Many on the Quay wore masks, others, elaborate head jobs. And some appeared to have claws instead of hands, wings coming out of their backs. I had heard about Altereds—they weren't a new species. Nats and even Nyets were resculpted by doctors into these creatures. I knew Heirs leased them, even bought them, and paid for the surgeries called "re-designs." I had heard they were banned in some parts of the U.A. proper. One spread his purple wings not fifty feet from me. He was a fellow about my height, very skinny, his teeth long and grey and sharp. I could see where the tendons had been attached, the fine detail. He'd surrendered himself to become a work of art. Someone had once described such elaborate transformations, before—told me about the strange parties in the Museum City he got to attend, from the time he was very young—

"Something, huh?" Serpent asked. "You wouldn't see me getting a scalpel, or a graft—"

I groaned aloud. I suddenly realized who must have caused the problem with my Trust.

Serpent thought I was in pain. It wasn't ordinary pain. He seemed to care. "Look, I will go get you the fuel. Okay?" He actually looked sad.

"I'm going with you," I said, my jaw stabbing me as I spoke. I wasn't going to be cheated by Serpent too.

"I am just getting over there, and coming back." He came in close, looked me over. "You should see yourself—ear all bloody, one half of your face twice the size of the other. You sure you want to run all round? You don't have such great balance, you noticed? Don't you hurt?"

Serpent was climbing onto the Quay from the rear of the boat now, the fuel can in his hand. I followed him. "I'm coming." I had to get that fuel, go up to Lazarus and straighten this thing out. I *knew* who was tampering with my life. Lazarus wasn't even aware, probably.

Serpent's fat hands were on the bollard he'd tied us to. Little birds with bent beaks scurried out of his way when his big boot landed on the slates. When I reached up after him, the pain shot down my already-aching arm.

"Hey, Malcolm," he spoke quietly, gently.

"I *have* to stay with you," I managed.

He closed his mouth and wagged his head. "Come on, then," he said. "Time's wasting."

I followed, with a new sense of purpose, and the marvels of the Sunken Quarter before me, gleaming.

II

April 21, 2111
Audubon Foundling House
New Orleans Islands, Northeast Gulf De-Accessioned Territory,
U.A. Protectorate

"*M*alcolm, dear, I want to talk to you about your mate, Ariel. He's got some problem with O. Please, go spy and tell me what." Lazarus had pulled me into the hall at lunch to tell me this.

I believed I was special by this time. Best actor among all the boys. A rising favorite in the Sims, much in demand. Eleven years by count. Peak of my popularity.

"What can we do?" Lazarus asked. "He's rejecting his holder!"

Ariel had been dubbed too unruly to be in the Sims, so, at Lazarus's urging, he had entered into a holding contract. His benefactor was a big extra-rich Heir everyone called O. Politically important, we knew. Ariel lived with O for long periods, in luxury. He followed him around on his travels, stayed with him at his glorious resorts, went with him to gatherings in the Museum City, the Sunken Quarter. He had the life of a pet, as far as I could see. The first time he came back, he'd said it was the easiest job in the world. Much better than the lengthy, repetitive comedies I had to act in. But this time he'd come back early from his visit and was upstairs in the attic, refusing to come down.

"Find out what you can," Lazarus said, his lip twitching, his brow furrowed. Usually his face was smooth as a plate, like other Heirs. I had the impulse to stretch out that overskin, and the prodermis under it, though of course I could never do that.

He shook his head. "Tell Ariel this is nonsense. He has to go back. O is outside right now, calling for him. It's a scandal, a spectacle. And times are hard."

I was Lazarus' confidant, his favorite. I already knew all the laments. *Times were hard.* There used to be other work for us boys. The Foundling House had a band, and some took up the building trades. Now enterprising enclavers did that work. He looked as if he would cry, which of course he couldn't, when he said, "All those jobs are over. Sims and holding contracts are all there is, nothing else. So Ariel should be grateful, do as his holder says. Not play the prima donna and ask to be brought back early. Unless there is something he's not saying—" His unblinking eyes moved around the room. "It's not as if many doors are open. As if there are any other avenues—"

I nodded. I would go talk to Ariel. I didn't mind. He was my mate, he used to help me. He was the first one who ever told me about the trick of *prologue*: he knew very well what it meant, but he only resented it, never mastered it. He liked to tell me we were found together, on the Old River Levee when we were little, both abandoned. I was three or less, he was around five or six. The legend was, we were in a long metal drawer, rusty—some said it floated there all by itself, from a ship wreck, or a boat that sank? Others said we were just stuck up on the bank by some ambitious wannabes trying to break the Procreation Laws and get to Memphis. So it would look like we came in from the Old River. They just weren't decent enough to leave us at the Foundling House Gate, which is what others did all the time with babies they couldn't care for. In other words, we were ordinary toss-outs, like most in the Home. Not survivors of some fancy shipwreck. Ariel insisted we were brothers, said he remembered we were together in some other place. That once, good people took care of us. I didn't believe. If they were good, then why did they throw us away? Not that I would have liked the life of the desperate independents, grisly Outliars, if that was who our "parents" were—those who scrounged for their slimy victuals, with their mangy dogs, their ramshackle hovels on stilts along the canals outside Audubon Island and the others. If Ariel and I had been born into an enclave, I wouldn't have liked that much better. They had easier lives, but they were "bound to the wheel." In the end, they were unlucky.

Obeying Lazarus, I climbed up to our place in the attic toward my mate. On my way in, I saw rats in a nest in the eave, little babies in a row along the side of the mother, a heap still as a carcass, their tiny tongues curled, and making troughs, to pull upon her teats. A few days before, she was running around everywhere, chubby as a little pig. We'd asked Vee the cook to get rid of her, but he said he couldn't, *she was pregnant.* I had only a vague idea of the meaning of the word. He said people were all supposed to have mothers somewhere, swore upon it. I thought it was a wonderful idea, but the sight of her here, her young feeding on her body, was truly strange. Her babies eager and pink, and so intent, and tiny, the size of my little finger.

I found Ariel stretched out on his mat, face down in a pillow.

I was about to speak to him, when I heard that voice. *"Ariel my dear!"*

O had a thick, uneven sound, broader than Lazarus's, an amplified whisper. I leaned out and took a look. Four stories down, at the edge of the central gate, the Heir calling for his pet. His physique was exaggerated, like a muscleman, the way a lot of them looked that season. Jeremy had only just explained to me that Heirs got a Re-job every two years, that was part of the Trust contract—a fresh new outer layer, a restructured prodermis, a new look if they ordered it. O's expensive peek-a-boo suit, antique gold, with its thick lapels, had lots of swoosh and drape, so we could see his "work."

"Ariel, Ariel, come back to me."

Ariel sat up, looking annoyed and said, "Don't look at him—I hate him."

"That's a lie," I said. "He's an Heir. A good Heir! How can you say *hate*? Even think it? He takes care of you. He provides for your Trust."

Ariel's round eyes closed in at the outer edges, as if he'd been struck. "Who are you to say? You just do the Sims, prance around — you—you know the story. Everything is explained in advance. You have a script. It doesn't constantly change."

"They always ask for encores. Jeremy says they have no sense of time," I said. The Sims exhausted me. But I managed to bear it, didn't collapse. I was tough. I could separate from my hungers, my appetites. That's what it took. Ariel was older, but I thought myself more mature.

"Do they make you stay awake for days, laughing at you, giving you orders, making you sit with them, while they are going over and over and over the same—"

"Same what?" I asked.

"Boring—" he started. "Taking you—" He looked at me, coldly, then said, shaking his head and sort of winding it up a little, so it rose into the air. "You wouldn't understand."

"O pays into your Trust," I said. I had heard some of this before. I had already decided Ariel was just lazy, weak, as Jeremy had said. "Maybe he tells you stories over and over—and then he sulks or whatever with you, but you know he's going to do it. It's nothing. Do you see what I put up with? Twelve, fifteen encores?"

Ariel turned, attacked. "What do you know? You get to be innocent, little innocent. Lucky, the little lucky one." He scowled at me, and then looked away, hiding his long face in his hands. I didn't know what he was doing there for a few minutes. Then I realized he was crying. I felt like crying myself. He had that effect on me, always did. But why? He leaned out the attic window, so O could certainly see him.

O called up, "Come, I'm so sorry, come, please forgive me, I am nothing, you darling!"

"Forgive him," I said.

Ariel said to me, "You idiot!"

"What?" I asked. "He's sorry. Forgive him, whatever it was." Yet, I saw the fear in Ariel's face.

I looked down again, saw O's large round eyes, blue-black, and all centers, no sides. Big, white-less, the eyes of a fly. Why did he have such hideous sheet lenses? He frightened me. I knew there were better styles. They didn't have to look like insects.

Ariel expanded, puffed himself out and yelled down, "Never again! Out with you!" Then he turned to me. "You don't understand."

"What? What do I not understand?" I lost all patience.

"He called me to his inner rooms—"

"When? What?"

"Two nights ago. He told me I was growing up. He told me he had noticed. My voice was cracking. My body was—"

"So? It's true."

"He said he wanted to see it all."

"So?" I said. I was always being peered at by their kind, inspected, by Jeremy's team, or even Heirs—I wasn't squeamish.

"Then he came closer," Ariel said.

"And?" I said.

"He grabbed for me. And he—"

"He absolutely did not. Heirs don't touch us. They don't. He did not!" It was not possible. Ariel might as well have been saying black was white.

"He grabbed me. He took hold of my—"

He'd had other lies for me before, but this one took the prize, I thought. How could a righteous, famous Heir, do such a thing, such a forbidden, dirty thing? They didn't touch us; they loathed us, I never heard the end of it. They despised our food. They said we stank. I had seen hundreds of Heirs in a single afternoon. They'd passed very close to me, stared hard at me, sometimes saw my nakedness, but they had never, never, ever— "You can't expect me to believe you," I said.

Down below, O's hoarse whining. "Anything you want, my dearest pet."

I screwed my mouth into a hard little knot. Ariel wouldn't look at me. After a long time of staring at O and saying nothing, not a thing, he managed, "Okay. Don't believe me. It's a story. Ha. Ha."

"You can't make up these lies. Stop it." I was relieved. "What do you think you are? You have somebody else to rely on?" Lazarus would have said these things if I didn't. "Look at me," I said.

He continued to look down, and something in his brain burned, I thought. I worried. What was it? I didn't know. I wouldn't for years.

Finally, after forever, my mate turned to me with the widest, oddest smirk. "That was just a test," he said. "To see what you would believe. Got you—"

"I know the Heirs," I said. "Don't lie. It doesn't work with me."

He wagged his head. "Tsk, tsk. Look at that poor creature down there. They have no timing. They lose their way. They have such long lives, they get lost in them—they need us, they forget—I pity them—"

"I love you!" O offered from below.

The statement stung like an attack, aimed at me. Nobody loved me, except Lazarus, possibly, and he never said so.

"See?" Ariel said.

Suddenly, I was jealous. Once or twice, Jeremy had called me "lovely." That was it.

Ariel arched out of the window, again, and shouted down: "No brosia on my plate—soba, holos. My own Broads."

So this was all a show. A way to bribe, connive. He'd been a little faker—drawn us all into his elaborate drama. Lazarus, too. I was about to scold him again. But then, I got another scare. I grabbed Ariel's legs, because I was sure he would fall, leaning out like that. It was a long way down.

"Anything," O called up.

Ariel had enjoyed the luxuries, seen how they lived. Lived how they lived. Spoiled. He wanted more. "Swimming in a pool!"

"You could drown!"

"Lessons!"

"I agree!"

"I want a soft cruise!"

"As soon as you say. I'll reserve tonight!"

"Genenfabric clothes!"

"They are ordered!"

"Those jewels that change shape and color!"

"Delivered tomorrow!"

"Living silk bedding!"

"You just have to ask! I need you! Just ask! Know I need you!"

"Sing me that song, *Bibbity Bob*—"

The Heir did what Ariel asked.

Then Ariel joined in. I realized I could let go of his legs. He was fine. That was a false alarm, too. No end to it. I looked out the window for myself. And I saw an Heir in full ensemble, leaning against the high wall of our foundling house, singing the Disney, *Bibbity Bobbity Boo*.

Ariel called down, "Let's do it louder! Louder!"

O raised his strange voice—one of them, obeying a little smelly one of us. In its way, a terrible thing, I knew, against all the laws of strats. But it had a certain interest, I couldn't deny—

*

As I followed my strange new friend Serpenthead through the Sunken Quarter that October evening, I decided that only Ariel could be behind the problem with my Trust. Last time I'd seen him, Ariel told me he was going to sue our guardian, and then he'd sent me that trinket he'd forced Lazarus to turn over, a pendant found on me when I was tossed out. I had the thing with me, in fact. I was bringing it back to Lazarus. He still kept all my records—the story of my life, and my fate, belonged to him. Lazarus would never do anything to harm me.

"No, he would not," I said out loud, maybe so I would believe it.

"No he would not what? Who? Come on! Who you talking to?" Serpent asked. I had just caught up with him on the other side of a new group of promenading Altereds. He was waiting, careful not to get too far ahead. He added, "I've still got some jancy gum, it works for the pain?" offering the foul stuff from one of his grimy pockets again—a bark colored rectangle, covered with powder.

I shook my head, carefully.

"Well they sell Q here," he said. "You know it?" He pointed to a structure a bit further down along the Quay. A cloth pavilion. "You can get it for a few crowns."

It was something the Sim staff took when they couldn't stand their headaches anymore. Jeremy used to tell me I was too young for it.

"Okay." I shrugged.

"Anybody here, please," he called when we got to the tent, which was lit by little weak-flamed copper lamp sitting on the pine board counter. There were medicines on it, colas for sale, masks. No person came. He called again.

An Outliar in a tight knitted cap emerged from the rear eventually. It was hard, at first, to tell if it was a female or a male, but then something about the eyes showed me. She wore several layers of clothes, as some of them did. She was dirty—hands, even the face. She offered me a small pouch with two yellow buttons inside it, and said, "Water, water only—five crowns," and I nodded, and gave over some of my Port Gramercy money.

She put the bill in her mouth. It must have tasted right because she slipped it inside her blouse, and handed me the pack. When I turned it over, it read—"Q: *Swipe away the pressures.*" I was happy with the hope of relief, told myself it was good to get rid of that money, too. I was ashamed of it. It brought back the whole Port Gramercy detour, and debacle. How was I going to explain to Lazarus the kind of trouble I got into there?

"Well that will do you, and one better," Serpenthead said.

"One better?" I asked.

"It loosens some people," he said. "I'm only—you plan to get to Audubon tonight, right?"

He was trying to shake me up, I thought. I dropped the disks in my hurting mouth and swallowed. Without water.

As we descended the steps to street level, he said, "People get waylaid in these parts. Pickers a plenty by the docks, all over. You have to keep sharp, keep up with me. Don't get behind again." He made his lips disappear, his eyes got bigger. "You okay?" he asked.

"Fine," I said. Just then, an aroma demanded my attention. Like the most wonderful things Vee ever steamed up in the kitchen, laden with herbs and pepper—all of us standing in rows in the dining hall back at the Home, little boys, hungry and waiting to grow, our plates shining, held up so to cover our hearts, in wait. I even remembered Vee's admonishments—to be kind, to share, and to keep our turn—

"Serp! Serp!" A voice from across the way. My companion froze.

A slender figure with a long white face and a thin ridged nose approached us through the arcade. His face, all beaks. He wore a little circular cap of checked cloth, and a black zippered shirt. He paused, oddly, when he reached us, nodding, as if he were keeping time with his pointed little chin.

"What? Peet? Why aren't you at the Palm Bar?" Serpenthead said.

"I'm headed there."

This narrow fellow looked hard at me. I didn't belong. He said, "Bebum." It was more a mumble than a word, rhythmic. "Who this?" His head jerked.

"My Malc, we come across from Port Gram, he had a boat he couldn't operate. Now he needs some compos."

Peet looked me up and down again, and nodded twice. "Bebum. What happened to him?"

"Shot at. I saved him."

Peet did not pursue it further. Such anecdotes did not surprise him apparently. "Bebum. Change of plans about the Palm Bar," he said.

"What?"

"Bebum. Cancelling, closing up, on account of a big underground Sim." He jerked. "Sim Verite." Then he nodded. "Never fear. Lordy's got us another gig," he added. "I'm seeing him right now. He won't wait. He'll hire other people we don't get there now. "

Serpent, crestfallen. "Shoot, came all this way and I can't sing?"

Peet shrugged.

"Well I have to see what it is," Serpent said to me. "You wait here? While I go?"

"Why don't we part here?" I asked. "I'll get the fuel myself. Just tell me where to go."

"Can't," Serpenthead said.

"Why not?"

"You can't be just anybody," he said.

"I am not just anybody," I said, and I thought, *I am a very lucky somebody, always have been.*

IV

November 1, 2117
Audubon Island Foundling House
New Orleans Islands, Northeast Gulf De-Accessioned Territory,
U.A. Protectorate

*T*he Sims business had collapsed. The situation was dire. Jeremy
had lost his shirt. He had been through his Boundarytime, and all
the initiations, his Trust had been in order, but at the last minute, he
couldn't make the payments. Sims were out of style, even despised as
old-fashioned. Virtuals, soft cruises, were all the rage. WELLFI had
invested in them heavily, and now there were endless advertisements
about how exciting and effortless they were. You didn't have to go
anywhere, deal with living creatures, actors. Like me. My career was
over. I was done for, in fact. I was sixteen by count, at the time.

WELLFI absorbed Jeremy's Trust, or eighty percent of it—they
could do that if you didn't keep up your end. He was too old to join
any open enclave. He was on his own, and no better than any Low Nat.
Recently, he'd come to say goodbye. He tried to be sanguine, showing
up on his little scooter, claiming he was going off to the Western Lands,
that he'd be fine. That he found something interesting about the "fast
dip in and out of life, so intense, so concentrated." I was very upset; he
ended up comforting me. Days later, though, I got the news he tried to
drown himself. Leapt into the Old River. Some Outliar fished him out.
A camp run by Gaist do-gooders had given him a bed. I thought I'd
never see him again. I also believed I would never have a full Trust, and

that my fate was going to be similar.

Then one morning in the spring when I was out in the yard, giving "acting" lessons to the boys—what use the skills were, I didn't know—Lazarus called me over.

"I have a few things to tell you," he said, leading me to his office.

He seemed excited. He didn't sit down. One of his small hands rubbed the other, both hovered over the blotter on his desk. He never changed. It was a joke—he had the same round little nose he'd had when I was five, never had it sculpted, never ordered anything new when he got a Re-job. He was so spartan for an Heir. Abstemious. Jeremy used to make fun of him. Which I didn't like, though I had to agree my guardian was odd. But my mind was on other troubles. I'd seen Ariel the night before. I was about to bring all that up, when Lazarus announced, "A woman could hire you. She might bother with education. She promises a clean barracks, a room in a dormitory if one comes open. The possibilities."

I tried to listen. It was astonishing—my luck. Lazarus explained how I would live, how I would look, how I would comport myself among Heirs all day long. In the middle of reminding me of things I should never say, and never do, he stopped. "What's wrong? Why aren't you listening?"

"Ariel," I said. "He came in late last night. Did you see him? I just don't know whether to believe what he says. He seems so unhappy sometimes, then says nothing is wrong."

Lazarus shook his head, looked out at the yard, through the open window. A gentle shower was starting. His gaze returned—stricken. "Listen to me, Malcolm. I know you are attached to the fellow, I know he makes that claim you are his brother—but—"

"But what?"

"Sometimes you have to—if you are going—you have to cut some off—"

"Cut him off?"

"He's going down the wrong road. I've asked him to leave here, not to return." Lazarus was grinding his blue teeth.

"Why?"

"He's afflicted," he said, too loudly. Then he waited, composed himself a bit. "There it is. You can't fix him now. I can't." He shrugged. "He will live with O. He says that's what he wants to do. O is not exactly on my side, you know, politically, you know—O's going to take over his Trust—"

Cut him off, I heard the words, but this didn't sound like Lazarus. He changed the subject. "You know what happened to Jeremy? And he was doing so well, and was vested—you are a rare case, you are on your way, *you* at least—" Lazarus was telling me to abandon Ariel. No job, no boss, no Ariel—much trouble as he was, we'd been through everything together.

"You have to think about yourself, your job. You can be saved. Don't consider anyone but yourself. I know you have trouble with that, but you have to learn. Listen to me," Lazarus said. "He's confused, he's attacking me."

I couldn't get him to explain.

"You love me, don't you?" he said, finally.

I nodded.

"Then ignore Ariel." When he said this his mouth was in a low, strange frown. "Please."

"Okay," I tried.

"Wonderful."

Something broke in my chest, when he said that word, "wonderful." I ached, after.

"Remember, you are on your way, don't think of the sad things! Don't you dare—this is Prologue—and an incredible opportunity!"

He handed me semi-translucent pants with a drawstring, and new slippers—it was an echo of the first day I went out with Jeremy. Except I wasn't coming back, so I was sadder. As I turned to change and pack, he called me over to say, "Malcolm."

I knew it on my skin. I believed it. He was going to touch me. They never touched us, of course, yet I still yearned for it. I dreamed of it, I burst for it, and was ashamed of myself for this. Once a boy grabbed Lazarus about the waist after he'd given him some toy, and Lazarus screamed, panicked, and called Vee to "pry this one off." The scene was awful, embarrassing, yet I wanted to re-enact it. I knew it was wrong, and it was too low, yet I saw myself doing it.

I turned and walked toward him, that hope in my heart.

He said, as if to ward me off: "Don't forget, don't forget!" In his old sweet rattling voice.

"What?" I wanted to know. If I could not get closer, to say goodbye, then, I wanted some wisdom from him, more than the rules.

"One day, but still not yet!"

How I loved him. I would take that sadness away. Someday, I told myself as I walked off, I would deserve his affection, earn it. One day I would be good enough, be an Heir, so he could touch me.

*

The Islands were still linked by a few bridges then. The next morning, I caught the Nat Car on the Sky Rail—lemon yellow, with metal seats. The Heir Car ahead of mine was brilliant white, with foam cushions. We went on a narrow cable strung along the hook of the shore of the shining Sea of Pontchartrain, which in those days was a fast slide, of two hours. When I arrived at the station on the U.A. side, I took the elevator down several stories. Through the glass I got a wide view of Re-New Orleans. It was crisp and pastel and full of turrets and verandas and pergolas—exquisite, clean, shining, and fashionable. Houses were close together and you could see the little patches of walled gardens behind them. I'd come into Re-New a few times when Jeremy took us over to perform in special, private Sims. This time, though, I had no lines to repeat to myself, no one reminding me what to say. Jeremy wasn't there holding my costumes, making me laugh. Reminding me to say Heirs, not T's, and never to say the worst names—*Shades, Bonesnakes, Zombos.* Vee wasn't in the dining tent, telling us to eat the breads he baked, the rice, the greens he stewed with fish. "Keep your strength," he always said. "Don't think you can eat that spun grass. That candy!" The "spun grass" was Heir food, brosia. Flax, not grass.

At Customs, I showed the appointment letter for the interview, and they let me through. I entered a Walled Urb alone for the first time. Outside the station, a few private vehicles, and one low, rubber-tired trolley rolled past, and Heirs waved their arms in greeting to each other, calling out, all smiles. They carried packages from the brosia merchants, the genenfabric stores. I contemplated their blank, open faces. Vee had told me once, "*If you make a man's face, his soul comes to you.*" It was quite the opposite of what Jeremy used to say, which was, "*All you have to do is look at them and figure out what face they want from you. Give them that, and nothing more.*" When it started to rain, I saw some of them open up the glowing shell umbrellas popular that season. In less than a minute, there were fifteen turban-shapes in the street, Heir legs poking out the bottom, all scurrying home.

As I waited under the awning for the very pretty rain to pass, I tried Vee's way. I fixed my eyes on the middle distance and held my mouth slightly open, hardly breathing, the way they did. I tried to investigate my inner emotion. But all I saw within was that silver skin the sun made on the Sea of Pontchartrain, that silver that was white, but also opal and pearl and steel, that silver that is no color at all of its own. I imagined it was a hint of what they felt: their *solid, obvious* ecstasy.

I hated the way my mind rushed about like a bird trapped in our old attic. Or one of those baby rats when they were finally set loose by their big tired mother. I was not an Heir, not yet. I still had thoughts of Ariel—what did he do or say that was beyond the limit? And of Jeremy—he did everything right, and he'd lost.

I was troubled. I felt no ecstasy at all. I did not even feel solid, or whole.

*

November 1, 2117
Curing Towers
Re-New Orleans, South Central District. U.A.

"**Y**ou are the one H. R. Gold Lazarus sent? You look young," she said. My new, possible boss, Dr. Lydia Greenmore, was speaking. She'd come to meet me in the reception area. An exceptionally handsome Heir. Slim, long legged. Doe-like features—a flared, very thin nose. Her beauty was practically an electric charge, an assault.

"My age is only approximate," I said. It was true. Nobody knew exactly when I was born. "They gauge sixteen this year."

"Of course, you wouldn't know, you were a toss-out, weren't you?"

Yes, that's what I was, all I was—I knew it, an upstart toss-out, nothing.

"Follow me."

I obeyed, keeping a respectful distance. She wore the standard WELLMED tunic. Underneath was a sculpted prodermis, in the current, dimpled, baroque style. She must have just had her Re-job. When we came into her vast blue office with the big marble desk, she turned to me and asked, "Are you hungry?" Then she raised her chin, awaiting an answer. Of course, she owned the conversation.

I hadn't developed a taste for brosias. I should have by now. I blamed Vee's influence. I couldn't forget that he'd said they were "good going in," but dissolved into "little slimies" in the mouth.

"Victuals, whatever you like," she said. "Go ahead, there is no penalty."

In no time she had ordered noodles in a peanut sauce and I was eating them from a white plate in my lap. They were very good, as Vee did them, spicy hot, with a little fish and big helpings of pepper. I began to sweat. She pointed to a napkin. I felt racy, daring, and awkward eating in front of her, but I couldn't help it. She didn't complain, not once, about how it smelled.

When I was done, I missed the slop, wished for more. My lips tingled, my mouth burned.

She had four orange lumps on her plate she hardly picked at.

"So this is your first day independent of the Foundling House? The Sim Company, Jeremy de Rayborn's Celebrations, went under, didn't it?" she said.

I nodded. I remembered what Lazarus had told me. *"Be brave. Answer, but don't elaborate. And never ask us about years, or count, never ask about family. Or what Wave—some of us are very touchy about where we came from after we enter this strat. When you go through your Boundarytime, you will realize you are not the same as your root self anymore. I know I'm open about such things.* He really wasn't that open. I knew very little of his Nat past. I'd asked once, and he said, *"There are all kinds of trouble back there. Sorrows. I've escaped and come to save all of you. From the uneven world, the world of consequences. We have found the way out of that. Never forget there is a way out."* I said to my interviewer, "Yes. I'm not in the Sims anymore."

"Are you attached to the sunken gardens you come from? The stenches? The floodwalls, the ring levees, the green courses, the raised roads, canals? Don't worry. Say what you think. We all know it's charming—even some Heirs can't leave it. Will you be able to adapt here? There's no point—tell me what you think," she leaned in, closer.

Say what I think. Everything I'd been taught went against this impulse.

I imagined the thin film, the mirror surface of the Sea of Pontchartrain I had noticed on the ride over on the Sky Rail. I knew there were lost towns underneath the sea that had lined the Northern shore and the Eastern edge of the old lakes—the Pontchartrain and the Maurepas—before they spread into a single sea, after the lands were lost and the Mississippi changed course. On cloudy days, I'd seen floating lamp posts under the surface, wrecked ancient cars, broken streets, the ridge pieces of old roofs. When the sun shone this morning as I was coming over, though, all I could take in was the shining surface.

"What are you thinking right now?" she asked and started to stand, which I found alarming. Would she leave so soon?

"That I will be happy here," I tried. I knew I sounded faint. I wanted to want this, but I really hoped to go home.

"Be truthful," she said.

"I'm thinking, I'm here to learn, to work."

"What?"

"Don't know what," I said, then I heard the voice in my head that got me into trouble, the one Lazarus disapproved of. Jeremy wasn't here to direct me. I added, before I could stop myself. "I am imagining that silver skin on the Sea of Pontchartrain."

"Why?"

I knew I should have kept my mouth shut. But I had too many things on mind. *Because that is how I want to be, to be like you,* I almost said. What I did say was, "I just was—"

She cocked her head. "Well let's play a game."

Women were awful, I thought. They read too well.

"The game, the game," she said. "If I was Jeremy, your director, and I asked you this, what would you say?" She had a list on a piece of paper. She read from it. "What is your first memory, Malcolm?"

"I don't have anything particular," I said. *Never talk about yourself. You haven't earned the right to be a subject.* I stared at her.

"Well I have a report that a Yeared assaulted you when you were five by count. Remember this? You pulled on her flapping skin? I don't blame you. The record says she was seventy-two by count, no surgeries! Who lets these abominations roam in the general population? I certainly sympathize. And there is a report you were found on the edge of the Old River with another child, older? There was a note you floated there in some kind of contraption? They theorized it might have been a drawer? You remember any of this?"

My whole life was written out for her there. "Not being found. Not much of the other, either—Lazarus told us not to bother with feelings and memories until we have the time to iron them out."

"He didn't," she said, throwing her head back, as if she saw the light, it was coming down from above. I'd know this gesture well in time.

"Yes he did."

"How brutal," she said, bending in. "That's what—your technique?"

"Lazarus was never brutal," I said. "He looked out for me. He still does."

"He was stealing something from you." She looked concerned,

upset.

"We all know we will have time to iron it out, if we—"

"Is that what he told you?"

"Everybody knows that," I said. I was chanting to myself by this time, *mirror silver, mirror silver,* but I still felt a sharp pain in my chest.

"Have I upset you?" she asked.

"Is this still the game?" I asked. I was losing!

This surprised her. But then, she took it on. "If you want. If I were Jeremy, this director, or someone else, what would you say now?"

"Stop looking at me that way," I blurted. I couldn't believe it. I covered my mouth, so nothing else so awful would escape.

"What way?"

"As if you want to *scour* me," I said—this line just leapt out. I knew I was dredging up the mess like what was at the bottom of the Sea of Pontchartrain. "You don't have any idea." I kept it up. What was I doing?

"Idea of what?"

"How *we really* are," I said. That was it. I was hopeless. I'd been hopeless since I'd come. I sounded like Ariel. As if how *we were* made any difference to her.

"I was Untreated once," she said. "I was a Natural until I was forty by count. I'm a Third Wave. Practically a Nuovo. I won the Albers Prize for my research. I am considered the inventor, or one of the inventors, of the process called Re-description, that Heirs go through. Heirs with bigger counts. Have you heard of that? That's how I got a Trust. Got this research position. Didn't Lazarus tell you who was going to interview you?"

"I'm sorry," I offered. "Truly. I shouldn't have said—"

"There's nothing to be sorry for." One eyebrow was raised. She started to stare then. She could do this all afternoon, and not be tired by it. She was scouring me. All I could do is look back, and try to parse out the song of those last lines, *didn't Lazarus tell you who was going to interview you? There's nothing to be sorry for.*

I knew there were people who said the opposite of what they meant. Heirs and Nyets and even Nats did this. You could tell what they intended only by the song. Jeremy taught me all kinds of songs for sentences. Sarcastic song, doubtful song, sincere song, insincere song. But she had a different beat from me, an Heir beat, and her voice was breathy and nearly tuneless. I couldn't be entirely sure.

She rose then. All I was sure of, was what an idiot I'd been. This disturbed me terribly, but something in me, also, didn't care. That awful reckless part I was always trying to kill off. *I'd had it bad since Jeremy lost out.* I was doomed because of it. She asked, "What did Lazarus tell you?"

"You might want to employ me. I'd help with your research. You would pay for some education. I would not get a better chance."

"I see," she said. She rose then, which disturbed me. "So are you going to obey Lazarus and work?"

"I always obey him."

"Why?"

"He cares for me," I said. I knew it was a weak answer. I was supposed to say that he would make me an Heir.

"I see." She was going. Finally. I was relieved. "Someone will come by."

I wanted to ask, *What about the job?* But I knew the answer, and besides, it was bad form. Heirs thought of all of us as beggars. Even Not Yets with large Trusts like me were beggars—some of them saw us as the hungriest of all, so close to the finish, the prize—

When she was gone, I believed I'd never see her again. I was confused, about that, about why I'd blown the interview, disobeyed everybody—I was miserable, but my misery wasn't going to last.

V

6:20 PM October 12, 2121
Sunken Quarter
New Orleans Islands, Northesast Gulf De-Accessioned Territory,
U.A. Protectorate

"*B*ebum, don't know what the job is. Gotta go see him." Peet shrugged, tapped his wrist, which had no watch. "Just heard of it, in the Crobster House."

"Let's go, then," Serp said.

"Hey," I said. The shadows of the wide pillars behind us seemed to be growing. I touched my face. It didn't clang quite as badly as it had. "I need my compos, remember?"

Serpenthead explained to Peet. "I got to get him over to Jeddy's lot. He's never been around here."

"Bebum. You wanna gig tonight or what?" Peet said.

"Okay," Serpent said, then turned to me. "Jeddy's ten minutes from here, tops. We'll talk to Lordy, come back, and then go get your fuel. Stay here."

Peet held up a tile that read:

CRAWLEY'S CROBSTER HOUSE
ON THE QUAY
NO. 17

He said, "Bebum. I was waiting on crobsters, not going to give up on 'em." He pointed to a restaurant. "Already paid."

"Okay," Serpent said, then his bulgy eyes surveyed the two of us. "Look Malc. You take the tile, you wait in the Crobster House—you see it over there?"

I could see the sign on the inner ring of the Old Market, the arcade Peet had come through.

"We'll go see Lordy, and come back to meet you, then go to Jeddy's. Promise." He was nodding, to reassure me. I think he saw I was a little scared, being alone in this raucous place.

Peet was eyeing me, in double time.

"He's a Nyet. He's going in for the Boundarytime ceremony. Fasting. He's not interested in your dinner! Let him wait for it. Then he knows we'll come back," Serp said.

"What, wait," I said. "I'll just get my compos. Tell me where the station is."

Both of them said, at one time, "You will never find it." Serp pulled on my sleeve, whispered into my good ear. "It's under the table. You familiar with this concept? They won't sell to you by yourself, see? One of us who knows Jeddy has to go to Jeddy's lot, get it, boy?"

I nodded. He was always ahead of me, somehow.

"Just sit anywhere inside and go up when they call the number 17. Got it? We will go talk to Lordy, get the job, then we come back, get the fuel, and the eats—" Serpent snapped his fingers. Before I could say no, they were off on the cobblestones, and I was going to a restaurant holding a wooden tile.

In Crawley's window, a short red-haired enclaver girl with a hat like a mushroom stirred away, the steam swirling up into her freckled face. Her smile greeted me through the hot mist. "Seat yourself inside," she said.

I lifted up my tile to show her.

"Ten minutes at the most," she nodded.

There were about a dozen picnic tables. People sat communally, where they could, many next to strangers, it seemed.

I took an empty one in the front so I could watch the street. It was a strange place to me—all strats together. I'd never seen this, only heard of it, and seen pictures in Lydia's (Lydia now, I could hardly believe it!)—picture albums. The ones from before the Troubles.

Some of the clientele inside were obvious Heirs, others, Nyets done up in decent, clean, expensive clothes to indicate their strats, their collars shining—the way I used to dress when I was working at the Towers. Seeing these clothes, I was ashamed, for mine were dirty, crumpled, from my nights in Port Gramercy, one in jail, and another on the wet, eventually bloody deck of Serio's boat. I'd been wearing them for three days. I counted, in despair. And with this gash on my ear, surely, I looked like an Outliar myself. I tried covering it with my hair. I plucked at my Not-Yet band, elongated my neck, so people would notice. But would they believe it? You could be anybody in this place. Altereds were strolling outside. One went by who was equipped with those wings—its clothing was cut out in the back so anyone could see the fine work of the surgeons. The muscles across the front of the chest were bulging, making him deformed—then I realized he'd developed that way to carry the weight of the new appendages. His spine was bent.

A set of three passed by in blue gowns, all exceptionally tall, with snouts like borzoi dogs. A group of four in yellow short pants, with dragonfly style double wings on their backs. Following behind them, a mascot on a leash perhaps two feet tall, a folded face like a bulldog, a gargoyle. I had never heard of an Altered that owned an Altered, but that seemed to be the case. There were also several Heir women with cut-out gowns which exposed their handsome custom prodermis breasts, covered in the latest eye-catching overskins. These baubles bounced and swayed. A few had three, one four. I couldn't keep my eyes off.

There were many normal-looking Heirs wearing genenfabric sheaths, and headjobs, with braids and cascades, as well—Second Waves, and Third, I thought. Also, what I took to be Nuovos fraternizing easily with their betters. All out for an evening watching the show.

At one point, a female Heir stopped in the middle of the sidewalk, bent down, and threw-up about three tablespoons of bluish liquid. Her companions didn't halt and scream, and pull the WELLVAC alarm on her pendant, order helicopters to the scene, the way they usually did at the slightest indication of illness. Instead, the other T's with her just stood there, a bit miffed. Then one, a man, put his hand in the small of her back and whispered to her to move on, which is exactly what she did. Never seen anything like it.

"What would you have to drink?" a new girl asked me as she rolled out a plastic sheet to cover my table.

"I am here waiting," I told her. I wasn't familiar with the protocols of restaurants. I had never been able to afford them. I held up Peet's tile.

But she said, "Drinks are on the house this hour. Joy Dusk—" With that, she picked up her two pitchers—in one the drink was pale blue-green, in the other, something pink. I chose the first. When she leaned over to give me a glass and pour, I saw the little brass pin on her white blouson, FREE WHEEL NORTH COUNCIL. And I recalled a sweet voice and when I'd first seen that symbol.

How weak I was once, I thought.

I was better now. Yes, I was over all that. Finally. (Though there was that incident in Port Gram.)

VI

Evening
November 1, 2117
Curing Towers
Re-New Orleans, South Central District. U.A.

She had a melody when she talked, it was constant, never too high. "You Malcolm de Lazarus from Audubon Foundling House in the DE-AX? Down in the drowning Islands? The Sim rental boy they sent? You had an interview with Dr. Greenmore at lunch?"

The office door had suddenly opened. This seemed miraculous—I'd been locked inside a long time. A round face. A brown haired Nat, in a beret. A girl. I thought she came from some kind of dream—her features so broad across her face, cat-like. Her arms, and cheeks, and her dimple. *Oh no*, I thought.

"I blew it." For hours, I'd been sitting there, wallowing in all the things I did wrong in the interview. I was sick, an idiot.

"If you think they hung the moon, you'll do fine. They think so too," she chirped.

But she was really going to show me out, not give advice, I thought. Back to the Sky Rail.

She added, "I'm here to get your body to your room. Okay?"

I had no idea who she was, or what she was talking about. Honestly, I'd never seen one quite like her: young, young as I was, plump, healthy, amber-eyed. She was wearing an opaque black shirt and slacks, cream colored. Loved the beret. Later I'd learn that all the attendants wore these. But that night, I considered it her personal style. She was carrying a cloth sack. The strongest, strangest scent floated up, filling my nostrils with a rich, blue-red warm explosion.

"Let's get you going," she said.

I was used to skin and bones. I could see the Free Wheel insignia with the words *Port Gram* on her lapel. I knew the logo Strict. Famous for adhering to the fertility codes. I'd only seen males from that enclave; they didn't let their women out often in the DE-AX. So she was something new. She took my arm and led me out into the hall. All the other doors along it were closed. The ceilings were high, glowing, and the floor, stone.

"This is a hospital, but they call it a Curing Tower," she said. "We take care of the Protos. Some First Wavers coming in now. Heirs only, of course."

A few raspy voices complained from behind the closed doors. *What are you doing to us? Why must we endure this? That stench again?*

I said, "They don't get sick—" as we pushed through the thick fire doors at the end of that corridor, and came outside. I was shocked to see it was night. The air was cooler, compared to the heat of the indoors.

"They don't like our food, how we smell, all that rot, you heard all this, before, I guess."

I nodded.

"Oh, we do mental here. I guess you will get to that. They are amazing in some ways. Alive in the age of Disney or Dylan, or Elvis, I mean, saw the archaic wars in the Fugue Age— knew Albers, personally, they—" she caught herself. "Sorry, I have to eat. Dr. Greenmore came up to me right at my supper hour, and told me to go get you." Without a hesitation she offered me half her sandwich. Then, she asked, "You eat regular victuals, right? You can't go in for years, right?"

Stunning inside my mouth, gelatinous, dark, dense. I remembered the name. *Hamburger.* Only had it when things were flush, when I was very young. Those last few years with Jeremy's shows, the commissary was spare. Vee almost always made fish at the Home, mostly shrimp and crawfish, he didn't allow flesh of beef or pig. Chef Menturians were Afro-Vietnamese, he'd told me. They had their "old Buddhist rules, modified."

"For an Heir, I think Greenmore's okay. Actually helps some of these," she said.

"You haven't said what's wrong with them." She had said *for an Heir,* as if she could judge.

"I said you will get to that. Didn't you hear me?"

"Well what *can* we talk about?"

She pouted, shrugged. Oh, her mouth.

I tried, "You an enclaver? Free Wheel. How is that?" Free Wheel had it pretty good, relatively speaking, I had heard. They got a Charter early, when the terms were more generous.

"We've got our system. The place isn't full of rapscallions. You been to Chef Menteur? Open enclave, everybody looking for an angle, leaving their own kin behind? And the rich getting out, the rest starving? All them poor houses up on stilts 'bout to drown? Twenty feet in the air? Not like that. We are orderly, we are on the cycle. We have a natural levee we live on, high ground, up here, north shore of the Sea. We don't toss out." She let her chin rise, then she dropped it. "Never. Criminal offense. Everybody gets a Procreation Certificate when they marry, that's the end of that. The same for all. We have the Free Wheel principles. Populations Stasis. I wouldn't have it any other way."

"Is *that* right?" I asked, mocking her. I knew every enclave tossed out, some hid it better.

"Yes, that is right," she snapped back. "A lot have the Free Wheel charter, we follow it."

Then she explained to me that she was born and she was going to have two children with her husband who was already picked out for her, and then, after a long life, she was going to do the so-long, which she called dying and later, her progeny were going to do the same. She used the word "dying" as if she didn't know she was cursing. She went on at some length before she said, "Why you looking at me like that? You never seen an enclaver who believed before? No Gramercian?"

"And the Fertility Codes?"

She drew back from me a bit, one open hand on her beautiful breast. "They are what make it all work. They are the core. We have enough for everybody."

Jeremy once called enclavers like her, "doctrinal lunatics." He didn't even like to hire the males to set up the tents, build the sets, work the props. They were too prudish, too by-the-book. Never stayed for the overtimes, put a limit in the contract on the encores. Walked away after mere 14 hour shifts. He used to ask me who they thought they were.

I mocked her. "You really believe all of it? Every bit?"

She hesitated. "Huh? Yes. Yes. Of course I do." Then she turned, sharply, and yanked me through another courtyard, and another, the walls covered with beautiful, intricate mosaic murals, abstract and swirling—greens, blues, reds. I was impressed to see the Towers were so well-designed. Her fresh cheek in that coral light, her hair lit from above, dark, shining. The whole time, she talked about her enclave and how wonderful it was—but I thought maybe she protested too much, as Jeremy used to say.

And, I couldn't put aside absurd, filthy ideas: a man like me, if he were another sort of man, could leave, cash in his Trust, get a fast electric, and go after one like her. *What if I were that stupid*, I thought. *Good I'm not.*

Jeremy tried taking back all he'd said about enclavers, those last days before his Trust was rescinded. *They have a kind of life*, he allowed. *It has its* sturm und drang, *its ferocious momentum. I mean, after all, imagine—NO encores. ONE chance at it all.*

She led me toward a tall building on piers. We climbed the stairs, entered, went down a corridor. She punched a code to unlock my door. Not much in there, just a bed, a desk. But mine, all mine. My own room. She stood back, in the hall, behind me, silent. As if I were suddenly a stranger, after all that talk.

"Good night," she said, abruptly, her hand on her collar. Then she pivoted, practically ran down the hall, her little beret sliding off. Well, she was trouble, I knew that.

*

The next morning, there she was again.

"Malcolm de Lazarus, you in there? I have to give you something." She paused. She had more to say, apparently. (*How was this a surprise?*) She was just outside the door. "You know, don't you, that I'm betrothed, you heard of that? My husband-to-be is named Landry. Landry from the Domino Clan. I'm here working on my dowry, that's it. You heard of that? We've applied for our P.C., that's for Procreation Certificate? You understand? We are due two babies. Two in the Domino line. Like I said, we have strict Fertility Codes and we enforce—"

Why did she have to go over this all again? I was not trying anything. I knew better. She insisted. "I am not an idiot," I mumbled through the door.

"Promise. Mean it. You know what I'm worried about?" she asked. "Or have you had it done—you know?"

"No not fixed." Jeremy had said not to get it too young, it was bad for your "drive." In fact, he'd told me even to the last, he had not been cut, he had been planning to get to Memphis for that.

I had *done it*, if that was what she wanted to know. The Sim staff found girls so I could *do it*. Outliars with sterility tattoos, certificates. *Just so you know*, Jeremy had said. *Just so you know and can put all that out of your mind. You know about the DNA Securitas? They find one living, or even so-longed, anywhere, even tissue—they look at it all, scan every piece that turns up, they have their ways—no poor girl gets an evacuation without them snooping around—they have dogs in the sewers, along the river banks, in the dumps, no form of disposal is safe— they find you produced offspring, even an itty bitty embryo, you will never be Treated. They will not let you through. All this is for naught. You understand? You are good looking, Nat girls will like your shoulders, your height, your hard brow, your hair, even your unusual mouth. These things get them giddy. They will try to trick you. So you will have to learn to keep them off—I have the tools."* And he handed me condoms thick as rainboots, which is what he called them.

Skinny girls with indigo S's on their chests, and shaved little pubises had shown up later in the evening, at my door. Another smaller "S" there, right above the slit. These were toss-outs, not from a Home. Sheltered by Outliars from the canal houses, probably, but had to work, or came from the floating slums. Who knew where they lived? They always requested hard currency. Enclaver crowns, U.A. notes, they didn't care—but not promises, no credit. And they examined the rainboots with a special light their agents gave them—before and after. Their eyes were flat. They always, always, even before we got started, had an obsession with the shower—how long could they use it when we were done? How many gallons of heated water, approximately? And they came with their own wads of paper towels. Cleaning up the fluids, any spills. Even with the condoms. Which Jeremy requested after, and threw into boiling water as soon as I handed them over, "to kill any cheeky survivors," he said. The girls burned the paper towels after they stripped the bed, put the sheets in laundry tubs, checked the temperature of the water, made sure it was close enough to boiling. I had tried to put it all out of my mind—except, except, the fact of their faces when I entered them—I looked, even though they told me not to, Jeremy told me not to, I did look. I hurt them. I knew exactly how much I hurt them, but it hurt me, too. That was my secret: I hated it because I saw how much I hurt them. That seemed weak, or wrong, but it was true. I didn't ask for them often. But now, in this girl's presence, things came back, from those awful shameful nights. Even seeing their pain, something broke open in me, even with those bored, scared, little reptile girls—and after, I knew it was wrong, forbidden, but I wondered what had happened to them—

I looked at Camille through the crack of the door, and all those explosive, shameful moments flew up at me. It occurred to me she was right, she shouldn't come in. She was just the sort I wanted to squeeze, hold tight. I could have sworn I had held her already, many times before. That was the funny thing. How familiar she was. Of course I let her in.

"You pick your husband? They let you pick?"

"None of your business," she said, glancing to the right. "Look," she said, her tone now meant to calm me, settle me. "I have my orders."

"What did she say? Dr. Greenmore?"

"She didn't let you know?" Pointing those pools at me. Which were not vacant—but daring, sharp. She quoted from a mobile screen she took out of her pocket. *"'He goes through an inundation, with Galcyon. He will be educated, formally. Camille, monitor him.'"* She looked up and blushed. "That's me, Camille." Then she continued to read from the screen, in a monotone. *"'His guardian Lazarus already gave permission. So say that if he asks. He does whatever his guardian says. The process will be four months, maybe. Then we will take a break, see how he does on his trials.'* Those are the orders, come right down from the Shade."

"You call her that?" I asked. "She's your Heir. You work for her!"

She said, "Not to her face." She looked down, then up again, fiercer now. "I am not taking any advice from you. You have no standing with me. I've seen Nyets before."

"What do you think of us?"

"Cold as a frosty morn," she said, and she showed me her chin. It was such a pretty chin, with a dimple. "That's what they say where I come from."

"Why?" I asked.

"Because they think they are like the Shades, they are stuck up—by association—rule over everybody when they got nothing but a lick and promise those snakes will break—" she said. "So I hear?"

"You heard lies," I said, stung. I changed the subject—I was scared of Galcyon. Ariel told me once it could kill you—addictive as well as expensive. O used to give it to him, he'd said once, without elaborating. For fun, O called it.

"So?" Camille said. "Like Heirs care you get addicted?" Her eyes cast about. "Now take a good look at this room, this space, this floor. Get used to it. This is where you are. Don't forget. It might throw you later."

I looked up at her, concerned.

"Don't worry. I take you through it."

I believed her.

It was charming how she stood back and thrust the cup toward me. The odor of almonds filled the air.

"What is it made of?" I asked.

"The chemicals? Don't know. Why don't you read the pharmacology screens in a couple of months and tell me?"

"Read?" I couldn't.

"Just you wait," she said. "This stuff will have you knowing it all in no time." She sat on the gray saddle seat at my desk, her short feet in soft slippers curling on the floor. "I won't leave you. Some are allergic." She whispered, leaning forward so I could see a bit inside her blouse. As soon as she realized this, she sat up straight again. "You'll do okay. Now drink up."

I obeyed.

Sometime in the middle of the night my dreams went from pastels to the most startling crimsons and emeralds and ceruleans. They took on amazing detail—the spinning of metal fans in the corners, the way the curtains blew, the color of the toenails of women, Ariel walking down to the end of an enormous hall, everything around him glowing orange. I awoke and saw Camille in a chair, her head down on my desk. She startled, then her eyes smiled at me, and she said, "Malc? Okay?"

Malc. (Ones at the Home—Vee, especially—called me Malc, how did she know?) I said, "Okay."

"Got you covered," she said, waving at me as if I were an old friend.

In my dream I grabbed her, held on tight, and began to fall, and fall—

*

The light. "*You are going to learn a few things this morning,*" a recorded voice said. "*You can go in any order you like on this tier.*"

A screen now where the window was. The pictures started. Jeremy had taught me some sight words. I knew perhaps a hundred. That was all. And I had the alphabet. But that day there were thousands of words, in order, in lists. There were mouths on the screen telling me the meaning of each one, at the same time as I saw those written—ten, twelve a second, then repeated. Every fifteen minutes or so, pathway trials. I recalled almost everything asked. It was easy. Somehow my brain had bloomed. The voice came on, said, "*Good for you, Good for you.*"

Blink.

The next week, arithmetic. I couldn't close my eyes for long, I might miss something. Parts of my head actually hurt but I couldn't rest—I was too alert, my awareness too crisp, too sharp. Division, around dusk. "*Good boy, Malcolm. Good boy.*" Percents. What one hundred was really, one thousand, how many years were meant by the number, the year, we were in: 2117.

*

At some point, days or weeks later, I had no idea of time at that point, Dr. Greenmore checked in, in the body, in the flesh, with a meal, a flat round bread with red topping. She said she loved "pizza" when she was of my strat. Friendly, it was odd. I was snot in our interview. I had no idea why she'd hired me, much less, why she was paying me this kind of attention.

She looked at me a long time, very curious, but said nothing. When she sat down in the chair close to me, she made a gesture, as if she were going to push the hair out of my eyes, but of course, she couldn't—wouldn't. I was surprised, interested, then, she pulled back.

"So is this pace all right?" she asked.

She was rather frightening to see in this state. I mean, in my state. Her rate of breathing, its awful threatening slowness, her fingertips, oval and circular underneath the beige overskin. The noise her transparent dress (golden) made on the paper blanket of my bed. The sad gush of her voice. She said to me, "Put out your wrist."

What was she going to do?

A small sensor, a tiny hat, over her index, and her finger hovered above the place where the blood went in blue lines into my naked hand.

Her eyes floated in their chemical syrup toward the upper left, then away, then back up toward the upper left again where the slightest piece of dust, actually two fronds of a down feather, each about three centimeters in length, floated down and rested on her long implanted lashes. My nail was sharper than hers and so I lifted my hand and reached to help her with this bit of dust, but then I remembered myself, I knew I could not, and so I hesitated, until the feather was far enough away—what was the safe distance? I'd forgotten. Eight, ten inches—

from her face as it fell. Eventually, I caught it on my finger.

When it was balancing there, I let go the smallest little package of air from my cheeks through my mouth and blew. The feather drifted away, from left to right to left. I watched it—I saw she watched it too. Everything was excruciatingly interesting. She smiled as if she were amused, and said, "Thank you Malcolm." I looked at her eyes— impossible yellow. Her overskin the palest taupe, just a few strands of silver. Jeremy would have said, "A very good Re-job was done on her."

Eventually she concluded, "You can have a little more. Your vitals are fine." She seemed to pull back, to increase the distance between us.

It tasted like vanilla this time. Higher dosage.

"You have to absorb all that," she said. "I'll give you about forty hours." She left.

I missed her.

After, I was supposed to sleep, but instead I watched the story of the day jumble itself into the most exquisite designs that eventually had nothing to do with the day at all. When I woke, I asked myself where I was, for I had lost track. But the whole idea of "I" seemed suddenly bizarre—a little vessel I decided to remind myself to go searching for, searching for "I," the Malcolm, as I was gloating, floating, in a sea of elementary details. Such as, how many thousands in a million and water vapor making rain and cirrus and cumulus and crystals, and the amazing meaning of the word "snow" and too and two and to, and to, and into, and forward, and toward and per and perpetual, and persuasion and perspective and persona, and person. And person. Dr. Greenmore. Myself. Person. Malcolm. The person Malcolm, the foundling from Audubon Island, which is capitalized, and here, Re-New Orleans Curing Towers, in the South Tower. The calendar year 2117 it was, one hundred and twelve years after the Reveal, when they claimed everyone could live forever. Then somehow drowsiness ambushed me with two huge paint brushes in its hands, my itchy eyes had to close so things mumbled into nimbuses, and I knew somewhere some things I'd never known. My head was ten times bigger than my little feet and hands and I thought I'd scream about this but I was asleep, and I had to give over to it. It was so delicious, to sleep, to have strange pizza in my belly, for I was aware, even, of all the explosions in my stomach, and the dissolving and the pressing on, everything. I also knew how to count and the word for the line around a square that delineates what was outside it and what was inside, like a fence or a border or a frame or a wall, or a skin. A skin was a perimeter, I thought. My skin was a perimeter, which must surround a being, a boundary, and that being would be Malcolm. And Malcolm was the name of the "I." What was inside it? Inside him? Any ideas?

Sometimes, I looked down and saw that chasm, where "I" was supposed to be. It terrified me.

✱

History. Review. For the exam. Two and a half months later. I spent my time suspended in a flood of images, except for Camille's longed-for visits (she came nearly every day) and occasionally, checkups from Dr. Greenmore. The solitude was necessary—all my attention was meant to be attuned to the endless screens, the hoods they put me in. I couldn't even be taken out into the courtyard—just looking out the window was too maddening. They locked the shade when they realized this. I'd finished elementary education. My trials had all been excellent, the screens told me.

Then one morning when I was listening to a lecture in Reveal History, something happened that changed me.

"Dr. Shamir Albers explored a system of life extension treatments beginning in the early 1960's. He began in secrecy at the Pfizer-Wellcome labs in Tacoma Park, Maryland (Now the Delmarva District in the United Authority). His firm was later renamed WELLFI, INC. Four decades later, his laboratory announced to the scientific community that their cure for the disease of aging had achieved extraordinary results. Mice that should have had a life span of 36 months were living twelve years. His discoveries were based upon the work of many before him. He relied upon metabolic manipulation studies that went back thirty years and more. In the 1980's, starting with a combination of therapies involving his original "cellular rinse" procedure, endocrine manipulations and nano level monitoring and feedback, Albers initially developed a method of periodic holistic treatments that could be regulated to postpone the onset of age-related conditions virtually forever. A further refinement was the prodermis and overskin, to provide cushioning and UV protection. He offered these to volunteers in his immediate circle, and then created a large group, who took the treatments covertly, and invested in Albers' company. Almost all are still alive today. They are known as the Albers Prototypes, or the Protos. They were first shown to the world in the year 2005, the date of The Reveal."

Camille walked in, and stepped in front of my screen. Not out of the ordinary.

But, her little jacket was tighter than usual. Or she had put on a pound or two. When she shoved her hands in her pockets, I missed them. "Finished with this review?" she said. The desire to touch her springy body, her more unpredictable flesh, so vulnerable and with a will of its own, not under her control entirely, compared to a prodermis. It was, what was the word? For *"possible to be perforated."*

I thought: all this education and I still hadn't lost my low traits. In fact, the education, or the drug, more likely, just made me worse. I was abashed, how much I wanted her. The screen: *"...Shamir Albers experimented upon himself, and did a so-long at the unfortunately premature count of 111. Some of his early working theories were later proved to be false, and even harmful... yet his research and the technique remains the foundation of longevity science."*

She put her fingers in the corners of her mouth, and pulled down. Mock tragedy.

"Stop," I said. "Have some respect!"

She made a loop with index and thumb. The other fingers rose, and the eyes went up. OK. She was awful, awful. I walked over and took hold of her hands. Both of them. I couldn't stand it if she hid them again.

"The shrine of this great man, who changed the entire meaning of being human, was permanently moved into the rotunda of the building previously used as a parliament of argument during the days of the old republic, when that unstable form of government was replaced by the United Authority Council, in 2047."

She let me hold her a second, the she pulled away. She was staring right at me. Up from my arms towards my shoulders, the strangest feeling—a kind of web forming. I couldn't tell if it were coming from her. Or from me. I could hardly breathe—

"The narratives of sacrifice, martyrdom and privation in the lives of the earliest subjects, the first Protos, are the stuff of legends. Collectively, Albers and his fellow scientists have changed the world, postponing possibly infinitely the greatest source of suffering—evolved beyond the simply human state."

"What bagasse!" she said, smiling, showing me something, dark like a bird at night, flying, and beautiful, I saw it in my mind's eye. I couldn't help it, I took her around the waist.

She inhaled the slightest bit of air, surprised, then kept my gaze. "That would make me tragic?"

"What is bagasse?" I asked. My mouth was dry. I was dizzy.

"The chaff of cane, pulp, garbage!"

Why were we talking about history? About anything outside what spanned us? I couldn't even think—

She said, "bagasse," again, and bit her lips. Her heart was pounding too. She had not pulled away.

"In the year 2005, the President revealed that he was a Prototype, as was most of his cabinet. Hundreds of scientists gathered to attest to the fact that the several hundred thousand who had been taking Albers Treatments had technically not aged at all in the 26 years they had been under Dr. Albers' care. Except for their replaceable prodermises, their low BMI, the First Wavers were no different from people around them who were only middle-aged or younger by count. Their mental and sensory capacities were the same, except for the absence, or decrease, through hormonal manipulations, of some of the lower appetites, which gave them a superior vision of reality."

"Superior? Bull," she said.

"Bull?" I asked, still holding her. She had not pulled away.

"Albers' subjects were, chronologically, between the ages of sixty and a hundred by count. An elevated age in the old world, but in the new one, young men and some women, in their prime! Public reception of this news was immediate and profound. The President announced this to be the greatest achievement in human history, greater even than the discovery of the Americas, or the ventures into space, saying, and 'All of history is Prologue.'

Acceptance of the new, Post-Reveal Age was not universal. After the first few years, protest groups emerged, forms of political/pseudo-philosophical objection, both based in what Arturo calls the 'Grand Substitutions' for Immortality—ancient mass religion and 20th century salvationist-plastimaterialism. The latter continues to be practiced today in foreign regions still in the throes of fugue capitalism and unregulated digital elaboration—both developments were outlawed in our territories in the early 2020's, in the start of the President's fifth term, at the same time of the New Constitutional Convention that established the first underpinnings of the United Authority and re-drew the boundaries of the former United 'States.' There were pockets of rebellion well into the late 2070's, and in the De-Accessioned Territories under Authority protectorate rule until the end of the last century, the final one being the long siege of the West Florida Federation, the Police Action of Perdido Bay, which, when WELLFI Security prevailed, was the end of the military phase of the partition, pacification, Enclavization of those on the continent still resistant to the Reveal. Internationally, today, all elites have begun to be Treated, and the struggle to transform culture has made great strides. Old philosophies are slowly dying out. The rearrangement of the economy away from the wasteful fugue cycles, and toward the preservation of the Heirs and values based on the Elysian Reality has led to a—"

She was in my arms. Our ribs were touching, our waists, our—

In that dangerous moment, this was my thought: if she were to kiss me once, I would be ready to throw it all over. Trust, hope, Lazarus, job, collar—I knew it was wrong, but I was willing, and purely, I didn't care.

She was still pretending this wasn't happening. "Greenmore says you should be ready for your tests."

I nodded. "I know." I knew all kinds of things now, including what something in me wanted to do to Camille, not just the mute and shameful desire, but every English word for it.

Finally, she pulled back enough to slide a drive in the slot. And blink. Trying to break the trance.

"Give me the Galcyon," I said.

"She said half a dose." But my arms were around her again.

"Now she's got you hooked, you gotta be unhooked," she whispered.

"Don't leave me," I pleaded. I could have sworn we had run off together already. "Just say the word—"

"Why you tease me like that? You know it's not fair—" But she was still in my arms.

"What's fair?" I said. "You and me, that's fair." I kissed her. Smack. She was sweet and rich and better than I could have thought. Smack again. No slap. She was on her tip-toes, she was pulling down her beret to hide our mouths. She kissed me back, she did. Twice. I slid my hand under that waist of hers, soft. Everything so soft. She was my girl. She was—

She threw her head back, snorted—but it was too late, said, "Don't."

"You kissed me!"

"Don't," she said. "It's a danger." She looked so sad.

"You want me," I said.

"I do not. I do not."

"But you know what's true."

"Wish I did!" she said.

"I thought you were so sure!"

"You think this is a game?"

"I don't, I don't," I said.

She said she had to go, and she left.

I was grieving then, truly grieving.

*

A week later Dr. Greenmore showed up after dinner. I was in my room, leaning against my desk. Exactly where Camille had been. She said, "You have done better on your tests that we had any reason to expect."

I was more normal, then. Not on so much Galcyon. They had been letting me out in the evening to eat, since I'd finished the tests. I was being detoxified, re-socialized. It was a process that would take months. Sometimes I believed my obsession with Camille was just an artifact of those druggy days. But there was such a certainty about it, at other times. She was mine. It would happen. I found myself seeing it coming true. I wondered could Greenmore see it. She was scouring, again.

"You—" she said, when she opened those gold eyes. "You don't have much of a dent on your lip, it's a bit odd, has anyone said anything to you about that? Ever?"

I knew that. Something so silly. That was it? That little dip between nose and mouth others had. Mine was quite faint, in fact, you could say, non-existent. But my upper lip itself had quite a peak, fleshy, and it hooked over the bottom one, which made my mouth interesting, Jeremy told me. Camille had kissed it, so it was worth something. "Somebody must have sewed it," I said.

"When?"

"Jeremy told me it must have happened. He said it must have been slit, cleft, a little bit, not much, and then sewed." He said I had a *period face*. Ariel had the lip, too. This was true, but I hadn't thought of it in years. Some trick the people who threw us away had done to us before they left us to rot. They circumcised certain tribes, marked animals to brand—that was one explanation, at least. Jeremy had suggested it. Some enclaves stitched a web between the first two fingers, took off the earlobes. Loose bands of Outliars did it too, marked their progeny with tattoos—the "S" girls.

"Well," she said, backing away, as if she suddenly smelled me, or took some other offense, I had no idea what it was. "That would be the fact of it, then. Though there isn't any scar I can see."

"I don't remember. My lip was like this when I was found," I said.

She raised her brow, she was done. "Well, what can it matter? Anyone who might say anything would just be superstitious," she said. Then she stood, without explaining, and said good night.

*

For a while, I eased into the Curing Towers routines. I took a job as a dishwasher in the Victuals Hall, which was for "Nats and Nyets." I was mentally and physically exhausted during these days, and couldn't endure much stimulation—I slept a great deal, and I was quite forgetful about everyday things for a while, though my education didn't fade.

I hadn't met any other real Nyets working or eating there though, I was the only one. They were all enclaver contract workers, like Camille. I sat with her at breaks. She let me, after some protest. She just avoided being alone with me. Never ever came to my room anymore. Since she wouldn't kiss me, I fought with her.

She said things like, "time is the medium of life." I said, "Time is what life is trying to escape." She said, "Time is on a cycle." I said that was her enclave propaganda. She asked, "Well how can you take the color out of paint?" I said, you can, and she said, "With what, bleach? What is paint with no color?" This was a Free Wheel bromide. I told her she wasn't original. I said, more than once, "There is such a thing as pigment—color in its ideal form, it's pure." This one flummoxed her for a while. I was even sorry. But then she came back. "By themselves I don't think pigments mean much. They are like, what, waiting to live, waiting to be brought to life? Before the cloth is dyed or the emulsion is brought out and blended and spread, when the pigment is still sitting in the closet—waiting to be color—what is it then? What?"

"What's eternal?" I asked.

"Well, those Shades don't seem Eternal to me, they seem miserable," she said.

"You'd be Treated if you could do it. Anybody would." I was being cruel. Free Wheelers weren't ever allowed to go in, no matter if they somehow got the money. That was what it said in their Charters.

"I would not," she said. "Go see them in the North Tower. Then you tell me."

I said she was exaggerating. No Heir I'd ever talked to, and I had talked to many, carried on long conversations with them I was proud to say—had ever mentioned such as what she described.

I'd been in the Curing Towers for months at that point, and I had never seen the "clients," as they were called. And I'd heard very little about them except Camille's extreme descriptions. Most of the workers refused to speak of them at all.

"I'll show you then," she said.

My ploy had worked. She said she'd meet me. We would be alone, sort of. Did this mean she'd decided something? That there was a chance?

We made a date for one night at sunset, when there weren't that many dishes to wash. I was still too sensitive to the day sun.

The gate to the North Tower garden was not locked. I was supposed to meet Camille inside. The orange–pink balloon lamps went on just as I approached the place. The stone pathways crossed. There were palm trees in the center in a ring. If I turned around I could see all the other Towers of the center, the signature gleaming mosaic tiles. No Camille.

Eventually, I spied a group of very quiet Heirs sitting on chairs in a row on a patio outside. Their pale grayish-blue organdium gowns blended with the dusky sky, which was almost like water. They stared, unresponsive.

In that light, they looked quite transluscent, not only their gowns, their skin. I felt more concrete by contrast. They were perfectly still, did not move. I saw a man at the far end, who did not have on the gown the others wore—instead a rumpled suit, fancy and very out of style. He was in the same trance as the others, though.

There was nothing really wrong with these people. So Camille was lying, but where was she?

Then, a low pitched wail startled me.

The figure in the suit trembled, then shook, then rattled, awful, like something coming up through him from a hollow place under the pavement. Louder, then softer, then louder again. He shook so violently I thought his limbs would come off.

The others yelled, in sympathy—a whole chorus of gravelly Heir voices.

I went in closer.

I recognized the white-less eyes.

Him. The only Heir I actively disliked. Now he was truly frightening, rattling like that in his chair. Scaring up his cohorts. O.

For old reasons and new ones, I wanted to run. I turned.

"You believe me then?" Camille had come up behind me. I startled.

"I don't know," I said.

"What would it take for you to?" she said. She looked at me from head to toe, drew me in with her eyes. I felt this in my arms, my whole trunk, something bright running down. It was awful. Wonderful. The web, like before, bigger now. I closed my eyes, opened them.

Only inches away. Cinnamon on her breath. She whispered, very faintly, "No, you can't, you can't believe me. I can't believe you. You can't believe in me. I can't believe in you. "

"Yes you can," I said. I took her towards me, dragged her away from the sheen of the orbitals, high on poles above, and kissed her perfect, perfect mouth. She stepped away, folded her arms in front. Finally, I said, "Why won't you believe in me?"

"You'll be one of those!" She pointed, and then she was running down the winding path.

I chased after her, the Heirs' moans rising, my face filling with tears—I never cried, but I was crying. My chest, my whole body gouged out, gaping, wanting. I had never hurt like that.

*

A few days later, I learned that Dr. Greenmore was "preparing" my assignment. The first news I'd had from her a month. I also heard that Camille had a new job, in another Tower. Nobody had any explanation—someone just said she had switched departments, and, "we thought you knew." A short blond fellow with a Gaist patch on his pale green medic's shirt took a urine sample from me, looked into my pupils with a little flashlight and said, "You are almost back, de Lazarus. Ready for adventure?"

"What adventure is that?" I asked.

"How should I know what the doctor wants you for?" he asked. "Who can tell what they want? I've never figured it out. They have what they want. That's the matter with them."

I came home one night a few days later, and found my door ajar.

I prayed it was Camille, but instead, it was the last person I'd ever thought I'd see. He'd broken into the Curing Towers, no mean feat, and talked a guard into letting him in my room, even though he looked a fright. Ariel.

I knew what Lazarus had told me, but I couldn't help myself. I wasn't unhappy to see him.

His hair was tied up in a bandana, his legs folded tailor-style in my chair. Tanned the color of fine maple wood, and his dark hair, which was not quite as curly as mine, wavy and long, had been bronzed in the sun.

An old ghost of an urge to hug him. I did it. He stank a little. "What do you want?"

"If you thought about it, you could guess," he said.

"Sorry, I'm no good at that."

"It's a little thing. But for me, life and death."

I was actually going to call Securitas, but then Ariel said, "Remember the last time we did a Sim together? There's something I need to say about that. "

I couldn't call any officers.

*

It was an awful story.

When I was at my peak, around eleven by count, I had really high billing in a Sim. With my influence, I had gotten Ariel a part. I thought he could try again, come into the business on my coat tails. It wasn't that long after the time I found him weeping, claiming he was permanently estranged from   O.

It was a funny-all Sim, with lots of extras, quite the sensation that year. Ariel's role was, "Walker, Religious Processional." He had to march around a track, with a huge puppet on his back, of a man tied to two crossed sticks. The thing must have weighed sixty pounds. Ariel didn't weigh much more.

No surprise, he wasn't grateful. He kept asking me if O, or friends of O, were in the audience, to see his troubles. He complained bitterly during every break. I heard him whining to Vee, who was doing the catering for the Nats on that set. Vee took him aside at one point, and told him, "They aren't like us, Ariel. They have no sense of time, no sense of proportion—it can't be helped." I knew Vee didn't believe in Sims, didn't believe in "mimesis." It was one of the rules of the Chef Menteurians, but he realized Ariel needed to play along.

This funny-all was like all the rest, we "mourned" around a coffin, and there were parades, and lots of mock tears—this would go on for days. Then, eventually, the one whose portrait we were all carrying, the one who had "so-longed," an Heir, would emerge from hiding at the moment the coffin was found empty, and say, "I'm still here! Ha-Ha! Ha-Ha!" And the music would go up tempo, we'd all dance. A "rough comedy," as Jeremy described it in the publicity "With Old New Orleans touches, and brass." A tragedy with a happy ending. The Heirs devoured these, loved the joke, and the part where they got to cavort with us low types.

It wasn't just Ariel. Things weren't so great for me either. I was playing the youngest "mourner" at the Sim. The "son." My shoes, these contraptions tied closed with wax string, were two sizes too small, and the blisters were excruciating. On top of that, Jeremy had given me a drug so I could cry, which was dehydrating me—I was ready to fall down.

The T crowds were huge. We had already done the whole Sim three times, because of encores, when the incident with Ariel happened.

I was standing by the coffin, wondering if I would be able to speak on cue—the inside of my mouth was a grave, a white salt dry gulch, my eyes were like dry rocks to drag my lids over. I saw Ariel trudge by, under the doll on crossed sticks. He was supposed to be crying, too.

I looked into his dark eyes when he came round, and his exhaustion entered me, I couldn't keep it out. Something terrible was going to happen, I knew. Just at my cue, Ariel collapsed. Mouth open, face in the dust. I thought he was biting the black. That I'd done him in. I was sure. I ran to him—broke character, a great blunder.

The crowd convulsed, with disappointment.

The Heirs, booing. Jeremy came out, tried to calm them.

When I reached my stricken "brother," he sat up. Sat up! And said, in a perfectly normal, not even a parched voice.

"What's got into you? What about the play?"

"You?" I asked. "You are okay?"

"I am fed up with this awful gig. It is so moronic. Give me a Disney in a flat any day," he said, then he sucked on a fluid tube, offered it to me. He had a camelback pouch of water hidden under his costume. I was ready to kill him.

Jeremy arrived then, terribly out of breath. "Malcolm? What were you thinking?"

When Ariel stood, some of the more sophisticated in the crowd decided the whole thing was a sort of parody, a play on the resurrection idea, and they started to laugh. Then Jeremy tried to agree, saying it was a "Variation." Critics were there. He had to do something. But only a few in the audience were that avant garde. They mostly liked everything played the way the script was written, and then, an encore, and another encore. The idea of "once," was beyond them. Even Jeremy complained sometimes, though he made them pay for every repetition.

All this time I remember Vee's look of horror. "Why always a joke of so-longs?" he asked me. "Why don't they joke about something else?"

After that, it was clear Ariel was never going to make it as a rental. Jeremy was furious. Ariel would go back to O. I recovered. I soldiered back. I survived. But the anger had never left.

*

"You deliberately tried to play me," I said in my room that night when
I'd discovered him. "I was working."

"I wanted to tell you I am sorry. I should never have done that. And
I am sorry."

He never apologized. "But that isn't why you came!"

"You know who is here?" Ariel said. "O. He's turned to a hard
Chronic. A while ago, Lazarus and he had a big fight. My Trust couldn't
have two sponsors, he said, couldn't be split. He said I had to choose. I
suppose Lazarus thought it was obvious I'd choose him. But I chose O."

I already knew some of this but not the reason.

"He bribed me. Said I'd profit. Isn't that the whole game? Anything,
anything, for...So Lazarus transferred my Trust, then, not so long after,
they had to haul O here. After all I went through with that wretch."

"What did you? Really?"

"You don't want to know," he said, shaking his head so fast his bangs
flew out. "You are lucky. You never knew anything else. You couldn't
compare. I always compared. I shouldn't have. Believe Lazarus. '*You
will have hundreds of years to iron everything out,*'" he quoted sarcastically.
"Don't ask me about the past. O's in here now, and he can't help me, or
run my Trust."

"What now?"

"I'm going to control the thing myself. Become an Unsponsored
Nyet Like Jeremy. Be emancipated. Run my own affairs."

"Jeremy didn't make it," I said. "You know what happened? When
you control your own Trust, they charge you all sorts of fees, take
percentages. It's better to have it in Heir hands. It is never worth it."

"Well Jeremy isn't me," Ariel said. "I can do it."

"Isn't it getting harder?"

"So? There's always a little nook or cranny somewhere. A way to
get through, get up. Didn't Lazarus teach you that? O has been here too
long. They haven't fixed him yet. He's got every anomaly. You've seen
him?" Ariel was standing now, pushing back his long frayed sleeves.
Part of me just wanted to give him a hot bath, clean clothes, and calm
him down. I knew what Lazarus wanted from me, to ignore Ariel, the
ingrate, but I wasn't strong enough.

"Brother?"

"I'll help you, but stop that lie."

"That is what we are," he said.

He was taller, and more slender and rangy than me. His body wrapped around the objects he sat upon, which gave the impression he was built of bendable bones. He wasn't strong in a square, straight sort of way, like I was. He didn't have the posture Jeremy forced me to have.

He touched his upper lip, which was exactly like mine—that I had to admit.

"I can't get there by myself. I don't have the codes," I said.

"Who does?"

"Camille Benoit, or she used to. Except—I've not seen her in a while."

"Well show me to her. I'll persuade her," he said.

"I don't want you to use her," I said. But I was thinking of seeing her, and I didn't care. I would tell her she ruled my dreams. I cared only about the delight of her, not her life.

"Please," Ariel said. And I nodded.

Soon after, we had sneaked over to the enclaver quarters behind the South Tower and were throwing rocks at Camille's window. I had only just found out that she'd moved there, where I could see her at night, and had been planning to go there by myself.

She poked her head out, surprised. She didn't frown when she realized it was me. "Exit door at the end," she said.

When we got to the east porch, she opened and leaned out. She wore a long shirt and white pajama pants.

"What you want?" she spoke directly to me, her amber eyes widening, then looked over at Ariel, whom she found suspicious. I knew this by the way her bottom teeth bit her upper lip. "What is this? Your brother?" she asked.

"Why do you say that?"

"You look just alike," she said. "Except he slumps." She pointed at him. Her nails were rough, broken. She was doing difficult cleaning work, I'd heard, and had to sleep on the premises because her shift was eleven to dawn. In the old days she'd gone home to Port Gramercy after work.

"We do not," I said.

"Get me in to see O? A Chronic in the North Tower. Please." Ariel, leaning in close to her. I didn't like that.

"Well Dr. Greenmore seems to think I spent too much time with you," she said to me. "What did you tell her? What did you say I said to you? Or did with you?"

"Nothing. Really," I said. It was true. I hadn't seen Greenmore, lately, or spoken to her of Camille.

"She's just harassing me then," she shrugged, smiling, believing me. "When I asked for a new assignment, she asked me a bunch of questions about you. Wanted to know did I have any knowledge of history? Did I talk to you about those things? What did you say when you came down off the Galcyon? She asked me did I know you were smart. Had somebody taught you? I told her I thought you had some privacy."

"You talked back to her?"

"What do I care about Shades? I say what I please."

My heart fell away, left me. I was cut. I was dying. She *asked* for a new assignment. To avoid me.

"My name's Ariel," he butted in. "I'm his brother, but he doesn't remember. He was too young." He was trying to figure out if she was the type to be persuaded by empathy or irony. He asked, "Will you help me? It's life and death."

The conniver, I thought.

"It depends whose life, " she said, looking at me as if to say, again, *who is this?*

She had asked to leave me.

Ariel tried to explain his plight. A Nyet with a Trust in a rogue Chronic's hands. I wasn't sure Camille would sympathize.

"What do I owe to you?" she said to me.

I was caught. I didn't think anything.

"I am going to lose everything, my Trust that I have worked for, if you don't—" Ariel was going on.

"Is he for real? Tell me." Her eyelashes catching the blue orb light, waves, like water.

I didn't want to say it. Ariel elbowed me. "He says something true," I mumbled.

"Okay," she said. It didn't take much. I thought she should have said no. I thought she would. My nod was very faint. Her upper lip, almost moist, inviting.

"Why don't we sneak in and see what astral plane the North Tower crowd is flying now?" she asked.

Ariel laughed.

She turned, stopped, and looked at him, so strong it seemed she might hurt him. "You owe me like I'm your momma, you hear?"

I was in love, I knew it. This was love. I had never been in love before. It was like, all the time, you were burning.

*

We got to O's private chamber at midnight. There were no windows in the room, only lights up at the ceiling, disks, illuminating the scene. Against one wall, a bed, and beside that, a shelf of ancient history books. O was in one corner, in a chair, his eyes open, but he did not seem to see us, or hear us. He was still as a stone.

"Shh," Camille hushed us, and she brought Ariel over to his old sponsor.

I stayed slightly behind, and scanned the titles on the shelf, "*Early Settlements in Pre-Reveal Louisiana,*" "*The Deaccessions: Concentration, Consolidation, Cleansing,*" "*The Geography of the Purchase, Quadricentennial,*" "*Federations Into Enclaves 2050-2093,*" "*One Hundred Years After the Miracle of the Reveal.*"

Ariel whispered, "Doesn't he complain? It's so meager here, so—I can hardly believe he lives like this. He's so used to luxury."

"I'm not sure he does live here, they go all over high heaven, you don't know about Chronics?" Camille asked, adding, "Shh, shh—" as she turned O around in his swivel chair, so both of us could see him, and the light would shine on him. Then she hunched down and looked at him square in his huge black-blue eyes. "Come here honey," she said. She sidled up to his ear. "It's me, come here, don't be out there now," she said. "See me." She snapped her fingers, came close to touching him, but refrained.

O jerked, his shoulders stiffened.

"Okay, he's in focus now. He will hear you," she said, reaching over and grabbing Ariel by the ragged sleeve. She brought him down to O's eye level. "You know this one?"

O's gravelly voice came, very deep, wavering, "Some time I knew him."

She turned to Ariel. "Speak to him. He's alert."

"Here," Ariel complied. "Here I am." He bent down and kissed O on the cheek—I'd never seen that in my whole life, one of us kiss an Heir, it gave me a jolt, made me slightly sick, I couldn't look, and O gushed, "You were the prince."

"Yes, I was your prince," Ariel said, and I could hear something in his voice breaking. "Your pet—"

"You flew, like Peter," O said.

"You wanted me to," Ariel said, pulling away, out of respect or fear or a sense of propriety, or all three, and in his face I saw a range of feelings—shame, and desire, too, wishing to be loved, the same as I felt that night, so I knew it. What a dangerous feeling. Then, I saw his pliant fingers, when he was seven, showing me the way, telling me what was in store, and then I saw his little boy's arms, now wide open, reaching for the air—"And so I did," he said. "Remember? I remember." He reached into his long cuff and produced a thick black pen and a rolled-up piece of paper. The contract that released the Trust. He placed the pen in the v of O's right hand. "Here," he said, pulling down a hard, dense voice from somewhere, a controlling voice, one that said some kind of *No* to all that. "Now. Do this for Peter. For Pan. For your little prince. Write your whole old name. You. Now."

I felt that thing I sometimes felt with Ariel. That he knew some heart I didn't know—at the same time, I wanted to reach over and pull Camille toward me.

"Why?" O looked up, his chin weak, childlike, trembling, his insect eyes bulging, questioning.

"To give me what you meant for me, because I flew for you," Ariel said. "I made you so happy. We played so many games, remember?" This was bitter and hard for him. He almost trembled.

"Why?" O asked once again.

"You meant it for me when you were there, in the Great Sunken Quarter, then, that day, remember?" Ariel asked, having to pull up the sentimental times. "We had a Creole rain and a bow?"

"Yes," O said. "Yes." And he smiled. "Yes, yes, yes."

Thank the stars. The surface now. The money. The answer.

I'd been holding my breath. My shoulders dropped, I exhaled.

Ariel raised his chin. Camille understood. She slid a flat book from the shelf into O's lap to support the paper, and closed O's hand around the pen. He wrote, mechanically,

Oscar Kingsolver DuPlantier. P.R.H.

So, O was Oscar K. DuPlantier (Proto of the Reveal, Heir). I had never known it. But now I had learned history. A founder of the U.A., fought the early fight to "customize the republic," back in the 2020's, before that—He was one who made sure that Heirs and Non-Heirs would never have the same rights again. Kept the rabble at bay. Set up the strat division rules. Trusts that gave WELLFI more and more and more power. Advocated for the de-accessioning of the Gulf Territories. They were dysfunctional, he argued, and should be "thrown back on their own reserves," though he himself lived in the Walled Museum City, most of the year. A famous, famous Heir.

When he had finished writing his name, O looked up at us all and said, "I see brights. They have flutters. Like Tinker, but they glow differently."

"Yes I am sure they do, baby," Camille said, patting O's hand as Ariel took the pen and document away. She just touched him, didn't ask permission. Her sweet amber eyes were on me. As if to say, "You know I did this for you." So there was hope. Maybe. Or she was just reckless. And why did I hope? How reckless was I? Lazarus would be so disappointed, if he knew.

O lost his focus for a few seconds, and sat perfectly still, as he had been when we found him. Ariel's face was all grief. I had no idea why. He had what he wanted.

Then, as I tried to pass new laws in my heart, forget Ariel, forget Camille, O trembled, quaked, the way he did the other time in the North Tower. Ariel saw a small bottle on the shelf near the bed, grabbed it up. "Here, he takes these," he said. "They always worked."

"You've seen him like this?" I asked.

"They make you promise not to talk about it. WELLFI doesn't even acknowledge—" He unscrewed the bottle of pills, counting them out.

"No, they make him sick now—" Camille said. "I have a better cure. It lasts longer. The walls are collapsing on them, it's like—" With that, she raised her hands, and bent down again, as she had when she first focused him.

"O," she whispered. "Come back to me. Hey, over here."

She waved her hands in front of his eyes, very close, right in his gaze. He erupted. "You piece of heat," he growled. "Get away. Get away." He quaked, shivered, raised his arms and dropped them down, then raised them again, like a pitiful bird, one I had seen once in a marsh, with tar on his wings, who couldn't fly. He shouted, cursed. Every filthy word. "Leave me here. Leave me here. Don't make me come back! Suck the—"

Camille, determined.

Her hands were dancing now, the way Vee's used to when he entertained us with shadow plays when we only had lanterns because the power had failed once again on Audubon Island. He'd call out the names of birds, or of animals, and say—"This is a mallard. This is an ibis, the bird of the so-longed," and there were the shadows of the creatures, on the inside of the foundling house wall. Camille was chanting. Time was stretching out.

When I looked again at O in the chair, I saw something strange— following the tips of her fingers: a greenish cast, a swelling color, glowing around his body, and then edging out a little from it. It had to be a trick of the lamps, something coming through one of them above. But they were clear pale yellow light, with no tint. I looked up to check. How could this color, this loose glow, be leaving a man's body through the top of his head, and going to dance with Camille's hands? It couldn't happen. Yet I saw it.

"Do you see that?" Ariel asked.

"Yes," I whispered.

"It looks like teal green."

"Not that dark," I said. "Fainter, the color of grass."

"It's that dark to me," he said, shaking his head in amazement. Ariel, who was always claiming he'd seen everything, whispered, "Whoa! What is that?" He was looking up, now—I didn't see what he was seeing, thought he was faking it.

"Shh," Camille said, in response, but not losing her concentration.

"What is it?" Ariel asked. "Why you put it there?" He was pointing at the ceiling. "Will it stay there?"

"You see it?" Camille said, hardly audible. "What does it look like?"

"Emerald now," he said. "What is it? What's the trick?"

Her head did not turn away from her task, but she said, "You see it? I've never seen it. I just feel it. It's green? You aren't supposed to see it."

For a moment, I saw a faint oval lozenge in the air above him. His lips formed a relaxed little ring, and his limp form uttered a gush. "Agh, agh." Then he went a bit limp.

The glow dissipated, vanished. Like the illusion it was, I told myself.

"Where did you put it?" Ariel demanded.

Camille dropped her hands. O was back in his stupor.

"You both see it?" she asked. "Somebody train you?"

"It was right there, like a big orb—you tell me you didn't see it?" Ariel asked her.

"I feel it. It is kind of wet, damp, like ghosts in a shut up house. But I never saw—"

"Where did you put it?"

"I guess I wouldn't call it, 'where.' It's like, folded, flat, thin, or thinner—I don't know how to talk about it, it's just away, for a while. I'll bring it back."

The whole thing made me uneasy.

Ariel said to Camille, "It's dark green, thick, very alert, and all in one place, but where did you put it?"

"It's right here, " she said. "If you must know." And she started to make a long sweeping arc down the left side of her body, about a foot out, then she brought her hand sideways, so there was a faint green flash. "I see," Ariel smiled.

Noise. A commotion at the far end of the room. Footsteps, three figures coming out of the dark.

"What's going on?" The first one who walked in had a high forehead, and beady eyes, red leathery braids, a long Egyptian style nose, a stretched neck enhanced with rings, silverish-black overskin. An assistant of Dr. Greenmore—Dr. Chotchko.

"Nothing. We were leaving, Doctor," Camille said in her work voice, her yes voice.

Then, from behind her, Greenmore's loud whisper. "Malcolm de Lazarus? How did you get here? Who is this?" She closed in on us, and eyed Ariel, looked him up and down, frowned at his moccasins. I hadn't even noticed his shoes before. Then she turned on Camille. "Who brought her here? What's she doing to the client? Malcolm? One of you tell me what you are doing." Ariel slipped the document, now tightly rolled, in the back of his pants. Dr. Greenmore missed this.

Camille's eyes wanted to ask me something. What was it? She was so open-faced, it should have been obvious. In a way, she shone at me, for a second. I blurted out. "It was all my idea, I brought Ariel here, made Camille. Don't blame Camille—Ariel is from my Foundling House—"

Greenmore's lowered her chin. "Don't be gallant, for heaven's sake, Malcolm. Don't shield her—honestly."

I went further, aware I was ruining things, half ashamed I didn't care. "It's true."

Camille looked at me for one more long moment.

"I'm not going to let you do this, Malcolm," Dr. Greenmore said. "I know who the culprit is. "

"But you don't—" I couldn't stop. I knew to stop, and I couldn't. "You certainly do not. This girl is totally innocent." I knew I'd done it then.

"You are foolish," she said. "Say anything you want, Malcolm. I am not believing you.—"

I ceased to be in the room, as far as she was concerned. She should have fired me, sent me packing. "I am guilty. I brought her here, made her show us—"

Greenmore was silent.

Camille's mouth became a single line. It was the way she looked when she made a mistake, dropped something, forgot a detail, and left her work unfinished. I knew all her moods, I realized. After a second, though, another attitude took over, and she changed her expression to that sharp one, the one she used the day she was mocking the history lecture. The one she used earlier that evening when she told Ariel he owed her. The corners of her eyes sank down, her lips pursed. Greenmore addressed her. "What was that thing you did with your hands? Something vile?"

"Just stuff a *traiteur* would know. I pulled him loose," Camille said.

Dr. Greenmore flashed at the word, *Traiteur*. I knew it meant healer, Camille had told me stories from her enclave. But Greenmore was the healer, not this girl. "And this, what, this Outliar? He a friend of yours?" she asked, accusingly.

I was thrashing. "He's from the Home, we grew up together— see, he has a collar—"

Dr. Greenmore waved her hand at me to get me to stop. She wouldn't hear me.

Camille jumped in. "Just to show them. He's my friend—a Nyet. I—"

"So this was your idea?" Greenmore asked. "This—prank with one of our clients?"

"It's not a prank," Camille said, holding firm. "All my idea," she threw in. "This fellow is my friend. He wanted to see what the Heirs turn into—"

I stepped right in front of Camille. "She is lying. Please, Dr. Greenmore. Listen."

Camille stepped out from behind me, and gave me a glance, disapproving, her lips still taut, as if to say, *don't you see?*

"You can go get your things, and leave," Greenmore told her, still refusing to hear me.

"No, no," I protested once again. "Please, Dr.—"

Camille said, "Malcolm, stop it now." She folded her arms. "I was leaving anyway. I am tired of this—" Her eyes swept the room, not landing on me. "Charade," she said. "This Shade Charade. As if you can't see what they, you keep pumping them full of whatever keeps them here, traipsing all over—why don't you let em go? Why? What do you have to prove?"

"That is just about enough you primitive little—" Greenmore stopped herself. "Just go, get out of my sight."

"Why, you scared of me?" Camille hissed.

"CAMILLE QUIT IT!" I yelled at her. To counter an Heir. She

could be stripped of her enclave rights—

"Out!"

Her face was blank to me. Camille pivoted, stalked off. Why had she tried to shield me? Why had Greenmore believed her?

Attendants gathered around O, propped him up. Ariel stood to the side, watching. Not saying a word. Afraid to.

Greenmore ordered Security to take Ariel to the Sky Rail.

Then she called for some others to come, so they could lock me up in solitary.

VII

7:12 PM October 12, 2121
Crawley's Crobster House on the Quay
Sunken Quarter
New Orleans Islands, Northeast Gulf De-Accessioned Territory,
U.A. Protectorate

I had to ask myself, what was I doing here, in the Sunken Quarter waiting for some Nat's, genetically altered, boiled shell fish? Instead of buying the fuel to troll up the Tchoup Canal to see my guardian, to tell him what I'd figured out about my Trust—what Ariel was trying to pull.

I was fascinated by the scene, of course. Such variety. I wondered if the Heirs drank the same liquids as the other. There were about ten true ones in there and, in addition to the Outliars and others, the enclave workers, there were about eight obvious Imposses who weren't quite succeeding in their goal, to pass for Heirs. I knew all those. Most of the others had the same drink as I did, blue-green, in tall tumblers. I was horribly thirsty. I could keep from eating, but I had to drink. I gulped it down.

A man sat down opposite me then—not directly across, but down a bit, to the left, away from the window. Strange looking. His hair or headjob was in a top knot, which was either very out of style, or something new again. His mouth was no bigger than the end of a thumb, and his upper lip very far from his nose, which made him look a little like the man in the moon. In truth, at a glance, I couldn't tell what he was. Heir or Imposse. Not in this case. He had a nacreous overskin, the hardest to read, but those were in style again, especially a certain abalone with lots of peacock blue in it. I knew all the techniques because it had been my job to pass as an Heir, at one time. I was good at it.

Something about the middle of this moon-man's eyes stymied me. They seemed so cool, the way Heirs' eyes always were. I wondered if a person just masking as an Heir would go to the trouble of putting in sheet lenses—these had been offered to me when I was a passing, but I found them too irritating. I always chose spot lenses instead. And I was crossing borders back then, being interrogated and inspected at close range.

I saw little wrinkles in the corners of this fellow's eyes—the skin wasn't perfectly tight the way it was on T's. So he was an Imposse. For sure. A very good one. There were whole communities of them, who mimicked every feature of Heir life, I had heard. He must have been one of those, a true professional. A perfectionist.

Jeremy had once told me they were often Nyets who had not made it, and couldn't bear the truth, so they pretended, got away with passing in Heir circles if they could, or at least existing at the fringes in places like the Sunken, living a parody. When he lost his Trust, he promised he wouldn't become a "travesty," like that.

"Allow me to introduce myself," Moonman said. "I'm Gepetto."

Why talk to a low strat like me so readily if he were trying to pass? Well, there was mixing here, I allowed. His voice had a rasp, but that was easy to mimic—larynx implant. So was the slowness easily copied—the monotone, the lack of rhythm. The staring, nothing so great. Imposse, definitely, I went over the whole thing one more time. An Imposse so meticulous he wore sheet lenses. Perhaps he had a patron. I had heard there were aficionados, connoisseurs, who paid for their ensembles, subsidized competitions. Gaists who once costumed me claimed they had worked for some of the winners, in fact.

"What happened to you?" he asked, gesturing toward his tiny ear.

"Accident," I said.

"You aren't getting it sewn up?" he said. "Don't they still use needle and thread on your kind?" He pinched his tiny lips, in a wince. His mouth was so small, it was in danger of disappearing. I had seen bigger ones on baby dolls.

I shrugged, tried to look in the glass of the window, but it just offered me a silhouette. One side of my face was swollen, I saw that much.

"You know where I came from?" he asked. "I mean, my name?"

I told him I knew.

"The Disney? You are a fan? So rare. No one has any culture anymore. The soft cruises are truly middlebrow."

"I know the Disney," I repeated myself. I was staring, still. This fellow seemed to enjoy the attention.

"I think there is a kind of story that draws you in by asking you to wonder what it is, and then when you stop wondering and have made up your mind, you are already on to other subjects—the story shows you more about you than you asked to know. Than you ever wanted to know. I think the Disney is one of those. The boy's name means knot of pine," he said. "And he wanted to be a real boy. I think it is the most metaphysical of all of them, truthfully. More than Alice. Have an opinion?" he pressed.

He was annoying, that was my opinion. "I saw it a long time ago," I said. "When I was a child."

"How long ago could that be?" he asked, with his smile, tight as the top of a tiny drawstring purse.

"A while," I said, looking over at the line under the large clear tank where the live crobsters were crawling, in their last moments before the servers fished them out with a long-handled net and tossed them into the cauldron in the window, to be stirred by the girl with a gigantic mushroom of a toque.

The sign under the elevated tank read, "Now Serving No. 12." Not much longer in this weird place, I thought.

"No, really," Gepetto interrupted.

Clever, the way he took so long to answer, I thought. "Years ago," I said.

"You a Nyet? Or you think you are?" he asked.

I was smiling. I stretched out my neck so he could see my collar. "You an Heir?" I teased him.

"Of course," he said. "So for fifty some years. Third Wave. Early." He nodded, pulled back a little. I thought that was a nice touch.

"Sure," I said.

"Well, you?" he asked, pretending he was recovering from the insult. "When is your Boundarytime? When you making the confessions?"

I nodded. "Soon," I said.

"You know they make you promise, then they give you secrets so you can't ever go back."

"Some do." Jeremy swore his heart to the Heir Ways, I couldn't help but remember. Then they wouldn't let him in—

"Well maybe," he said. "But you have to believe. Leave all the rest at the door. You ready? Gonads? Heart?"

I nodded.

"Don't see too many of your kind anymore," he said, shaking his head. "A lot of *wannas*, not too many *gonnas*. What is your count?"

"What you think?" I said, shrugging.

"Don't know. So many elixers now, so many fountains of youth."

"Twenty," I said.

"Never, so early to be mature!" he said. "What did you do? Where did you get the Trust?"

"Rental." I was bragging. "Sims."

"You're really old," he said. "Thirty. I bet." He was silly, I knew he was fake. I understood that, and despised it, pretty much. I couldn't get this place, all these danger-seeking Heirs and Imposses and Altereds—it didn't make sense. In a flash I wondered if I could find a water taxi this time of night—but couldn't afford it. I ought to get out. I was being corrupted already.

"Well, I am telling the truth, unlike some people," I said, winking. "I'm young. I'm what I say I am."

He winked back. So that puzzle was solved. He as good as admitted it, that he was Imposse. I looked down, to avoid his gaze for a moment—after this exchange, these secrets, how could we go on talking?—and I saw the dirty floor of the place. Then I looked up and saw a line of Heirs forming at the counter where the brosias were sold. It didn't make sense for them to be in this place, the true Heirs, so well-dressed and turned out. The kind who inhabited every Walled Urb in the U.A. It was risky, beyond that—

"You using telemeron?" Gepetto asked me.

"What?" I said. You didn't ask things like that. "It's illegal," I said. "I am twenty. That's my count." I could have been put off by this invasion of privacy, but curiously, I wasn't. I looked at my glass. I had drunk about half my second, or perhaps my third blue-green drink. The girl had come by with the pitchers. Things were getting—what—more fluid.

"Come on—" Gepetto said.

A shell was stuck on the floor. This was some kind of crisis. A puzzle to be solved. I saw rather quickly, with no evidence, actually, that the shells all over the floor were glued to the paving stones, under a thick clear varnish. The pattern of them was too interesting to be random. This came in the form of a revelation. The broken shells and little puddles and discarded feelers were there to give the illusion of a dirty floor. That made the most sense because, otherwise, how could it exist at all? Since it had such a fascinating pattern. Like so many other things in the Sunken Quarter, designed, for the highest effect. Like the Altereds, like this Imposse, like the shining picturesque coated buildings, the gleaming stadium style stairs that rimmed this place, kept out the Old River. I touched the table under the mat the waitress had put down. On the face of it, it was carved with initials by old lovers, but it was obvious this was a replica of a rotten old table, rendered by an artist. There was something too—studied about the carvings, the placement of the grime. It had to have been made that way. How else could this fit into itself so well—an artist had done it. A producer. Like the way they made the weather in the big Urbs. But on a more meticulous scale.

I could practically see the artist doing the whole room, making it the perfect replica of a seedy dive where all kinds mixed, and creatures were boiled alive, and at the same time completely sterile, safe, so the Heirs could come down to the Sunken Quarter and mix with rough types and have their dangerous evening. All this dirt and these cracks and the seediness and the costumed creatures were a form of trompe-l'oeil. I saw it all.

"You *have* some telemeron?" Gepetto asked me. The drug was popular with Imposses. The Venus Gaists had mentioned it. It kept Imposses looking young.

"I don't take anything!" I said. "I have been living in the country, nothing is available." And then I was thinking, *so this isn't dangerous, this is play-dangerous.* One day I will live where there are tunnels for bullets, where there are domes over the cities, where sunset is designed months in advance, and rain showers come with music—even the dark side, the danger, is covered with polymer—I was getting closer. It was what I'd been promised, and I would have it. I was breaking out in a sweat, remembering my traveling days, my working life—

Then, I heard a voice, scolding, saying, "Drink the blue drink—what, you crazy?"

Serpenthead was at my side, somehow. I hadn't noticed his approach. He took the drink from my hand. "With the Q, the Quanderie? Nobody ever tell you anything? Oh my Malcolm, you think you going to steer that boat up the Old River, or the Tchoup Canal? Where you been, you don't know this?" He reached over and tried to take my pulse.

"I'm fine," I said to Serpent. To Gepetto, I said, "As I was saying, in the country. I've been in the country."

"He's a rube," Serpent interjected. "Don't even know what Q is."

"I'm not familiar with the nomenclature," Gepetto said, using a haughtier tone with Serpenthead than he used with me.

"No experience in rude life," Serpent said, jutting his chin at him a bit. "A rube. A bumpkin. He trusts the wrong people. Perfect strangers, weirdos too. You know what I'm talking about? What really goes on? He's idealistic." He paused, turned to me. "Malcolm. Let me get a look at you." He cupped my chin in his hand and peered into my eyes for a second. I let him, it didn't bother me. Why this concern? He glowed a little, when I looked straight at him—odd. "Oh," he said. He shook his head. "My boy, you are in for it."

VIII

March 6, 2118
Curing Towers
Re-New Orleans
South Central District, U.A.

Solitary confinement was rotten.

I repented, reminded myself what Lazarus promised: that we could work with the surface. Only with the surface. I had to return, be reasonable, material. I tried. Sometimes I couldn't keep myself from having the fantasy that I'd run away with Camille, that I'd lose my Nyet status and take off, like Jeremy, pick her up on the way to the wild west, or whatever territory we could find that would let us in.

Eventually Greenmore called for me. To fire me, I believed.

She was in her summer office, in the North Tower. I trekked over there in my baggy prisoner clothes. I'd hardly eaten while alone. I was gaunt. She seemed happy to see me, told me I was a free man, then went on.

"Well, after the other night, I know you are aware that we treat very old Heirs here, who are called Chronics? The technical term is 'Clustered Anomalies?' I guess I don't have to explain too much. We need to talk—about them."

"May I speak? Freely?" I asked.

"Yes. What is it?"

"You aren't sending me out?"

"No, I'm not sending you out, if you mean back to the islands, no," she said. "I punished you. Why do you have that look on your face? What happened to your body? You look so miserable." Eat. You have to eat while you are a Not-Yet."

"You aren't sending me out? You aren't?"

"No. I have a job for you."

I could not understand her generosity. I felt enormous relief, and also, to my shame, disappointment—there would be no running away, no finding Camille.

Dr. Greenmore obviously didn't think any of it was worth discussion. She was going on with her monolog. Her nostrils narrowed. She was so phenomenally smart. I saw all the things she knew organizing themselves into armies, nations, in her brain.   She knew about Heir lives. About what was important.

"I'll be frank. The disease—if it is one disease or a group of them we don't even know that—is not well understood. After all, these are people over one hundred and ninety by count. We have never had to deal, in the history of man, with the conditions of people of this count."

She described the syndrome. With Heirs, very old, from a certain era, even when the Re-jobs went well, and the Re-descriptions, a small percentage were returning home and developing catatonia. When they were conscious, they also exhibited knowledge of remote events, also, less well documented, rapid changes in temperature—metabolic chaos. There were even a few examples of Heirs in New New York "catching on fire in a closed room." Also, unexplained heat and moisture about the body, like a very local atmosphere, noted by caregivers. When they were given sedation, they sometimes demanded to be taken off the medications, so they could have their "anomalies" again. They apparently got addicted to these altered states, claimed they were— "achieving something," "getting somewhere."

"We have to confine them. Frankly," she said, rolling her beautiful crafted eyes, lids taut, streamlined. "WELLMED and WELLFI dismiss every single case as an isolated incident. They like to say these effects have been seen only in Albers Protos, and many first tier Protos are unstable. But now some of the Chronics we are seeing here are First Wave, I'm getting more and more reports of cases in the northern U.A. Now, about where you come in," she said.

"Me?"

"Yes, you. Are you ready to travel for me? Can you go to the other Curing Towers and collect the raw evidence? It can't be done on the Net or the Broads—WELLFI is listening. I have correspondents in every

Walled Urb—New New York, Snow White, Memphis, Upper Houston—
Can you do this for me? Pose? Be a spy?" she asked. "You understand
that to travel in these areas of the U.A., the interior, is going to require a
disguise. They are more rigid in the north—they don't have any mixing.
Strats are strict. Nyets cannot move freely in most districts. If you
went as you are now, they would have all kinds of suspicion. Securitas
doesn't look the other way. You will have to pose, be an Imposse, in
other words. Have the Heir privileges." She smiled. "I want to trust you
Malcolm. And think of it—you get a taste."

She expected me to respond. I couldn't think what to say.

"You don't think you can handle it?" she asked. "You don't want the
opportunity? To see all the Urbs? To travel?"

I sat up straight. I said, "Of course." No matter how bad I was, no
matter how low my fantasies, some good Heir was always looking out
for me. It was true. I was lucky.

"Well, then," she said. "I'll have the technicians come see you. Get
you outfitted. The best, so no one will detect you. Would you like some
lunch?" she asked. "Brosia?"

I'd try it.

"I'll have the girl bring some in," she said. "Come over here, to the
table." She'd never offered me a seat at a table with her before.

"About the other night, you do understand." Her lids dropping,
her chin back. "How enclaver Nats such as that girl can't be given any
freedom, they don't understand our enterprise.   They are enemies
among us. It's best not to fraternize. Certainly it is always a mistake to
take a Nat's part. It's—for Nyets, it's a betrayal. It isn't done. No matter
the circumstance. You heard her. She has false beliefs, she's mad—"

"I was at fault," I said.

"I won't hear it. Forget that stupid—forget—You are a Not-Yet,
aren't you? Committed? Right? You don't have any—scenarios of,
intimations of—" She looked at me rather strangely. It was not so much
scouring as watching, waiting the way fishermen did, for one swimming
by.

"Intimations?" I looked back at her. Did I have to confess?

The brosias came then. I shoved one in my mouth, then another. I
was very privileged to be eating them, I reminded myself. Odd, exotic
flavors. Fish, caramel, spice, some I didn't recognize. I concentrated,
tried to enjoy.

But it was always the same with the stuff—no matter how exciting
the pieces could be going in, they always melted into fuzzy, toneless

lumps before I could swallow them.

She was a fisherwoman, letting me off the hook. I had to do better. I wanted another nature. As an Heir I supposed, I'd have one. I hoped.

"Lazarus trained you well," she said, after a silence. "Even if I disagree with his methods." She paused. "You have never travelled in the Walled Urbs much. Now you will have the chance. Cheer up. Change of scenery is what you need. Forget all the complications you've encountered here. All the fraternizing with Lowns like that smelly girl. I would never have let her near you if I could have imagined—your poor taste—"

That stung. I wanted to protest, shout at her, but she came very close to me, scared me a bit—her hand formed the curve, as if she were going to cup my cheek. She stood, while maintaining that gesture, looking at me very deeply. To make sure I was with her. Her face was all points, her eyes, golden, slanted, perfect. "Don't stand up for her," she said. "It's not right. It's just not right. You betray your strat and your fate." A long pause. I squirmed. "Don't speak of her to me ever again. I won't either. Now to work."

*

It was about a week later. There was a knock on the door, and I answered it.

"WE ARE HERE TO FIT YOU," a pair said almost in unison, a man and a woman. They both wore fuchsia, with Venus Gaist insignia on their breasts. "H. R. Dr. Greenmore sent us? For your assignment?"

I had been sleeping. I'd worked until very late, cleaning the kitchen. What did these fancy people want?

"We do specialty o-skins." The woman said, the taller of the two. She was broad-shouldered. "Would you like to see?" She carried a portable screen. She opened it, so she could show me the styles.

I sat down to look— a few gaudy T's, or so I thought—

"No," the other one said. "Stand up." His hair was burgundy, in a frizz around his head. A Gaist fashion. "I have to measure you. Arms up."

Jeremy had measured me hundreds of times, but not for an o-skin. Heirs were offended if we played them, even though they found Imposses amusing. Jeremy could never overcome the prejudice. So he always produced period pieces. I was typecast, strictly twentieth century, with a few excursions into the nineteenth. Once he put me on a raft and set

me out in the Old River, in honor of a "Classic of the Ancient Regime."
I was a ragged boy, with a straw hat. They put pale makeup on me, and
freckles. A big Outliar man whose body they blackened with dye was
beside me.

The burgundy-headed one took out what looked like tongs, and
jabbed me in the waist. I thought, but didn't say, ouch.

"High tolerance, huh?" he asked. "Figured you would scream."

"He was a child rental," the woman said. "The old Unabridged Sims."

"Oh, that explains it," the man said.

"Can he wear one?" the woman asked.

"Wear what?" I asked.

"P. P. D.," she said. "You are Malcolm? That's what they call you?"

"Yes."

Burgundy said, "Sit down." He lowered his tongs. "You don't know
what we are doing here? What they hired us for?"

"They?"

"We don't like to name our clients. People, persons, Heirs, you work
for. Those *they*."

"Yes?"

"If you are thin enough we will fit you with a P. P. D. *Pseudo-prodermis.*
Full suit."

"What do you think? Should we fast him?" Broad shoulders said,
as she pressed the tongs to pinch one of my thighs. She got about an
inch. "It's up to you. How would you be more comfortable? With a
full dermis overlay—we have about fifteen styles, extremely lightweight,
virtually the same material? Or would you just prefer some cosmetic
patches and filler? Our patches never slip. You are good looking, how
much work have you had?"

"Work?" I asked.

"Surgeries, amplifications, augmentations, refits, stretches?"

"None," I said.

"Well you are one lucky—" Her hand slid down my torso. I didn't
like it.

Burgundy asked, "Why don't you let him take a look?"

They sat me down so I could see the screens. She pressed a button
and keyed on a fashion show. Display after display of handsome Heirs
in a variety of styles—hard-edged, rippled, sculpted, hyper-defined,
all the pseudo-prodermises completely visible, because the Heirs were
in transparent sheaths. Some were loudly dressed, a few were rough
Nuovos, with the gold braid they were wearing lately, the barbaric "troll"

headjobs from a few years back. Except they weren't Heirs. They were Imposses.

"Every one of these pictures is a Nat, do you believe it?" Broad shoulders asked.

"Amazing," I said. "But I'd rather not fast." I was already underweight.

"Fine, really. We can work with filler, patches here and there. You are a nice cut to start with. Good outline. I think style 92."

Burgundy got out the calipers again, and a measuring wand. "Just a few centimeters around the chest."

He made me raise my arms again. I was starting to sweat. She noticed, and said, "Not to worry, not to worry. All of us are Nats here. These overskins have a wicking system. Never hot. And they shine just like the real thing. They breathe. The pores are as invisible as any in the UA. See we wear them just for the comfort—you thought we were Heirs?"

"No," I said. I didn't think that. They touched me. "But why don't they just hire an Heir to do this job?"

"Maybe somebody wants you to get out of town," one of them mumbled.

"Say what?" I asked.

"We didn't say anything," they both said at once.

*

The suits did breathe, I noticed later that month, when I was transformed into the (Imposse) H. R. "Lucretius." I was disguised as a Second Wave professional, patterned on screen 92, complete prosthesis for my face, that thick look Heir faces had, that made their expressions so subtle and *slightly delayed, entrancingly out of sync,* Jeremy used to go on and on about how beautiful they were. The pores of my fake overskin were larger than the overskins on true Heirs—my metabolism required more porosity than a true Heir would, but the fabric was iridescent, and the shine camouflaged the holes.

I travelled for months, went to Curing Towers deep in U.A. Territory. The raw landscape was horrible, I'd never seen it. Sometimes, I caught a glimpse of the empty ruins, the garbage towns, that weren't needed anymore. Why not just knock them down?

But mostly I travelled in the bullets and saw nothing of these depressing scenes. Instead, gorgeous rolling hills, populated by galloping herds of fanciful creatures—lavender elephants, lions that

shone like silver jewels—which did not seem to be holos at all, but real
landscapes of amazing depth. They were projected onto the walls of the
tunnels. On some lines, they continued right up until the moment the
bullets pulled into the huge terminals, inside the domed cities, none of
the offense of the raw land.

The cars were practically empty, even though travel was easy. Why
had Greenmore been concerned? Nothing ever happened. I knew
WELLFI had been discouraging travel for a decade—it was what brought
down Jeremy's Sims. Risk brought injury, which was costly for Heirs—
required switching out the metabolism, speeding it up, Re-description,
millions. WELLFI needed to save.

*

My story was, I was a WELLMED courier. Under the lid of the case
on my lap were fifteen vials set into foam. These were supposed to be
experimental elixirs. So precious they had to be personally delivered.

Usually, there was no trouble, but once, a Securitas approached me.
He wore a black suit with bright yellow lettering on the back and the
yellow collar and cuffs. Contract enclaver logo: *New Phase Mercenary*.

"This way," he said politely. For some reason, he'd singled me out.
He had to inspect me, look hard at my overskin. I was certain he was
counting pores, looking at their size.

I wondered if he could hear my heart. I was far too fast in that
department—dead giveaway. I held my breath without raising my chest.
My rate of respiration might bring questions. Heirs were so incredibly
slow.

"What division of WELLMED do you work for, H. R. Sir?" the
fellow asked me.

"Varietology." That was my script. I nodded, and fished the ersatz
ID-pendant-transmitter out of my loose shirt. He made that gesture
with the backs of his four fingers, touching the palm that said to me,
come a little closer. I leaned forward. I knew if he looked at the nape of
my neck, he could possibly see the seam on me, the lack of prodermis
sutures. I hoped he didn't see where the patches were. The false flesh
they'd pasted on me.

But then, I realized I didn't have to put up with any of this. I drew
up all haughty as if an Heir, and asked, "Isn't this enough?" The way
Greenmore would say it. And that put him off.

That was as risky as it got. My boss thought this was some kind of test.

    Easy to pass.

*

A thousand miles took less than a day. I went to all the major centers, saw all the architectural wonders, things I'd read about.

    I knew I should appreciate it all, but my mind was on her amber eyes, her blue black lashes, the way she said the word "bagasse," the way she walked out of my life and never said, never said—

    Around all the cities were the very high walls, fifteen stories. Most had balloon domes above that, a sky projected. Re-New Orleans, where the Curing Tower was, had a partial covering overhead, and a primitive system for weather styles. It was, by comparison with others, a small town, on the very edge of the U.A. These wealthier Urbs had more complex displays. Styling the climate and all of that was a great art: synchronizing it, making it more like music, factoring in enough chance and order, a branch of varietology. The larger cities competed for the most innovative composers. There were fashions, like everything else in Heir life. If I had to choose, I liked the more unreal places, the ones with fanciful rains—something besides ordinary water—genenfabric petals, shining crystals of sweetener. Once I saw a moon that morphed into a white rose right as it hung in the sky, over the course of the evening. By morning, it had turned back into a bud.

    A few Urbs didn't have producers for the weather. They actually lived under the real sky because the climate was considered ideal. Snow White in the west was one of these. It was in a deep dramatic valley, at the Western edge of the U.A., right next to the Pacific DE-AX, lands that were "let go" after the Great Rim Earthquake.

    It was late in my travels that I visited there. Securitas sentinels stood on top of the wall—holding rifles, with headsets and sight glasses and night vision goggles. Keeping out the Western Bands. I had heard by this time that some of his friends had helped Jeremy recover from his despondency and gathered up the money to give him passage to the Western DE-AX, the mountains.

    One morning when I was out walking, I saw a scrawny street vendor outside the Urb gates. The mustache was white, but the brows were still black, and I saw that funny "M" across the ridge at the top of his face. I was about to call out to him. Of course it would blow my disguise, I knew I was a fool, but I was lonely. I was half an inch from it.

I saw his eyes, and I was sure.

And he recognized me. He understood. Or he understood I was already an Heir—which would have been quite extraordinary, as I was only eighteen. But I looked the part.

But then, the next moment, he waved his finger at me, wagged it back and forth across his face, like a metronome.

He was being generous, magnanimous. I knew his expressions.

No. Don't. Come. Near.

Beat.

No. Don't. Come. Near. Forget me. I am lost.

I knew that was right. I could hardly bear to obey him. I stood there and burst into tears: Lazarus would be furious with me, I knew, but I wept anyway. I was weak, like that. I wanted to get better.

IX

7:30 PM October 12, 2121
Crawley's Crobster House on the Quay
Sunken Quarter
New Orleans Islands, Northeast Gulf De-Accessioned Territory,
U.A. Protectorate

*G*epetto wasn't that concerned about my inebriation.
"Why don't you let the boy be at peace? A little Q plus some aguacalicali? Not so bad. A buzz, that's all," he said to Serpenthead. They went back and forth a few times. Serpent took my chin again, and asked, softly, "Malcolm? You know who I am?"

"What?" I asked.

"Your pupils are big big big, ya know what that means?" he asked.

"*Number seventeen*," the girl with the toque called out, before I could respond. Serpent reached for the tile I'd left on the table. Peet appeared—from nowhere, it seemed—and said, "Bebum. I'll get them."

I looked down when Serpent released my chin. The floor was even more interesting than before—studded with crobster shells which suddenly seemed the size and shape of the elbows of small children swimming in a pool. To me they moved, ever so slightly, and the floor was liquid, and each little scrawny arm in its turn got out of his way, an illusion done so very well, so very well I thought. In the street under a green glazed faux copper lamp, I saw a pair of musicians also in green—golden green, actually, and one leaned in while the other leaned back, and they chatted that way, compensating for the other's movements, perfectly choreographed, and I thought of the beats in Peet's and sometimes in Serpent's speech, which were part of the same phenomenon, and I asked, "Who is the artist? Who *did* this night?"

"Artist? Artist?" Gepetto's pencil thin eyebrows rose, with a question, then he said, "You are right. It has its charm. That rough thing they are doing now, that danger that people find so entrancing. It's the same aesthetic as the big new Underground Sims. You have been following them? Ginger? Perhaps?"

"You hear something about Ginger?" another fellow asked in a tiny whisper, one who had just sat down, by the eyes and the teeth and the headjob, undeniably an Heir, slumming. Perhaps he assumed Gepetto was one of his kind. I wasn't going to tattle. The new Heir was in a costume for the night—a fancy cultured overskin, which had white feathers about the face. He was a mad owl, his eyes wild.

The two of them started in on gossip about a big "Ginger" Show, a Sim, something I knew nothing of, when Peet returned with his sack of crobsters, and said, "Come on, let's go. We can't waste time. We've got another job. It's that thing over in the Far East DE-AX. Everybody has been following it. Updates for over three years. It's finally been called. The finale. The tickets went on sale six hours ago, and already sold out. There were bidding wars, the cost— It's tonight. Lordy's got us hired as bouncers—pay is good. We got to find a ride over there—"

"Where they putting it on?" Owl asked. "I heard they changed the venue. True? Bigger theatre?"

Peet turned to him and said, "Not at liberty to divulge."

Serpent said to me, "Come on, we got to hurry, scare up a water taxi. First, we gonna get your compos fuel? Come on, you can walk can't you?" He gestured to the fuel can against the leg of the table. It had an ugly stink.

I was trying to take all the information in. It wasn't easy. I had to go to the fuel place. Had to move. I would. Of course. I'd be seeing Lazarus in an hour or two. Find out what was behind this mess with my Trust. Redeem myself.

White Owl said, "There are no water taxis left tonight. They are all taking people to see Ginger. The whole Quarter is clearing out. I'm looking for a ride—" He pulled out a ticket, the size and shape of a playing card, which read,

ADMIT ONE
THE SIM OF A LIFETIME

**FAR EAST PLAYERS PRESENT
GINGER'S GOODBYE
DATE AND VENUE TBA**
✳✳✳✳✳✳✳✳✳✳✳✳✳✳✳✳✳✳✳✳✳✳✳✳✳✳✳✳
**NOT-YETS, ENCLAVERS, OUTLIARS,
NOT ALLOWED UNLESS
ACCOMPANIED BY AN HR.
PROPER ID, WELLVAC MEDALLIONS REQUIRED**

Gepetto took a hard look, held the ticket up to the light, and told the rest of us the thing was "counterfeit."

"So you idiots think." Owl stomped off.

"You can do it? Walk?" Serpent asked me, when we were back to four.

"I am fine," I said, trying to stand, then sitting down again because of dizziness.

"Bebum," Peet interrupted. "Hate to say say say this, but he's too drunk. Put him back on his boat. Let him sleep it off—"

"Yeah," I said.

"He'll get rolled. They'll strip him," Serpent said, chewing his lip, then he asked, "You gonna steer that boat? Get up to Audubon Island? You able?"

"Let me go to the Ginger with you. I have a transport," Gepetto said.

"You have a ticket?" Serpent asked.

Gepetto shook his head.

"Excuse me H. R. high, you offering us a ride?" Peet was interested.

It was impossible, that was true. An Heir proposing to ride with our strat. But he wasn't an Heir. "He's Imposse," I blurted out, then realized the faux pas. Again I tried to stand. I managed this time, head swirling.

"The fellow said there are no water taxis. I have a transport up by the ramp to the ferry, get you there quick," Gepetto said, not bothering to contradict me. Then he turned to me. "You want to talk about artistry, these new Sims are—you really should come along. You sure you don't want one last adventure? You'll love these new Undergrounds—entirely new concept—" His eyes were lines drawn by a fine pen.

"And you know this guy?" Serpenthead asked me. "You trust him?" To Gepetto: "What you gonna do when you get out there?" To me: "You trust him?"

"We just met," I started. "We are still going to this compos place, right? Jeddy's is it?"

"Who trusts Imposses? You?" Serpent asked me.

Peet looked at me, then Gepetto, trying to make up his mind.

I could only shrug.

Gepetto took mock-offense. "I'll drive you two there, or three, you get me in. Deal? What have you to lose?"

Serpent said to me as if Gepetto weren't really there. "He's a T, an Heir. Imposses don't dress that rich, never, no."

Peet looked me over. "*Who* is this Nyet to you?" he asked.

"Saved his life," Serpent said.

"Bebum. And so you gonna do it again?" Peet asked, nudging him.

Serpent said, "I promised I'd get him to Jeddy's fuel place."

Peet didn't want the detour. He was eager to take Gepetto up on his offer, or quit all of us. "Whatever. We have to go. Jeddy's quick, then we head off." He shook his shoulders, as if he had a shiver, said, once more, "Bebum."

We set off, gas can and sack of crobsters in tow. Serpent and Gepetto were in front, Peet and I behind.

"So what is this guy?" Peet asked again as we stomped into the crowds.

"Imposse," I said. "I already told you. Look at his eyelids—wrinkles. Crows feet. Dead giveaway."

Peet paused. "That rich why doesn't he go to Memphis?"

"Ah, very perceptive question," Gepetto turned back and answered us—he'd been listening. He had very good hearing, as good as an Heir—did he even have the implants? He continued— "One day I will explain."

Serpent, Peet, Gepetto and I turned off the main street and proceeded through the narrower ways of the Quarter to the Northern Basin Rim. They marched, I staggered. I learned from their conversation that the build-up had been quite spectacular for this show. It was technically called a "Sim Verite," whatever that was. Apparently independent operators had been putting them on for the last few years. They'd discerned some portion of the Heir population still had a hunger for the "living production." Soft cruises didn't do it for everyone. Unlike the old Sims, those I was in, where artificiality was the hallmark, these were very gritty. People in the Sunken Quarter had been following bulletins broadcast every few weeks, detailing Ginger's "progress." There were a great many subscribers to the saga, running commentaries—bets laid on the day. The Far East players never put on a Sim before, yet the screen installments were riveting, had drawn in a huge audience, of all stripes.

I was the only one of the four of who knew nothing of this sensation.

"In the story, she has what they call cancer," Gepetto told me. "An ancient disease Nats still get. Only here. They've cured it in the fugue countries." He elaborated that in fugue countries the society spent money to keep the Nat population alive, curing all kinds of diseases, when the people weren't going to have but seventy or eighty years in the end. I knew that WELLFI controlled common doctors as well as Heir doctors, didn't believe in wasting resources that way. I'd heard at the Curing Towers that sick Nats had to go overseas for care, the few enclavers who could afford it.

"Who are these Far East Players?" Peet asked.

"Chef Menteurians," Gepetto said.

"No, not Chef Menteurians," I slurred. "They don't even have pictures on their walls." I protested.

Peet interjected, "Bebum. It can't be them. I heard that whole enclave was shut up, closed, or something, what was it?—big doings over there, no visitors these days—can't be putting on parties. What you think?"

"I never heard of this *Verite*, what is it?" I asked.

"Where have you been? Why are you so out of it?" Gepetto asked me.

"The country," I answered. "West shore of Sea of Pontchartrain."

"And what brought you to the end of the earth?" he rasped.

Part Two:
The Grand So-Long

I

September 22, 2119
Curing Towers
Re-New Orleans
South Central District, U.A.

Greenmore's exile brought me to the country.

She was hounded out of her position at the Towers after she gave her talk about the Chronics.

It was a year after I started traveling for her. I thought it was a perfectly wonderful talk. I helped her write it, in fact. I was thrilled she wanted my help.

She gave it at the *Re-New Orleans Curing Towers Conference on New Therapies for Clustered Anomalies*. A conference I helped her put on. Many were watching from a distance on a limited Net, all over the U.A., but several hundred had come to this assembly live.

We'd planned her speech before the entire group for the afternoon of the second day, when attendance would be at its height. I had even edited her phrasing. For the first several minutes, she gave examples about Chronics—showed holos, read eyewitness accounts, case histories—things I had helped her distill from the data I collected. Sitting near the front as she spoke at the podium, I thought it was a persuasive beginning, excellent. At one point, for some reason—perhaps I heard a whisper, or a sigh—I looked back at the faces, the audience of her peers—doctors in the field of Reveal Psychology—and I saw, to my surprise, that it wasn't going well.

"It is incontrovertible if you look at the data, that Clustered Anomalies are not random as others have postulated, but actually a sequenced syndrome with regularized, even predictable, stages. Typically, the subjects begin with retreat from normal identity interests, including the denial of previously-held truths."

She described their complaints: they say they are "enclosed," no matter what sort of setting they are in. They have hallucinatory conversations. Next, the Chronic Stall. Personalities become erratic, diffuse. When she mentioned that they often skipped the rules of sequence—reported things that had not happened yet, as if they had already happened—there were quite a few louder gasps in the audience. She went on, she was brave.

"We see those finding normal physical barriers objectionable, or insisting they are unnecessary, or illusory. There are also examples—too many to be dismissed, I believe—at this stage, of remote viewing." (More groans.) "I will admit these run against our present understanding of the physical universe, and gravity, and even the conventional view of the ineluctable direction of time." (A loud sigh. A laugh or two.) "But this is what is happening to our pioneers in the Elysian Reality—and there are reports, and records, as I have shown. And should we dismiss all of it? Testimony of scores of experts in this now-growing field?"

"What?" a woman next to me asked at that point. An Heir with silver corkscrew curls, shaking her head. "All this has been explained." I turned to look at her. I was wearing the sort of headjob I often used on my travels, but I wasn't disguised. When she realized I was a Nyet, she turned away as if she had seen a monster, and asked the Heir on her other side, "Why is the seating mixed? What is wrong with these down here?"

Rumblings began throughout the audience; Greenmore soldiered on. "My hypothesis is this: we have come to a new boundary, in Heir development. Their minds are so mature, they are testing the limits of the normal range, if you will, of existence. Because these growth spurts are irregular and uncontrolled, we are seeing symptoms of a new, previously unclassified, psycho-soma-metabolic illness. But our very mature patients' consciousnesses may be expanding in ways that challenge their physical status. Revolutionizing their metabolisms, their relationship to time, once again. Once again.

"I plan to use this hypothesis—that they are not sick, they are growing. They are continuing to expand. I want them to experience, without impediment, the radical nature of this new stage, of their inestimably rich, epochal lives. We need to guide them, chart the territory, and not ignore it. Help them, from an enhanced perspective. The over-self has been part of our theoretical framework for some time in Post-Reveal Psychology. Indeed, it is part of the foundation, though often un-discussed, of my original theories of Re-description. Here we can see that a region beyond is actually being traversed by our Protos, if you will allow the metaphor. I see more of an opportunity than a malady. A new frontier—"

I thought that line brought it back. To facts. To the correct view. Everyone would see she was still in the mainstream.

But, when she was done, they stared at her. No applause. Then, in a few moments, the protest was unified, the growl of a mass. She was shouted out of the pavilion.

*

The screens came out with their version the next day: "*H.R. Doctor Lydia Greenmore, Winner of the Albers Prize, discoverer of Re-description, Posits New Unproven Theory, and Claims Obscure Common Cause for Clustered Anomalies among Protos.*" "*Lydia Greenmore Cooks Up a Syndrome.*"

Her research was noted by all who were interviewed in the article to be "questionable," based on "unreliable sources." There were references to widespread reports of her history of association with "fringe experiments"—at this she went into a rage about her rivals who spread "these lies, this libel." The cartoons came next—cruel, offensive:

Greenmore was depicted in the clothing of an H.R., but with a wheel you could see behind her legs—the image used by the FREE WHEEL movement, with infants and old people and copulating couples at different points. "*We are trying to understand the Protos,*" she was quoted as saying. A little man, a Yeared, ugly, meant to be a caricature, stood behind the wheel like a gnome, and he was saying, "*We know what's wrong, tell them Greenmore—*"

The people who came to her defense were the last straw—the philosophers on the radical side of things, some from a university near the Canadian Border, who had been discredited years before.

These were all "crackpots," Greenmore told me. "Nobody listens to them. Or funds them," she said. Their endorsement was "the kiss of death."

I was by her side through this entire trial. We attempted for several months—every major and minor grant, every foundation, even the remnants of the ones Lazarus used to write off to. Some from the Free Wheel movement came forward, but, she told me, that if she accepted funds from them (and they were poor enclavers, hardly money at all) she would never be able to get even a dollar from any reputable group. They accepted the Cycle!

In the end, after months of attempts, she made a request of me. She was giving up, taking a sabbatical. A hiatus. Would I follow her out to the Wood Palace—her Estate in the DE-AX, and be her personal research assistant? It was quite unorthodox, in a sense. I was young, and a Not-Yet. She insisted it wasn't a holder contract. I'd be working, not entertaining her. "You are smart. You've been terribly helpful. I'm going to be looking into the life of the ancients. Philosophies Pre-Reveal. Particularly the esoteric typographies. The maps. See what they say."

"Well I wouldn't know anything about any of that—"

"I have been curious. About certain theories of—"

"Of what?" I asked.

"Older psychologies, and cosmologies—and the correspondence between the two," she said. "Come. We'll study together. You are so bright." Her golden eyes flashed. "Do you know what your I.Q. is? Completely out of the expected range. Most need implants to do as well. Without hiring an Heir, I won't get anyone more able."

Why didn't she hire an Heir? Perhaps I should have asked. The answer would have been helpful, in the end.

For several days in early November, we cleaned out her office. It was emotional. Her old colleagues, Dr. Chotchko chief among them, came up to say good-bye. As soon as each one got ready to leave, Greenmore would remind them they would all prosper in her absence, have more of a lump of the brosia, now.

Finally, one Thursday, in the early morning, we set out in a transport, which she drove herself. I sat in the back with several boxes of her files.

Her land was about fifteen miles past Re-New Orleans along the Westernmost edge of the Sea of Pontchartrain.

On the way out, we passed ruins of old towns from the fugue era— she pointed out towers where petroleum had been refined once. I'd never seen that. Then we drove through stands of oaks and even some fields of cane—enormous grass, was what it looked like. Gaists and some Port Gramercy cooperative farmers grew it, but the bulk of the crop was for the bute refineries in Brazil. Past this ocean of tall grass, a narrowing wand of land, in blue water, which she said was part of her estate.

Soon we were going along the middle of an isthmus, fortified on each side with piles of limestone rocks, in the midst of low reeds dotted here and there with standing pools, and then the land widened once again, and there were neat patches of green on either side. Crops I didn't recognize. Then, rather suddenly, a white house rose up out of marsh. Handsome and wide shouldered with white columns, a copy of the ancient French Colonial style, square, on stilts, and one story.

The plank road became a bridge, the house's only tether to land.

When we pulled up, two servants came out, who introduced themselves to me, shaking my hand heartily. Klamath and Mimi. Like Vee and Marilee back at Audubon Foundling House, they had citizenship in the Chef Menteur Enclave.

"Give him a tour, I need some rest," Dr. Greenmore said when we'd put down our bags. "Feed him." She was mistress of this house, she was queen.

The place had one huge main living area, Dr. Greenmore's suite. All the other rooms were narrow enclosed galleries with glass windows on two sides which could be shuttered for privacy. When the wooden jalousies were open it was a completely transparent house. Everyone could see everyone else in it. All had views of the water.

In her main room, besides her bed and the armoires and closets, and the small brosia-only kitchen, was a sizeable, swimmable, pool. Next to her room on the opposite end was a long room like a hall of glass, with a little pallet on the floor. "You will sleep here, I assume," Klamath told me.

A little later, he took me on a walk

She had given him permission to cultivate the land, he said. He showed me his plots of herbs—some I'd seen when we were driving in. Every basil plant was as high as my chest. Other fields had healthy cilantro, others lemon grass, also parsley. While we were trekking through the fields, he told me that his son, Serio, who fished the Sea of Pontchartrain, came to the Wood Palace frequently and gathered this herb harvest to sell at Chef Menteurian restaurants and shops.

I had never seen a father speak of a son born to him. Vee, I knew, had a daughter or two, named after spices—I'd never met them. He had no son. Klamath was a lot like Vee, but shorter and stouter—a barrel-chested man, with long salt and pepper hair, and large, almond eyes, brown skin.

When we came back into the house, Mimi's expression betrayed some tension, frustration. "It just passed," she said. "They are going to go through with it."

Klamath clapped. He turned to me. "The Exodus application!"

"I don't know why you are so happy about it," his wife said.

Chef Menteurians' territory was under siege by rising waters. This had been true as long as I'd known anything about the place. I'd seen pictures from Vee, heard Camille describe it. There were no trees at all in the main village at that point, just the blue-white oaks—dead ones, killed by salt, "pickled." I gathered they had taken the radical step of proposing an application for an Exodus Agreement—which meant asking permission to purchase new, in this case, higher, ground, to eventually move their whole community. The U.A. Council, which oversaw such events in the territories, took a long time to consider these proposals. Apparently after years of inaction, they had said yes.

Mimi said the Exodus itself would never happen; the window of opportunity was so short. More money still had to be raised. They would have a narrow time frame to get all the financing together, purchase the new plot, have it ready for development, and then, resettle. If they failed, they lost the option to move. The agreement expired. Other threatened enclaves had got the U.A. approvals but were not able to buy enough land. The expenditures had depleted the enclaves' treasuries. They were worse off than before, and they were still where they were to start.

"Oh be quiet, sit still," Klamath told his wife. If we all just work, and pay our part—one day at a time—those other enclaves didn't have what we have, the population—"

He started pulling off the collard leaves for dinner. He liked looking on the bright side, and he liked to be doing something. I could tell he appreciated the facts, not the feelings.

"You fear it too, don't say otherwise," she said, shaking her pretty, shapely head. Her hair was in small rows of curls, very close cut.

Klamath didn't answer.

"He does, he does fear it—look at him," she said, trying to bring me into it. "Exodus Agreements are very tricky. Everything is on the table." She turned to her husband. "Tell him of the risks."

Klamath shrugged. "There are those who live after us."

"Well we bet everything we have for the hope of something better? That may never come?" she asked. "Heirs would never do that. Would they?"

The question was directed at me. I shook my head no.

"Our future is of another kind." Klamath tried to sound reassuring.

Vee used to say similar things. He didn't want to live on and on, and on, he'd be bored, he said. He wanted each moment to have a certain savor. A beat. A tone.

I felt at home in this kitchen, listening to Chef Menteur politics. It all seemed familiar—enclavers talking about their limited lives. Me, at the table, waiting to be called out for a new role, and waiting, and waiting.

*

"Fancy seeing you here, scene of so many crimes." It was Ariel, on St. Charles Avenue, months later. He'd accosted me outside the floodgates at the entrance to Audubon Island. Walked up on me out of nowhere.

"What crimes?"

"What they did to us when we were young—those Sims, those sickening operas—lending us to people—enslaving us—"

"I never saw them like that," I said.

"You were always the hero, Malcolm, weren't you—to Lazarus you still are—"

"What do you want from me now?" I was arming myself, preparing for my "brother's" belligerence. Lazarus had written me again to avoid contact with Ariel, somehow he'd heard about our adventure at the Towers. He'd specifically said, *"Malcolm, I have asked very little of you. You have always been obedient. But for your own good, do as I said before, and cut him off."* I was still furious with him over the incident with Camille. Almost a year had passed. I blamed him; I overlooked the fact that it was my choice she got involved.

"Well, going to see our *benefactor*? The young hero returns? He's not there. In Memphis for his shoring up. New prodermis, new cheeks, both places. His Re-job. Considering going in soon again for a total Re-description, you hear about that?"

"You," I started, and then I held back. What would be the point? I didn't feel like a hero right then—more like a failure. I did not have the same faith in Greenmore now, or in any of her research, and for that I felt both disappointed and guilty. I had been out at the Wood Palace for a season as her "assistant." But essentially, I had nothing to do, except occasionally help Klamath and his son Serio in their fields, bundling basil, chopping cilantro, tending watercress. I was just a place-holder.

But now that I was put to work, it was worse.

I'd come to the New Orleans Islands on an errand I considered completely dubious. I was to go to a sale at the library at a former university and buy up the books on the following subjects: "Egyptian religion," "Greek religion and mystery cults," "Christian mystics," "Kabala," "Buddhism," "Reincarnation." There was a sale because the books were not technically approved—considered "garbage from before the Reveal"—and the library couldn't keep them dry anymore. Because of their useless subjects, the books were offered by the pound, not by the title. If she had asked me to acquire pre-Reveal pornography for her I might have felt slightly better about it—it was used sometimes by the Varietology community, I knew, and it wasn't in any way questionable, the way these books were. She wanted to pursue the gross superstitions of past Nat ages. That was what she'd meant by "esoteric topographies." A horrible idea.

All morning I had been sorting through the moldy spines. I had managed to get eighty-two volumes, for a few crowns. At this moment Klamath and his son were lugging the boxes back to Klamath's boat.

I'd decided to take a break, wander my old haunts, and get some fresh air. I knew Lazarus wasn't home, and Vee and Marilee were back at Chef Menteur Enclave, apparently, because of a family illness. So I wasn't going by the Foundling House.

I never traveled for recreation—every dime I made went into my Trust, so I was sorry to have come at such a time, when nobody was around.

I was just going to take a look at the park where we used to perform. It was all a huge lake now. Closed to the public. The Sim business long forgotten.

So, obviously, the islands were still sinking. For a while things had been stable, when I was a boy, but now there was standing water everywhere, even though it hadn't rained in a week, and St. Charles Avenue was a pair of little healthy brooks divided by the median. In the far distance, I could see the Museum City Floodwall.

My good shoes were soaking wet—new ones Greenmore had bought me, very fancy, genenfabric woven top, made from a mold of my entire foot.

And now, worst of all, Ariel, in clothes that were even dirtier this time than when I had last seen him. His hair, even shaggier. His beard, even stringier. Why didn't he care for himself?

I knew I shouldn't let him catch me up. I was angry, and anger always catches you up. But then, I had to tell him: "Camille lost a lot. She couldn't complete her dowry. She had to leave. That was all she wanted and if she married, she must have married with a deficit." I didn't know the facts, just that Camille had left within a day of that night with O.

"Why did she take all the blame? Why didn't Greenmore listen to you? Have you ever asked her? Why was Greenmore so partial? She hired you for another job?" Ariel turned his palm to the air, for an answer.

I had no idea except what she said, that I was bright. And I didn't say that. She had spent on my Galcyon, my high-speed education, my detoxification. I was an investment, maybe. But I knew Heirs were profligate, I knew they could afford to overlook the tiny sums they spent on us, and hire others. There were plenty of desperate, better behaved and willing workers around. She'd been loyal, that was unusual. Ariel was right to ask, but I wouldn't grant him that.

"Port Gramercy doesn't let its betrothed girls out and about for very long. She got to marry? Exercise her Procreation Agreement? Follow all the Fertility Laws? She came out okay?" he asked. "Right?"

"I don't know" I said. The thought of her made me feel weak.

Greenmore had sent me on those junkets right after I got out of solitary. Nobody had information when I got back at the Towers. I assumed she went back to Port Gramercy.

"It hasn't been easy for me since that night," Ariel continued. He meshed his fingers together, held them at the mid-point of his chest, stood directly in my path. I couldn't pass. "Aren't you going to ask me how it turned out?"

I asked.

Ariel described the troubles he'd had setting up his Independent Trust. He started with the point when the Trust had passed from Lazarus to O's stewardship. Then he said, the signature on the documents had half-worked. "They still don't want me to control my own Trust. They have it rigged every which way. They don't want any new Heirs. You are fooling yourself if you think it will work for you."

I was well aware of Ariel's paranoid constructions. I was not going to comment, but then I blurted out, "If they didn't want anyone else paying in and becoming an Heir, why do they have the status Not-Yet, why do they have the Boundarytime ceremony, why do they have initiations, and centers like Memphis that still do the Treating? You don't have an answer do you?" There were egrets up in the trees that

were out in the middle of the lake. At that strange moment, two took off
in one glorious motion.

"Oh don't use that superior look with me, Malcolm," he said. "I
know it's a defense."

He knew how to get under my skin. "Well now? Every last drop of
what Lazarus was holding for you? All those fights, that night, and you
have your Trust, in your own hands?" I mocked him. "What was the
point?"

"No, I'm going to have to go after Lazarus again," he said.

"What?"

"The money has been in limbo since O signed that paper. There's
a U.A. WELLFI Bank officer in charge. He's taking fees to manage, but
he's not doing anything. Come to find out that before I can get complete
control of the money, I have to show where I came from. What enclave.
Or prove that I come from none. Hard to prove a negative. The courts
won't take at face value that we are charter-less, you and me, any of the
foundlings. The burden of proof is on us. They say they need to see
any records, any materials, about the day we were found, how we were
found. What we were wearing—clothes, notes, features of the vessel we
were found in—anything. DNA samples, of course— they said mine
were anomalous. I can't have my money until I can prove who I am.
People from enclaves aren't allowed to have holdings in WELLFI. "

"Even if they were tossed out?"

"We weren't tossed out."

"I know you think that. Just tell me what I don't know."

"If you are in an enclave, not just raised in one, if part of a group
only by DNA, it doesn't matter, you are under that Charter, that Treaty.
New rules. You can't get in, be an Heir—"

"Why didn't you just let Lazarus keep your Trust? Let him run your
money. He never did you any harm." I knew that WELLFI bank had
never required any scrutiny like this of my identity. What if we were
discovered to be enclavers? Most Charters swore off ever being Heirs,
in perpetuity. Strict castes. Ironclad. I screamed at him. "What are you
doing? You can ruin me, you thought of that?"

He paused, he realized. I could see the regret it in his eyes, for he
didn't want to harm me, no matter how angry he was. "I'll tell Lazarus,
if and when he turns the stuff in, not to put us together."

"Not put us together? The records all say we were found together.
Everybody knows—please, go back to Lazarus."

"I've dissolved it. That's over. Listen—" He wagged his finger at me.

"We were saved, not tossed out."

"Oh, this stupid fantasy of yours."

"It's a memory. Guns going off. Green explosions. There was a woman weeping—well-dressed, long dark hair, she set us afloat. Palm trees. Palms, those tall ones. Sand."

"Come on."

"You never missed them. I did."

"The myth of the eternal return," I quoted, showing my education. "You were a prince, a woman cared for you, only tried to save us, from the guns."

I surely should have gone on my way, off into the splashy streets, but I heard at that exact moment, an old and slightly melodic note in Ariel's voice, which I associated with nights when we were very young, when he looked out for me. Which made me pause.

"It's your history too," he pleaded.

I pushed passed him. Now he was following me close on the old streetcar tracks, splashing mud on his own cuffs, tugging at my sleeve. I could see in the distance the dirt path he'd trod with that huge puppet sculpture on his back in that funny-all. That day he tore me down into his doom, then mocked me—and I was there again. Now that path in the park ran right into the new lake.

I turned to him. "There's nothing there! We came from nowhere! What did Lazarus ever do but try to save you?" I had had enough. "Why do you have to ruin everything?" I meant it. "If you had ever worked hard enough, and followed the rules, you wouldn't—"

"Like you? Hole up with some cranky Heir—delusional? You know what they say about her these days, your Dr. Greenmore? Rumors of her radical associations in the past? Worse than Lazarus. Really nuts."

"Did you know I was coming into town? Are you following me?"

"NO! You are paranoid, Malcolm. How would I know where Greenmore sends you? Lazarus might just hand the facts over, to avoid the courts. You'll hear from me soon I hope! Besides, if you believe we came from Outliars, what have you got to worry about? So don't!"

He had a point. A perverse point.

"There you are!" Klamath approached on the tracks, in his high rubber boots. He was signaling me it was time to go back to the dock on Freret Street. Serio, his son, whom I was just getting to know, a small fellow, with long, strong arms, and a small head like his mother, was right behind him. "Malcolm, now!" He called for me, and I strode quickly to him and his son. Leaving Ariel behind.

"Why do you act as if you don't want to know? You do!" Ariel called after me.

"Leave me alone. For now, forever!" I shouted back and ran. At that time in my life, I truly believed he was dangerous, against me.

But about wanting know who I might really be, I wasn't as disinterested as I was supposed to be.

*

About a month later, on the narrow pallet where I slept at Greenmore's estate, I found a package waiting for me. There had been a U.A. Post delivery, unusual. It was a small box, about six inches in a cube. "A. de DuPlantier," it read on the outside. And my Wood Palace address. With dread, and also some kind of shameful elation, I opened the thing from the top. Amidst the stuffing made of curlicues of pink paper, I found an envelope. Inside, a note, which read:

Malcolm, sorry about the argument on so sadly soaked old St. Charles. Here you will find a missing particle of our lives. Were you looking for it? Sorry if you weren't. I was WFRSN 19068, and you were a few digits later. Same brood, I'd say. Don't yet know what it stands for. Obscure enclave if it was one. Ariel AKA your Brother with Proof.

P.S. I have asked my lawyer to request the judge keep these facts sealed, as they pertain to you. The judge doesn't have this tag, this evidence, because you do. I think the F is Florida. I don't know who the hell we are, now. Palm trees were right.

What was he talking about? I knew what Lazarus would want me to think. That Ariel was ruining everything.

Yet, I felt my heart beating fast. Furiously, I fished around in the shreds of paper until I found an antique mesh bag with a tiny set of ridges at the top that laced together with a wire cord. When I felt the object, inside, I was tantalized, excited. It was so strange. Why did I care? I shouldn't—but—inside, two metal charms on a chain, each with a green tarnished nickel backing. One was a plain square, one had an enamel surface. The enamel showed a white star with five points as the design, set out in a field of lapis blue. When I turned over the second square plain charm, I found the letters and numerals: WFRSN 19077. Well, was that the answer? Was this a stamp of an enclave? What were their rules? Why did they get rid of us? Why didn't they love us?

I couldn't quell these Nat concerns. My mind raced: if we came from an enclave, were they Free Wheelers? Did I have a Free Wheeler's rights?

Lazarus would be so disappointed.

II

8:17 PM October 12, 2121
Sunken Quarter
New Orleans Islands, Northeast Gulf De-Accessioned Territory,
U.A. Protectorate

*O*n our trek across the Quarter, Serpent, Peet, Gepetto, and I arrived at a corner where a parade was going by—about fifteen Heirs paired with Altereds, both in pink satin, genenfabric, walking tiny little dogs half the size of normal shoes. Some new genetic innovation, dogs smaller than rats. They were giddy, giggling wildly—the Heirs, that is, not the dogs.

"There have been updates every few weeks, and scans of Ginger's body, you wouldn't believe, something growing on her natural places like a tree, very convincing, common doctor's reports—it's got so half the Quarter would greet one another by saying, 'How's Ginger? What's up? She gonna make it? A real rollercoaster.'" Gepetto was trying to get me interested. Why did he care? "You won't believe how Sims have evolved," he went on. "Being outlawed was such a boon—you won't recognize the art!"

"Like, bebum, they would have ever *not* cashed in, like this night *wasn't* gonna come," Peet interjected. "Whoever the Far East Players are. I never believed she'd get better. Where was the profit in that?"

At that moment, I smelled the steam coming off the bag of crobs Peet was holding. We sat down right on the curb of the cobblestone walk while the parade was passing. I reached in and grabbed one from

Peet's sack, pulled it out, crushed the fat tail-shell of the creature in one hand and liberated the huge white clump. At the thought of what it would taste like, after so many days of not eating, I was afraid I might cry.

I felt Gepetto's eyes. Remembered how guilty I'd feel after I ate. So I offered it. I had already blown his cover. Also, I'd avoid my craving, get rid of it. Or more perverse, enjoy it by watching him eat it.

But Gepetto looked through it, didn't even see it. He was leering at something else. The silly dogs, the ridiculous costumes.

"And tonight," Peet was going on, as we still waited for the last little row of marchers. "Finally the night. The so-called finale." The tail meat glistened, jiggled. Peet grabbed it and said, "Thought Serpent said you couldn't be tempted."

I let it go, stood. We staggered on.

"There's Jeddy's!" Serpent called out not long after.

I saw a green flag and a hand-lettered sign. *Jeddy's BASIN-STREET-ON-THE-BOWL BUTE/BIOS/VICTUALS/VROOM Transport TIRES REPAIRED. Locksmith Pawn.*

An ancient tiled building lit by street lamp had three doors, all closed. On the side and at the rear of the building was the Basin wall—here the graduated Quay dwindled to a single narrow border that kept off the waters. No lights were on inside this place. At this my heart sank.

"You brought him here, now, let's move," Peet insisted, shoving his friend forward.

"I made a bargain," Serpent retorted. "So what if he's a Nyet? Keeping up my end!" Then he pulled me across the big street with him. Peet and Gepetto, now a faction, refused to cross. They were too eager to get to the transport.

Debris everywhere, stacks of it, high piles of old bricks, of trash, of huge thick tires people used in the DE-AX because of the horrible roads. I tripped on a crowbar. Serpent took my elbow, kept me from falling. "Come on, boy, this is what you want, hey?" he asked. "Go up there tonight on that tub?"

"Yes, of course," I said. In hours, I'd be home, I told myself. Lazarus... answers. Tell him what Ariel had done if he didn't know it.

"JEDDY," Serpent stopped suddenly, yelled. "WHERE YOU?"

"Come on!" Peet shouted from across the way. "What's the hold up?" He had lost his rhythm.

A single bulb came on. I celebrated. The door opened. A very large man appeared. His outfit was coveralls, tomato color, blotched with black stains. He had only a few teeth in his mouth and all his fingernails that I could see were perfectly black. "Who is it?"

"Serpenthead Louis," Serpenthead said. "Played with the Vipers band? Remember me? Got some compos?"

"Vipers band?" he asked, pushing his greasy hair back. "Well what did they play?"

This was a test. Some kind of ID. I hoped Serpent wasn't bluffing. My whole future depended upon this strange Yeared. I was abject, but the odd thing was, I was so pitiful I almost wanted to laugh.

"Come on!" Peet clapped his hands across the street. "Bebum. We are leaving! One minute!"

"*I grabbed the tuna/ I grabbed the cell/ but that Kat was toting hell hell hell*—" Serpenthead sang in his very smooth baritone.

"Hah Hah." Jeddy smiled in recognition. "What happened to you guys?"

"Can't talk now, this fella here got to get up the Tchoup to Audubon— needs some compos—you got?"

"Shoo," Jeddy said. "All out, buddy."

"How can you be out?" Serpent asked.

Everything I'd done wrong had led to this catastrophe—gone into Port Gramercy in the first place, all of it—that *Me* that got me into trouble—"Out?" I stomped toward the fellow. "You can't be!"

Jeddy pulled back his bird-like head, turned to Serpent. "What is with this guy?" he asked.

"Nyet, 'bout to go to his Boundarytime, swear off the likes of us, you believe it? How can he give this great life o'ours away? Help him, huh?"

"True is, I got no fuel, none. Of no kind. All these launches and yachts and little cruisers and water taxis and what not just come through here the last two hours. Going to that Ginger junk."

"Every last drop?" I pleaded.

"COME ON," Peet cried from across the way. "Me, and this Imposse are moving, Serp!"

Serpent waved. "Give me another minute bro!" Then he asked Jeddy, "When will some more come in?"

"Morning, late morning. Sell to you then."

"Yeah? What price? What price?"

"Discount, okay," he said. "I'll give him the good price all right! Night." He shut his narrow door, and locked it.

"LEAVING NOW!" Peet called from across the way.

"Yes!" Gepetto's hoarse voice.

I looked at Serpent, bereft. "You got two choices," he said to me.

He was fair, honest in his dealings. This seemed impossible—an Outliar like he was—but I knew it was true. "What are they?" I had no thoughts. I'd come to the end of the ride. I'd be here at the Basin wall forever. What was I going to do? Swim back to Audubon?

"Sleep it off, here, outside Jeddy's. You could get rolled; about ninety percent chance this edge of the Quarter."

Jeddy said through the door, "I ain't letting no Nyet loiter here, you take him. Sorry there are thieves." He shut off his outside light. "Like I want to have some bait in front of my store?"

Peet called. "LEAVING. 5-4-3-2-"

"You can come, we'll be back ten hours from now, in the morning—" Serpent said.

"I can sleep on Serio's boat," I said.

"It's certain you will get rolled on the Quay, one hundred percent chance there, pickers galore!" he said. "You think Gramercy docks is rough? Make up your mind. I got a gig."

And so, almost weeping with frustration, I left, crossed the street with Serpent. I consoled myself it was just a setback of a few hours, an evening.

"You'll get here first thing in the morning," he told me. "Jeddy will sell you—you in no shape to drive that old boat anyways tonight. You better off—"

"What? Better off?"

"I know," he said. "I am sorry, but we got you this far—not long now—"

I looked up and saw Peet and Gepetto—a narrow, beak-nosed musician in a black jacket and a low beret, and a tall, emaciated shiny-skinned pseudo with his hair in a bun, and several bracelets on his wrists, and slippers, along with Serpent, with his wide head, and the thousand pocket tunic, and his awful bowl legs—my gang, now.

"Quite the wheels, bebum, quite the wheels," Peet said, a few minutes later, as he and Serpent climbed in the back of Gepetto's strange transport—a plain grey metal outside, with luxury inside. Nutria fur on the seats. The thing was parked about a quarter mile from Jeddy's.

"Oh, we do what we can," Gepetto said to Peet, proudly as he gunned the thing up the ramp set into the terraced well of the Quarter. At the dock at the top was a large rusty boat with smokestacks like a tugboat, but with a broader deck. A sign on it read,

**EAST NEW ORLEANS/FAR EAST DE-AX FERRY
CAPACITY 11 TRANSPORTS FOUR AXLES EACH.
CLOSED**

He parked again, yanking up the brake, on the steep incline.
"It's not running!" Peet exclaimed. "Too late. We got to be there by
nine! Show starts at ten-thirty. Can we make it if we take the long way
round?"

"Maybe we can get them to take us across," Gepetto said. All around
as far as I could see was open water except for the Quarter directly
behind us. Gepetto got out of the car to talk to the ferryman. I thought
he might stumble, the ramp was that steep.

We watched him bang on the door of little rusty-roofed house on
the top of the ramp—a stall, really. A fat man appeared who asked where
we wanted to go. "Mississippi!" Gepetto shouted. "Far East DE-AX?"

"Not scheduled. Wait until tomorrow."

"I *told* you to hurry," Peet said to Serpent.

"I heard you," Serpent came back.

Gepetto took out a thick wad of bills to show to the man. Peet
catcalled, "That's one rich falsetto! Where'd he get that kind of DOUGH?"

Within ten minutes we were the lone transport on the deck of the
ferry steaming across the Industrial Pass, a fifteen-mile wide expanse
that took us to the wilder part of the territory.

"Look out there," Serpenthead said when we were in the middle.
From that vantage point we could see a glow to the Southwest. The
wind on the water was fine, even cool—I opened the door to feel it. It
woke me a little, brought me to my senses. Then I saw the hundred
masts of the armada: approaching slowly across the waters from the Old
River, a fleet of pleasure boats, yachts, steamers, small cruisers, and a
swarm of water taxis. "Those the ones bought all the compos," Serpent
said. "This Sim must be huge."

Just as the illumination on the opposite shore began to appear, a
feathery fog started to creep along on the surface of the channel. We
were going into the deeper country, the truly abandoned places.

It was as if I could feel certain things coming to an end.

*M*y discoveries did not begin propitiously. My discovery of my other fate—or at least, its first intimations.

It began with Ariel's package, that charm. And Greenmore's questions. She called these conversations "bouncing things off of me."

"Oh they could talk to this thing 'god,'" she said. "Gave their every word and deed to this it, this 'god.'" She slowed. "What do you think they meant by this word, Malcolm? Have you any idea of it?"

It was late winter after I found all those books for her at the sad rotting library on Audubon Island. After having been silent for several days in a row, she'd called me into her room to tell me she had discovered in a book I'd found, *Catholic History of New Orleans*, that the building where the Audubon Foundling House was, had once been a convent for "contemplatives"— mystic nuns. They had a "vow of silence" and were "cloistered." They gave their every word to "the god," she said. The building had survived the various floods beginning with the Great Katrina, and later, when the Mississippi changed its course and the general rising of all the seas took the last of the land south of the city, and New Orleans was broken down into islands. "The building had one of the highest walls in the whole city, it saved them over and over," she said. "They prayed all day, and all night, too. They didn't meet with outside people, except for a few benefactors."

As a boy at the Home, I was always grateful for the high wall around us, especially when there were hard rains which turned the streets into streams, the canals into rushing rivers. I had never wondered why it was originally built. I had always been interested in the little niche at the side of the foyer, though. Set in the wall at waist height, it had two pairs of doors, between the outer foyer and the dining hall. These doors slid up and down like double hung windows. But not of glass, of solid wood. There was a little space in between the two gates, not more than a foot and a half in width, and about four feet in height. There was a bell to ring, and beside it, a hole for peeping through. It was Ariel's favorite place to hide.

Greenmore told me that when visitors from "the outside world" came, they rang the bell and then raised the door on their side of the niche, and placed their money, then closed the door. The nuns would open on the other side and replace the money with "divinity," then close it again, thus keeping themselves in seclusion. She said, "It seems to me they thought of prayer as the work of calling on something invisible. Then they produced that candy, something in honor of the invisible: made of sugar and egg white, sweet as heaven, like little dollops of cloud."

"Like brosia," I said. I want to remind her who she was. She seemed to be having trouble with this lately. She seemed to want to speak to me as if I were an equal.

"I think sweeter," she said.

I told her people always forgot about the place in the middle, didn't realize a small boy could wedge himself between two sets of doors, and stay, as it were, inside the wall for hours. And if someone started to open up one set, the boy hiding could go behind the second set, and run off. He always had a warning, and an escape. Actually, Ariel and I were the only two boys who could stand that enclosure—the others were afraid of being inside, couldn't take it for hours. We always could. Neither of us was in the least claustrophobic.

"Is that so?" she asked. "Do you know why that is?"

I shrugged.

"How else were you and he different?"

I shrugged again.

"But where is our secret door?" she asked. "It must be here someplace," she said, pressing on her chest. "No one sees it. How does 'the god' come and go? Or the soul, which is I think, the same thing but from this direction. They all have different names for it. The soul is the part that participates in the larger—a little tiny connector to the whole, so to speak. They say it exists. We don't believe—" She put her fist near her heart.

I had no idea what she wanted to know, or why she was asking me.

She looked at me very hard and said something quite strange: "I would have thought you might have thoughts on such things, or have images of them."

"All this was long over when I got to the Foundling House," I said. "Why?"

"But what if you think back?" she asked, looking at me in that way she had before, fishing.

How could these things matter? She was confusing. She made me uncomfortable. "I don't know," I said. "Klamath needs me. We are working on the coriander." I wanted to go back to the barns where he spread bushels of leaves of the spice on thin cloth, and we boiled water underneath them, and then captured the steam. I liked the work; I liked helping Serio and Klamath.

"I make you nervous, don't I?" she asked.

I wanted to say I was worried, about her, but that would be too bold. In any event, she could tell from my expression, apparently.

"How can you worry about someone who is seeking the truth?" she asked. "Don't."

In general, this was the entire content of my position as "research assistant." She was mining mystical literature, and the rest, and then she called me occasionally to ask me what I thought of things she'd learned. I never thought very much of it. It was written by Nats, it was all idiotic. She seemed to think that because I was a Nat, or for some other reason, I would have answers she couldn't come up with on her own.

"Religion, so I was taught," she went on. "Was what we had to cling to before the Reveal? It had to do with tying yourself on to some story, some myth, and repeating it so many times you believed it. And the myths were all about immortality, finally, so I was taught. Once we had that, or something this close, we didn't need religion anymore—it was simple. Everyone was taught this. The word religion, after all, comes from the same root as ligament—people tied themselves to a story so they could live, as if forever. An act of group imagination, group self-hypnotism. And now it has no function. But what if it there is something to it? In their mystics, in their esoteric—"

"There can't be anything," I said.

"If I can crack the code of it. I'm going to posit there is something there, see where it goes. There are so many mystical testimonies—all

these were liars? In fact, I'm not even going to have my Re-job this year.
I've written them and told them. I am too engaged in my project to be
interrupted. If I am going to try these practices, I'm going to have a
Natural body, or as close as I can get—"

"What?" I had never even heard of such a thing.

"In due time," she said. "You will see." She picked up her tiny brosia
plate, and handed it to me, to let me know I could take it with me when
I left her suite.

Have scraps from her table. I took them. It was an honor, it seemed
to me.

That afternoon, in the kitchen, I confided in Klamath, and asked,
"Can she do this? Not go in for her Re-job?"

"She can do anything she wants," he shrugged. "She's an Heir."

"Will her—"

"It's not going to kill her. Not right away. She can skip a cycle. It's
been done. Not by her, but I have heard—"

"Why would any Heir risk something like that? Couldn't it harm
them?"

He shrugged. "The thing about them is they aren't like us. Not like
us at all. They don't even have the same truth."

*

"You are taking this too far," Chotchko told Greenmore later that same
month. Someone had to say it, and I couldn't, and Klamath couldn't.
So we were thrilled she was here, saying it. She stood in the middle of
Greenmore's suite in her bright red leathery braids, her cherry colored
sheath, her travel cape. I never liked her at the Curing Towers—I didn't
think she had enough deference to Dr. Greenmore, but now I loved her.
She had heard of Greenmore's plan not to get her Re-job on time, and
she'd come to get our boss to change her mind.

I was watching all this through the blinds from my little
room.

Greenmore just stared at Chotchko, tightlipped. Chotchko pressed:
"Is it masked despair?"

"Will you stop condescending to me? You aren't listening. *I* at least
understand the problem. None of your crowd even does. What if some
Protos have evolved to the point they can't help but seek to expand—
or whatever you want to call it. What if there is a natural imperative
after a certain number of years in this consciousness—their physical

entities, their minds, are expressing this, what, this climax, th
transition. Look at the evidence, the way they are breaking out. I
know it. There must be a conduit. Someone must have found it. Once,
stumbled upon it—the mystics. A clarified path. The boundary can
become the corridor. This must happen. There are so many who say
so— and perhaps the ones who took the mushrooms knew. How to do
it in a healthier, less chaotic fashion, in a way that doesn't harm. Or the
Tibetans, they wrote a whole book about the territory, I think—but it
has to be decoded—"

"Oh my Albers," Chotchko said. "That is the book of the Dead. They
were dead. They died. You know? Bit the black? So so so-longed?"

"Those who wrote the books didn't, or if they did, they came back.
They wrote directions! Just how do we translate them? Everyone wasn't
an idiot before the Reveal—think about it. How could they have been?
They produced us? Nats have reason. Malcolm—look at him, his
I.Q., given everything, is completely unexpected, there is no ordinary
explanation for it, did I show you that at the Towers? Have you ever
read Swedenborg?" Greenmore was raising her hands again. Her gown
made wings. I felt exposed, being discussed like that.

"What is this now? You want to figure out how to do what? And
without the—so-long? That's your research? So you are going to try to
so-long to see?"

"If you are going to call me names—and, not, *not so-long*, expand.
I have never mentioned *that*. That's the whole point! There is reason
to believe some consciousness loosens from the body after old death—"
Greenmore's raspy voice rising. "This would explain some of the
experiences of the Chronics, their erratic voyaging, their insistence that
the dimensions that hold them in don't count—we have to do something
so they won't continue to destabilize. Or the First Wave. You don't
recognize sacrifice, do you? Is that it? I'm willing to go out, chart the
territory—find the way—"

Chotchko: "Honestly Lydia. You are not making sense. *Loosens
from the body*? We know there is no consciousness without the body.
Perhaps you should see someone. Dr. Jeremiah has openings—come
back to the Towers—perhaps if you rethought being redescribed. And
certainly it's lunacy to skip a Re-job."

Greenmore leaned forward. "I am planning on the body being alive,
of course! I believe in the Reveal! Of course! Don't you understand?
You, of all people, fail to see the importance of what I'm trying to
discover—the First Wave will be hitting this limit. We are going to have

millions all at once, filling all the beds. And think of the varietology possibilities, if these methods can be taught, and I think they can be taught, especially if one of us learns how they work, and how to adapt them to Heirs—and reduce the risks."

"You know as well as I do that the most we can do is find a drug combination to calm them, slow them down, keep them in the normal range," Chotchko countered. "When we were working at the Towers, working on the data coming in, we all thought it was chemical. You thought so too—"

Greenmore said, "Mental events have chemical consequences, you know this. Just think, we can give them a tour, so they don't have to fear, or experience anything as messy as—"

"You sound like a heretic. Please."

This was all too difficult, things between Heirs. I was actually on Chotchko's side, and I had to be against her. I would have much preferred a play, if things were going to be dramatic. In a play you knew how things ended. That everyone was pretending.

Greenmore called me in. I obeyed.

"Pick her up and take her out," she ordered.

"But Dr. Greenmore I can't touch her," I said.

"Did you hear what I said?" she asked.

Chotchko stood, looked right into me, her bright ropes sprouting from her head.

Greenmore said, "Move," but I did not.

Chotchko and I passed through a few more moments like that. I was throbbing, with confusion. What if she didn't relent? I would have to carry her, a horror for us both.

At the last moment she said, "Oh, you fool," and stalked out.

I followed.

A few minutes later, out on the pier, she said to me, "She has to get help. She just can't stand to be wrong."

Chotchko's transport was at the end of the plank road. The driver had gotten out—he seemed alarmed to find me there, alone with an Heir. "I'm okay. He's all right," she called him. To me: "Perhaps I went too far, but she's going off—do you see it? Off in her own world, it's megalomania, worse. If there is some realm—who is she to travel there alone? Solo Columbus?"

I was shocked Chotchko would even entertain the ideas. It was hot, almost dusk, noisy with frogs in the marsh, and cicadas in the herb fields and low trees out in the firm land that the marshes were connected to.

"Do *you* know what she's trying to find, Malcolm?" She was speaking to me as an equal, or closer to an equal than I was comfortable with. "Do *you* see the folly? You do, don't you? I can tell. Why don't you tell her?"

"She won't listen to me," I said. The whole idea that I could tell Greenmore anything and that she might act upon it was disconcerting.

"She's disturbed by how far she has fallen. The reception of her research. It has devastated her. It's her pride. She certainly doesn't trust me. She may think she has her reasons. But I have always given her credit. I will, I'm not going after—explain this to her—she has something right about the Protos. And she was right it was going to hit the First Wave. That's already starting. I have seen the reports. I didn't want to tell her. Yet obviously, her approach is absurd—we can find a drug. We are trying some already."

"But I can't stop her. I'm just—" I said.

"She trusts you," she said.

I shook my head.

"But she does, you don't know?" Chotchko asked.

"Know what?" I asked.

She looked away, gestured for the driver to open the wide burgundy door of her high-wheeled vehicle. She made that noise, that click with the tongue at the top of the mouth, to know he should come and meet her, escort her back to the car. He ran up to her: he was a Gaist, wore that blue tattoo on the lids. I didn't know what enclave he was from. He didn't look her in the eye—he seemed surprised when he saw that I did. Out in the country, I had lost my manners. She turned back and looked at me before she set off. "Just, take care of her," she said. "Will you?"

I swelled with pride, to think she felt she could ask me something like that. Then fear, because, who was I to take care of a grand, brilliant Heir?

Walking back to the house, I was still thinking about the fact that Greenmore had asked me to pick Chotchko up. The taboo was so strict; I was having trouble with it. I recalled a story from years before. An Heir had fainted into a puddle at a Sim. Vee had been the only one around. Two Heirs gave him permission, ordered him to handle her. None of them had anywhere near the strength. He didn't want to. He never had touched one, not in forty odd years of life. Once he handled her, the Heir would have to go through a whole purging, purification—it was quite a tax on them, being defiled by one of us. But he did it. "*They are so light,*" he had told me later. "*No more than a wet dog, the skin*

*is not fat and muscle, what you call it, the prodermis—it's like foam—
they are very light, full of air, just like their voices"*—and he had smiled
when he said this, even laughed a little. It had been late at night at the
Foundling House one of the many nights when we had no power and
were huddled in the kitchen, with candles. He had just entertained us
with a shadow play earlier. I was about twelve, or thirteen, and he was
having a little orange-basil wine which they were still making then at
Chef Menteur. He was giving me a confession, letting me in on a secret.
"No substance—" He had shrugged. *"I always knew in some way, but
to touch—"* He shrugged again. *"There's that moment when what you
always knew, somehow in your mind, but it didn't work to know it, or it
somehow goes against your own view, yet it comes forth, it's a revelation, a
gift, when the knowledge arrives, the world rights itself."*
    "What did you always know?" I had asked Vee.
    "They are ghosts," he had said.
    "You can't say that," I had said.
    "I know, I am sorry, I should never have said that to you." He was
turning over his palms in gesture of resignation, but still a vague smile,
a flash of pride. *"Will you forgive me?"*

*

After Chotchko's visit, Greenmore redoubled her efforts, said she was
putting herself in a "cave"—adapting this from a mode of Tibetan
sensory deprivation. We were not to go in to see her, only slip the
brosias and hot water under the door. There were certain draughts she
was taking, Klamath confided. She'd had them sent in from Gaist allies
in South America. Smuggled, actually.
    Even Mimi was excluded, except for every few days, to bring her
fresh gowns.
    I watched her sometimes through my blinds. She was in there for
forty days and nights—chanting, and walking, and weeping, taking
meticulous notes. When she emerged in late July, the relief was palpable,
at least to me.
    It was actually a beautiful day, not as awfully hot as it should have
been. I saw her on the plank road. She seemed strong and alive. I was
energized by the sight. I thought her decline must be over.
    The house was high—we'd been working on raising the
foundations—and the water level seemed to be stabilizing. The fields
were well-drained. We had dug new lagoons, and the swamp irises and

the gray night herons and the ibises and the dark beautiful ducks and the roosting egrets in the evenings filled the swamps around us. Greenmore was beaming. She had a new calm, perhaps. Okay, it was over.

I was watching her from the small dining table on the deck beside the open windows of Mimi's galley kitchen. At this point, Greenmore had been out walking for about half an hour—off the boardwalk, and through the basil gardens, the collard patches, the mounds of cilantro, out to the marsh, and then back.

She came inside the house through the French doors off the kitchen. She never went into our kitchen. After a short tour past our stove and sink, she exited again and pulled up a bench at my outdoor table, and asked, blithely, "What are you eating?"

Shrimp and crawfish with herbs, and rice, thick and spicy, which I had an impulse to cover, to hide.

"Can I have some of it?" she asked.

"What did you say?" Klamath blurted out, through the open kitchen door.

Greenmore said back, "I want some of what he's having—what is it? Okras, thick noodles, crawfish, shrimp with what? Ginger, basil? Cilantro?"

I had no idea she had these words in her vocabulary. I had never heard her speak of our food with any word other than the general term, "victuals," a slur in their eyes.

Mimi was over at the counter peeling shrimp for the restaurants. (Serio had inspired his parents to start processing them, for the Pond Gaists and the Chef Menteur restaurant trade.) She turned so quickly she knocked some shrimps on the floor, where they formed a gelatinous gray mass.

I was disgusted, the way Greenmore should have been disgusted—the clumps and filth I still put in my mouth. I couldn't stand her to be here, to see it. But she didn't seem to mind.

I saw Mimi's grooved and dimpled face, looking over at Greenmore, shocked. An Heir, asking for our lowly fare. What could it mean? The world was crazy.

Klamath came to the table, and offered his mistress a taste from a stirring spoon. He must have thought that would sour Greenmore on the general idea. She surely had not had victuals cross her lips for fifty years, or seventy, or more. He leaned in so close to her it seemed forbidden to me.

But she sucked up the broth he offered, and said it was "incredible."

This whole scene was incredible.
But there it was, and it was going to get worse.

IV

9:20 PM October 12, 2121
Mississippi I-Road
Far East De-Accessioned Gulf Territory, U.A. Protectorate

I woke in the front seat of Gepetto's car. The shock of what I had gotten into, with these Outliars, spread over me—an electric stealthy chill. I wailed inwardly.

This was the part of the DE-AX everyone warned everybody about. The Far East—Heirs never went there.

When the fog lifted some, I could tell we were on a double road. The lanes on the outside were straight and the other road opposite just the same, across a little earthen divide. Every three or four miles, we had to stop and drive around some obstacle, or hole or ruin or crack or mound of garbage. That, I was used to, I'd had to drive a few times around the vicinity of the Wood Palace where the roads were abysmal— travel by boat was usually much easier around there. I was just not used to the long stretches, which reminded me of pictures in books of the way things had been once when things were connected to each other, before the Heirs had to keep safe from the rebels. When they used to have airplanes in the sky, large passenger boats with thousands in the waters, when the Broads and Nets were all connected, so everyone could communicate with everyone else, regardless of strat. And nobody was listening to every word. I could only imagine the chaos of all that. At one point, I saw motorcyclists in cone suits zooming on the opposite lanes, flipping out of the fog, and then into it again. Images from the far past, anachronisms.

"Good we are in this tank, in these parts. No Securitas out here," Peet mumbled in the back.

Finally the good road broke down, and we bumped along on a detour with wretched little signs: *"NEW OCEAN SPRINGS EX-ENCLAVE Of hOLE KNOWLiDGE STOP at TOLL!!"*

"They tear up the roads like this for the revenue," Peet said. "Make you stop." We pulled up to a tiny shack which stood before what I could see was a wooden bridge under a single pinkish lamplight. We couldn't go over it, though, because a portion of the bridge was hovering practically at a right angle up, leaving quite a gap. The sign said, *"Caution Wolf River Drawbridge."*

In the car, as we waited, the fog came in heavy again, as if on cue.

"Hate these goddamn people, worse than Free Wheelers or gypsies. Bebum. Don't let them get started," Peet put in.

Serpenthead tapped me on the shoulder from the back seat —I had given up on objecting to this. "They aren't many left. Real specimens. Relinquished their Charter. Turned in their Procreation Allotment. Went off every grid. Moved into the DE-AX on purpose, didn't get stranded here. Strange beliefs."

"Such as?"

"The sun and moon are conscious, we go to some sea island when we die, turtles have the big spirits, I think."

"Bebum. Why are they even still living here? On what land?" Peet said. "This is all swamp."

"I think they are about to so long out of existence. Harmless, though, I guess," he whispered. Serpent seemed amused by all of this.

A man in a long shirt with a hood adorned with nubby deer horns, emerged from the hut and came towards us. Serpent continued, "They have the idea there is a way to go be a hermit in the pine forest and dance alone, and know something. Always going out to the islands, sitting alone in holes in the sand. Waiting for the *throb* they call it."

Peet contradicted, "Bebum. There can't be any more islands. Gulf's too high, rising seas."

"There are the islands," Serpent said. "We are going to one—"

The man took Gepetto's bills, and started to talk.

"Always get a sermon with these," Serpenthead said, rolling his eyes. Gepetto turned to me with great amusement.

The Ocean Springs Ex-Enclaver poked his head into the driver's side, near Gepetto. His eyes' whites were pure pink. He began his lecture in a growly shout, as if the intended audience were twenty feet away, not eight inches.

"In the beginning a Great Tortoise came up out of the water according to our founder, W.A. and he was made of gold and he saw the god in the trees and the god in the bushes and the god in our faces, and the crabs and the clouds, and he called them alive, and they woke, and when they woke, they knew they should abandon the dominant mode ashore. For they were not separate, they were one. Chapter One Verse 1 and 2."

"Okay, enough," Peet covered his ears, barked at the preacher. "We got the picture."

"Chapters One Verses 3, 4, 5," the horned fellow shouted on. *"One is not divisible but is a singularity ...."*

I looked over at the woman inside the shack, her eyes deep in her head—marbles at the bottoms of two wells. She was lit by an old cornosene lamp she held in her hand. Her long arm thin as a twig, a sickly yellow white. "Please, please," I said to her.

She reached up to turn the large wheel that drove a crank that made the drawbridge slowly lower, and she called to her mate, "Come over here darling tell me! Don't stay so far away!"

Gepetto said, smiling wide, "Far East DE-AX. M, I—crooked letter, crooked letter, I, crooked letter, crooked letter, that's what we used to say in the old days."

"Bebum. Never know what will crawl out from under a rock out here," Peet said, sitting back again when the car started to move.

Then we were rolling past the man with the hood—he seemed astonished we were leaving—the rhythmic chant of his poem beginning to fade, and eventually, we stopped being able to make out the words.

After the bridge, which we crept over at two miles an hour, Gepetto went forward at a pretty good clip under trees so thick they covered up the sky, so the darkness was almost total. Then the woods opened out a bit. Taller pines, then. Later still, we were going across a grassy marsh, the kind I was used to from the shore of the Sea of Pontchartrain.

Eventually, no trees at all.

The fog again, thick, so we couldn't see anything. "Bebum. Chowder," Peet called it. "Hate these roads, all kinds' criminals out here—"

I was reminded of nights at the Wood Palace: I felt the same old uneasiness, the same sense of apprehension, or was it anticipation. Dread was part of it. And loneliness, another part. The incredible loneliness I'd felt there. I saw it, somehow, for what it was—and out of it, I'd promised things. Serious things. The gravity of my promises seized me then, made me almost want to weep.

I thought of what Vee said that night about lifting up an Heir: *Sometimes there is something you always knew, but it never worked to know it—*

Since, I have heard people say that important events ripple out in all directions, forward into the future, and even back into the time before they occur—they create waves, the way a pebble dropped into still water makes circles. If that is true, what I was feeling then—excitement, a strange clarity— was something of the before-effects of an event that had not arrived at me yet.

Now, I call it my alchemy.

V

December 28, 2120
Wood Palace on the Sea
Western Gulf De-Accessioned Territory, U.A. Protectorate

A few weeks after she started eating some of our food, Greenmore started asking us to "liberate" her—that was how she put it. She said Mimi knew how because she once worked in Memphis.

We protested, gave her every excuse. She became enraged, so we said we would, but we must postpone.

Finally, she said, if we wouldn't do it, she'd hire people who would. She had her contacts.

We had a meeting. Mimi, Klamath, and I. Klamath said if others were called in, there could be reprisals. Arrests. We were better off doing what she had ordered ourselves. Later, we could undo it—this was the hope, at least. And we could keep it secret.

A few hours later, we filed into her suite together. Instinctively, Mimi closed all the blinds so that this secret thing would be done in the dark.

"Look at you Malcolm," Greenmore said. "So frightened. Calm down, I'm a doctor."

"But why?" Klamath asked her. These things she was doing to herself, were an assault on him.

"I have my reasons. I have them, you must trust," she said, closing her eyes for a second. "Now, leave if you don't want to look. Mimi? Now."

Klamath and I decided not to leave. We needed to see this. Face it. Deal with the consequences. Be there in case something went wrong.

"Madam Heir," Mimi said, in a ritual I'd never seen. "Madam Heir, for your wishes to be fulfilled I must have contact."

"I allow it."

"Madam Heir, for your wishes to be fulfilled, I must have contact—" Mimi hated saying these words.

"I allow it, and I have my purification planned."

"Madam Heir, for your wishes to be fulfilled, I must have contact—" At the third voicing of this same phrase, Mimi became visibly distraught.

"I allow it, and I have my purification planned, cover your hands, and shield yourself, speak not of it," Greenmore said, with a kind of boredom. These were lies, she had no purification planned.

Mimi got down on her knees, put her forehead to the floor, then lifted her hands above her head. When she stood, she bowed a second time, and put on pink gloves, like rubber. Then she said, "I will do your will." And she placed her hands on Greenmore's sculpted heart-shaped face.

First, she removed Greenmore's protective lenses, which shielded her whole true iris, and the white.

Immediately, Greenmore started blinking, and blinking, like a Nat. I hated this.

Her whites were really the yellow of dirty teeth, on a Yeared. That part was strange, and ugly, but the real irises were not: they were the very darkest brown, just like my own. I had always thought her eyes were that cat color, gold, wheat. To match her hair. Not true. Then Mimi took off her entire headjob, which, surprising to me, was all one piece, a great hard helmet, with her silken yellow hair falling out of it. Greenmore's true hair was tiny white tufts, very scant. It would have been more dignified if she were really bald.

Next, Mimi found the two little seams, the sutures, behind her ears. If you took a certain special kind of pick, you could work your way in under the microscopic stitches, and begin the process.

Greenmore had something in her jewelry box. She made Mimi go get it.

Mimi returned with a y-shaped pin, and stood on a small stool from the closet. She said, "It's going to hurt. I'm using some lubricant. Grapeseed oil." She had it in a little dish. Mimi loosened the prodermis first with the pick, then with her fingers. She worked quickly, with precision—the gloves didn't trouble her.

I saw the whole separating from her forehead, her neck. Mimi took hold of the prodermis and started peeling the face away, and then the front of the neck, then, the chest, shoulders, and down, and down, her torso, and down—

I was curious, but ashamed to be. I was looking at my future, after all. My future physical self. The prodermis was actually in three layers. Each was attached to the next by a moist gelatin, living glue called cartiliform. I had never seen this, only studied it on the screens in a short lecture called "Heir Physiology." The layers had to be taken off separately, and then reassembled. I could tell by the ease with which Mimi handled them—they were, in fact, quite light. As Vee had revealed to me.

"Do you want privacy?" Mimi asked at a certain point, after the first layer was down around Greenmore's shoulders, the other two loosened at her hair-line.

I was still a Nat, a man. I knew this. I was sorry about it. I stared.

Greenmore was looking directly back at me from behind the prodermis face, with her real face. I had never seen it. And I didn't think of it as real. "Okay," she said, to Mimi. Yeared, brown eyes. How very, very old, those raw eyes.

The process continued behind the screen. They took the entire envelope, three layers.

Now all I could see was Mimi reassembling the layers she brought out, and hanging them on hangers. "Eventually it will wither, Madam," Mimi said. "I can't keep it alive off of you for that long. You know this?"

"Of course," Greenmore said. Her body had shrunken—I could see this in the silhouette behind the screen. But her voice was the same.

Then she came out.

We had been asked to flay her. We had done it. There had been the formalities, the permissions granted, the care taken, but in the end we had flayed her. How vulnerable she was, without the layers. She had lost an inch in height. Her grand head job sat over on a tray, all by itself. She had no curves or turns in her form. It was not horror I felt, I realized. It was tenderness.

It was as if I were witnessing the reverse of the world. I was disturbed in places within me I didn't even know existed. Before us— no powerful, beautiful Heir, instead, a small, mineral-blue figure with a tiny waist, a white feathery pubis, a scant cloud of white on her head— our magnificent Greenmore pale, slight as a sea sprite.

The underbody, covered with the "real" skin, which had hardly an

ounce of fat on it, was moist, sweet smelling, thin, blue-white, like scalp.
The veins were visible, everywhere close to the surface.

For a moment I thought of those sterile tattooed girls, the way they
were scribbled all over with tiny blue lines. I thought many terrible
things, that she was an emaciated little child, a little stick of a blue
goblin, that she was ugly.

"What's wrong?" she asked. What was wrong? She was so exposed,
and so slight, no more than fifty pounds, a starved, wiry one. Her curvy,
slinky elongated figure separate from her, hanging over by the shuttered
glass walls, a wilting corpse.

"Nothing's wrong," I lied.

"There is no shame here," she rasped. "I gave permission."

Klamath was as upset as I was. He picked up a sheet, but Mimi said
that would chafe. "I'll go to the barn, cheesecloth. Just hold that on
her a while." Mimi pressed past me saying, "You tend to her, help my
husband. Don't just stand there."

I couldn't move.

Greenmore said, to our further dismay, "I want the sun light."
Another being had stolen Greenmore's voice. "Raise all the old blinds
in the house."

I just couldn't keep in my mind that it was Greenmore. Her small
bluish face, which came up to the height of Klamath's heart.

He shook his head. He was very close, holding a sheet around her,
not letting it touch.

"Do it," she rasped again. She didn't even seem to understand we
were so astounded by her appearance we could hardly follow orders.
"Klamath? Do it. I'm right here." Her breath on his chest.

"Yes, Heir," he said finally, reconstructing his old tone. "Will you
take this?" he asked, and she nodded, and took the sheet out of his wide,
competent hands. Then he walked off to the corner of the room and
started turning the cranks that opened the blinds from inside.

"I have not looked at light with my eyes bare in seventy years," she
said.

"Your skin, you can burn—there is no re-generating it, you
understand." Klamath tried. But then he was done, and the sun pressed
in, bouncing off the marshes, doubling the brightness. So everything
was brilliant, searing.

She screamed at the light, cowered.

"Please, I'll close them, now," Klamath was still in the corner. "Let
me."

She shook her head. Then she wrapped the sheet round her, and tucked it, held her blue-white hands to her eyes, to form a visor and said, "I will get used to it. Malcolm, don't look so forlorn—so upset, I'm still here—"

Mimi came back, then, with the netting, to swaddle her. Cheesecloth we used to strain herbs we were boiling in the barn, trying to extract their essence. Greenmore dropped the sheet and allowed Mimi to wrap her up like a blue baby, round and round, use a whole bolt of the feathery cloth.

"Sunglasses, perhaps," Greenmore said when she was covered.

Mimi said she had some. I knew they were one of her most valuable possessions—plastic, from Canada, she'd paid a weeks' wages for them.

Greenmore didn't know this—she just put them on, and looked in the long mirror.

Her silhouette: a small head, a long neck, a column of fabric, two sticks for arms.

I was thankful her eyes were hidden.

VI

9:55 PM October 12, 2121
Mississippi I-Road
Far East De-Accessioned Gulf Territory, U.A. Protectorate

*I*n a flash, now, a roadway on pillars was rising up out of the marshes, and in the distance, there were several buildings high as mountains.

I had seen pictures of the huge towers that scraped the "sky," in the fugue countries, heard that one nation was always trying to build one higher than the last, win the record. An example of the backwardness and idiocy of such societies.

The fog descended again, then lifted one more time and I could see the top of one of the buildings, and the letters which read,

N W R ENCY C SINO & RESORT

It was, like the others, growing out of mounds of white drifting sand.

The landscape became enormous. The moon was far far above. We were under stars. There was a glorious roar. Around us, in all directions, a huge swath of black satin pulling up and then pressing down, and then riding into the shore. At the sight of it I felt a strange desire to dive in.

A tap on my shoulder from behind. Serpenthead again was saying, "Hey Malc, okay? You coming in? Never seen the ocean?"

"Up there, that's the entrance," Peet was telling Gepetto. "Park, and park."

We drove up to the hotel, but it didn't seem to have a door. Then Peet found a pathway dug in sand, a tunnel. "That is the new entrance," he said. "The old real entrance, with the marquee, all that is underground or under-sand ha-ha. Bebum. I played a gig here once, couple of years ago. Looked real different."

"Well?" Serpent asked me as he opened the door of Gepetto's transport. "You probably better off inside with us—"

"Sim of a lifetime—" Gepetto called out again.

"Oh, shut up, he's got other stuff on his mind," Serpent said. "Come on, Malc. They will hire you, I bet."

My feet landed on the black, cracked pavement. I was going in, of course. I didn't need persuading.

We went single file behind Peet to the entry way, a narrow walk covered in a dirty carpet. We opened a crude door. Inside was a dull corridor, with a sign pointing to the elevator, which we took down into the actual lobby, which was coated in slick tan stucco. There were fluorescent lights across the tops of the large black squares. I realized, when I looked again, these were the hotel's plate glass windows, now buried.

The whole place had the odor of old beans, a filthy wall-to-wall carpet, two couches in one corner, one with a broken leg in the front. Peet led us all over to a short man with a very long pair of eyelashes who was standing behind the Reservation Desk.

Leaning in, so as not to be heard by the other clerks, he said, "*Sebastian*, Penthouse Arena." And the man immediately gestured to a service elevator in the corner. It was filthy too, with thick gray blankets on the walls, and crushed boiled egg and empty brosia bags on the floor. We all got in together—Gepetto was planning on being hired along with me. Two extras, hardly likely. Imposses were considered decorative beings, not good for any employment. But owning up to being an Imposse was his only shot—an Heir would never be allowed backstage at a Sim of any kind. He didn't even have a ticket.

The elevator door refused to close the first few times Peet banged on the "Penthouse," button, but finally it did and we heard the sliding whir that meant we were moving.

Just when the brass panel of lights beamed the number 8, we stopped dead. And the lights went out. There were five more floors to go.

"Power outage, surprise," Peet said. So there we were in a box in the sky in the dark. Gepetto started to moan. Peet mumbled something, might have been prayers.

"So'kay," Serp reassured me.

"I know," I said.

The elevator noises came on again. "Well," Gepetto said in his low sliding voice. "A bit of excitement." Then we jolted, and were grinding upward again. I lost my balance. Serpenthead caught my arm.

"That drink with Q, I'm surprised you are standing," he whispered. "Young and pure and chaste a man as you? Empty stomach. Giving you credit."

After several more starts and stops—doors opening, no patrons standing on the landings, my heart rising and falling at every rattle—we arrived at the very top of the building, and walked into another bare corridor. As we came around a corner, a slender woman with long silky dark hair and a wide round white collar appeared. She came up and asked, "Word?"

Peet knew what that meant. "Bebum. *Sebastian.* Security."

"Sebastian. Like Ariel's companion in *The Little Mermaid*," Gepetto said to me, excited. "Remember?

I said, "Yeah, it just keeps coming—"

The woman with the collar had a long silver ring with a dazzling pear-shaped stone on her right index, which she waved in front of us as she led us though the winding halls until we reached a door that said, "MIRAMAR PENTHOUSE ARENA. BACK STAGE. AUTHORIZED ONLY." There were two big Nat men with black stretch shirts inside. They paid no attention to us newcomers. Our guide turned to all of us, finally sizing us up, preparing to introduce us.

Gepetto paused—would he be hired? Would they accept him? Could he go where honest workers went?

"What's this?" our guide asked, noticing him.

"Bebum. Imposse who drove us," Peet said. "He insisted on coming. Wants to be backstage."

She looked askance.

Gepetto's tiny lips were quivering.

"You vouch for him?" she asked.

"Please," Gepetto said, under his breath.

Peet shrugged, turned to the moon face. "Bebum. You ever worked? The likes of you? Tell her—"

"Sure, sure," Gepetto said, nodding wildly. "I'm Imposse, but I used to work."

The girl said to the rest of us, "I want someone on him. How do we know he's not undercover? You understand?"

"Yes, I'm under no cover, no cover," Gepetto said and wagged his head. Then he turned to us, for she still looked dubious. "Let me back here with you, or I'll go now. I won't take you back!" he threatened.

Peet's eyes rolled around. Then he looked at me with a new urgency. "Listen, you stick to him, like glue—that's your task." He had my wrist, held it tight, squeezed.

"Well?" the girl with the collar asked.

"He'll get in no trouble. Bebum, he'll not get near—" Peet said.

She looked us all over one more time, said, "Okay, follow me." And then she was leading us through that first gathering room. After that, we were backstage.

There was an area in the center of the stage, curtained on four sides with white canvas. I could hear murmuring and grunting coming from inside the cube. Several pairs of feet and something that looked like two sets of wheels were revealed by the few inches gap between the canvas and the floor. "That's the talent," our guide said, and then she turned around and called out, "SEBASTIAN, the muscle is here."

So Sebastian was a person. He appeared as if out of nowhere, down among some seats. He had a head like a soccer ball, wore a tight black shirt, similar to the others I'd seen, but he had epaulets. "We are the *muscle*," Gepetto said as an aside to me, with delight.

The house lights were turned on higher. I could see we were playing to a wide steep arena—perhaps three thousand could be seated. There were two aisles leading up to the doors at the top.

Although the set-up was different here, with the formal stage, the audience more or less in one place, I felt an excitement I always felt before a performance, from my acting days.

A new woman, this one in a dark green dress, dark brown skin, her black hair in a tight ball at the nape of her neck, emerged from behind the tent of canvas. "I'm Tamara," she said to me. "I'm with Ginger. Part of the family. Her husband is my brother." She offered her hand. "Sebastian promised—we demanded extra security. You?"

"See how they keep it up? Stay in character? Dazzling," Gepetto said, ignoring her. "Thank you for letting us be part—"

"Who is this Heir?" Tamara asked.

"Imposse," I said.

She relaxed.

I was actually an actor, so I wasn't that impressed. I would tell Gepetto that when this Tamara was gone. In fact I thought it rather silly. We all knew who they were, the parts they had to play, or we would soon enough. They didn't have to fake it with the technicians, the stage hands.

"You are *all* the extra security?" she asked, glancing at Gepetto, whose long, ridiculously skinny arms were dangling out of his sleeveless, semi-transparent gown. He was simply too well dressed for this occasion, this task. And too weak, to look at him. And why did they need security? Or have a fear of undercover inspectors—who gave a damn what happened in the Far East? She said, "We wanted someone right up on the stage, in case—"

"You know why you are here?" the Sebastian fellow offered—he'd bounded down the left aisle, climbed up on to the stage, and joined us. "You know what to do? Hey, you, what happened to your ear?" His eyes were fast, and bulgy.

I hadn't felt my injury for hours. Instinctively I reached up, tried to cover it with my hair. The Q. I thanked it. "In Port Gram, got shot at—" I said.

Sebastian was not surprised by this report, apparently. "They get ugly up there, got too many rules," he said and nodded, then moved on. "If anything goes on, and I tell you, pull this lever." He strode to the right wing, to show me a gray metal wand sticking out of the wall, and ropes. "Drop the curtain, put up the house lights. Understand? Very simple."

I didn't know what all the fuss was about. Gepetto tailed me over to the edge of the stage with Sebastian. He noticed him, finally, and asked, "What's this one? He with you?"

"Imposse," I explained.

Gepetto looked at Sebastian with his most pitiful face, his tiny lips disappearing into a bite. He looked so nervous he seemed mock-nervous.

"Muscle?" Sebastian asked.

"He drove us here. He volunteered. I told him he could be backstage. It was the deal, or we would never have got here on time."

Sebastian looked at me hard, to see if I could be trusted. Apparently I somehow passed the test. "And you are? Is that a Nyet collar?"

"Yes. I'm ready for my Boundarytime. "

"Is that so?" he asked, unbelieving. Then he turned to Gepetto and said, "Don't get in the way."

"No, no sir!" he said, timidly.

Sebastian moved on to Serpenthead and Peet. "I want you standing down there, in the orchestra pit," he told them. "Keep an eye on the entrances, and be flexible—go up to help the ushers, or work the stage if—"

"If what?" I called to them.

They acted as if the question had no meaning. "Okay. You are the last resort, if I give the signal—"

"Pull down the lever," I said. "Do the ropes."

He made me practice opening and closing the main curtain a few times, using the long loops. "That's right, quick study," he said, nodding. "I'll be up there," he pointed to the catwalk. "I don't have those curtain controls. I'll have all the others. Don't ask. I didn't design this place." Then he went to the opposite wing of the stage and climbed up a ladder along the wall. Soon he was right above our heads. From there he could oversee cues for changes in lighting, in music, sound effects. Orchestrate.

I squatted down on the edge of the stage. Peet had left the crobster bag there. A few tails remaining. I forgot myself. I started to pull one out.

Immediately, Tamara came over. "What do you think this is? A picnic?"

"Look, you don't have to—I was an actor. I understand. You don't have to keep up the character," I said.

"What are you talking about?" she asked me. "My brother's wife can't bear the smell. It's disrespectful." She stalked off with the food.

Gepetto hunkered down beside me. "They are good, aren't they?"

I said I thought they were way over the top.

Not long after Sebastian's ascent, about 10:15, the doors opened. The house lights were suddenly bright, piped music came up, and the audience rushed in, all either Heirs, in costume and regalia—or Altereds of every description, on leashes. The jewels and headjobs were impressive as ever. I always liked the glory of seeing them in large groups, gave me an old rush from my boyhood.

Eventually, Sebastian ordered the house lights down, the canvas "tent" parted. So I saw the set and the Sim. This touted Ginger Sim. The costumes were drab. Current day, not period. Nothing special. Maybe shabby was the point. Tamara was still wearing her green outfit, the best dressed of the bunch.

A skinny woman—terribly skinny, emaciated, the way Lydia looked when we flayed her, possibly sixty or seventy pounds—lay on a hospital-style bed, which accounted for the two sets of wheels I'd seen showing at the bottom. Her color was not the delft blue Lydia was, though, instead, brownish pink, like bleached cypress. They could be Chef Menteurian, that was true, to look at them. But Vee had always had that prohibition against copying. Perhaps it was just the makeup. Perhaps they were from somewhere else. No variety in the grouping. I wasn't used to that. The emaciated one was set up on pillows, propped up rather high, so the audience could see. Her hands like claws were hooked over the white sheets and a single knitted blanket. Bags hung beside her on a pole, from them, intravenous tubes, which appeared to run into her at places along her arms.

"Let the grand *so-long* begin," Gepetto quipped. I tried, but I couldn't laugh. There was something about this dull little tableau that upset me deeply, but for the life of me, I couldn't say what it was.

VII

 W e went through winter, spring, and summer with the "Natural" Greenmore. She continued her "research," insisted she was getting somewhere, having marvelous "excursions." And we were scared all the time something would happen to her, that she was about to dribble down. Also, she was kind of interesting, a little tiny woman who bustled about along with us, ate at the table, like a bird, but still—spoke in a different voice, had quickness, a different kind of vitality. She was vulnerable, she felt everything. I got to like her that way.

Then, WELLFI found out and stepped in. We got a certified notice. Klamath and Mimi suspected Chotchko intervention. Klamath told us we would all be accused when they saw her stripped like this, eating this way. And what if she wouldn't go for her Treatments? Heirs left exposed eventually reached a tipping point, different for everyone. Then they deteriorated rapidly, and could not be saved. The judgment went first, he said. As in Greenmore's case, he implied. "They will twist it all around and say we killed her," he said. "You are our only hope." We were in the kitchen at the time, peeling the perpetual shrimp for the East Menteur market, but he turned up to look at me straight on. "You. The only reason she hasn't leapt into the lake."

I had no idea what he meant by that.

The same day the messages came from WELLFI, about her

Treatment times, I got my first news about the trouble with my Trust,
wrote Lazarus for a clarification. No answer.

It was a hot day, muggy, no wind, but a storm was approaching. I'd
seen it reported.

Hurricane Horace. I asked Klamath if he'd heard. Of course—he
followed the weather closely. Everyone from Chef Menteur had to.
A whole team of tropical storms had formed this season, worse than
the previous years, he told me. Most collapsed out in the Atlantic, but
the last two hit Florida—Fantasia and Gilbert. "And now Horace," he
said, nodding. "They say it is a very organized storm. Not a good sign.
Nothing these days is a good sign. So, talk to her, please."

I finally got up the nerve. I found her on her bed, her tiny body
folded up near the top under layers of fabric, mummy-like.

She had a stack of books spread out over the blankets—not those
she was always reading, from the dismantled library on Audubon Island
that day I last saw Ariel. They were wider, broader, and they had little
pieces of paper sticking out on all sides—things stuffed in, markers.

"These are scrapbooks of when I was a Not-Yet, but I didn't call
myself that. I didn't know I'd ever be Treated," she said. "This is what
I looked like." She opened one book. I had to sit beside her on a stool
to see it.

Flats on paper, fading. A young woman with dusky skin— sort of
the kind mine was. Dark, wavy hair. Dark eyes. Her features were
different—flatter and wider in the photos than now. What remained
the same was something about the bridge of the nose, how the eyes
met together there—intelligence in her gaze that she had not lost in her
transformation from Nat to Heir.

In one she stood on a shore, bright green behind her.

"We used to go see what was left of the beach, I mean the strand, the
sand," she said. "There was still a little left along the Panhandle then.
It wasn't summer. We didn't care. We liked it in winter. No one knew
how long it would last. It was as if we were saying goodbye to it. It was
a pilgrimage. The sea was rising then, so quickly."

She wore black stockings without feet and a long tunic, and a small
stone, a little moon pendant around her neck on a black cord. "Blue
Mountain," she said. "It was the last of the old beaches to survive,
without artificial means. It was high above sea level, by comparison."

The sea was green as baby grass.

"I'd just graduated university," she said. "Decided to take a post-doc
in Advanced Extension Psychology. We were having a vacation. This

was a man I met at the Defuniak Research Center."

Just the dark sloping shoulder of a man's jacket, and those collars I'd seen before in old photos, starched and broad, pointed, standing up, exaggerated. The picture had been torn. The body had no head.

"I was going with him. We used such terms, as *going*. Can you guess what the year is? Twenty forty-five. Before the Great Transfer. That's years away. None of us knew then how we would, or if we ever would. Make it. So many resources had dried up. The Troubles had started, the rebellions, the bombings, and the combat in the old cities— all over there being no 'economy,' no fugue cycle. Heir communities just started to wall themselves in. No jobs but in WELLFI. Psychology or Physiology, or Endocrinology or Extension Studies. And there was Varietology, which was big. I was lucky, I had an aptitude. I thought I would be special, have a chance, break out, and be someone. Arrive. Come up with a theory of everything."

"You did," I said. "Re-description."

"I thought I did, too, for a long time. He—the man who is missing here—was very brilliant, too. He was in genetic studies, and we spent our spare time watching the old flats. He had nostalgia, somehow, for the mess life used to be, the redundancy. He was the one who had the theory about how we could evolve. We couldn't just live on and on—the goal was immortality. Different. He made this distinction, between our epochal lives, and immortality."

I felt something strange, awkward, a little fit of rage, in my consciousness. I was glad that he had no face in the photo. "Where did he go?"

She put her fingers over her mouth. "I don't know," she said. Then she put the photo down, slipped it under a thin clear film. Jeremy had once told me that covering one's mouth was a good signal of a liar—I had used the gesture in a play. She turned the page.

A restaurant in this photo. I still didn't find her easily recognizable. She seemed older. A plate in front of her, spread with victuals. Curlicues of fried things—fish or shrimp. Still that dusky skin. She wasn't an Heir, not yet. I liked the way she looked: smart, authoritative. A man beside her. She hadn't torn out his image. He had a big head and broad but sloping shoulders. His jacket was close cut, with a severe "v." The high wide collar again, this time slightly less exaggerated. He had a very dark brow; it almost merged, like Ariel's. And his skin was pale, ivory. "There he is—the only photo I didn't destroy. We had such a bitter falling out. He thought my invention—Re-description—was a 'superficial version' of his theory. I'd appropriated his ideas, and 'cheapened' them. We stopped speaking. But at this time, he was my mainstay," she said. She pointed to another picture on the opposite page: Treated men, early Heirs, Protos—I could tell by the teeth, and the puffy stylized skin, the tight popped-open eyes—sheet lenses were cruder then—otherwise, they dressed like everybody else, like Nats. The tablecloth was the same; it must have been taken at the same, or a similar restaurant. They had plates with little dollops on them, which I recognized as early, crude brosias.

"There are the others—the ones I worked with, helped me with my first big grant. Everything was about to happen for me. I was about to become well known, about to win the Albers Prize," she said, pointing to a row of bearded men in ancient style suits, that ridiculous boxiness male clothes had at the time. She continued, turning more pages. "Oh, here he is again. I guess there are two I didn't destroy," she said. In this one he was in profile, looking at her, touching her arm. I hated that, for some reason.

"What's his name?"

"John Ottoman. Some town where he settled took up his causes— it's one of the shore towns that have since gone under." She looked as if she were going to say something else, then she thought better of it. "Have you ever heard of such a name? John Ottoman?" she asked.

"How would I?"

"Just curious," she said. "He had a reputation. But he went off the deep end. Got involved, finally, in a rebellion, a late and futile rebellion. His science required a politics. His politics posited a science—"

"What sort of science was that?"

She didn't answer.

"I thought you didn't know what happened to him," I said.

"Well, we cut off communication, mostly, so I don't really know—"

"Did you marry?" I was never supposed to ask things like that. I knew it. It was almost as much of a breach as touching her would have been. Or about half as bad.

"Of course not," she said. "What would have been the point? There were so many regulations already; it was clear where things were heading. He wasn't going to be an Heir, and the Procreation Acts had come in—there was no having children. I was being Treated, how could I have married? He was a radical, anyway. He stopped believing in Albersian—"

"Free Wheel?" I asked.

"Not really—" she said. "We fought like dogs, over politics, economics, after that first fight over his ideas. Things were very unstable. No one knew how we were to keep it going. We still had some idea of a nation, but it was fading. The two kinds had so little in common—those on, and those *hoping to leave*, the cycle. The original Protos, the first Heirs, the aristocrats. It was just before the outbreaks, all the bombings—I said that. The lines were being drawn. You have no idea what civil war is."

"No, I don't know," I said. "But we have our own conflict, here and now. Klamath and Mimi are very concerned; they want you to consider your health. And what could happen. And I think you should consider—What can I do to help you get ready? For WELLFI? The transport to Memphis?"

She looked up from her reverie, mildly surprised that I'd changed the subject. It wasn't my place. But she shrugged. She was done. She had shown me what she was going to show me. I had no consciousness of its significance—she seemed to accept that.

"Don't you see I'm not ready to get ready?" she asked.

*

It was late in the evening. More dire reports of Hurricane Horace. I sat in my room, thinking about the worst case. The flooding could increase, the Sea could rise, and storm surges were predicted. And there had been no answer from Lazarus. I wrote again, said it was urgent.

She was in her room. I could hear her stirring occasionally.

I had never been exasperated like this at an Heir. What had she discovered? With all her retreating and regressing? Her chanting, her meditating, her "mystical attempts," her elixirs from South America? I was willing to tell her it was enough. Continuing to put her health, her very status as an Heir, at risk , was foolish. I would even mention how her deterioration would be blamed on Klamath and Mimi, and even me. I went back to see her, found her lights were on.

She was sitting at her desk. I could see she had taken out her luggage, which was encouraging—I had not expected that.

But then I saw there weren't any clothes inside. Just a cloak I recognized, spread out on the bench by the pool. It was a romantic cloak, of some antique fabric, bronze, brocade. I also saw her wooden shoes, the platforms, the ones she used sometimes to stalk across the marsh, to keep her feet from getting wet. Mimi called them "Japanese"

Two large valises were wide open, and empty, their satin genenfabric pouches attached to the top lids, drapes above an empty stage.

She was lit from below. I still could be surprised by how wizened and tiny she was. Her almost hairless head and her obvious skull made her look like a water bird. She moved to the bench by the pool so I could come over and sit beside her.

It was odd. How focused she became when she looked up at me. That old sharpness. She asked, "How old were you when you got to Lazarus's Foundling house? To Audubon Island?

"They decided I was two or maybe three. What difference does it make?" I asked.

She didn't answer. She picked up one of her albums. "Some of my books say there were many lives in a line, one after the other. Or that the life force goes into a wide sea, and then comes in again, reforms, condenses, nothing is ever lost. And we meet the same ones over and over. And everything and everyone is connected to everything else—what does that mean to you?

I said I had no idea.

Then she touched the place between the bottom of her nose and the top of the pink of her own tiny bluish lip. "Do you know what this is called?" she asked.

"No," I said.

"The philtrum," she said. She traced her own indentation. "On you it is very shallow—you told me once you thought it had been sewed closed. That was your director Jeremy's explanation. But you don't remember that, do you? A needle pinching closed your lip? Lift it up," she said.

I did what she said although it made me quite uneasy. I was ashamed of my heat, my scent, my saliva. She came in close—as close as she had when I was confined, on Galcyon—inspected the place inside my mouth, where it was attached to the gum. "Oh," she said.

"What?" I asked.

"It's attached all the way down—it isn't sewn, that isn't scar tissue, it's a ligament—"

She let me let go of my lip. So I could speak. "Oh?"

"See mine?" In her mouth there was a shallow web of flesh at the top where the inside of the upper lip met the gum. On me, that web came all the way down to my teeth. I'd never known I was different. "Do you know the legend?" she asked. She reached to touch my lip—

she *touched my lip.*

I shook my head, pulled back. She was so tiny, and her skin so transparent, crimpled cellophane.

"The legend is that you know the other worlds before you are born, or reborn. But a force, an intention, something, comes down and touches you right there, on your upper lip, and says, *shh, shh. Forget it all, forget*—think of it as the place where all the rest we could know, we once knew, is filtered out. That trap door in your foundling home. So we live in the place of solid things, of one direction, of closed gates. Of yes or no. The Chronics are seeping back to yes *and* no somehow, I think, or into some in between."

She noticed my agitation. "I'm sorry. I'm so sorry," she said. Then, "You are such a sweet boy. Young man. So terribly, so—what is it? Reticent, patient, withheld. Do I make you nervous? Did I come too close to you? Was it terrible that I touched you?" She took a breath, leaned back, and withdrew her finger. "My friend insisted we could evolve. Or that some could. Evolve so that we could still hold that all within us. The memory of the passage in and the memory of the passage out. And we would know the way. Some of them say another world is right here, right next to us, and we can't see it, our reason keeps us from seeing it—or there are many, not just one, as if enfolded in another and another. What would we have to do, if that were true? To find them? Where do the near-so longed go, for example? The ones the common doctors occasionally revive? If they see worlds, where are they, if not right here, beside or inside this one?" She brought all her narrow fingers to a point. "What is the mechanism? Where are the directions?"

"Why talk about things we can't see?" I asked. "We should be talking about Memphis, you need to get ready, and go. I have to go talk to Lazarus. There is a problem with my Trust. I've written, but he hasn't answered. I'm going to leave soon. I have to—but I won't until you do."

"They got in touch today," she finally said. "Chotchko's team is about to announce a new drug combination that keeps them down. They haven't had an uncontrollable case in six months, all of them are remaining 'within the confines of ordinary experience,' she is very proud to announce. They've reversed them, put them through Re-description, stopped all anomalies in several cases. Everybody is content. Or at least manageable. They are fine, although she does say, '*They all express a certain yearning on occasion, like a trace memory, for that unfocused, inchoate state. For its "intensity," which I believe we can address, with right enhancements, the right probes in place when we do their Re-descriptions.*

And of course your research on "mapping," these "other states" could be
of great use, perhaps to give them something of what they want, some
simulacrum, which could pacify—' Of course, now that they have found
a 'cure,' they are happy to admit that my research—our research—was
not doctored. In fact, she needs every scrap of it and is willing to give
me credit. To claim our data was real. She can send them back to their
normal Heir lives, and she has."

"Well that's a triumph," I said. "There's no reason not to go back."

"The problem hasn't been solved," she said. "Chotchko's just
postponing. Eventually, eventually, they will continue down that path—
do you see? Immortality is an entirely different—"

"John?" I asked. I thought of the man in the pictures, and I had,
again, a certain pang, like anger.

"What about him?" she asked.

"Wasn't he the one that thought immortality was different?" I asked.

She paused. "He was willing to give up too much. He was willing
to wait for another generation, to work with genetics, not Albersian
techniques—he was willing to—he did, so long—he could have
surrendered, he could have been Treated—"

"Well then don't take a risk now," I blurted out, at that very moment.
It was in a moment of bravery, or clarity, or bravado. Everything seemed
to come together, for that second. Fall into place. "Please, go to Memphis
for my sake, because of—us," I said. "Us."

How shocking what I'd just said was. I felt a jolt.

Her expression started to change, to widen.

"I don't want you to—to—," I said. "For my own sake."

Inside, then, the jolt was gone. In her face I saw the consequence of
what I had said. I saw forever. I felt something falling in on a surface,
and breaking through, and then that breaking through another level,
and so on. "I want to live forever with you," I heard myself say. And
then I said something that seemed to come from another place entirely,
not from my own body, not really, but from the farthest reaches of my
hopes, far out at the tips of my thoughts: "I love you. Or, when I am
worthy I—"

I watched her face, then, trying to take it in. Her round skull, under
her thin blue skin.

I had said something I wasn't allowed to say, ever, never, not until I
was an Heir.

She looked down. Even when I became a Nuovo, the gap would be
enormous—we'd be ostracized for the match. It would be us against the

world.

I saw her smile. "Is that what you want?" she asked. "I never knew that." Then she said, mysteriously, "Well perhaps it would be so." Smiled, and in a few moments, she said, "Yes."

I was trembling. *She said yes.* She opened her tiny arms. She expected me to fall into her lap. I thought for a moment, of kissing her small lips, now so papery and delicate. I thought for a minute, *she's not really an Heir, she's not covered in a prodermis*—but I couldn't. It seemed like a theory, an experiment, when I'd said, "I want to live forever with you." A gambit, a try. It had worked. Now it was true. So quickly. So strangely. She'd taken my up on my offer.

I felt again the thrill and fear I'd felt the first day she'd interviewed me. But if I held her, I would crush her. I said, "Wait until you are back, in yourself again."

She said, smiling more, now, "Oh, of course, of course, but call me Lydia."

"Lydia," I said. That was our greatest intimacy. I said, "Lydia." Then she touched my cheek. She touched me, and I did not ask her to take her hand away, and she did not take her hand away. I think I trembled.

Any question of what I'd do when I was an Heir, was solved, now.

But the question of whether or not I'd be one, was not solved.

Her fingers were very cold.

*

The storm, Horace, went south of us, but we had terrible weather for three days—swirls and bands of rain, and rough seas, so rough WELLVAC wouldn't come to take her away. So we waited, and got her ready, put her skin back on her bones, and all the rest. Mimi put her in a beautiful white dress, and she wore a long cloak with high wings at the top of the shoulders, with a brilliant purple lining. A queen.

It was Tuesday and hot as it could be after a bad storm, blue, and very dry. And exactly noon. The transport was a handsome, black and gold vehicle, almost two stories high, square. It was mud-splatted and fouled by the time it parked at the gate at the end of the boardwalk. The officers came out in their elegant black uniforms, with handsome collars and cuffs, three of them, silver stripes down the pants legs, and immediately started cleaning.

Then the side doors opened and two WELLMED nurses lowered the chair that would carry her. She could walk, of course, but this was part of the ceremony, the pomp, the service. I knew the chant, from the days when WELLMED had come to get Lazarus for his Re-jobs.

We all meet the Reveal on our own, and our renewal, alone. They said in unison, and she was to respond:

So I come now alone, to be restored.

"We can't see the rest," Klamath told me. "We are not allowed. It's a ritual—private."

But I was hers now. I was different, now, wasn't I? Didn't I deserve?

The chair was a throne, with a high back decorated with a huge sideways-eight figure, the infinity figure, WELLFI'S emblem. There was the sound of horns—a recording, I guessed.

"We have to go inside or they will chase us," Klamath said.

So I went to my pallet and thought about the promise I'd made, the future I'd have, forever.

VIII

11:00 PM October 12, 2121
Miramar Penthouse Arena
Mississippi I-Road
Far East De-Accessioned Gulf Territory, U.A . Protectorate

"*I*t's just like in the old moving flats, hospital dramas, with those crude little tubes," Gepetto was saying.

"Ginger" seemed to be asleep, but then, when Tamara spoke to her, she nodded, closing her eyes tightly.

I could hear Sebastian from the catwalk say, "Lighting Check. Sound. Malcolm—curtain going soon."

The stage lights went on—red, pale green. Tamara came over, waving her beautifully manicured hand at me—the nails were darkest green, curved as claws, I noticed this time. "We aren't ready, tell them to hold off."

"Curtain in two minutes," Sebastian hooted down.

"I've got to get her comfortable!" she called up to him. She looked over at me at my station in the wings. She was about to talk to me again, but she'd forgotten my name.

"Malcolm," I whispered.

"You ever worked one of these?" she asked.

I nodded.

"Well, help me with the bed."

She was beautiful, if annoying, and I followed her. She squatted near the wheels, reached under. "Can't find the lever," she whispered.

Crone

"I don't want to jerk her. Her bones ache—" When she stood back up, she was close to tears.

I got on my knees, and I found a small handle on the rail of the bed, which released the crank so she could elevate the Ginger, who smelled terrible, really, it was awful to be near her, my nose level with the mattress.

"Thank you," she said, batting her eyes for a moment. "You are?"

"Malcolm," I said for the third time.

"Yes, I have a lot on my mind. I'm going to depend upon you. Help me if I need it," she said. "I suppose these parasites want to see everything, don't they? I hear her father is coming. I think she's waiting for him… "

"He won't come," the man beside her said. "Too angry." He had the same fierce green eyes. He wore his hair slicked over the high dome of his head, the way Serio did. He took Tamara's hand, then, and his face seemed broken with sadness.

"This is my brother Naroh, he's Ginger's husband," Tamara said. "This is—" She still hesitated over my name, then retrieved it. "— Malcolm, to guard us."

I nodded hello. He had one hand on this Ginger's body, and the other was holding Tamara's hand, so I didn't offer mine to shake. He repeated himself to me, "Her father won't come. He's been against it all along. Ginger insisted—"

"These parasites—" Tamara said. "I wouldn't have encouraged it if I could have imagined it. No shield. No privacy."

"I wouldn't—call them that. They pay. And you don't have to keep in character for me—"

"What?" she asked.

Before I could elaborate, Sebastian called down, "Curtain now."

And the last chapter in the Ginger saga, the "Sim of a Lifetime," was center stage. Recorded horns, then violins. The lights that hung off Sebastian's bridge came up even brighter, illuminating the area around the bed, and also spots beaming onto the stage from the back of the arena, which were so bright I could not see the audience anymore. They became that familiar Heir choir of gasping and whispering I remembered from my youth. Tamara's face gave me the shivers. She was so convincing, and so consciously unconscious—her surprise at the curtain when it finally rose. She really seemed horrified to find herself on stage. They all did.

*

Several hours had passed. Heirs were milling around in the aisles, subdued, though excited.

"'Sim Verite,' huh?" Gepetto asked. "Can it get any better than this? You know of course what everybody says." He looked up at me. He was sitting on the floor, holding his knees near his face.

"What?" I asked.

"Can't say," he said. "Get people in trouble. What do you think, true?"

"What do I think about what?" I said. "Repetitive script. That's my review."

His eyes widened, he put a hand on each cheek, opened his tiny mouth into an oval.

When my boredom had set in like a hard freeze, about three in the morning, something new came. A low, stuttering sound, like one stick being dragged across another jagged stick, but in a kind of echo chamber. And then, softly, Ginger shuddered.

Tamara put her hands around both of Ginger's shoulders, and held her, tightly. "He will be here," she said, rather loudly to Ginger. "I know he will."

"No he won't," Naroh whispered back.

There was a call out from the back of the auditorium, like a cat call, then a whistle.

Tamara looked over at me, her green eyes articulating: there was some disaster. But where? She was an excellent actress of her kind, I concluded. Almost at the same time, a figure emerged from the rear of the stage, a man in a white tunic with a u-shaped placket, and simple trousers. He wore a hood, and his hair was long, silver white, curling, falling out of it onto his breast.

"What is he doing?" Naroh asked. He covered his small button mike in order to say this, so the audience couldn't hear. "*Now* he shows."

When the figure got to the bedside, he wrapped Ginger's emaciated fingers inside his large, wide palm. I knew the hand, I did. It didn't make sense.

"What I have always wondered," Gepetto was going on, "was why he wanted to be a real boy when he didn't have to do that—"

"Shh," I said. "I'm trying to understand what she's saying." Tamara had just taken off her mike. She was facing me in the wings, mouthing words, wanting me to do something.

A deeper, growlier shudder this time, without melody. The man with the hood was nodding. I still had not seen his face, neither had the audience. Then suddenly, he left the stage, head hidden in his elbow.

Oohs and ahhs from those watching. Very bad form, how the actor just left like that, without a reason. Had he forgotten his lines? Next, Naroh stomped off.

Somber flute music came on. The first soundtrack in some hours.

"Water" was Tamara's unvoiced request, I finally realized. Poor thing having to carry the scene alone. Everyone was so unprofessional.

There was a fountain by the fire exit door. When I came back with a cup, it was time for an intermission. I dropped the curtains.

In the next moment, Tamara asked me to help her hoist Ginger up so she could take a sip. I told Gepetto to stay where he was. His response: "This is heaven, and how could I leave?" I went over and took Ginger's sad smelly shoulders. Tamara brought the cup to the lips, but the actress would have none of it. Even with the curtain down, she was completely uncooperative. Tamara tried twice more, then handed the small vessel over and asked me, "Is there a place for air? I'm going to faint." All this improvised, unrelenting drama. Where were Naroh and the hood?

"I can't go through with this," she said. "Her father wants to stop it. We can't stop it now! This was my brother's idea, and the younger enclavers," she said. "And Ginger's, of course, she *wanted* to do this for us. Our sacrifice for the Exodus, she said. So we can be resettled. Her father was against it. I see now why. Naroh said, 'I never knew it would be this hard.'"

Such a method actress. I said, "You can't just quit. You have to have an ending."

She looked at me. "Her father thinks we can."

"Well you are improvising, no? So just stop now. It's not so complicated. You are going to have all the encores, if I know anything about Heir audiences. So you might as well come to some conclusion about the main production."

She asked me, "You a Nyet? That collar? Where did you come from?" She was hostile, but I had no idea why.

"From Audubon Island."

"A Nyet from Old Lazarus's place? One of those he trotted off to work at five or six years old?" she asked.

"You know Lazarus's Place?"

"Yes. All about it." She stalked off. How had I offended her?

Music—the curtain. I had to open again.

*

Around four a.m., Gepetto defined the sounds coming from the stage as "agonal breathing." The crowds had been riveted since the last intermission. It was quiet, I could hear the two men arguing faintly, off stage—Naroh and the hood.

There was a slight shift in Ginger, then. Peculiar that she moved on her own, after being still for hours. Then, a sudden kind of expansion in the air about her and—amazing, as if for a moment everything got bigger, and more vibrant, I didn't know how they managed this illusion. A slight color—white this time, bluish-white, really, but otherwise, like what I saw that night with O.

The lights went out, then, not just those on stage, throughout, all except the exit lamps. Another electrical failure. Yet the white-bluish glow remained. *"Please take your seats,"* Sebastian called down through a battery megaphone. Some in the audience lit small pen lights, and lanterns, so it was possible to see their very similar faces, their narrow noses, their glistening teeth. Standing up, talking excitedly, and gasping. *"Please take your seats. This will be the final intermission. Auxiliary generators will be up and running momentarily."*

Tamara shouted, as soon as the curtain was down, "NAROH, NOW." She faced the back of the stage, the direction Naroh and the hood had gone. Then she turned to me and said, "I can't leave her now. Go get them. Find them!"

"Where—?" I asked, under the spell of this dull skit. I mean, really, I thought a minute later, why didn't she just leave the "dying woman's" bedside and go find them herself? They weren't far, I'd heard them arguing.

In the corridor directly behind the stage, I collided with the "father." "Malcolm," he said.

How did he know my name? He removed his hood, then, and his face formed itself into one of the most familiar in the world to me. But now, it was inside an old, sagging, Yeared's visage.

"Vee," I hugged him. "Why are you here?"

"Why are you here?" he asked.

"I am on my way home. I have to talk to Lazarus. Something's wrong with my Trust—"

He looked confused. "Oh, that. I can hardly see in this hall," he said.

"Lead me to the stage. Tamara was calling me. It's time, it's Ginger." His large brown hand fell over my arm, and I led him where he wanted to go.

"*PLEASE TAKE YOUR SEATS,*" Sebastian hooted from his megaphone as we passed beneath his catwalk.

The sudden boom and rattle of a generator.

"*HOUSE LIGHTS,*" Sebastian yelled. "*CURTAIN, CURTAIN.*" Someone else opened it—I didn't. I was still linked to Vee. A few Heirs out of their seats gathered around the apron below the stage. They were saying, "*Let us up there. Let us touch. Help us.*"

I asked Vee, "Did Ariel do something—did you hear?"

No comprehension.

Tamara was now on the bed, folded up behind the Ginger, who was panting, and not very regularly. And more alert. Naroh on his knees, holding one of her skeletal hands, and weeping. Vee was on the opposite side of the bed from Naroh, also holding Ginger's hand, speaking softly into her ear. Chants of his, I recognized.

I remembered what he had told me, once, that you make the expression another makes—and I made his grimace.

Ginger sat up, and opened her eyes, and said, "Here, all here!" loudly, clear as a bell. After all that silence, she finally spoke. There was something remarkable, profound, I couldn't deny. And then she closed her eyes, jerked a little to the left. The white glow I'd seen before widened around her head.

Vee and the other man threw their bodies over her form on the bed, clasped hands, and wept—some symmetry there.

The applause, deafening. It took forever, but in the end, a very good show, I had to give it to them. Gepetto stood and started slamming his two thin hands together, elbowing me to clap as well. Eventually, after a rather stretched-out, recorded, violin interlude, Sebastian called down to me to close the curtain.

All of them were still holding onto the body. I saw the crowd from the edge of the stage. The houselights were up: about a quarter of the audience had now gathered around the apron—very eager.

"Announce an encore," I called up to Sebastian.

"WHAT?"

Tamara came over to me to say, "Stop them. Make them go." I peeked out the closed curtain and saw two Heirs, un-athletic as they were, were trying to crawl up on the stage. I had never seen such a thing, so undignified. They were on a ledge near the top of the orchestra pit, trying to move some stools into place for steps.

I saw Serpent walking out in front, below, trying to pull himself up. "Need me Malc? Need me? Stampede coming—"

I did need him. I went over to give him a hand—by the time I got him on my level, there were four trying to crawl over each other and up. But they weren't coordinated enough.

I called up to Sebastian, "Don't know what an encore is?"

I felt a presence on my left. Vee. "I thought you hated Sims," I said, rolling my eyes.

"I came to stop this travesty. The money is there, now. So Lazarus—"

"You came to tell me about my money? How did you find me?" I asked, thrilled for a moment. "It's there? There's no lien? It was a mistake?"

His eyes were bulging. "She's my daughter."

I looked into the sweetness of his ruined face. He was truly a Yeared now. His lids were so long and heavy they only lifted so you could see half his eyes. The bags beneath were swags of skin, loose downward loops. I said, "You were so well cast. Why didn't they change your name?"

"Malc?" he asked. He was looking at me with what almost seemed pity. Then he shrugged, as if to himself. "Why do you have that bloody ear child?"

"Shot at in Port Gram. Long story," I said.

"You were shot?" he asked, reaching for my shoulder—

"You said something about my money?" I asked. "Do you know why Lazarus hasn't answered me?"

Tamara called for him before he could respond..

"This is my cue," he said, lightly, and he walked away.

"Well, thank goodness, encore," I said.

*

"Encore, we agree, we all agree with you—" an Heir in a purple gown, a very fancy embroidered vest, and a gold headjob, the first of that huddle who had managed to get on the stage, was saying. I encountered him in the wings near the front curtain. A small entourage followed behind him. They were in pale lilac gowns, like uniforms, all the same. Six or so of them. The gold head had taken over as leader.

This little crew pounded their hands together, made that thudding sound. "More, more, and more."

"I'll see what I can do," I said.

"No you will not!" Sebastian screamed from overhead.

Behind the canvas, under meager lights, Naroh, Tamara, and Vee were trying to cover Ginger with a blanket—why didn't she just get up, play was over. As I reached them, they realized the hospital style bed sheet was too short, so they couldn't pull it high enough to cover her head—last gesture in the drama, apparently. Naroh took off his shirt to cover her face. Why these touches, at a time like this. No one was watching—I interrupted them, said "You need to do an encore. We'll have a riot if you don't. I'll announce it, Vee, listen," I said. "Convince that stage manager up there," and I grabbed the little button of the mike off the bed where Tamara had thrown it.

"Help them out of here!" Sebastian barked.

"YOU! PROTECT US!" Tamara shouted, livid.

"I am trying," I said. "Just give them what they want."

The crowd led by goldhead who had followed me was right on top of us now, all saying, *"Can we feel her? That would be better, much better. Even than an encore, that's what we think. Just touch her before she gets hard, we heard they get hard! OH PLEASE!"*

"This is a Sim," I told them.

Naroh, who was covering Ginger with his entire body by then, to keep them from touching her, used one arm to swat the leader away. They gasped, shirked, but didn't stop coming. "Help us get out of here," he yelled to me, with disbelief. "Get them off of us."

Gepetto in the wings, starting to pound his hands with glee.

"DON'T YOU MAKE THEM GO AWAY? ISN'T THAT YOUR JOB?" Tamara shouted, struggling to loosen the brake on the bed, to roll away, to safety. Naroh, taking out the tubes, knocking down the pole, to get the bed out, but he was only using one arm—as he was still guarding Ginger from the Heirs' probing hands.

"Can we touch? Why are you doing that? Can I feel her heart? Why are you doing that?" came the lilac Heirs' breathy voices. *"Please explain why they are doing these things. Please."* The number of Heirs on the stage had tripled by now—they wanted to paw this scrawny little actress, this—

"YOU!" Tamara said to me. "WHAT ARE YOU?"

"Don't yell at him, Tamara," Vee said to her. "He's Lazarus's boy—"

"What? Is he blind? You a Bonesnake? One of them?"

"I'm a Not-Yet, I'm Malcolm, you know—"

Vee facing me, shaking his head.

Blind, Tamara had said.

She had said, blind. It was such a strange thing to call me. I'd always had fine sight.

Then, something I can only describe as a sooty cloth, perhaps, if you can imagine that, was lifted, from my lungs, first, and then from my neck, and my mouth, and my nostrils, and my eyes.

My life turned back on itself, like a sleeve.

A more impressive voice than mine shouted into the discarded button mike, "AWAY." I startled the lilac team and the better dressed Heirs down below, for a moment. I rushed to pull the curtain closed again, and explained to the rest of the ones milling below, "There's no encore, you've seen enough. Don't you know what you saw? IT IS THE END."

The first lilacs came after me in front of the curtain, saying in unison, Goldhead at the front: "We paid our money, we watched her, and we are fans, Ginger Fan Club—" There were easily fifteen of them now.

I begged Gepetto, who was idle at the edge of the stage, to talk those below.

He asked, "And stop the entertainment?"

"It's not a show!" I screamed at him.

"Even better! Of course! Let me touch!"

They finally had the bed unstuck, and were moving it, wheeling it away, but every few inches, they were blocked by the fans who were trying to pull down Ginger's sheets, her garments, hoping to touch her skin. I couldn't even count how many surrounded us. Naroh started swinging at the swarm. Vee tried shoving the whole bed at them, a battering ram. A few Heirs fell down, got right back up again. That was when I did it, after the whole bed didn't work—

I just picked one Heir in lilac up, and took him to the edge of the stage, and threw him off. He tumbled over and over in the orchestra pit. For a second, my assault froze the rest. Hah! What Vee had told me so long ago was true. They were practically weightless.

I went ahead, tossing Heirs right, left, so Vee and Naroh finally got out the rear way wheeling the bed, with Ginger, and locked the door.

Sebastian, bellowing, "*PLEASE TAKE YOUR SEATS. PLEASE TAKE YOUR SEATS. DUE TO THE NATURE OF THIS PERFORMANCE THERE CAN BE NO ENCORE.*"

Two Altereds with implanted feathers—these were big, hefties with muscles, not wisps like their masters, pinned me. They were huge men—warts, big teeth, beak noses. Nearby, Gepetto cheering: "*Go go go.*"

One of these was strangling me, literally, pressing down on my neck with a claw. The owner called out from the apron of the stage. "Get him, get him, traitor—" I was the enemy now, the target.

Out of nowhere, Serpenthead was crawling down along the stage floor, sneaking between two onlookers. The monsters had turned their heads for a moment, to get further instructions on torture from their owner below. Serp spoke into my better ear, said, "We can pull them off for a second, I'm going to come around behind, Peet too, you have to scram. Get up when I say—" He was signaling for Peet, in a fist fight about ten feet away. He said only, "Now's— " And when Peet got there, they threw off the two of them, and in the next moment, when I was free, Serp took out the lovely knife with the thousand blades and tools, and slipped it in my shirt pocket, "Go north."

"What?" I asked.

"But cut yourself loose if they get enthusiastic—"

"What?" I wasn't sure what I was hearing.

"Go," he said, and I started to.

But then, the same two feathered monsters had him by the throat— blood filling his face. He couldn't talk; only mouth the words, "Get out! North. They will know you!"

"What? Who will they know?" I asked. For a second I believed he had answers, he had them all along.

I grabbed the two of them around the chests, and held them off long enough for Serpent to escape. When he had his throat back, he urged, "Take that Petto, drive—they mean to kill you—"

"Will kill you—" I said, pulling him with me. We made a break—I led Serp, and Peet followed— but only a few seconds later, on the steps backstage, two more took Serp by the shoulders—his bowl legs dangling—

But I was surprised, he gathered his strength, and cast them off like old clothes—they fell off the steps, literally, and their Heirs below were horrified, shouting at us as loud as Heirs could.

"We'll make it out," I said, as we got onto a balcony where you could glimpse the sea. We had a moment. I said, "She called me blind."

"Not now you aren't!" he said. "I see that, so do you."

"Dock over there! Bebum." Peet pulled Serpenthead away. "Split up—mob coming." Dimly, in the distance, I saw some of the launches and yachts that brought the audience.

"Malc? Don't follow me! Get North!" he shouted galloping over the wall between balconies, in the opposite direction from the parking lot,

Peet behind him.

"I'm going with you!" I said to Serp, for I wanted to follow him, but one stray lilac had found me, grabbed my bad side, my injured ear, and I screamed—pushed back. He covered my eyes. It was a struggle to overcome him. When I looked up, Serpent was nowhere, and I saw Gepetto, fresh from his cheerleading. I said, "Your car!"

"Okay, if you are going to be so dramatic."

I covered my head in my jacket to protect from the assaults, and with my other arm pulled Gepetto off the balcony into an empty office.

I rushed down the steps, all eighteen floors—no more elevators—found the lot, Gepetto beside me. For a moment, we were by the sea, and everything was eerily calm.

"Why can't we stay for the fun?"

"They were trying to kill me," I said again. "Kill Serpenthead too. Peet."

"The best part. Nothing like it. Don't believe it really happens anymore. It's so unlikely. So spooky."

"So you knew?" I asked.

"Of course." Cruel little grin.

I dragged him to his car. He didn't want to leave.

"START THE THING," I shouted. He opened the door, and I pushed him in.

"Okay," he said, turning it on with a slender key, beginning to edge out of the lot.

"Please. Can't this thing go?" I asked, pushing down on his knee, which pressed on the fuel, so we pulled out. I was giddy with the energy of anger.

"How many in the audience knew?" I asked once we were moving.

"Knew what?" Gepetto paused, and then he raised his ridiculously thin eyebrows. "Oh that of course," he said. "All of them I suppose, though they would deny it. The Far Easterners were very clever, escaped the censure of the authorities. After all, who was going to complain? So popular these days—tickets to births, to the removal of bloody tissues, very delightful, the rage. Everyone likes the way it's underground. Sometimes, of course, these deceiving enclavers don't really, really—I mean, I think we have a right to have it verified, to feel the body. Don't you think we paid for that right? Don't you think that should be understood? If the Heirs are willing to be defiled like that. I don't know why they got so touchy right there at the end. Do you realize what we paid?"

I couldn't bring myself to answer him.

*

REG++CY in the rearview, now. "Don't you think there is something wrong with—" I asked.

Gepetto said, "Wrong isn't really a current term." We were out past the marsh, past the elevated highway, on the same pot-holed road we'd come on. The sky still an umber, even more brown than black now. The compass pointing "north."

"Speed up," I ordered him. He'd seen me manhandle Heirs, think nothing of it. I hadn't had time to think anything, anything. I'd picked them up and thrown them down without asking— "Wrong was always such an uneven word," he continued.   "I love these shows. We go to them all we can," he said. "But being backstage—ultimate. I owe you."

"Where do you all get the money?" I asked. I'd heard "we."

"Oh, that," he said. He turned to me, said nothing else.

In that sharp, focused light, I saw the secret of the loose folds about Gepetto's lids—he had added wrinkles, so he looked like an Imposse. Makeup. Thin rubbery pink layers, now coming off in shreds—glue weakening, all those hours under stage lights.

I reached, and ripped them off. Underneath, the tight lids of the T's. I didn't even think of the fact that I was touching him. "Why are you wearing that stupid Imposse stocking? Aren't you hot? Aren't you embarrassed by such cheap—?"

Gepetto jerked away, lost his grip on the wheel. "I had you fooled. Ha-ha to you. Just some rube Nyet. Think you know things. Too clever by half. You think what's real is made, what's made is real—you thought that wretched creature and her relatives were—"

I tore off his fake stocking, and got to the real one underneath.

"Stop, stop, I'm trying to drive," Gepetto said, swerving. I stretched over and stepped on the brake. Gepetto was too weak to stop me. The car screeched it stopped so fast, skidded.

"What now?" Gepetto asked, in more of the natural rasp of a true Heir, not with the other tone, the high-pitched "Gepetto" voice he'd been using most of the night.

"Get out," I said.

He was out of the car, standing in front of the scrub forest, the buzz of cicadas solid as a wall. "What now you scaredy Nyet? Stopping?" he taunted me.

I grabbed Gepetto's actual overskin, yanked it off from his prodermis. He said, "You didn't answer. Why did he want to be a real boy when he could have all the excitement without that? He really, really could. I do." "What?"

"Knot of pine, so foolish, I think. That's metaphysical. He was a fool. Better off if he had stayed wood. He would have lived forever if he'd stayed wood—but he wanted to be bleed-able, pierce-able—sloppy, able to be crushed, cut, changed. He could have run away. He didn't. Real, you die. You defended those diers! You woke up and defended those black biters, those—"

"What do you want?"

"I am just as you are," he said, pleading. "I am just as you are. Sensation," he said, pleading. "All that is boiling in you right now, what a recipe: indignation, rage with a dollop of pride on top—"

I had his prodermis right at the seam. One rip and it would be off.

"I dare you," he said, puffing up, eyes getting round, rotating towards me.

We were beside the rough little road, a few feet from the car—high pines on both sides. No lights in any direction but our headlights. The car still running....

"Not pain, never pain, but the intensity, always that—so delicious, even the longing is delicious—oh, you are going to do it, aren't you? Flay me out here? Aren't you? What are you? I heard that Tamara ask. You know what I am but what are you?"

The gesture had to be over. I threw him down into the ditch beside the shoulder. He rolled over a few times, his thin gown catching in the weeds. His prodermis unattached a little, so his face was losing all expression, sagging like a sock pulled off the toes.

I scrambled away before he could stand, drove off in his car.

Not ten minutes later, as I was speeding down the road, the WELLMED helicopters appeared, calling out to their poor lost Heir, searchlights rolling. They wouldn't look for me, not right away, only there to rescue him, in these hinterlands, lower a chair on a cable—I'd seen this before—and haul him up into the arms of two or three nurses, so he could ride back to wherever he came from, his palace, his remove. They might charge him some fines; use some cartiliform to reattach his prodermis, fill out reports. Slumming in the DE-AX, an old story—rescued—

North. "They will know you," Serp had said.

At some point while driving, hours later, I realized the trees I'd just passed, were the ones I'd already passed hours before. The same for the clumps of abandoned houses behind them, the same for the holes in the highway.

Around daybreak I parked and got out of the car to urinate, heard a growling noise in the woods, like a wild dog. Packs of them in the empty towns Peet had told me, places where they had taken over completely, the old brick slab ruins were their dens.

But two figures in dark shirts, big Nat men, at the periphery of my vision, held a ridiculous wide yellow net. When I turned to look, one jumped on my back, brought me down. I heard, "Don't bang him, don't bang him, don't you see his face? Who he is?"

A hood around my head, a needle in my thigh.

"Ooh, his ear is torn, he bleeds," I heard a high voice say. And then, "Don't hit him so hard, he's good..."

Everything started to fade. I felt some relief, since the war inside me was ending. I was conquered, bagged, like game. I couldn't fight.

IX

3:20 PM October 10, 2121
Port Gramercy Customs House
Northeast Gulf De-Accessioned Territory, U.A. Protectorate

*T*hat very afternoon, after Lydia had finally been hauled off by her equals for Memphis, I asked Serio to take me to the New Orleans Islands. He said no, that communications were down, towers out everywhere, problems because of the predicted storms—but I begged him. I had already waited a very long time because of Lydia, and Horace. Then in the morning he woke me early and said he could take me, if I didn't mind a stop in Port Gramercy to pick up a tool, a miter saw, that he was buying from a man named Thibodeaux. So I put on my pale stone-colored jacket, my transparent black shirt and canvas pants, and took the little bit of money I'd saved, as well as Lazarus' note, and the tags Ariel had sent, to return to my guardian. I packed no bag. I'd wash the shirt when I got to Audubon. As we sailed, Serio mentioned I could stay on the boat in the harbor in Gramercy, or come into town. It didn't matter to him.

It was a beautiful, breezy day, the grandest possible blue, as it could be after rains, especially in October. I wondered later, if it had been overcast, and mean, would I have had such bright, dangerous thoughts—I asked if they didn't have a good sugar café in the city. He said, yes, the best. But wasn't I going to start fasting?

"I can have some sugar in my coffee," I said. But I had already started thinking of possibilities. Port Gramercy wasn't a big town—I was ashamed of myself, my conscience came by—

After we did pull in, Serio and I had to wait in line in front of the Port Gramercy Customs House to get day passes. There were Nats in front of us and behind, in all sorts of rusty, preposterous vehicles—cars pulled by mules, others spewing black cornosene exhaust, electric motorcycles with cabins on the rear and seats for three or four people, ancient terrain transports with makeshift benches built out from the frames. There was apparently a party, for the next few days, Cycle Fest. Something to do with the cane fields, the harvest. It had been postponed because of the storm. The officials let most of them through pretty quickly. When it came to our turn, they told us to get inside. Someone behind us said, "Go, move on."

"Who does this guy think he is?" Serio asked to me. He was talking about a bowl-legged dark-yellow skinned Yeared behind us in line.

Serio turned and snapped to the fellow I learned later was Serp, "Back off," using the tone enclavers used to those below them. Surprising, Serio being rude.

Then a captain with beady eyes, a head fat and wide as a cantaloupe, and a tight khaki suit, took a look at my Nyet collar. He used the code on it to get into my basic ID screen. "What's the story here? Twenty by count give or take? Still have your nature? Don't you Nyets have to declare and go under," he asked, his small eyes tightening. "The knife?"

"I haven't put in yet—so I haven't—" How attached these were to their reproduction, how superstitious.

"You close?" He seemed skeptical. "Give me your financials pass."

"I won't," I said.

"You want to get into Port Gramercy?"

I was interested in the world she came from—wanted to see it. Camille. "Just for a few hours."

He didn't like me. "Okay, you type it, I won't look."

The screen light cast on the captain's broad and ugly face suddenly went from chartreuse to a cold blue. He said, "Look. Your numbers." His face relaxing, his shoulders dropping, his neck stretching out, so he was suddenly looking down on me. "Why didn't you say so?"

"It's there," I said, though I was ashamed.

"But got a lien on it. Your jack, your dinero. I wouldn't get any operations done either I was you." He rolled out the word "operations," as if it were a marble in his mouth. "Maybe you better make other plans?" Bead-eyes, like a pigeon's going round in mock delight.

"There is some mistake. I'm going home to get that matter

straightened out."

"You, right?" He held his hand over the figures at the bottom, and showed me my documentary existence: *Malcolm de Lazarus/Registered Enrolled Full Dependent Sponsored Not-Yet/WELLFI TRUST #1329087666.... Trust Sponsor: H. R. Lazarus De Gold of Audubon Foundling House Audubon Island, New Orleans Islands, etc. etc.*

"See that right there?" Meaning the color orange, an oblong field, running behind my big healthy number.

I was humiliated. "It's a mistake. Why don't you call?" Perhaps I could get through on their lines. Maybe Lazarus would answer them.

"Towers out to the Islands, Horace the Hurricane. Got to wait for the Rouge Gaists to come fix them. What genius in the U.A. put out that contract I'd like to know?" He paused, continued, "Your kind are kinda on your own till your ship comes in aren't ya? All or nothing bet? I'd keep my options," he said, making an obscene gesture with one hand, and then he picked up a tiny mike, the length and width of the tip of his smallest, chubby digit, and spoke into it to his deputies. "Bring the little guy over."

In an instant, Serio was between two deputies, bristling. They'd made him take off his shoes, his belt, even unscrewed the precious ink pen Mimi had given him, into three parts, turned the lining of his hat inside out. His bright smile was missing.

"Out of town by sundown. Before the Festival—hear?" Leaning over, the captain took a slim pad of blue newsprint out of his pocket with a roughly stamped FREE WHEEL insignia on it, and scribbled his signature on the bottom. He handed one to me and one to Serio.

"Like this is some paradise," Serio said under his breath as we were turning to go, but he wasn't daunted. I saw the thought of adventure in him, after everything.

All I wanted to do was to find a screen and write Lazarus, again. Serio was telling me about the pleasures of this sad town, while I berated myself—

But then I was forced to stop thinking of my trouble, or rather, to stop thinking.

*

As if it had been pre-set, pre-arranged—

She was so lovely, lovelier than I'd never seen her, sitting there in a black dress. In her hometown. In the sugar café. At a table with a checked cloth. At the same moment that I rejoiced, I accused myself of wanting this, of planning it.

At first, I felt a sinking song of a feeling, dipping down like a weight tugging on me.

You were younger then—and besides, there was nothing between you—nothing compared— I said the words to myself, but looking at her, couldn't believe them.

"Well there you are. I was thinking of writing you. Telling you. How could you know that?" she asked directly as if there was no reason to be formal with a person you hadn't seen in two years, a person of another caste. Was there a reason? In her presence, none.

"Tell me what?" I was as direct as she was.

"I lost Landry," she said, softly.

She was a widow. Black, of course.

"It's been ten weeks," she said. "First day I'm allowed by the custom to be in public, see people outside the family."

"I'm so sorry," Serio interrupted—or to me, it felt like an interruption. For Camille and I were the only people in the room, didn't he see that? "How long were you together?"

"Married two years next June."

"What happened?" Serio again.

"Get your coffee," she said to us, eyeing the waitress. Everyone in the cafe tracking her— "Go on, please, order."

Serio's quick slight body an asset, his sweetness, his attentiveness, apparent again, like the sun coming through clouds. "He had an accident," she said. "Welding a seam on a syrup tanker. Underwater. We already had enough from his family's cane fields. He thought we needed more. I married without my full dowry. He was all hung up about that. You remember." She looked at me. And that web grew over me, but I was going on, to my life. I was in love with Lydia. I was going to be with her. I had promised.

Her husband had broken the first rule—welding, he had pulled back before the current was turned off, and been electrocuted. Repairing a vessel of syrup for the fugue countries, where the prices were rising—

Then, I felt it again. I was anointed, when she looked at me. Camille's plump arm, the wrist that was showing at the end of her sleeve, obsessed me. I trembled.

"Staying? Come for the festival?" she asked, when she had finished the recitation about her husband. Or perhaps to cut my gaze short, stop me from thinking.

"On the way to see Lazarus."

"Your Boundarytime?" she breathed quickly, leaned away, said what seemed false, "Oh. Wonderful." Then she turned to Serio. I felt abandoned.

Behind us, two entering the café.

"Why you still here loitering?" The captain from the Customhouse. "Stand," he said.

"You know who I am. Honestly, there is no need—we were leaving. No need—"

Camille straightened, blooms of red out on her neck. "Ronny, leave them alone. They aren't—"

"He's a haughty Nyet, not fixed," the Captain, Ronny, shouted back, and the women in the café gasped in a chorus.

"No respect?" Camille asked.

"My brother hardly in the ground. You shut up. You sit down," this Domino said.

"They did nothing to you."

Serio's rage rising. "What is your Lownat problem? We came here, giving you our business—?" Serio pulled away from Captain Domino's grip, but in response, the bully threw him on the top of a table. "Take him, Charles," he said to his big-toothed deputy, then turned to Camille: "I told Landry you were a whore."

She was shaking by then. Everyone looking on.

I reached to strike him. He grabbed my wrist, and said, "Attempted assault on an officer." They got me into cuffs.

Serio ran, which made him guilty of "resisting arrest." They rounded him up, marched us both off.

*

"Well I couldn't live if I didn't know my kin," the amazingly ugly fellow, whose name tag read *Lou Rae Ducorney, STEWARD*, was saying to me a few hours later. He ran the Port Gramercy Jail. "What you got is that pile of money. That's all you got. And Captain Domino said something's hanging on it. Claiming it. WELLFI has everybody by the short hairs. You don't know that? You think they gonna let anybody rise when they got the keys to the kingdom?"

Outside, fireworks of the festival, people walking by, laughing drinking, talking. Boom boom fireworks, and accordions.

"Starving the enclaves. That's their strategy. Control our currency, keep us embargoed, restrict our exports to Brazil, Haiti, Cuba, put up the Broad Walls, fuck up the Net, make sure we can't hardly breed—tied our balls up with all this Procreation Act baling wire— "

"Nothing's wrong with my Trust, that's a mistake," I said, knowing I shouldn't respond at all.

"I heard all kinds a stories about them busting people's Trusts. Get right up to the threshold, they slam the door," he said. "But let's say for argument, you get through the eye of the needle," he said. "What you going to do then? Who you going to be?"

I wouldn't tell him. I knew it: what I'd promised, what I wanted.

Ducorney looked as though he was lowering his snout to sniff something. He said, "You don't answer because you don't know who that is. Where you from? Just say and do what they say, say and do?"

I still didn't answer.

He stared at me. I wasn't going to say a word, answer him, fight with him. He saw it. Why wasn't he leaving? I suppose it was possible he was thinking. But I doubted it. Finally, he raised his head up again. "One more thing," he said.

Silence from me.

"I got a bet going. You the first Nyet I've seen in a good while. You get a lotta fakers out there, you know. Imposses galore. Epidemic of all kinda freaks. But I think, in this matter you settle our question. You spent time with Heirs, working in them big outdoor operas? Captain D. told me you a star."

I still didn't answer, though it was hard.

His long face breathing thickly, scent of his oniony supper. "You tell anybody I asked you this I will kill you." He looked down to the far end of the hall. "You get T-pussy? Heir snatch? How does it work?"

"What?" I asked, blushing.

"I knew it," he said. Then he hollered down the hall, "Sy, you gotta get in here."

Sy, slumped, bloodshot eyes, shuffled up. "What is it Lou Rae?"

"Come on, he going to tell us how it works," Steward slapped his thigh. "I knew they put out. But do you take that off? That proderm what ever it is? Don't that kill them? Tell us. We got a bet."

"I'll tell you," I said, breaking my silence, "if you let me get to your screens. All about it—you have no idea."

He asked, "How they like it?"

"Show me the screens first."

When they took me, leg irons, to a small room off the front office, and turned on their ancient, moldy Broad screen, in complete shame over my predicament, I tried to send another message—who know how long I'd be here?

Dear Lazarus, Glorious H. R., Guardian, I hope this note finds you well and that you are back from Memphis? I am detained in Port Gramercy, but I want to make sure you know there is a lien on my Trust? Some claim? Any? Please communicate. Do you have any idea—

I sent that before the connection fizzled.

Later, I told them things I knew, not everything. Caps. What the Venus Gaists told me. Or Jeremy, who talked about these advances when he explained to me how much better it all was than the "functions" I would perform with the little tattooed girls he hired. I didn't tell them what was better. I didn't really know. In fact, when I finally was allowed to leave them and their endless, pornographic questions, I listened to the Fest outside—people talking in the streets, calling out to one another, string music, horns, accordions—and I wished they would tell me something. If they had any idea, which probably they didn't, but what was it like if you had a real Nat girl and she loved you, if she could love you? In that ordinary, old way? How would it be if you kissed her and she kissed you back all you wanted because she wanted to and it would make her happy, and you too, and it wasn't forbidden—I wondered about all that, though I believed I'd never know it.

Sy came to my cell at dawn and said, "Listen, I didn't appreciate all those fibs about T's. The caps and the dials and the elixirs, the probes, but on the bet, I won. He paid up. And he didn't like losing. Said you were cheap Nyet slime, Outliar in truth, I'm saying get out of town. They said to release you, and you had better get. Fair warning."

Steward called my name, butchering it, "DeLazarai you piece of DE-AX crap. Landry Domino's widow's here for you."

*

She was standing outside at the bottom of the long front staircase of the jail, shading her eyes, the sun was rising behind the building, wearing a long dark blue dress with sleeves to the wrists. I saw the wetness under her raised arm, which engendered within me a terrible kind of yearning. A desire for her temperature, somehow.

"Free man, you liar," Ducorney shoved me hard going out. I stumbled for a few steps. He threw my jacket after me. Camille said, "Oh! Malc!" And at that second, I found my balance.

"That Lou Rae—psychopath. Your friend shouldn't have ever run. Really pissed Ronny off. They hate Chef Menteurians on principle around here. I sprung you. Ronny'd be here with me to chaperone if he'd woke up yet. He's still sleeping off the Fest. Why I came so early."

I asked, "Can I talk to Serio before I leave?"

"You better get out," she said. "You can't wait for visiting hours, that is for sure. I made a deal—"

Her hair was up, and falling down as well, the darker roots showing at the neck, I noticed. "Last night at the festival. We made a truce. He said you could go. I can talk to him." She paused, looked down. "Sort of. And that's the mess. He likes me."

"What's the mess?" We were moving at a quick pace across the asphalt square to the gates. The town was quiet and littered after the Fest.

"I don't own my Procreation Certificate. It goes back to Landry's family and that means, to Ronny, the only living brother. If I had my whole dowry, I might have bought it outright, instead of the Dominos getting it. He doesn't have any sons. He's going to use sex selection this time he says, even though it costs a year's wages, you have to go to the lab in Upper Houston in the U.A. Planning to start trying on me soon, went to see my doctor without asking me." She looked as if she were going to cry. "Landry said he wasn't ready for a child. He wanted to get going on his welding, have more money. I said I was twenty-two and when was he going—" She broke off. "If I had got pregnant, this would be different."

A man in a t-shirt with a very graphic Free Wheel on it who was walking across the street, waved to her. She picked up her pace.

"What is Ronny going to do?"

"I have to be the mother of the child. He will have to make me his second wife to do this. He could cut me some slack, but he's not—"

"What about his wife?"

"She will just have to put up with it for the line. You never heard of Levirite marriage?"

"What happens if you marry somebody else?"

"Who is going to marry me?" she asked. "I have to get Ronny's permission. And anyway, I can't have anybody else's child, just one in Landry's line."

I was ignorant of this enclave arcana.

I asked, "Are children the only reason to marry? Don't people say it's love?"

She looked around—my question didn't seem serious to her, or it was too serious. "Called me a whore like that in a public place. That's so people turn against me. So if he marries me nobody thinks it's unfair. I never was any kind of—you of all people should know—I am sorry you got pulled into this. And that Serio, he wasn't—"

"What's Levirite?"

"You heard of the Bible I guess."

"Lydia had a copy of it," he said.

"Well there you go. It's Lydia?" She rolled her eyes. "I knew—"

"No, no," I said. But it was true, wasn't it? Or it was going to be true. At that fact, I was desolate, suddenly.

It was a cool, and sloppy day—threatening rain, or, possibly, worse—for October. Debris strewn around—beads, hand bills. Still dressed from last night, two girls in scant skirts stumbled by as if on their way to another party.

"Why did you claim Ariel? Why did you say—? Why did you—"

Stalk off? Tell Greenmore what for? Take the blame?

I nodded.

She stopped walking, looked at me. "You don't have the slightest, do you?" She did that thing where she tightened her lips, bit down.

I asked, "Why don't you leave this place?"

"I have thought about it. But you know what Closed Enclave means, don't you? I could never come back, never see my kin."

Under the thick cloud cover the dismal little town seemed even more forlorn.

"You still love all your rules."

"No." Her pupils got big. She was mad. "No. Okay. I don't like these. These are horrible rules. I hate Ronny. Landry hated him too. He's a bully. I hate him. He doesn't just want a baby from me. He wants to run my life, every aspect—"

"What will you do?"

"Like you care?"

"Of course I do." At that moment, I was willing to—I didn't mind what Lazarus, what anyone, Lydia—I'd throw all that away if it could save her. At the same time, I knew what a fool I was. I said, almost inaudibly, "I do care."

She shook her head, as if to erase my words. "Well there is nothing to be done, now." And she put her two hands around my neck, and kissed me softly on my mouth, warm.

"Goodbye, Malcolm," she said, pulling away, shaking her head again, slower. "Sorry it has to be like this. Sorry." She handed me forty Port Gram Crowns. "The jail guards took all your money, didn't they? Here. You gonna be an Heir. Get what you wanted. Good for you. You spent every hour of your life on it, didn't you? So far? Come on—"

"I am sorry, about Landry," I said. "And my part—"

"Go on Malc," she said. Then she took me by the neck, again, kissed me another time. A shock went through my torso, down, bright, fast, tense. Lightening.

I couldn't let go of her. I never would. I knew it was wrong, but inside, I never would.

✱

I had a long walk after I said goodbye to Camille.

The money she gave me worked in one of the metered Broad Screens at the corner near Gramercy docks after I left the gates of the city. I wrote Klamath, to tell him about his son.

"*Heard from a lawyer already. And a bail bondsman,*" was his reply.

"*We were pulled into a feud this woman is having.*"

"*Well some looker I hope for this trouble. Lawyer has standing in the Free Wheel Syndicate Circuit. Said show up at the arraignment. You should be there too that would really help. Nine days from now, ten a.m. Serio says use his boat—he heard you were released.*"

The screen went blank. I put in a few more of Camille's coins, but the machine had jammed.

✱

I went for hours, seeing only salt water and bare shore. I needed water, started to feel faint. I found a trough at the marina where they cleaned fish, drank from the spigot like a dog. Despondent, I went back to the deck of Serio's boat, and planned to sleep until the holiday was over, then try to persuade someone to go up to the jail, see Serio, ask for the key—

When I woke, I heard a voice from above, two shadows pointing at me from the dock. "GET YOU GUN, SEE HIM DOWN THERE! Liar here for our women. Don't let him get away with it."

A loud "brraack" and then another.

Then, I heard a new voice, a melodious close-at-hand voice at the rear of my deck, and then from above, another, "*I can hit him from here—*"

"Get down—what, with your rotten aim? Hiding in that little deck—see?"

BRAACK, BRAACK, over my head, and then, "I GOT YOU COVERED," and the boom.

Part Three:
The Gate in the Wall

I

The two who had captured me took the sack off my head, so I had
the benefit of my senses again. I was on the floor of a cave with high
ceilings. The walls were jagged and moist. Mosses like carpet and
some like tiny ferns were growing up the sides. I could see them
close at hand, by my hurting head. On the wall about twenty-five feet
away, a very old moving flat was projected—hardly more than Vee's
shadow plays. A group of raw, dirty, scrawny figures sitting on a thin
wide mat were watching the film, in which a good-looking man by
the antique standards was taking a shower with his boxy suit on. A
very skinny woman—almost like an Heir in her elegant emaciation,
her bird-like neck, was looking on, asking the handsome shadow
of a man why he was soaping and soaking his suit and still wearing
it. There was laughter. I saw that the watchers' skins were wrinkled,
rippled, grooved—stretched over sticks of bones. They laughed and
fell back and sat up and laughed again, in unison, chained to one
another. Occasionally one would look away, at what was going on in
the rest of the cave, and his large toothy blue smile would, for a second,
fade, until one of his cohorts or one of the guards—who were also the
same, emaciated, scribbled with veins, sheathed in rags—would come
toward the one out of line and slap him back to look at the ridiculous
handsome man showering in his clothes. I saw that they did not blink.

A shackled flock of flayed Heirs. I shuddered.

"We saw you with that hideous Shade in Imposse disguise. You had him, bravo! But then you had mercy," the shorter of the two who had captured me said. Both were gristled Yeareds, about fifty or sixty years old, burly fellows who smelled bad. The one who spoke was stocky, the other, tall, skinny with a pot belly that flapped over his belt.

"That's how we know who you are," the shorter one went on. "On account of the mercy you showed."

"Just like his pictures," the tall one said. "Even the lip."

"I never believed the lip," the shorter one, whose hair was white-silver, with bangs. "And see, it isn't quite."

"That's what it looks like. That's what it says. Shallow."

"Who are you?" I finally asked. "What *what* looks like?"

"We ask the questions. Why was that one driving the transport? We know it was your transport. Why did you come into our territory? Were you looking for us? Someone by any chance send you this way?" the taller asked, his heavy wattle jiggling.

"Who are you?" I asked again. "What someone?"

"He's pretending he's surprised we exist," Silver-hair said.

Then a stocky woman came in, with hair shorter than that of either man, a denim shirt and black pants, her skin dark. "Well, Salamander," she said. "At last. "

"Who?"

"You," she said. She turned to those I'd been talking to, her underlings. "Did you do this to his ear? Did you think that was a good idea? Intelligent? Did you hit him on the head?"

"Only the hood on his head. Just the hood—we had to steal the car," Silver said.

The other added, "Ear was like that."

"Look at him, so unworn, so young," she said, her hand coming to my cheek. "And oh, he's hot."

I winced when she touched. I had been in pain, since I woke. Dry heat, a few small fires underneath, burning into the blanket.

"Like his pictures," Silver said. "Like his pictures."

"What about the top of his head?" the tall one with the wattle asked.

"They say it's tiny, take you all day to find it."

She glowered at them. "Shhh." Then she asked me, "What is it? Do you think we are a myth?"

"You should have seen him. One that was passing-down, a surly dandy mocked him, soon as Salamander took off, the filthy Shade, popped his body alarm." Silver raised his arms, spread his fingers, to show how the WELLVAC copter had zeroed in upon Gepetto. They had been following me even then, but why?

In the flat on the wall, at a distance, the skinny woman with a long neck and the man who washed in his suit were now on a representation of a boat, with a representation of bridges and building of old "Paris" passing by, in the background. I knew this because there was a facsimile of "Paris," in one of the western Walled Urbs—river, cathedral, boats, islands, all of it. The chained figures watching it were rapt now, humming.

The woman in charge continued, "A show like that, tickets to a deathbed. Pay a hundred million for ringside to a childbirth, like to see the woman's parts open—didn't think it possible, but they are getting worse."

"Who are they, watching that movie?" I asked.

She said, "We take Bonesnake prisoners when we can."

"We use them for ransom," Wattle said. Silver offered, "We flay them and keep them down, show them flats, pacify them—so they lose themselves."

"Did he do that to the Shade who was passing down?" the woman asked.

"No. He had mercy. That's how we knew for sure who he was."

She looked around, just as the prisoners rattled out a great, uniform laugh. "We need more quiet. I have to clean that wound. Let's go. Can you stand?"

It was slow, the standing part. I was stiff, achy all over, the fires within me flared. She helped me to my knees—gently. On two feet, I was dizzy. She led me out of the cave with the captives and into the open air.

The place was in a clearing carved from scrub forest, a sort of village, made of the ruins of old trailers with ragged awnings and tents attached, as filthy and messy as any Outliar settlement. There were empty ancient cars, lean-to shacks, some little houses on platforms up in trees, huge tires carved into chairs, and flattened into pallets. Nearby, the ruins of a scrap yard made a forest of rust. A few fires were set about, embers, smoking.

She led me across the open area to the single concrete building. An acclimatizer on the outside spewing steam was the only sign of electricity I'd seen except for the flat projector in the cave.

Inside this building, fourteen limp sacks on hangers suspended from chains attached to the rafters. In each one, a hull of an Heir. Prodermises, in some state of preservation.

"Trophy room," she said, without stopping. "We wanted you to see it, Salamander," she said. "So you can tell Neil."

We passed by a woman in a dark blue jumpsuit who was using a mop to swab the hanging skins with a viscous solution from a bucket. My guide continued—"He needs to understand it is war against the Bonesnakes, very clear, without mitigation—there is no compromise in this camp. It's under my command. We have men and women and children who will fight, tear them down, strip them, they are not immortal, we know who is immortal, he who goes past, goes through," she looked at me when she said this. "But here, we must fight. And we will help. You. That's all we want."

"The Ocean Springs people?" I asked.

She shook her head, almost violently. "Why do you ask such questions? Do I look like a lunatic to you? I know who you are, so don't insult us."

I could smell the coconut oil, the thick greasy ooze the worker used to coat the prodermises, which made me a little sick.

"Say who," I said. I hadn't any choice.

"Do you have amnesia?" she asked, closing her eyes for a second. "Did you lose your memory? Did they strike you? Is it the fever?" She reached for my forehead, calmer for a moment, and then she withdrew. "Or do you just distrust us? Come."

We left the warehouse, went out into the clearing again. On the other side of a turned-over tireless WELLFI transport truck, she showed me the entrance to a a a small hovel with scrap metal walls. Inside, she lit a lamp, and told me to sit on a stool.

"Now," she said, holding up a mirror to me. "Look," she said. "Who do you see?"

I saw my unshaven, grimy face, my brown eyes, my thick hair, my brow, my tight, too-tight Not Yet collar, and also my bloody, painful, swollen ear, and puffed-out cheek. My lip—what was it they had against my stupid lip? It was as it had always been. One day, when I got to Memphis for the Treatments, I would get the web inside fixed, have the surgeons to give me an indentation, so I looked like everyone else. But after what I'd done, would I ever get to Memphis now? Assaulted several Heirs. And didn't care! I didn't. Lazarus would condemn me. I could see it in my reflection—I didn't care. I was a different man. And ashamed of it, as well.

"I'm going to numb you," she said. "And disinfect the ear. Then, I am going to sew it up. It's swelling, going to get worse—if I don't. That's why you have a fever. Do you have any objection? There could be blood poisoning, it's angry here around your neck, red—"

She was touching it, which was excruciating. In truth, strange as everything I'd seen so far was, I trusted her. Couldn't even explain it.

She went on, "I won't let Salamander be imperfect." Then she leaned over me, the weight of her breasts impressive. "Put your head back. Open your mouth. You won't remember this—"

I did not fight.

She dropped a small lozenge underneath my tongue. As it dissolved, I began to float. I watched her carefully, though I somehow lost interest. She drew out a long flexible needle, threaded it, bit off the ends, and pierced my lobe, then drew up the needle and thread very high, before she went down for her second stitch. I started to get groggy.

As I drifted off, she said, "My name is Mo Lion. I know who you are."

II

I had lain on the floor of the hovel for three nights and four days. I had been awakened a few times and been given liquids to drink. I was lying still on my mat, and the dull throb around my jaw was improving.

I'd had my share of visitors over the days, mostly more of Mo Lion's little army, it seemed—fellows in black or yellow vests with thick soled shoes, short or long brown or blonde or silver hair. Skins caramel, ebony, pink, and plaster white. The men were more likely to have long locks, but the adult women had hair no longer than a fingertip. They were mostly Yeareds, a few my own age. They came to gawk at me but said little. They had started calling me "Salamander." But when one was about to utter the word it seemed, Mo Lion would appear and tell them, "Shhhh— he's incognito."

This morning, Silver, who had captured me, came in with a very small auburn-haired girl. Her green eyes had long lashes. She, too, had short hair, but not as short as the older women's. It was the first child I'd seen in this place.

"I'll show you, honey," he said.

"Yes Charlie," she said in her little voice, which was musical, charming. "I want to see."

They thought I was asleep, but my eyes were only half-closed. I watched what they were up to.

Charlie went to a calendar on the wall and flipped through the pages with pictures of characters from history—one was of Abraham Lincoln—until he came to a portrait of a man with a five o'clock shadow, dark skin, brown eyes, thick hair, a familiar brow. "See? He looks just like the Great Neil," he said to his small companion. "He's traveling with false identity, as a Nyet, see the collar?"

"What is his name?"

"Shh. He's a Salamander."

"I don't know what that is," I spoke up.

"See how he keeps his disguise? What a soldier," Charlie told the little girl. "We have to go now, we can't bother him." They scurried away.

These were insurrectionists, some last remnant from the Troubles, I guessed. They couldn't imagine anything else: I had to be a soldier, one of them. I was tired, I was sick, I was even willing to indulge the fantasy as I lay there. If I were a guerilla, working for the Mo Lion clan—what would I do? I asked myself. Raid Port Gramercy and haul out Camille, get her away from Domino, find her protection. Spring Serio from jail. Among the Heirs, I would stop those horrible new Sim Verites, expose the audiences, and purge those from the ranks. But I wasn't a guerilla. I was myself, that was, someone waiting to be alive.

The pair came back, not long after, because I was I dozing. The child touched my engraved collar, called out the numbers of my Nyet Enrollment. I woke.

Mo Lion entered, yelled at them.

"You must be awake by now, the stuff has to have worn off," she told me when they had left the second time. She knew me.

She shoved some mush in a bowl at me. Rice and brown meat. I asked what kind.

"Horse, a little deer," she said. "We are overrun with both herds. Eat everything; we have no fields on that account. Might as well eat them. Near here, they live right inside the old slab and brick ruins. They have fine shelter, finer than we do. They prosper."

"Why don't you live in the ruins?"

"The U.A. mercenaries always look there. You don't know this? You do know this." She had very thick hands for a woman and a large square head. When I looked at the mush, I thought I might be sick. It had been so long, so very long, since I'd had solid food. I shook my head no, and asked for the broth again. She came back with a new bowl, a metal one this time. I sat up and drank it directly, without using a spoon, and asked for more. Delicious.

She pulled the misshapen screen door closed and clipped the hanging curtains at the other opening, so she could give this hovel a little privacy. "You don't have to be secret with me," she said, when she touched my stitches to examine them. It didn't hurt as much as even yesterday. "We aren't your enemies. We are not upset about who you are. We consider it a privilege to care for you. I sewed your ear back together. Stopped the infection." She held up the mirror again. "See?"

I was gaunt, my eyes were hollow. I wasn't as swollen. My neck wasn't red any longer—wasn't "angry" as she had put it. I thought, overall, that I looked quite strange, like someone I didn't quite know.

"Would I save someone I wanted to harm? I know how to harm. We just want one thing."

"What?" I hoped I could offer her something. Of course, somewhere, I knew I had to get this matter with my Trust fixed, go to Memphis, do the Boundarytime ceremony—in fact, the last few days alone, when I had been awake, recovering, I had gone over all my mistakes since I left the Wood Palace, and tried to explain all the errors in judgment—I was drunk, I was confused, I was light-headed from fasting, under the influence, etc, etc.

But over and over, I had come up against a single, glaring fact. At the Miramar, I'd thrown Heirs down and later, I'd stolen a transport from one and I would have killed him if I'd had to—but I couldn't find the guilt in me. I kept looking in the mirror, even, for it, but it was not there.

Camille—I wanted to see her, save her. There it was—

She was ready to speak. "When you leave here, go to your cohort, Neil of Pensacola or Jude—we did lose John, didn't we? That's not a myth, is it?" she asked, conversational now, less emphatic, for a second, then returning to the formal tone: "Tell him to join forces with us, or let us join with him—we can be his guards, his higher corps, his shock troops," she said. "And you—you see what we have. We wouldn't harm you and we wouldn't harm him. Ultimately, we know your nature. So how could we harm you?"

"To join forces, exactly, to do what?" I asked. It came to me she'd given me some potion, that's why I wasn't outraged. At all I'd done, at what she proposed, I should have been horrified—

"Take the transport that belonged to that abomination," she said. "We filled it with cornosene. Go to your leader and explain. Will you do that? We can't use the Net, messages intercepted, no matter what code we use. We have not gotten through in a long time."

"How long?"

"Seventeen years I count," she said, with no note of futility.

I nodded "yes." I felt terrible, having to trick her.

She took up a piece of paper with typing on one side, which she intended to reuse, and a long stick, a homemade pencil.

She put the paper on a book near her, and began to write with the concentration and intent of a child. Her lips moved often, tightening while she formed the difficult letters, or came up, I supposed, with a complex phrase. I liked watching her compose. In fact, I wanted to do what she asked. If she hadn't been insane, and hadn't believed me to be some mythical person, I would have tried to do what she asked. After great effort, she folded the long letter in half, and handed it to me as if it were the most grand and elaborate scroll engraved by calligraphers, and said, "Tell Neil of P. Give him this. Read it now, make sure you understand."

I took it and read it, aloud.

"*To HIGH NEIL BY WAY OF THE Glorious Younger Salamander we found wandering in the Picayune Hills, Incognito—*

Mo Lion of the Picayune Hills Clan by the Bullet Tracks near the Pearl Tributary beseeches you to let us join with you in the cause of the Greater Rebellion. We want you to reconsider your present doctrine of restraint— we want to fight for your glory, we want to be engaged in the great slaughter of the totalitarian Elysian Shades, the monstrous venal Usurpers of all the thriving, of real, conditional, transmutable life, the cowardly Bonesnakes here to prey on sacredness, which is, more than anyone alive, what you know. We want war not with you but with them, to your kind we surrender. We will be subjugated, we understand your sovereignty. Yet, we want you to see our desire for the greater cause of destroying the rubber-covered reptiles, cold blooded, flaying them, handing them their ending.

Here is our magazine: two thousand liters of cornosene, a ton of thick nails, twenty-three shotguns, sixteen pistols, two gross shells, plastique, ammonium nitrate—three tons. Troops, one hundred and two alive, no disease. And fifty-one Shades ripe for ransom, to negotiate, prodermises preserved for fourteen. And hatred for the enemy, which is the only thing we are not prepared to lose. With your Salamander, we send three young recruits, so you can see our mettle, test it.

Mo Lion, General, Picayune Hills Army

October 18, 2121"

When I had finished reading it aloud, she said, "Good. Say we did not seek to harm you. Say we know our place, say we know your gifts, his gifts, we understand their meaning, and acknowledge the divinity. Which is why we are willing to fight. We are believers," she said. "And if he's quiescent as you are, will you tell him why we have to fight? We know these things—we have read all the chronicles of Defuniak, of Pensacola, the Rebellion—the fight cannot end—that's our position— the Bonesnakes cannot prevail, it is death if they do."

I nodded. Didn't know what to say.

At that point she put both her hands on the crown of my head—and parted my hair at a certain place slightly forward of the swirl on the top. She weeded through it as if she were looking for lice, the way Marilee used to do. I did not fight, somehow. I wanted her to find what she was looking for as much as she did. But, I couldn't want that—

"Here," she said finally. "I have it. I see it. I was just making sure."

Some small indentation on my scalp. It seemed to be about the size of a mole, and until I felt her fingernail exploring it, I had never known it was there.

But this was odd—when she rubbed it hard, a steely thrum went down my spine. As if she were plucking me like a string. I straightened, jerked slightly, got a little scared.

"I thought the reaction would have been stronger," she said. "It's not completely closed, just a slight membrane on top. You can't deny it now."

"Tell me who I am," I said. I believed her, for a moment. Though this had to be a parlor trick.

"You lost your memory?" she asked and stared, sharp as Lydia. "I'm tired of you being coy."

I was frightened. I shook my head no.

"Well?" she asked. "Say who you are."

"Salamander," I lied. The distinct feeling I was not lying.

"Where born?" she asked.

"Florida," I said. What else could I say?

"Were you in the latter set? We have only read the twenty -nineties records, say they all died. We only hear about Cuba now."

The nickel tags Ariel had sent me were in my jacket. I showed them to her.

She read the number, examined the white star on the blue background, and said, "Well stop your act, okay?"

"Okay," I said.

"We don't know the tray numbers," she said, which meant absolutely nothing in the world to me. I nodded, as if it did. She gave me my tags back, and some tablets to stop the infection, and then she patted me on my breast. I wished she would explain to me what I pretended to know.

Charlie came in then, without the little girl. He held an ancient map sealed in wax paper. It showed what the roads had been sixty years before; I saw the date on the back. Meticulously, someone had marked out the many routes that were no longer viable, and drawn new ones in, using crude pen and ink. He included the toll stops run by the Ocean Springs Clan and ways to avoid these. He indicated he thought I would go into the hills outside of the abandoned city of Mobile. There was a circle, with the marking, *"NEIL OF P?"* where they guessed Neil or his minions were hiding out, or had been once. There was an arrow, as well, pointing south, which said, *"ISLA DE YOUVENTOOD?"*

"Do we have it right?" he asked.

I didn't want to lie.

"Don't make him divulge," Mo Lion instructed from the other room where she was talking to the woman who swabbed the hanging prodermises. "He's the real thing. Wait until we are allies, then we can share intelligence—he's their prince, don't expect—besides, our passengers will be with him—"

"What passengers?" I asked.

"Some of our army will come, keep you safe, and talk to Neil direct. Escorts."

"Escorts?" I asked.

Charlie's gray eyes looked up at her as she came in. "How many are there?" he asked her. "Salamanders?"

She said, "We don't know. He's younger than any of our intelligence has ever—" She turned to me. I was still studying the map. She pointed to the markings outside of the ruins of Mobile. "Well, do you see it there? Or the way to it?"

I nodded again.

She seemed satisfied. She gave me some cocaine salve for my ear, and told me, "Godspeed, give our highest to your brethren."

Another man came in, one I'd never seen before, said, "Come talk to them, they are restless..."

"Who?" Mo Lion asked.

"The escorts are having an argument about the weapons. Which ones you want them to take? They all want to carry the magnum—if it works, they want to test it—"

A shot, then, and Mo Lion called, "Those wasteful idiots—"

I didn't have the keys to Gepetto's, had no idea who did, but found Serpent's gift, his knife, with that curvy razor wire. The transport was just behind the concrete building where the prodermises were hung.

After Mo Lion and the others went out to break up the fight, I fled. At the other end of the camp, I saw the "army," a group in black with shoes made of silver duct tape and soles of pieces of tire, their heads wrapped in mesh helmets. They each held a pole, like the handle of a hoe, with a curved crude blade attached to the top.

This was my moment. I pried open Serpent's knife. He'd kept it well, hardly any rust. I found the wire he used to rig Serio's boat. It wasn't hard, I got it in. The car turned over, I rolled out. I was a good thousand feet away before any one of them even heard the engine. I watched in the rearview as they scrambled to one of their pitiful vehicles. I almost wanted to stay, to help them. What a sinner I was, I knew.

I floored it, found the I-Road—for miles it was unblocked and entirely empty.

*

As I drove, heading south and west, using the compass on Geppetto's dial, I gained confidence that I would find my way out of the Far East De-Ax, and back home.

But I wasn't calmer, I was more troubled: the whining faces of those Heirs and Altereds looking upon Ginger's body, and Geppetto's sneer, and the gargoyles going for Serp—

I drove through uninhabited, overgrown lands, punctuated now and then by cratered-out villages, mountains of brick rubble, and flocks of deer in some of the empty towns. Packs of dogs came at my transport on the road, sometimes as many as fifteen strong, willing to kill themselves for the delight of nipping at my tires.

I took a white gravel road detour from Charlie's map to get around the Ocean Springs Toll Booth, and headed into the lowering sun as the day aged.

I had to return to my original plan. Go to Lazarus, get my Trust straight, go to Memphis, my ceremony, and go back to Lydia. Lydia.

I left Gepetto's vehicle not far from where I'd found it parked along the Elysiana Canal, and I took the gas can that was still in the back seat, and went to the small shack Serpent had taken me to, days before.

There, I chatted with the Jeddy fellow, who wore a peaked hat and many necklaces this day, and still the filthy red jumpsuit. I reminded him how Serpent had sung to him, and that Serpenthead and I were very good friends—saying these things, I missed Serpent, mightily, and wondered if he'd made it. I told Jeddy all he asked about the Ginger. Finally, he sold me the untaxed, illegal, compos fuel, which I paid for with the last of the money Camille gave me.

And at that moment, on the edge of the Basin, beside the Elysiana Canal, I made the resolution I would not ever see Camille again, or have anything of hers again, and though this thought gouged a great hole in my chest, so that I didn't believe I could ever breathe, I managed to march across the Quarter and find Serio's boat tied to the bollard. Exactly where we'd left it.

And, as I headed home, all that had happened in the Far East seemed to fade—that horrible Sim, that wild band. As if everything that had happened since I'd come to the Sunken Quarter almost a week before, had been a dream, and now I had awakened.

*I*t was close to sunset. The canal stank, and dogs barking from their roofs seemed to have organized a chorus: when one led off with a howling tune, the others yelped in response. The noise of generators blended with talk and laughter. Some of the squatters were sitting outside on the decks and terraces. The dwellings in general seemed ramshackle and temporary. Anyone living here must re-evaluate his circumstances every season, I thought, and discuss with his neighbors other possibilities—houseboats, dry land up north outside of enclave territory. I saw some of the women smoking in the dark, I smelled meat grilling. One of them called out to me, "Hey, cut that off," meaning my motor, "Can't you see we're living here?" Then, "What you want boy? What you looking at?"

It was almost as if nothing had happened in the last one hundred and twenty five years—I was aware of history, now, I hadn't been when I was a boy—I knew what things looked like long ago, in the dark times, the Pre-Reveal. A few children waved at me, delighted by Serio's boat, assuming I found it exciting to be steering a weather-worn vessel through the canals and swamps and flooded houses that a great city had come to. They thought this was an adventure—I knew the feeling. But I was tired of adventure.

There was something glistening and sweet, though, about this place and how these citizens clung to it. I had not seen it when I was a boy, either. I had not even seen it a few days before when I had come this way with Serpenthead. But now I felt what life was like before, when all were on the same watery, unsteady footing, when everyone knew that things could change in an instant, that all was vulnerable, not some completely vulnerable and some not vulnerable at all. When the moment could impinge upon people, bring them along, when that was common—it had been more like that here in this part, in the DE-AX, than anywhere else, the U.A., or anywhere, Lazarus had told me once. Which is why they let him alone here to start his little home. They did not molest him for his antique beliefs, for taking in toss-out children, a salvage operation, as the U.A. world saw it. This was a place on the edges, as they saw it, where what was past could be discarded, forgotten, ignored, occasionally visited for the thrill of the exotic. A place with the fortune, or curse, of not-mattering.

I passed the last occupied house. The only sight then, besides the water and the trees, were the peaks of old roofs of houses nobody could live in anymore. Then I saw, across the way, ruins of the bridges and the smokestacks of old industries Serpenthead had shown me, metal scaffoldings and towers that were part of the old ports. When they were out of sight, I felt more alone than I ever had, for some reason.

At a point on the Tchoupitoulas Trench, I came in upon a cinderblock floodwall with great brown-orange rusted iron gates, where I thought the Foundling House should be. At first I didn't realize what it was, and looked around for the old brick circumference, the original wall of the cloistered nunnery, that Lydia had spoken of. Then I realized the old barrier was inside a new one, for I could make out the high tower of the chapel poking out above the enclosure. When I steered in near enough to look over, I saw the new retainer was necessary—the height of the water in the Trench was easily seven feet above the level of the earth in the play yard. There was the old sign, in case I had any doubts:

AUDUBON FOUNDLING HOUSE.
LAZARUS DE GOLD, FOUNDER.

I called over the top of the white blocks, "Marilee? Marilee?"

No one came.

I tied the boat onto one of the rusty loops of rebar that formed a crude ladder sticking out of the mortar between the concrete blocks. I climbed up on these, crawled over. There were wide ponds on the grounds inside, and innumerable puddles. Along the paths, bright blade-shaped leaves of pink caladiums were still vigorous despite the standing water.

As soon as I was in the old yard, I remembered being a boy. No—I *was* a boy. The things around me were solid, and in possession of their own spirit, their own mystery—the veined pink leaves, the tall complicated oaks with their hollows, and low branches, the big magnolia trees with their crotches, for climbing and snoozing and hiding in. Even the inanimate things had life—one swing was more ambitious than another, it could take you up so high you could see over the old wall, another kept you down—

I saw one antique swing set in a corner: it had been meticulously disassembled.

Then I recalled the day I went to work as a child, the day Lazarus told me my life wasn't real, for years my it was going to be shadows—my real life, would be later.

I should have felt elation, to be returning. I felt some dread.

What was he going to tell me now?

IV

6:00 PM October 17, 2121
Audubon Foundling House, Audubon Island
New Orleans Islands, Northeast Gulf De-Accessioned Territory,
U.A. Protectorate

"*H*ello, anyone here? Marilee?" I called again.

At the sight of a certain tree I used to climb, actually, a bush—a crape myrtle—I flashed on Ariel sitting up in it, and I imagined I saw Vee as he was in the old days, standing at the back door, with the bread he used to bake, or a plate of his cellophane noodles. I entered the empty hall— tile floors and high, arched doorways—and more memories came back. Above my head, the murals I'd forgotten, of the "Sights of Audubon Island and the Museum City," that Lazarus had us paint one summer when he thought we could develop ourselves, and become "creative." It was one of a million schemes meant to save us. Fondly I recalled a few others. We would become a twenty-seven piece band, we would learn to sew costumes for the shops in the Sunken Quarter, we would become upholsterers and drapers and carpenters for the Heir homes inside the Museum City, which were always being redecorated, redesigned.

"Can it be Malcolm?" Marilee appeared in the woody darkness of the interior hall. It was at the sound of her voice that I finally felt I was not in some dream, but was home.

"It's you!" she said. As I came closer, she added, "What are those stitches in your ear? So thin! Hungry? Something to eat?"

I said I'd run into trouble in Port Gramercy. I would describe my

exploits in the morning. I needed to eat something, but what? With Mo
Lion I'd only managed broth. It was hard to think of food, at this point.
  "Is Vee—?"
  "Not here." Marilee shook her head.
  "Still with Ginger?" I counted back how many days since the
Miramar Arena.
  "Well then you know about that, very sad, very sad," she said, her
face buckling. She looked away. "Come into the kitchen." She looked
down then, to mind her steps in the dark hall. She was past middle age
now—this shocked me. There was a time when I would have thought
the sight of her ugly—women Yeareds were said to be the ugliest. But I
didn't find her so now, the opposite.
  "I met Tamara," I said. "Saw Ginger, Naroh—"
  "How were you there? You were there?" She came alive.
  "I ran into some fellows in the Quarter, who were going to work—I
didn't know the Sim, the—"
  "How was she at the end? Ginger?"
  "Strong," I realized it as I said it.
  "He told me the crowd was very ugly. He told me they came on the
stage, wanted an encore—"
  "We beat them back," I said. "Why didn't you go?"
  "Lazarus would have been alone. He's not well. Have you not heard?
So I decided to stay. And the way, the stage—neither of us wanted it.
Naroh her husband, and the younger ones on the Council, and Ginger
herself, she wanted it." She was leading me back to the kitchen, through
the old dining hall. The absence of the sounds of children, the emptiness,
had begun to sadden me.
  The shades were drawn, and the tables had been stacked in the
corners, ends up. "He's fired all the rest of the staff. I didn't think I
could—abandon him right now—"
  "Exactly why did they—"
  "Sell the tickets? Do the Sim Verite?" The kettle was already on the
stove, over a tiny purple flame. She liked to keep it on low, I remembered,
fondly, but not let it go out. She got up and went to it, and began to
prepare two cups of tea. With her back turned, she said, "I think she
wanted to be a sacrifice. She was going to so-long—that was already
known. So why not give something back? Give to the community?
This is what she said to me." She shook her head, coming toward me
again. She was smaller than I remembered. Her hair was still black and
in several thick braids, but there were a few unruly white hairs near her

temples. There was a long window in the kitchen. The sun was low now, and it streamed in between us through the long window. She sat down, propped her cheek on one hand. "We never wanted her to be on display. Vee's first wife died of the same thing—that was how he came to marry me. It was so tragic, that we should go through this again—and then have Ginger's illness a cause, an entertainment—"

"Tamara, and Naroh, and I—we got her away from the crowd, eventually. She was just with the family. At the end, we got the Heirs off the stage." I saw the pain in her face. "We don't have to talk about it."

"No, it's all right. You handled Heirs?" she asked, snorting a bit, to take it all in, then waving her fingers over her cup. "Well, I understand it was an extreme situation, everyone says so. Stories have gotten out. WELLFI Securitas is going to '*crack down, on Verite,*' the whole practice. But of course, if it goes on in the DE-AX, it will only be talk. The Heirs get their earthly delights. This place just exists for their variety." Her breathing changed. I realized she might cry. She managed to ask, "Anything else?"

"Tea is fine," I said. "Just sugar. A little sugar—I had to touch them. The Heirs."

She shook her head. "It is over now. What were we supposed to do? Our enclave, people can leave, it's not closed like the Free Wheel Charters. Those with wealth went years ago. Joined the Heirs, when they could do that, or sneaked into Brazil or Mexico to work in the bute refineries, or in construction. So we have little, so little, we have to sell whatever we have that is useful to them, you boys had to do the same—it is the way the world is now."

"What did you think we sold?"

Her eyes were tiger's eyes, golden brown. She shrank them. "I thought it was terrible. I remember that day Jeremy marched you off over the ring levee, to the Sim tents. Those transparent clothes they made you wear. I had cleaned you up, washed your head, combed out your nits. I was hopeful for you, but sorry. I thought you were lucky, but I when I hugged you goodbye, you were trembling. Ariel was more sensitive, he couldn't even bear it—you were tougher, or you were the better actor. "

"Lazarus said—"

"I was sorry that you would have to turn your childhood into—you had to act being the child. You couldn't be the child. At least Ginger knew what she was about. We thought there was no other way. Then, at the last minute, Lazarus had an idea. He heard about it." She tilted her head to one side, as if she had decided something, stopped for a moment, took a sip of the tea, which was dark green.

"Can I see him? There's a problem." It was not the custom for anyone to barge in on Lazarus. Marilee would have to announce me, and Lazarus would have to give his permission for me to come in. I felt the old formalities of the house still pertained, even though there were only three people in it.

She breathed quickly. "You should rest first," she said. She sipped more tea. "He is sleeping."

There was something in how she said it, a low melody in her voice, which betrayed exhaustion and an appeal to our old relationship—times she would comfort me, give me soup when I was sick. She was pleading in a way. But I had to ignore it. "I have to see him now." She was confused by how my tone had changed.

She turned her cup from the front to the side to the back, pretending to admire the design. It was a scratched-in bamboo stalk and leaf. She had seen it a million times, so had I. She was avoiding me. "Not right now," she said.

"What is it?" I asked.

She paused for a long breath, began, "Last spring, when he decided he couldn't keep the house going, he signed up for a Re-description— you know this? They did quite a job. He's been back a month and a half, and he hasn't evened out yet. We are worried about him."

"What is his new—?"

"I don't know—rugged sportsman, lots of adventures, a safari type, man's man. He has an inch wide mustache." She almost smiled, mimicking the pinch of the thing under her nose, with two fingers.

"Lazarus?"

"They did the tests, and decided that was a good translation for him." She shrugged. "But it is not taking well. Sometimes, the old personality is too rigid, it doesn't give way, no matter the number of memories and probes they use to program. He's having troubles, not sleeping, and then he takes pills, and once he took too many. He is supposed to shed his old biography. He says he doesn't want to! Or he can't! In fact, quite the opposite. He's obsessed with it. Maybe he's afraid he will forget. That's why I couldn't be with Ginger. I had to stay with him. He's very erratic. Ariel thought so too, when he was here."

"Ariel was here? What did the WELLFI judge say? Did he tie up my money? My Trust?"

She pulled her shoulders out of the position of the conversation, at that point. She wasn't huddled with me anymore. I thought it had to do with Ariel's perfidy. She had helped him—she often took his side— "Ariel?" she asked. "He was here." She nodded, and all the wild white hairs at her temples caught the low light.

Marilee was hiding something. I pressed. "Yes, Ariel. What did he do with my accounts? Do you know anything about this? Did the courts freeze them? Just let me see Lazarus. Just let me—"

"Wait, Malcolm," she said. "Just wait. You can have the old attic room—or can you even stand up in there now? You have gotten so tall. Why don't you sleep?" She looked outside. It was a rose and gold sky, flaming out before dark. "Go see him in the morning."

"Please, what is it? Did Lazarus fight with him? What about my Trust?" My voice was my voice when I was a boy, when I wasn't ready to go to sleep. "Has it been decided? I am not eligible? Is that the story?" I was willing to take the truth, to learn that it had been settled.

She put her hand down and held her lips tight. "I don't know of these things," she said.

"Yes you do."

"What is it?" she asked, slightly defiant.

"There is some kind of lien on my Trust. Is it because they say I came from an enclave? I'm not qualified? In Ariel's suit to run his own Trust, they had to look up our origins, he told me—"

Her eyes closed. She did not say anything else. She wasn't going to answer. Her nose moved downward, too—it was part of the sealing up of her face, which I remembered she'd do when we were boys and we'd tease her or make her mad. She looked younger, when she opened her eyes again. "Talk to Lazarus," she said. "I am not the one. But I can tell you I didn't have anything to do with your Trust. And Ariel was in and out, he came here for a few hours, then he went to Florida, to find records they have there—or something—"

"What do you know?" For some reason, for the first time, I had the feeling the whole thing had to do with something she knew, I just didn't see exactly how.

"Look, he can't be awakened. You could try, but he's on sleeping tablets. It's not going to happen. He will be out until morning. I dose him very carefully, we have to regulate his mood—"

I followed her down the hall.

"He distinctly told me, 'I can't let anyone see me like this,'" she repeated, and then she opened the door. "Go ahead. Look."

My guardian, my "father," was lying supine on the bench with the green cushion.

The mustache was almost funny. He had a healthy-looking new prodermis, orange-brown, a slight potbelly, which was exposed, as his robe had fallen open. His forearms were thick and resculpted, the wrists beautifully veined. Middle aged, not young, that was the look. There was a pen on the floor, near his hand. It sat on top of a group of papers spread out like a fan. His large-lettered handwriting, full of loops and flourishes, decorated every page I could see.

What had Lazarus been thinking? Or what had the doctors in Memphis been thinking? A man's man? An adventurer? It was as if he'd given up his will to the varietologists.

Then, the soft snore of an old, old man. A true Yeared. Where was my guardian?

"He's been writing, you see, it seems to calm him," Marilee said softly. "He was dosing himself with these pills to sleep. He took too many; we had to splash water in his face. Stand him up and force him to walk, to bring him around. Vee and I were very upset. Now I give them to him. He can't be roused, I know. At six, he will awake."

I defied her. I went to him, grabbed his thick arm—touched him, I didn't care. She was shocked. "Lazarus. Lazarus."

"Stop, please," she said.

He wouldn't wake. He was as limp as one of those hanging skins of Mo Lion's.

I followed her wishes—I had to. Full of questions, I closed the door.

V

7:00 AM October 18, 2121
Audubon Foundling House, Audubon Island
New Orleans Islands, Northeast Gulf De-Accessioned Territory,
U.A. Protectorate

I woke in the attic I had slept in as a boy, at dawn. The light came
in stripes through the jalousies, and across my thighs. That had not
changed. And neither had the noise—the cawing and whooping of the
birds announcing the morning on Audubon Island. Louder than ever
now, since the park had gone back to the wild. I was just as I was when
I was a boy—except I had been dreaming about Camille.

I lay still, paying attention to the tiny explosions all over my skin. I
could feel whirling movements passing from one spot to another, and
thought of them as exchanges among my busy cells, as a kind of business,
an economy. Behind my eyes, the buzzing of my brain—whirring, high
pitched. Once, Lazarus had told me that lying awake in bed was the
epitome of idleness. Rebellious, I lay there, listening, remembering. I
had the sense, and I wasn't in any way drunk, that every event in the
recent past fit into a pattern, that I was watching evolve.

I pushed it back. I thought of my Trust. Marilee knew something.

I crept down the stairs. It was so early the kitchen door was closed,
which meant Marilee wasn't yet up. I pressed my hand on Lazarus's tall
office door, and entered. I saw him—still apparently asleep, inside his
strange new physique.

I went to the desk, and was about to turn on the screen, to see
if I could break into the Home accounts, get some answers—when he
stirred—

"What? What?" His familiar rasp. "Malcolm? My lucky Malcolm? How is it? How are you? My one success?"

His tight Heir eyes smiled. They were more crusted over with crystals than usual—the silicon syrup, dried. He waved one of his new thick hands, wiped the sand out.

"It's okay," I said. "Success?"

"Oh, my, how can you ask? Isn't it your Boundarytime in a month?" Lazarus asked, rising into a sitting position, closing his satin robe. His old optimistic voice, the tone rising as if he had a joke. He was wide awake, ready to launch into a speech (because he'd been lying awake, in idleness). "Of course success. How can you ask that? You always did what you were told, always bore up under the worst, anything Jeremy or the audiences demanded, devised. I envied your, your—" He searched for the word. "Obedience, doggedness. How you never wavered. How you held to the principle, in face of everything—" He spread his arms out as if to hug me. "Prologue."

Of course I wouldn't come to him. It wasn't done, and I had to follow the rules, forget that wild night in the Far East, in Mississippi. And Mo Lion's madness. Lazarus was never one to breach decorum, to break taboos. Did he know of my adventure? Did he know how far I'd strayed? He couldn't.

"It's all right," he said. "The rules don't matter anymore. You want a hug? "

What did he mean *the rules don't matter anymore*? "I am fine," I said. "Not accustomed."

He put his arms down, and sized me up with his eyes

"You are just skin and bones, boy," he said. "Fasting for the—"

"Yes, and a rough journey," I said. I looked at him hard. Something was very off, wrong, besides his new strange skin.

"Well," he said, in expectation. "And the ear? What there?"

I minimized my encounter in Port Gramercy, didn't want to confess all my transgressions. My greatest sin, of course, was wanting to see a Nat girl. I wouldn't admit that if I didn't have to. He'd be so disappointed in me. I wasn't over the offered embrace. Why would he want to break a rule like that? So fundamental? I just blurted it out. "What's the issue with my Trust?"

He crossed his feet, folded his arms. His eyes scanned the room, as if he were looking for a prompt, a subject. Finally he asked, "How did you hear about that? I can explain."

Finally. Reality. My voyage behind me. "Yes, did Ariel do something to it? Show my background to the WELLFI officials? It's the courts, isn't it? How can we fight it?"

"Ariel?" Lazarus looked as if he couldn't quite make this question out. As if he had expected me to say something else.

"It's encumbered. It's claimed—"

"Ariel?" Lazarus repeated.

"That plan of his for taking over his Trust—"

"I didn't give Ariel anything, except my apology," Lazarus said, and sighed deeply. Then he stared at me. "He left, in a hurry, for Defuniak in Florida. He has some investigations. He believes you two have history there—or something—probably true—he located the archives, finally. You came from the West Florida Federation, he discovered that—" Then, rather abruptly, he fell silent.

Even for an Heir, it was a big pause. I could feel time actually creeping along, light changing in the room; I thought hours were passing us by. Finally, he unfolded his arms, so he looked more vulnerable, and then, he said it. "Okay. I promised your Trust, to Vee's enclave. I put all the accounts of the Foundling House in their hands—so they could go ahead and move. Before they drowned. I took your Trust and made it part of the guarantee to get Chef Menteur out of that water-logged— so they didn't have to go through with that monstrous exhibition. I couldn't bear it. I just couldn't—"

"You did what?"

"I put up—collateral. So they could move, build on higher ground. Not lose their option—"

My chair was leaning back on the desk, balanced on two legs. At the shock of this statement, I came forward; almost fell out onto the floor. I got up and stood against the desk, so I was looking down on him. "You did what? Vee? He doesn't—"

"Well they were going to drown when another surge came. We are going into another era like the one of the Great Storms—Katrina, Rita, Jerome, Isadora, Althea of 2016—you don't go back that far, but I do. There are five thousand in Chef Menteur; I suppose some have already gone on the Exodus by now. And there was what I had left in the Home's accounts and your Trust. That was my calculation. Vee didn't ask me. I did it on my own. It wasn't fair to you. I know." His voice sagged, scratchy but familiar. I played this voice in my mind all the time. To hear it saying such a thing, that he hadn't thought of me— "I know I am not the kind to do this sort of thing, and to steal, and to disappoint you, for I have disappointed you—I see it in your face."

"You? You took my Trust for them?"

"Ginger wasn't doing the so-long according to the prediction. Wasn't—on time. The Sim Verite wasn't going to come off in time for them to move—the option, the window, was expiring, so when Vee told me this, I—" It was so peculiar to see Lazarus this way, justifying himself. His falsely tan, thick face, his unblinking eyes, looked so awkward. "They were selling tickets to his own daughter's—think of it."

"I was there, I know what they were doing." I paused. "They made the money. They made it, the place was packed."

"Well then, she had a turn for the worse." Lazarus looked expectant, as if he were waiting for my approval. He was an Heir—he shouldn't ask me for approval. Then he said, "I am so terribly, terribly sorry you had to ever, ever, I never wanted you to ever, ever, witness—"

I ignored the apology. "Well then what?" I could feel something like an old armor, closing around. "What got into you? You would never do such a thing. Isn't, wasn't, my Trust close to mature, and wasn't it mine?" I felt a white fire, anger, thrusting in me in flashes, the way it had when I went at Gepetto. Strangle the little man inside this sack of a Hemingway? What did Mo Lion call these creatures? Bonesnakes? Was I a guerilla now? But I loved him; I knew that I loved him, at the same time as I came around toward him in anger. "What about me? What about the one who did everything the way you said?" I was shouting. "You handed my Trust to Chef Menteur? To diers?"

"I know I was wrong. I know I was wrong," was all he could mumble. "There was the possibility that Vee's people wouldn't need it, but it had to be there, to be their guarantee—What if the patrols stopped the Sim altogether? Was it awful—?"

I nodded. It had been horrible. But how could I agree?

"I know my gesture was completely wrong, as regards to you. Completely, it cannot be justified. And look—even that gesture was meaningless. She went ahead and what did you call it when you were boys? *Bit the black* for an audience. All my projects have been rather hollow. I believed in them all. I did. That's the irony of it, they turned out to be hollow."

"Don't call me hollow!" I was shouting.

He was startled for a moment, but then, quickly, he nodded, agreed, weakly, with that ridiculous new "handsome" face of his. "If they made their money that monstrous way, if Chef Menteur has its security, then, I can remove the pledge," Lazarus said. "It is ten minutes on the Net. But do you see how I might have felt I was right? Thousands were doomed?

Simple people, Vee and all his cousins? People we sort of love?" His airy voice went even lower. "You were the only success of your generation, all the rest have been set off roaming. I did them no good at all. Sometimes you feel you can make a decision that will save you—but it wasn't mine to decide. That one single move in a long life can set the whole of it right—a long long life. But can't you see, Malcolm? What I was thinking? I know it wasn't mine to decide."

I understood what he was thinking. But he was wrong to think it. He was wrong to think those things as I had—as I had been wrong to think I had a right to assault Heirs, to throw them off stages, to protect dying Nats at Heirs' expense. Which is what Lazarus had done: protected them at my expense.

After a silence, Lazarus asked, "Do you think you might ever forgive me? One day?"

The old order had to come back. It had to be one way or the other. He had to see. "You couldn't do this," I shouted at him, to clear my own confusion. "You going to go on now and liberate all the enclaves? Is that what this he-man body is about? You going to free them? Start a rebellion? Give all the Trusts out there to the cyclers so they can run them into the ground? Is that what you want me to do? Finally see the light and give everything to the diers? That's what it is now? I am not you. I am what you made me. I am stronger than you." I knew at the same moment that I had thought these things in the last few days. I had seen Mo Lion's part. These very things I was shouting at Lazarus about. I was having this argument with myself as much as with him. This fact enraged me more. I had not been stronger than these sympathies. I was ashamed. I had felt every one of them. I knew why Lazarus had done what he'd done. I remembered the moment when I realized the hooded father backstage was Vee and the sorrow in his face.

"Of course it isn't fair," Lazarus said. "I said I will put it back. I swear to you. As soon as I can get on the screens, get to the WELLFI Bank."

"You better," I threatened.

"I will, I will." Weary, exhausted.

I had to allow my heart to slow; I had to put aside enough fury to find what I wanted to say. Ultimately, I looked straight at Lazarus, began:

"I am your son. You told me never to give in and I didn't, and now—now, that is just what you do. Desert me. You told me to put off my very life, for now, for now—feel nothing—" It was another layer

of confusion: I was showing him my feelings, which was something he
taught me never to do. "You said I could iron it all out later—"

"I told you that?" He seemed surprised, horrified.

"You told me I was supposed to postpone—I was supposed to—"
I was angrier about this than the Trust, really. I backed away, toward
the diamond-paned windows in the alcove that surrounded the desk.
If I got too close, the anger would magnetize me, draw me to hit him.
Something in me wanted to kill him. I didn't know what he could do
and not do, anymore. I hated it, that I loved my anger. "You told me
to put my life into the Trust. I am waiting to live now because of you.
Because of you, I am still waiting—" I started forward again. "Don't
give me that expression, as if you deserve no blame—" *You are speaking
to Lazarus,* I told myself, but it didn't help.

Lazarus covered his head with both of his orange-tan arms and a
strange sound came from him, gravelly, and slightly like a horn. I had
no idea what was going on. The oddness of it. I wasn't sure the sound
was coming from him, even. I hated it. I despised this man. More than
I had Gepetto, and in the same way. For not being what he said he was.
For not apologizing for his false life.

I became aware of a line, only just vaguely aware. On the other side
of it, was cruelty. I went up to it, right up to it. I did not know which
self—the armored boy I once was, or the other new one—would cross
over. I was so furious I couldn't distinguish. One part of my heart,
against the other part. "You destroyed my life," I said, finally.

"But you are fine, you are alive," he said, trying to be happy.

"You told me, *not yet!*" I said.

His old eyes flashed up at me. "Your Trust will be back. I'll put Dr.
Greenmore in charge, how about that? She'll keep Ariel's lawyers away,
your record sealed. She has a thousand times the influence I could ever
have." He paused, looked pitiful. "I don't know anymore what I believe.
You are right. I am not to be trusted. Right to be furious, even. We live
a very long time, but we are not gods—we think we are, but we are as far
from it—every day we get farther—all this time doesn't even make us
wise! I thought I was wise but I wasn't!"

I said, "You have to believe in what you told me." In the fury of this,
I saw all the things I would have done differently if he had released me,
let me go—told me he was wrong. I saw for a moment Camille's wide
eyes, looking up at me, from the bottom of the jail stairs, there to free
me. Free me. I needed—a core, a center, a constant sense. One heart,
not two.

I wanted to kill Lazarus. I really wanted to kill him. I had never met that much rage within me, never—
I left, so I wouldn't try.

*

"He keeps saying these things," Marilee complained when she came back from Lazarus's office holding the luncheon plate he had not touched: elegant brown brosias. Tucked under her arm was a slim folder—I wondered if it were some paper records of my accounts she put there on the kitchen table where I sat. "That his efforts have come to nothing— that if you live long enough you are there to see everything you have built go back to ruin. Things fall apart." She paused, looked forlorn for a moment, continued, "He came back from his Re-description, and everything was all right for a few days—we were sending the last children off, doing the best we could. Then he started saying he didn't want to be somebody new, it was all posturing, costuming, without meaning. He said who could be fooled by such hocus pocus? Two-hundred-year-olds were supposed to believe in these charades, this programming? Take on a new personality? The drugs and probes were supposed to erase it all? He grabbed me—grabbed me! It was in the hall one night. He asked me, 'We are just this? This shallow? That's what they think?' He said perhaps we could build up the foundling house again. I said we could get more orphans—the boys might be as fine as you and Ariel. I said we could start over. But there is no money of course. Where were the Trusts going to come from? From putting them out to be Altered? Lazarus deplores the surgeries. Money was a question, but there are always more orphans, the enclaves throw them out all the time, it hasn't stopped, I told him. We could round up a group in a week, if he'd allow it. I could go out in the boat or to the U.A. border and find ten in two days, I told him. Then he asked us about our family. He had never asked before, like that. We told him about Ginger—what they were doing with her cancer on the Undernet, gathering an audience, a fan base. It really set him off. He insisted he would do something, so we wouldn't have to 'Put on that horrible display,' but we said we had no choice, we'd been advertising it for a year—" Her shoulders relaxed. "But then one morning over two weeks ago—he told us the guarantee was there—" She nodded, vigorously. "We shouldn't wait. We should move."

"He used my Trust. If Ginger hadn't—my Trust would have been spent. You knew, didn't you?"

"I suspected,when I heard him talking to bank officials. But Vee had gone to tell Ginger not to go through with the show—I didn't ask questions."

"What do you think?" I asked.

"I think, I think," she said and looked down, at her own small breasts, then back up at me—as if she were asking her heart for the answer. "I think Ginger should not have put her—she should not have been their show. Horrible. I think exactly as my husband thinks. And I also think that your money is yours and Chef Menteur has no right to it."

"Even if you would drown without it?"

"Don't make me answer that," she said. "I have to believe in my own life."

"So do I," I said.

I decided I would go back in, and talk to Lazarus about his life. I would do this for myself, so I could see, and so I could understand, and I was going to listen, not yell. I was waiting for self-control. It wasn't easy to muster, anymore.

Marilee was going on. "Ginger said she wanted to give her so-long meaning. She had her wish—the enclave will do well, it will have a start—and what more can we ask? The land they have given us is very high ground, with pines. We are supposed to start settling in two days, going north, all the transports. The boats will go up the Pearl River. We can make our gardens again, without the saltwater killing them. We can put in the dams. All this is very good. But you should have what you worked for," she said. "Lazarus was right *and* wrong. He has been writing this." She handed me the folder that had been tucked under her arm. "Why don't you figure out what he's been going through? Read it now, before he gets here."

"Who gets here?"

"Ariel, coming today," she smiled.

Always was her favorite.

VI

My Life, Beginning With the Early Pfiswell Trials, In Short When It's Been Very Long, Very, Very Long—

I was born in 1920, spent my earliest years in the first optimism of last century's profligate plasti-materialism, saw war, saw one wife, Rachel, die, married a second, Alexis, much younger, with whom I had children in the late 1960's, boys, who wanted me to live forever, so they said. Who wouldn't? I was a rich doctor, good-looking, sixty, young seeming when I first heard of the Albers trials. I had big gas cars, a house with thousands and thousands of square feet. Life was very good. I had contacts in the medical field, people who said the new longevity science was solid. Albers, a genius. I heard through the grapevine that he wasn't going to go public with any of it; put it out into the refereed journals—I could see why he wanted it to be proprietary. It could be a goldmine, after all. And of course he needed human subjects. I paid a million—imagine, a million! What I could do now with the equivalent!—to go to a seminar. I heard what they had to say. I knew they wouldn't kill me. It was a huge investment. You had to be at least forty—mature, very sane, to get into the program. Some as old as sixty-eight got in. I could afford it. I thought I'd try. I didn't even tell my wife, because she was too young to do it. I said I was going to a study course in London, in my specialty, cardiology.

So I went in, went under—they put you into a coma for two weeks then for the RNA interferences. The surgeries were hard, the nano-monitors. But I came back good as new, invigorated, though I'd had my balls replaced with neuticals, and had to go to an analog testosterone. The first thing anyone noticed was that my hair stopped turning gray. My boys thought my secret was that I ran, ate the right diet, and looked fifty at sixty-five, *then at seventy, then at seventy-five. I wasn't running. I faked that too. I jogged out of the driveway, and then hid in a culvert in the park.*

Alexis didn't know. She had her questions, as I could perform, but not exactly in the same way. But she didn't ask too much of me. I was the doctor. I had the answers. She knew she'd married an older man. The probes, the enhancers, all that hadn't been invented. This was still the dark ages.

My boys were the ones who couldn't get over it—in the nineteen nineties, I still looked fifty. By then the Albers techs had decided we needed prodermises, because of the UV, and the lack of fat. I got one that looked aged. I appeared to be perhaps sixty-five, finally, in the year 2000. I was eighty. We had to get these prodermises ordered, custom detailed in Malaysia. Each tiny hair was "invaginated" into the fatty layer back then. Even at that, of course, the hairs didn't grow. I pretended to shave.

When Alexis was old enough, I explained it all to her. I remember that night. I took her to the beach, Rehoboth, in Delaware. It was winter. People still enjoyed the beach back then, they weren't afraid of it. We were on the boardwalk, the wind was hard—I told her we could do this forever, and she said she didn't understand. And I said forever, again and she heard me out but refused to believe it. When we got home, I had to show her the place where my prodermis had its seam in the crack of my ass—they weren't behind the ears then, the seams—I showed her the way she could pull my hair and I didn't feel a thing. "Let's see you really," she said then. "Let's see you really. You have been hiding?" she asked. "I knew you were hiding from me, hiding, you have always been hiding—" She pounded on my chest. But in the end, she went in to get it done—she was too late for the trial, I had to bribe them. But it turned out she had ovarian cancer, early stage. So she was not a candidate. We did not win that war. I felt great grief about all the years when our love had been synthetic, when I pretended my ecstasy. It was the first true grief I felt on account of my commitment to the trials, my transformation.

I could hardly bear burying my second wife. I remember my boys at the funeral, though, were less grieved than amazed, or perhaps, dismayed, by my vigor. I still looked far too young, regardless of how well "distressed" the prodermis was. "You always look the same, Dad," they said to me. It was hard to seem frail, hard to fake it. Some members of the First Wave trial just staged their own deaths and went off and lived in some other country, passing for young, marrying one woman and then another, sneaking back in every year for checkups, the rough, early Re-jobs, with Albers. I heard about this but I thought it would be lonely, I thought I would miss my sons. So I kept up appearances. There was the great difficulty of pretending to eat, and not eating. Pretending to have functions you didn't have, appetites you didn't have. There were no decent brosias then. You just had to scatter your plate. If you did eat anything significant, except the vitamins on the regimen, they would kick you out of the trial. It was hard, a great challenge. But most made it. The major problem was the loneliness. There were almost no women in the same cohort, except wives, at least not any I knew of. Pfizwell—Albers' company—didn't give us too much to go on, in terms of helping us contact each other. We were all underground. They thought it would be better that way.

Of course it was fun to travel, to do everything you had ever wanted to do in life. But eventually I learned that there are only so many things in this world, only so many pleasures in this universe, which bring you happiness when you are alone. The number is not infinite.

"What's your secret father?" my sons asked. "How did you find the Fountain of Youth?" It was getting lonely—so many acquaintances died. I didn't know how much longer I could go on, but then the Reveal was announced. That was my hope. I could meet my cohorts. For four years, we waited until all the data was in, all of us were examined over and over, by doctors who knew about the trials and doctors who didn't. This was all very clandestine. This issue of our health was a distraction from the loneliness. We were all followed around, our intimates interviewed. Albers' agents were given the same leeway as the FBI. My sons even asked me if I were involved in something illegal. I just told myself to wait. To hold on. Eventually the Reveal would come down, which I thought would be our liberation. We could share our secret with the world. Make the whole world immortal—just like us.

I told my sons a few days before the trip to Washington. They were flabbergasted, and curious, amazed. But most of all, angry.

I thought at most there would be a few thousand—

But Pfizwell had over four hundred thousand in the trial. A group of senators who were all in Pfizwell's employ, it turned out, as was the President, who ran the country then, and his father, and all his cabinet. They made the announcement, said that it was one of the greatest events in the history of the world, greater than walking on the moon or finding America or penicillin or flight. And they marched out the specimens— men who were chronologically close to one hundred ten, who were physically fifty. We all left our distressed prodermises at home, and came out with fresh cultured ones, which used our own DNA—Albers' team had finally perfected the process—and we looked terribly natural. If you call "natural" how we look today. No sign of aging, all the doctors announced, inside or out. My boys saw me on—they were called TVs then. I thought now I would be free of the isolation, the weariness of keeping the secret so long. Now that the trials were public, our medical histories and conditions were clear—that we had stopped aging, my stock in Pfizwell soared, broke every known record. I was terribly rich.

I gave my sons some stock, and soon they were comfortable. They settled down, got married, and had children quickly. Saul was a lawyer and he was doing well. There were many suits between couples, where one was Treated and the other not—many more men than women had been done. There was a whole new area of the law—a new kind of breach of contract, of grounds for divorce. I told my sons they could be Treated. Access was open. I could pay, I told them. What more can a man give his children than this long long long long long, possibly infinitely extended life? I thought that would make them happy. "You are as rich as gods," Archie said. He always had some disdain for me, for my judgment. He was the artist. You are guinea pig gods," he said. But when it was time to be Treated, he got Treated.

I did what I could for the others in my family. And so did most of our cohort, those who hadn't hidden out in other countries, divorced and disowned their relatives somewhere along the way. We were incredibly rich. The giddiness of the predictions was absurd, in retrospect. The whole world would be immortal, the Pfizwell-owned newspapers and the Net declared. The horrible burden of death finally lifted from mankind. All the strain upon the natural resources, all the difficulties caused by disease and by debilitation, over. That was the official version. We could plan to live between two and six hundred years, they said. But in two hundred years, even a hundred years, we certainly would have the mechanisms to live even longer, and then, even longer. Our lives expanding and expanding, like rubber bands. And we would just have to limit population growth, which would be a natural outcome of the Treated process, which required sterilization. The argument went—why reproduce when you will live on and on yourself? Pfizwell, Albers's personal corporation, had already expanded to WELLFI, and WELLFI merged with the banks, holding companies, media. All the laws to keep things separate had been overruled by the government, which was controlled, entirely, within a few years— more than we had ever imagined possible-by WELLFI's interests. There were millions and millions Treated over the next eighteen years. WELLFI encouraged it—the Trust system was set up, the contracts for perpetual care, the warranties. WELLFI knew it needed a statistical majority

Treated. As long as it was the United States. It was still a democracy, then, and without a majority Treated, there could be problems. Cheap offers, easy access—it was never as cheap again to buy in. The rule was set that the earliest you could be Treated was twenty-six, and the maximum was forty-five. This staggered the pace a bit, so it took almost two decades for the great bulk who could afford it to be Treated.

Around 2030, we started to notice that numbers who could be in the elite, had started to dwindle. People blamed the single-focus economy. There were no investments in any other area beside Treatedness, and upkeep of Heirs, and lifestyle research for Heirs. The non-Heirs— still a majority, then, but just barely—began to get anxious. Their life expectancy was dropping and dropping. We could all see it coming, before it actually happened, but once the economy was so single-pointed, and so shrunken, the task of developing anything else seemed so big—after all, we were just individuals, what could we do? The system broke down. I had grandchildren. My Trust was where my money was now tied up—mine, that is, and my sons' Trusts, and their wives' Trusts. I couldn't afford to pay for my grandchildren. They started calling it the Manic Depression— inflation, deflation, inflation again. WELLFI tried a series of policies, each one more disastrous than the last. I started to realize around then, I think, that WELLFI's policy toward those Untreated, regardless of what their propaganda said, was to let them die off, so they could just grab the political majority. Suddenly there was no money, except in the Trusts. WELLFI itself had to diversify—its own investments weren't growing enough. It had to start investing in fugue capitalist states, overseas. About this time, the tide shifted—all our laws were to accommodate the ease of the Treated strat, the wealth and leisure of our strat. That was when they coined that ugly word, "strat." "Class" not even "caste," was sufficient for the "magnitude of the difference," so they said. There were more than a hundred million who had never been able to afford being Treated, and all our own children couldn't, now, afford it. That didn't matter somehow. All that mattered was that our "strat" kept its privileges.

My grandchildren were Lucian, Michael, and Jennifer. I couldn't do anything for them. It broke my heart. They couldn't even live decently— they had no money, couldn't get jobs, even though we managed education, which cost two million— that was all we could manage. Some of my fellow First Wavers said the young Nyets—our children—were selfish and unthinking, didn't respect what we had sacrificed, had brought forth on this continent, this new age, this supreme gift. The problems in this world as far as my "strat" were concerned were these: having enough variety, and finding ways to remain excited by life when you were a hundred and ten years old in the approximate body of a forty-five-year-old, or finding ways to have sex that felt like sex, and love that felt like love, and food that tasted like food. The great Untreated saw the world differently, obviously. VERY DIFFERENTLY. Then, I guess, it was about 2044, the potential Third Wave, my own grandchildren, stopped playing nice—even at the time, I didn't blame them—

VII

7:15 PM October 18, 2121
Audubon Foundling House, Audubon Island
New Orleans Islands, Northeast Gulf De-Accessioned Territory,
U.A. Protectorate

*T*he pages just ended there, I wanted more—I was fascinated, for I'd never known about Lazarus's root self. He had always said it didn't matter. I had been told that, when I went through my Boundarytime, I would see that light, too—that the past didn't count, what I'd been, once I became an Heir. Another lie, for he had not forgotten a bit of his own story. If I hadn't been so angry at him, I would have barged in to ask him questions—but I was afraid of what I would do—but just then, in the yard:

"What? What? Vee? Yoo-hoo!" Ariel's liquid baritone. "Anyone at home? Anyone?"

The first thing I saw was the black bandana. Then I saw he was wearing the smile he used to have when he was six—a too-big smile, wide and face-stretching—dating back to before he'd met O. I watched him descend the ladder of rebar loops poking out of the concrete wall— his long narrow legs, his slouchy shoulders. After the last step, he had to jump. When he landed, his feet slapped and splashed the muddy ground.

He rushed up and grabbed me by the shoulders, in a gesture not of anger, or competition, but of delight. In my ear, "Brother," he said. "I need to see Lazarus, alone, for a little—then we will talk. I have the secrets of the universe!"

Secrets of the universe and he was going to make me wait to hear them? He galloped off, to Lazarus's office, but said to me, "Fifteen minutes. Wait for me."

I had met him in the entry hall, near the old closed-off dining hall. I went in and found the sill of the double windows where we used to conceal ourselves during hide and seek. I used to sit there sometimes when I wanted to think. Remain alive, but not be part of the world. I climbed in, or tried to. I sat in the old spot, facing into the dining area, too leggy now to close the wooden gates. But it was almost the same as before. Ariel was with Lazarus a long time. I could hear their voices, but not the words.

I listened to other sounds echoing in the house. Vee arrived, back from having buried his daughter. I had heard Marilee tell him something, and then I heard him go in and talk to Lazarus. Ariel was still in there. Vee went in, and he came out. I heard him say to Marilee on the stairs, "Lazarus used Malcolm's Trust. Malcolm's! "

"He knows," Marilee said.

"Where is he?"

I did not come out.

"I don't know," she said. "He must have gone out into the garden."

"I'll find him after I rest, I can hardly stand," Vee said with great weariness in his voice.

It was getting to be dark.

I heard Ariel call my name one time.

And then, I think, he figured it out.

He came to find me—he didn't even ask what I was doing there.

"Lazarus is in an awful mood, you spoke to him?" he asked me, and then he shrugged. "Marilee said there was some drug for it. Do you want dinner? I brought all sorts of goodies. Those Gaists in Florida can cook."

I shook my head no. I was still fasting, I insisted he should know this, but I came down into the kitchen anyway. I had been fasting for so long now food seemed impossible, in fact. I couldn't believe I had ever eaten it. Tea was my mainstay. I could also take broth—it was the smooth, bright part of the fast. I had no interest in thickening up things now.

Ariel's hair was unwashed as ever. He had a spindly beard, even more unkempt than the last time I'd seen him, and a remarkable tan. When he came into the kitchen, he slung his hand-sewn black sack onto the back of a chair, started digging into it and brought out a great many canned and jarred foods—fish, fruits, delicacies from the Gaists of Defuniak Shores, where he'd been visiting. Some of these were in recycled glass jars, and some were from smugglers who brought in tins from the free Caribbean islands, he said. He had mussels, stuffed olives, smoked oysters, canned claws of crab. He opened a half dozen with little keys shaped like the letter T, rolled back the tops, and offered them to me. Of course I said no.

"Getting that little shrunken Heir stomach?" he asked, teasing me. "What fun is that?"

I knew the flavors of the delicacies—hearts of palm, anchovies—were intense. Too intense.

"You'll shrink yours too when the time comes," I said.

"We'll see," he said.

I explained what Lazarus had really done. Then I asked him how his Trust was.

"Well, that can all be rethought, maybe," Ariel said, nodding his head assertively, "because everything we think could be wrong." He looked about, as if to see if there were other listeners, and then settled his gaze upon me again. "I'm just now wrapping my head around it—what I learned in Florida—" His eyes were glistening. He was like he was when we were little, when he was explaining the fancy rules of some mad game he'd just invented, as I said, the way he was before he met O. He assumed I knew what it was about. "That charm—you said you had the key, what was that?" I asked.

"Listen—" He spread his fingers apart a few inches above the wooden table. "There were hold outs. They had their own ideas—*status quo ante* ideas. They didn't sign anything. They didn't recognize the U.A. Never—"

"So we weren't in an enclave? That makes me an Outliar? That makes us—?"

Ariel continued. "There was a conflict within the West Florida Federation about five years before we were born, two factions. Some were willing to sign on in enclaves. Others were standing with a researcher named John of Pensacola—the main one. We come from his band. That's the start of what I found out." He reached down inside his sack and retrieved and opened another tin. Mussels this time. Orange and green in their sauce, I saw, when he turned back the lid. "You have to try these," he said, nodding.

"Did you say *John of Pensacola*?" I asked, pinching up one, and putting it back—it was greasy, shimmering. Why was I even touching these? "What, our parents were in his band?"

"That's tricky. Let's go back a few years. The leaders of this place were the scientists from the labs in Defuniak. They worked for WELLFI's interests—they were subsidiaries. But they were becoming too independent. Hated the bans on research. They also didn't like the strat laws, hated the anti-mixing. They wanted to make Treatments cheaper—or, really, they wanted them to be unnecessary." At that strange idea, he shifted his eyes away, and then back, as if he needed to find support for such a claim on the highest shelves of the kitchen, or in my eyes. For myself, I wanted to be blasé, but I couldn't. "Albersian treatments were a crude method, something more elegant could be developed, that was their line. Genetically. Genetically. They felt they had found the gene for aging, for dying. They were looking for some cure that didn't need to be updated every two years. But of course, this would mean, something that wouldn't make the Protos and the First Wave any more money. The U.A. wasn't having that." He shook his head so hard his dirty hair flew round. "Some alternative to the Albers' Method? Never. Eventually, WELLFI shut down the lab, accused them of smuggling, piracy, selling WELLFI secrets to foreign entities. In fact, they were selling their genetic therapies for Nat diseases to clinics all over the world. That was why Lazarus didn't want anybody to know where we came from. He was afraid we would somehow be found out, and harm would come to us—I mean, he resisted until just lately, when he said I could see whatever I wanted to see—I mean, just a few months ago, after I ran into you over on St. Charles? He switched his policy, I guess."

"He seems to have been changing a lot lately," I said.

"WELLFI was livid about these renegade researchers. They were persecuted. I see that now, even more than when he tried to explain it last week." Ariel squinted, which he sometimes did when he wanted you to know he meant what he said. "I'm not furious. Not with him. The prejudice against anyone associated with West Florida still exists—on this last trip I encountered it, everywhere I went. Rebels. Smugglers—"

Ariel got up and put more of the contents of his sack onto the table. He was looking for a particular tin or jar. He lined up one whole row, and then dug down again. Finally, he pulled up some fat peaches stuffed in a jar as round as a ball, pried off the paraffin-sealed top, and offered them to me. I knew they were very sweet, with that thick chewy suede-like skin. I couldn't remember the last time I ate a peach. Yet, it would be hard to start, so I resisted. He shrugged. Sorry for me.

"John of Pensacola and the others got more and more radical. Said their science was going to change the whole model. Two of these were his sons, Jude and Neil. Who are of myth, I would have to say. Of legend, perhaps—"

"Neil of Pensacola? Jude of Pensacola?" I interrupted.

"Both huge in Cuba. There's supposedly a small band on the DE-AX border, other scattered ones, part of the diaspora—I guess you could call them— followers. You hear of them? "

"Long story," I said, nodding.

"Pretty late in this negotiation, WELLFI said they would give them some autonomy, like a little fiefdom in the DE-AX, if John would give them revenue from his discoveries. But John declared West Florida could be its own land—he'd have his own country, thank you very much. West Florida was a country before there was the Louisiana Purchase, like Texas. It started north of here, and went all the way to the Perdido River. The U.A. surrounded them immediately. A blockade. They were still selling their therapies—couriers were coming up to meet them on little skiffs from off-shore islands. From Cuba, from Haiti, from Mexico. He made a flag, printed money, and had a bank. He decided the new country needed people, and so he started unfreezing embryos he'd stockpiled from his early days, his genetic research days, and finding surrogate mothers to bear them." He took a deep breath. "We were two of those, as far as I can tell. Many were born during the blockade. Then, when you were not quite three and I was maybe five, by my calculations, the U.A. decided to roll in with firepower. Go after the holdouts. Boom Boom Boom. I remember some of this. When I was in Florida, I saw things I'd seen, or felt I'd seen—" He gazed off. "I know it's true. You were younger. You always thought I lied. We lived there. I recognized some of the buildings, the plaza—all ruins now. I didn't lie. They hugged us, held us, there. Treated us like humans." He looked hard at me, asking a question. His mouth drew into a little "o," his thick brows lowered. He said, "You still don't believe me. You say it's a myth. You say—"

"No, no, hear me," I said. Then I wasn't sure what I would say. I shuddered. It was true. Somewhere, inside, I knew it was all true. O— All of it, true. He had never lied to me. Never. All of it was true.

This rushed through me like a bright, vigorous wave. Pain, sorrow—

"I took pictures. I can show you. Just as I had remembered, everything, palm trees—"

"I believe you," I said. And for that moment I loved him more than I ever had. I had been blind.

He stopped. He heard what I said. He almost started to laugh, the release of a kind of tension, that sort of laugh. "You *do*?" he asked. His eyes went up to the ceiling, as if he were looking for help. He would have to get his bearings.

"Yes, I believe you." I nodded. "I should have before." I remembered Mo Lion's missive. I would have to show it to him. It was upstairs in my jacket. Yes, I knew about the myth.

"When the U.A. gun boats came up Perdido Bay, they sneaked us out, I am not quite sure who took us. There were others, too, but it's not known if they survived. But the boat we were in was pursued into the Gulf, and then ran up into the Old River to hide for a while, and, as far as I can tell, our escape boat was sinking, but somebody set us out in little blankets, with our ID medallions, put us on the levee in a drawer of metal and then, I don't know, Marilee found us in the mud."

I leaned forward, eyeing some anchovies in a tin Ariel had left open. I considered how Ariel's information would tear apart the already thin, shredded plan I had for a future. Ariel. Always there to ruin my life, though he'd only meant to once, that time in the park. What was I going to do? What was I going to be? I felt it all disintegrating. I was falling, falling, nothing underneath me.

The anchovies were salty, like the sea. I thought of Klamath's cooking, and I missed, for a moment, that simple life of waiting, of suspension, at the Wood Palace. Now I'd come to learn that I had been born during a war. This seemed apt, to me. I was still in one.

"I suppose you have something to worry about if Lazarus wanted to give your money to Chef Menteur. He can, you know, technically, until you go in and declare, and commit to Memphis, he can do anything he wants with that money. But you don't have to worry from this investigation. Your Trust is still sponsored by an Heir; you didn't come under some Charter. You came from complete outlaws, pirates, and renegades. Hah! So relax." He snorted, and grinned his boyish grin. "The West Floridians found ways to make diabetes easy, to conquer certain cancers, ways to zap genes in the egg, to make the next generation more perfect than the one before it—they even got some of their money out. But there were consequences."

He brought out coconut, started to eat again. I knew it would be very sweet. My mouth would pucker. A word flowed out of my consciousness. "Does this have to do with the Salamanders?"

"Well then you know. The legend of the Salamanders. They are also called *second born*. I don't know what that means. The ones, who know, won't tell you. It's their mystery, what they believe, what they pray to in secret: it's a cult. Around our brothers. These are much older brothers. Some in Cuba say it's high Santeria, others say they have another vision, it arises when they are about twenty-eight. They say, in Spanish, these are able *'to pierce the boundary—to know—within and without.'* I think it's something to do with what John did to those genes. Those of his sons, Neil and Jude, and maybe the genes of those he caused to be born during the blockade. In other words—us." He was running his fingers through his stringy hair, applying some oil from the coconut inadvertently, making it even stringier. He was excited. "I mean, wouldn't it be ironic?" Ariel asked. "After it all—our whole stinking lives, our lives lower than slaves, if it turns out—we are priests, leaders, by birth? We have a vision?" Suddenly, Ariel reached over and ran his fingernail along the top of my head, until he found the tiny indent Mo Lion had found, and he scratched it with his fingernail, hard, like he was trying to pierce it, and I felt the same peculiar shock Mo Lion gave me. "Did you feel that?" he asked. "Down your whole spine? And our lip—all the Salamanders I saw in the pictures have this lip—"

I nodded. I touched mine.

"Well, then, it isn't just me," he said, shrugging. "That's a sign. But what does it mean? And that thing, that thing we saw around O? Nobody else saw that, not even Camille—but you did. I did." He shrugged again. "I've seen pictures. They look something like us." He cocked his head, his eyes widened. "No, exactly like us. People cling to them, follow them everywhere. Say they are the second born, which is a kind of—I don't know, there are several interpretations. One is—*'undying.'* Imagine, we don't have to be Bonesnakes. We don't have to starve, be Re-jobbed, have our cells rinsed, our RNA screwed with, wrapped up in dermises, sealed up like, like, living—be one of them. I know you love some of them, but—" He shook his head. "This whole life, everything Lazarus planned for us, every horrible thing I suffered with O, for the sake of—all of it has been a huge, huge, huge, detour, a byway, a vast distraction from our real—it's like a cosmic joke." Ariel smiled. "So, I'm going to Cuba. Want to come?"

"What about your Trust? What about your money? The suit for control?" That was what I asked, but I was about to run up the stairs and get the letter from Mo Lion, show him what I knew—

He cocked his head. "Maybe I don't care—maybe I want my real life—"

"And if it's just a legend?" I asked. "You don't know if it's real."

At that point, he brought two hands up to his own neck, grabbed his Nyet collar, unhooked it, took it off, and laid it down. There it was, then, just a green tarnished hoop on the table. It was as if the tremors in me started to spread out, so that things around were beginning to crack, to fall apart, and I was afraid to move, I was terrified—"It is just a legend."

"Not if you believe." Just then a loud shout. There were other noises at the same time in the background—banging doors, screams. Footsteps, getting closer—Vee burst into the kitchen.

"Lazarus, it's Lazarus!" he shouted. "It's horrible."

VIII

*I*n my memory, the next few days dwell in a dark blue, deep, deep river, where they will always be.

This is what I saw:

The tips of Lazarus's orange-pink toes, suspended about two feet above the armrest of his bench. His strange form, his foam-wrapped skeleton, hung from the upper beam of the library. His ladder was lying on its side, on the wide-planked wooden floor, and there was a rope around his neck. Apparently he had used the ladder to climb up to the rafters and thrown the rope over, and then to fashion the noose. I thought of the shock of the moment when he kicked the ladder out from under himself. The noose had squeezed—how did he know how to do this? Where did he get the resolve, the intention? From the force of the knot tightening about his throat, his sheet lenses had popped out and landed on his cheeks like large dark dots, like the ones clowns have. There was a thick, naked clown in a he-man suit. He hung there where our father, our king, had once been.

Ariel yelled first. "Cut him down. Where is his WELLVAC alarm? Call them now!"

I wanted to move, but my body was not responding to commands. I heard Marilee say, "He threw it away, into the Trench. Days ago. I saw him. I ordered a new one! I should have seen the signs!"

"We'll get him down," Ariel said. "Come on." He gestured to me. "Come on, we have to—" He picked up the ladder. "We can call them—"

"He's dead," Vee said. He stood there in his pajamas. He had been awakened from his grieving slumber by Marilee's discovery. His whole face was now even more assaulted by grief than it had been when I had last seen him—he was gnarled, grizzled, and hardly recognizable.

"I know," Ariel snapped, setting ladder right. "Help me Malcolm."

Somehow, I responded. The ladder had steps on both sides. We climbed up—Ariel got to the top step and then grabbed the body around the upper torso with one arm. With the other, he was trying to reach the knot, loosen it. "Help me," he said. "Brother."

I was aware how my arms reached to grab the top knot of the rope, to release Lazarus' head. But in another realm, I was disappearing, that was the sensation. Or more like, fading out. I thought remotely, of how, a moment ago, I'd been a man, with opinions, enjoying Ariel's optimism, his tale of legends, of rebellion. I was watching our old world fall to pieces, with a sort of glee, and now I was erased. I felt the impulse to wipe the present away, I felt myself obeying that impulse. I saw the room darkening around me. Then, for a moment, I came back to the present, where my arms were holding Lazarus' lifeless thighs, and Marilee was handing us a muslin drape, a sheet, and we were wrapping him—Ariel supporting the bruised blue neck, closing the popping eyes.

In part of myself, I saw these things, in another, I had vanished.

*

It was perhaps four and a half hours later.

The body was on the floor, now, in the dining hall, and Vee and Marilee were seated on the bench. We all were silent, except for Ariel, who could not sit still.

He paced back and forth in the cypress hall and called out, "I only just understood him, only a few days ago, now he's gone! Gone!" And to me, he said, "What is wrong with you, don't you understand? He's gone! Is this that cave you used to slip into when we were kids? Wake up. Come out Malcolm. Come out!"

The words were in my mind: *I am here and I know he is gone.* But a second later, I wasn't even sure if I had said them aloud or not. I had said something, but I couldn't remember what it was.

The body was on the floor. We had no idea what to do about it.

We couldn't bury an Heir. Heirs didn't die. They didn't.

And I was thinking this: I had wanted to kill him. And here he was, dead. Dead. So-long wasn't the word. Dead, that curse, was the word.

*

The discussion was a horror, but a necessary horror. It came the next day.

We had replaced the muslin sheet with a plastic tarp. Ariel had just finished explaining that we had to remove the prodermis pretty soon, because the Heir body underneath "will make it stink—we won't be able to get rid of the smell." I had no idea where Ariel had obtained such information. I didn't ask.

We had concluded that there was no way to tell WELLFI, and we would have to keep it from Lazarus's sons, as well. Vee described the consequences we faced. Unless pure accident could be demonstrated, we would all be accused of Heir Murder—a thousand times more serious than any other kind. If Vee and Marilee were implicated, they would both be put to death. And Vee's other children, by his first marriage, Ginger's sister, Ginger's sister's children, would all be jailed. All procreation certificates for all of their progeny would be abrogated. If any of these events could be traced to Ariel and me, we too would be put to death, the Trusts we had taken back by WELLFI, distributed to living Heirs with diminished Trusts, by lottery. "You should have thought of this," Marilee said, pointing her chin as if addressing Lazarus's corpse, which now lay on one of the dining tables. She used a very rare tone of low rage. "He said he wanted to save us, and here he does this! Here I was, doing everything to keep him alive, and here he goes—"

"We just have to be smart," Vee said. "I am sure he thought we were smart."

Ariel proposed water burial.

Vee said we could throw the body overboard past English Turn, where the Old River took on the currents of the Gulf. Something in me recoiled at this proposition, still, but I couldn't voice it. I couldn't say that Lazarus's dignity and proper respect was worth the fate of Vee and Marilee and Ginger's children, and all that came after them.

"We do it at dusk tomorrow," Ariel said. He had been strange the last twenty-four hours—in turns furious, and then calculating, and then inconsolable, and then calculating again. Somehow, we all agreed. We would bury at night. Throw the body overboard.

"The WELLFI investigators might come looking," Marilee said. "When they bring the new pendant. They would have to deliver it in person, to check his identity. They said it might be a week."

"For that, for them, I'll come up with something," Ariel said, calculating again. A moment later, he asked me, "Did you see this?" showing me the papers written in Lazarus's hand.

I realized it was the second half of the manuscript. I told him I had seen the first half.

"Read this part. You should see why he did it."

He understood. He saw my guilt. He was my brother. He understood me.

He always had.

IX

My Life, Beginning With the Early Pfiswell Trials, In Short When It's Been Very Long, Very, Very Long—PART TWO

The Troubles weren't really started by the stubborn fundamentalists standing up for the Wheel, nor by the fringe philosophers of the Cycle, nor by the radical Gaists with their protests, as the history books say. The Troubles were mostly fomented by the potential Third Wave. An entire generation had no future.

As I have said, we only had controlled sources of news. But underground, they were gathering in some cities, and in cells all over, making plans, beginning civil disobedience. The normal ones—by normal I mean like us, secular, materialistic, educated, modern—joined in the end with the Luddites, took up their retarded creeds. They all shared the goal of defeating us, they had nothing to lose—this was so clear to me. Of course I could see their position. My own boys couldn't, and they disowned their own children in the end, but I saw their case. I suppose the rebels figured once they had defeated us they could sort it all out between the secular moderns, Heir children, and the fundamentalists. It didn't turn out quite that way. As Yeats said, "The best lack all conviction, and the worst are full of passionate intensity."

I didn't believe in the violence, was terrified of the riots. I had kept myself alive so long; I couldn't bear to be violated now. Didn't know what to do when they bombed WELLFI headquarters. Knew less when I learned my own granddaughter Jennifer was in a cadre in what was once Chicago, one of the first to join forces with the Wild Oats, a fringe group. Terrorists, anarchists. They didn't care. They had no future. I tried to plead with her. She wouldn't answer.

I kept switching sides. At one point I even took what funds I had and sent them to Michael, who was in San Francisco, having joined with Free Wheelers out there, a more liberal branch, eventually defeated. I suggested he find his sister Jennifer and just go somewhere there was a cycle— England, or Canada—the old life was apparently still possible there. Most other nations were our enemies, and there was, internationally, a hue and cry about the power of WELLFI, so exile was difficult, but in those other places there were still economies, jobs, professions. Michael trained to be a common doctor, followed in his grandfather's footsteps. That was considered something like being a veterinarian, by then. WELLFI gave them strict codes about what they could treat and what they couldn't. He showed these to me. I was infuriated. The great Untreated, as we called them then, couldn't even get decent ordinary care—blood pressure medicine, chemo. The Cyclers, the Mass, the Diers. Some of my cohort even said publically it was a blessing they were doing the so-long in such numbers. "Reducing the strain on our resources," they called it.

When I spoke to my grandchildren, to that generation, it was hard to know what to do. I understood their frustration—and what kind of country is it when the only thing you can imagine your grandchildren doing is leaving it so they can grow old and die on foreign soil? While you stay home and amuse yourself and amuse yourself? There were years of turmoil. I couldn't make up my mind. Heirs slaughtered in the streets, flayed, set on fire. The WELLFI media started saying that the Treateds couldn't intermingle with the Nats any longer. It was just too risky. The collars were introduced. I was more sympathetic than most of my Wave who just built the great new Walled Urbs—Memphis, Bright Phoenix, Kingston, North New York, Snow White.

After the first set of uprisings, there were several more—things were unstable, dangerous, for years. Heirs couldn't travel without being assaulted, so the bullet trains were built. The Untreated started organizing itself into affinity groups, barter syndicates, communities, economies. They couldn't riot and wage war all the time. They traded the commodities they still needed and tried to train the doctors and teachers—their standard of living was much lower than it was before, during the fugue age. It had just gotten worse over time. Like the English who let the Irish starve at their back door while they helped their colonies improve, we let our Nats nearby waste away. Meanwhile, we fed fugue economies a world away with investment. Eventually, since there was no changing WELLFI and its interests, a minority, a few of the stronger federations, the more fundamentalist ones, just invented their own way of governing themselves.

The enclave treaties were the last thing, not a good thing, entirely. Heirs preferred to make peace with the most conservative, the most ideological. By the time the treaties were being offered and the disbanding of the idea of the nation had been seriously considered, I was pretty far in the North Camp. I had broken with my sons. This was in the late twenty sixties, early twenty-seventies. The second wave of Procreation Laws. If you had children—not that many did, during the Troubles—then you couldn't get Treated. There were a great many riots about that, though. People didn't like having their "generative freedom" as they called it, taken away. The word from Washington—I guess it had already been renamed New Albersia—was that the nation was just ungovernable as it was. And the new black economy didn't pay any taxes, didn't contribute. Eventually, the most conservative elements won. They abrogated the Constitution, set up the United Authority. I wasn't on that side. This was a rich country, this had been a rich country. Nobody could see clearly because of the violence. I thought I could work for that: the goal of everyone being Treated. See if we couldn't get the potential Third Wave Treated. There probably was a way. But people got scared. Heirs, that is. The people who scared people always won. They always win. They have all the money.

There were stories about my grandchildren's generation. Lots of suicides. While the enclaves were still open, some fled to them, signed on to their rigid rules to stay alive. Some of course managed to scrape together the money to be Treated—begging, borrowing, stealing. They stopped rebelling, and started lying about their status, men disclaiming their own offspring, mothers having their pelvises surgically changed, so it would seem they had never borne a child, everybody scrambling, lying, changing their minds. So many infants were murdered, tossed out. The DNA Securitas was checking everyone they could, so children who were adopted, were saved, were added to the files. Samples were taken.

I didn't care about the rules anymore. I went out into the open country. I saw what was really going on. What I write here is not the official version. I was all alone. My boys wouldn't have anything to do with me—they still hardly speak to me. Michael, my grandson, I know for sure, died of natural causes in a Gaist commune in Kentucky. That galvanized me. He was only sixty. I had lived to see my grandchildren die. I had lived too long, I knew it then. But I kept up. I am a man of fixed ideas. I decided there was something I could do, good I could do. I was full of pride. Grandiosity, more like it.

About the time of the Great Rim Earthquakes, which took so many, including my granddaughter Jennifer, I got started. The U.A. had long ago deaccessioned these Gulf lands but had not really let go of them. I left the U.A. and came here.

I gathered together some of the children. And I began.

I went back to my oldest beliefs, those that had made me a doctor in the first place, back in the 1940's. (Can you believe how far back that is?) That you can always do something to help.

And I tried, from the start, " to make a difference." I had all the schemes, the mailing lists, the appeals. I trotted out the foundlings and said they deserved a chance. "I-I-I," it was always me, my heroism—I just kept going and going. Trying to save the boys, trying to find them work. I survived in this enterprise for forty years. But then, lately, the charities started to claim, along with everyone else, that there was no toss out problem anymore, and if there was, what was the point of salvaging? Salvage, that was the word they used. That was what they told me. "Why save them when they have no future, or they are only going to be Altered or become slaves or just quietly so-long? Why?" So, this year, after we sent off the most of them to labor camps in Brazil and Mexico, I went off to be redescribed—one of my sons suggested this in a letter, an attempt to reason with his ridiculous father. He told me I should stop cavorting with the great unwashed, those who are going to do the so-long anyway, it was bad for my soul, he said. Didn't I understand the Reveal? The Elysian Reality? My associations were muddying my mind, he said. I was just living in the mire. When would I uplift myself? So I tried. Perhaps I was an old fool. But then I found myself the last few months in Memphis cavorting with my purported peers, and I couldn't bear them. I stayed a few months to honor my son's request, but when I came back, Vee let the last few boys go. I have made no difference at all. My last attempt, giving Malcolm's Trust and everything else I had to Vee's people, not needed, not needed at all. But it was Malcolm's! I betrayed him!

So it comes time for me to arrive at my conclusions, and to complete this litany of regret, and to find what illusions I had and to grasp what their consequences were, no matter how innocently I believed them. How innocently I acquired them. Now, I think it is the greatest gift of all to have a sense of time, to know when some way of seeing things, some set of goals, is worthy, and when it has worn out its worthiness, when it no longer fits the circumstances, when its very existence is a kind of distortion.

And so I have decided, after two hundred and one or two (I've lost my count, along with everything else) years, that I would rather have that unchartered terrain where all my true boys are going or have already gone, and my grandchildren, and my wives. I want that undescribed place, where none of the theories pertain. Out past the last perimeter, the last of the last, for they keep building a new boundary, past the last, and past the last, so nothing is ever real, there is always more, I have lost what I believed in. I have lost, lost, lost, and now I am lost, and now I join them. This is the short of it: I am sorry we ever rebelled against the sweetness of the long night, the place past the boundary. Sorry we were ever so afraid. Sorry we chose to be so vigilant, to never sleep. The nightmares came anyway. The nightmares came in the daylight, in the nation. Exactly because we chose to wall ourselves off from them. Everything good has been lost because of a few who devised how to stay awake all night, how to prop their eyes open, to watch and watch and watch but see so little—go absolutely blind—

    Goodbye to those I did love still in this mortal coil, I try here and now to shuffle it off, pull it off if I have to—Lazarus Newbirth de Gold HR WELLFI ID 237,678. October IN A VERY LATE YEAR—

X

4:20 PM October 19, 2121
Audubon Foundling House, Audubon Island
New Orleans Islands, Northeast Gulf De-Accessioned Territory,
U.A. Protectorate

*T*he next day, I sat with the scrawny, true body in the dining hall.
I had helped Ariel take off the prodermis. He took it outside and
burned it. Then, much later, he brought in the ashes, said we were
burying them separately, "Just to be sure." Then Marilee came in
with cloth she'd washed by hand, and she moved Lazarus onto it and
started to sew it into a shroud around him. When I watched her do
this, I realized she had done it many times before. I found this—a
familiarity with death, with its rituals—completely incomprehensible
and completely ordinary at the same time.

I joined Ariel and Vee as they carried the shriveled frame (corpse,
to even call him a corpse!) out to Vee's boat, and hid it under a pile
of debris and furniture from some rooms in the Home that Vee had
stacked on the deck. Since these actions felt so impossible, they were
almost easy to do. I employed that *pretend* I used to feel in my acting
days, as a way to get through.

We trolled past the houses with the women smoking cigars and the
dogs howling and down into the Tchoupitoulas Trench, and then away
from the Quay of the Sunken Quarter and into the deeper stretches of
the Old River, where, Ariel said, the Gulf traffic used to come up to
the Port of New Orleans, to Henry Clay wharf right at the end of our

street, and the Napoleon Wharf. He said he'd heard there used to be cranes taller than ten story buildings to pick up boxes bigger than three transports full of goods that all the people, in the regime that was here before the United Authority, used to consume, eat, dress in, break and throw out. The fugue country, the old one.

Ariel was telling all these tales while standing on the prow of Vee's boat. Vee was agreeing that things had been like that once, very long ago. For a while they were arguing about the exact year things did happen— when the river moved its course, when the ports actually shut down. I was crouched in the stern, holding onto the grommetted tarp, which was threaded with some cord and covering the old mattress and chairs from the unused rooms of the Foundling House. We were hauling all this to hide the body. If we were stopped by any WELLFI vessel we could claim we were just taking some furniture to East Menteur's new site. I was watching the wake of the boat, the white furrow in the water. Nothing I could think of felt worthy of being said. A bruisy thick liquid surrounded me—how I remember this day. I could not see light, even when I looked at it. Every so often, I would poke my head up, and say to myself, "You condemned him, fought with him—and, finally, you wanted to kill him. *What are you?*" as Tamara had accused me, and then I would sink back down into the brown and purple flow.

Finally, we reached the place in the river where Vee said the currents were infallible, always spun back out, toward the Gulf. Vee came to the stern and told me to help him slide the body out from under all the stacks of furniture. It looked as if it would be difficult, but it was not, really. The furniture was old and in places rotted, and it broke apart easily.

When the time came, Vee called Ariel back from the wheelhouse, saying the boat could drift for a moment.

I did what Vee told me to do—I took Lazarus' feet, and Ariel took his neck, and Vee cradled our guardian, our king, our father, under his tiny waist, and we counted, "One, two, three." Vee lifted him up on "four," and put him over the side of the boat. Then, all at the same time, we let go and watched the sack that held Lazarus's frail inner, true body sink in to the river's brown depths beneath the foam, toss up, feet first, and disappear.

Vee had said a few chants, repeated a single mantra over and over, on the way back. I learned it by heart although I had no idea what it meant. *Ohm mane padme ohm*— And then, we sailed back to the Foundling House.

*

When we got home, very late that night: I went into the kitchen. I found all the tins and cans and jars Ariel had opened, which were still open, and in the refrigerator, and this is what I did:

I ate the anchovies: pungent, salty.

I ate the rest of the peaches, thick-skinned, blush pink, in cloudy sweet terribly rich syrup, delicious. I was devastated when they were over.

I ate mussels in olive oil—orange and swimming in pepper sauce, ten at a time in my mouth.

I found the hearts of palm, and fished every one out of its juice in the can.

I saw Ariel had four kinds of rum. I drank white, I drank pale yellow, and I drank the brown, and then, finally, the garnet-colored rum, which I liked best.

I finished off the white greasy coconut.

I smoked a long fat cigar, smuggled from the islands.

I lay my head on the table, at the end, in my satiation, in my stupor, my longing. What would Lydia think of me? How could I go into my Boundarytime with so little discipline?

Then, in my great grief, I fell asleep.

XI

8:00 AM October 20, 2121
Audubon Foundling House, Audubon Island
New Orleans Islands, Northeast Gulf De-Accessioned Territory,
U.A. Protectorate

"*M*alcolm? Malcolm? Are you listening?"

Ariel woke me. I'd slept at the kitchen table the whole night, my head cradled in my arms. I could hear him, but he seemed very far away.

"We can't stay here. Do you understand?"

I nodded again.

"You understood last night. You have to agree, and snap out of it, and come. Didn't you tell me you were due at Serio's arraignment? Back in Port Gramercy? Didn't you tell me—If you don't show, they will be around here, asking for you—"

For a few minutes, I managed to forget what was wrong. For a moment, I was awake, and in daylight, not in the bruise-brown world. I made a few remarks, a few plans. We had to leave the house, I knew that. We had to let Vee and Marilee leave. WELLFI could be coming soon, to deliver the new pendant, they would start looking for Lazarus, put out an alert.

"Where are you going?" I asked, sitting up. I'd forgotten. Or wasn't sure Ariel had told me.

"Cuba," he said. "We have our brothers—right? Maybe? You should come. Remember what I was telling you? Remember anything? Did you believe any of it?" He rubbed his bare neck, where the Nyet collar had stained it.

I did, or I half-did. But I said, "I have to see Lydia. I am still going to be Treated."

I was afraid I was going to be Treated. I was afraid of becoming what Lazarus was, what Gepetto was, what any of them were, except Lydia, I thought. I had promised her—I had to honor something.

"But your Trust was transferred to Vee's people, didn't you—" Ariel said.

"He told me he'd put it back," I said.

"How do you know he did what he was saying he was going to do? You think he was in his right mind?"

Entering the office was almost unbearable: how everything closed down around me, how I could hardly hear Ariel now, nor make sense of his remarks. I was haunted by the things I had done in our last encounter. How I had shouted Lazarus down, for what, for changing, for exactly what I myself had started to do. I could not deny it. Although now I had had enough of these changes. Being Treated was the only change that made sense. I was going on. It had to be one way or another. I would be an Heir, if it could be. I wouldn't make the mess of it at the end that Lazarus had made.

I had wanted to kill him.

Ariel rushed to the chair in front of the screen, opened the files, got to the accounts. He turned to me. I was standing in the middle of the room, remembering the scene of the crime. "Look, he took it out of the funds for Chef Menteur. He put it back to you. He's not the sponsor anymore."

"Who is?" I asked, and inside, I felt both at once—relief and terrible guilt and trepidation. It occurred to me my guardian had done this last thing before he killed himself. That afternoon. Listened to my harangue, taken it to heart. This made me very sad. Made me want to give the Trust away. Made me want to do what he'd wanted to do.

"Greenmore. Your queen." Ariel looked at me smiling.

I asked, "Why do you call her my Queen?"

There was a wand of light in the room from the top of the jalousie blinds, and in it dust was floating and tiny feathers, very beautiful and silvery. I was staring at it, this beam, it seemed as if it would help me somehow. Ariel said, "I'm not mad at you. You know, it could all be a story, about the Salamanders? I don't know what I believe, really. I just can't follow their way." Ariel's long, handsome face pressed into the streak of sun and his long lashes and his brown eyes were illuminated by a bluish white, almost a film, coating them. "You think I am desperate because I have less than enough Trust, I'm grabbing at straws, don't you?"

I was the one who was grasping at straws, I knew.

I looked away from the screen, and away from the sun, as if I could find the answer somewhere in the room, but the room was dark. Only sadness was there, no information, no instigation to make a plan, to form an intention. I had been so confused when I was here, that last argument. I'd told him I hated him. But I hated my own confusion the most. I wished I could tell Lazarus that. Once, I had known what I wanted. To be with Lydia, and before that, forever, to be an Heir, what Lazarus told me to want. That wasn't so long ago. To be with Lydia, in Re-New Orleans. Or in Snow White, or some other deathless urb. "I don't know," I managed. "I don't know."

"Well, get your things, you and I are going to Port Gramercy. Vee and Marilee have to leave too. We all have to leave together."

"Why are you going to Port Gram?"

"Finding a freighter that will take me to Cuba," he said, blinking once. Then he waited a minute, he pursed his full lips. He was concerned for me. "And you—?" Ariel asked. "And you? You are going to the arraignment, remember, for Serio? Testifying? And if he gets off, we can give him his boat back. We have to leave Lazarus's boat here, we can't let them think he left, can't let them think he was off somewhere— we will all be brought in a dragnet. He killed himself. It is no crime. We can't be blamed for it. He had a right. He lived what, two hundred and some years? He'd had enough. You read the letter." He paused. "You know it is nothing you said. You know, right?"

I didn't.

He took my shoulders, demanded my gaze. "Look, you read the letter. Come on. Come on."

I nodded and followed him.

We came out of the office and saw bags in the hall. Vee and Marilee were there, ready to leave. Ariel told them, "Go upstairs, and mess up a few rooms—toss the kitchen, the office. The story is you were both at the Ginger Sim. The story is Lazarus was alone." Vee nodded. "Do you have something long, metal, a crow bar?"

Vee thought for a minute. "There is one of the poles from the swing set," he said. "We struck it down."

"Is it rusty? Does it still have strength?"

"I think it will do," Vee said.

"Then help me get it to the boat." Then he turned to me. "Didn't you hear what I said? Didn't you read Lazarus's letter?"

I nodded.

"Well, then, we have to move. Move."

The time had come for the last element of the scheme: leaving the Home, abandoning it.

We left Lazarus's office a complete mess, everything still there, sans the testimony, the rope and the body. We also went through rooms upstairs, at Ariel's insistence, throwing open drawers, breaking dishes and keepsakes in Vee's and Marilee's private quarters.

I took the testimony. His story, that he left for us. Ariel instructed me to keep reading it. According to his directions, we walked out and left the doors open, and the old brick perimeter, and the fancy iron gate, we also left ajar. We climbed up and over the newer floodwall to where the boats were tied to the outside rebar steps. We carried our few possessions with us, plus tins of Ariel's for dinner in the evening and meals the next day, and more, on the open Sea of Pontchartrain. Ariel got on Vee's and Marilee's craft. I was by myself, piloting Serio's. Ariel had the ashes of the prodermis in the several handsome jars that had once held the whole peaches. He was planning on dropping these into the deepest part of the Sea.

He told Vee and Marilee to take grappling hooks and hold on tight, keeping the side of our boats close to the cinderblock floodwall.

He called out to me to start the motor on Serio's boat and sail away. I managed, and steered out from the Home, then I cut the motor after I was about one hundred feet distant.

From there I saw Vee and Marilee holding tight to the ropes that were attached to the grappling hooks. Then I saw Ariel raise the rusted post from the swing set over the heads of Vee and Marilee, as if he was going to hit them, knock them out. For a moment, I thought I'd read everything wrong, and Ariel *was* completely insane.

But then Ariel did a very sad and clever thing.

While Marilee and Vee held the cords attached to the grappling hooks tight, keeping the boat close, Ariel had the leverage to attack the gates, with the steel pipe, and pry them open from the outside. When he got them apart, the canal waters flowed in, slowly at first, then with more force. In a few minutes, the water opened them wide. The canal rushed in. The Home took in seven feet of water. All this, while we motored away.

I was not able to see it, actually, because I was too far away, but I saw it anyway, in my heart, inside. I saw water quickly moving in and overtaking the entire Foundling House—play yard, main house, dormitories. Brown-blue water, claiming everything—the tables in the dining hall, the wooden counters in the kitchen, the old black stove, the carpets and books and hundred files of lost children in Lazarus's office, the bench with the green cushions I'd sat on the first time he called me. Ariel hadn't explained beforehand that he was destroying the entire Home—perhaps because he didn't want anyone to protest, to complain, he didn't have time for any more emotion. But the pried-open gate—sign of forced entry, and the flooding—would probably convince WELLFI investigators of malfeasance, of brigands who'd come in, and inadvertently caused a death. Should they ever inquire as to what happened to the person, the Heir, Lazarus de Gold, the answer would be that he was the victim of a break-in and the flood that followed.

When Ariel told them to let go, to haul in the hooks, they did so. Vee went to his helm, and steered his boat out into the open water. I saw a glimpse of Vee's jaw thrust forward, as they passed me. His expression was hardened, ready for the rest of the journey. Steeling himself. Saying goodbye. I fell in behind, steering Serio's tub, for they knew the way.

Their house was gone, their past was gone, his daughter was gone. There was only the future. Marilee was beside him, her face also unmoving.

It occurred to me how WELLFI would cover this story, how they would say this old decrepit, shameful Foundling House beset by robbers was a very good example of why Heirs should not live in hazardous, water-logged islands where Outliars were prevalent, an excellent example of the terrible risks of living outside the U.A. proper, where things like this happen, the risks of running a house full of abandoned children from who-knows-where at the edge of the Heir world. Proof no one should attempt to help the doomed, the lower strats. Maybe one of the ingrates had done it. Proof they should be left to their own ends.

At a certain point, when we turned into the Carrollton Trench, and out of the city, I felt a stabbing pain in my heart. It was all gone. I had nothing, no home, no father. I had my Trust, my future, and all this was supposed to be Prologue, and not matter. But I couldn't help it. It was all that mattered: what I had lost, not what I would get.

About halfway to the Sea of Pontchartrain, Vee's boat slowed so I could catch up. When I was beside him, he said Ariel was getting on—they were going to have to veer away now, not go North to Port Gramercy, but further east, to Pond, which was the port closest to the new Chef Menteur lands.

Ariel swung the grappling hook over the rail of the deck of Serio's boat and then brought our two boats so close together he could climb from one to the other. I appreciated how Ariel could swing around like a monkey, climb aboard like a pirate, cling to legends, be certain he was going to get his due some day.

He would get his real life, the one he might believe in. I didn't know what I believed, not yet. I gave him Mo Lion's strange letter, let him read it while I held the wheel. I asked him what thought.

"Good, all good," he said. "See, there are believers out there. These brothers of ours must exist."

I told him I didn't know what I believed.

"You will. One day it will just be clear," he said. He put his arm around me, as the sun started to blaze pink and orange, its last dazzling net thrown wide, before it sank into the Sea of Pontchartrain.

XII

10:55 AM October 21, 2121
Port Gramercy Enclave Civic Complex
Northeast Gulf De-Accessioned Territory, U.A. Protectorate

*I*t was shocking to see what they had done to Serio. His wrists were bound with wide black metal bands, and from these, a tongue of leather led down to his ankles, which were also shackled. He was marching out of the courtroom with the other prisoners when I first caught sight of him. The bailiff had told us to stand, because the judge—a thick Port Gramercy matron, with a slight lisp—had been called out of the court and was coming back in.

I had been in the place for an hour. It didn't have paneling and vaulted ceilings like courtrooms in the flats I'd seen—it was low-ceilinged, humble, with gaudy mustard colored walls, that seemed to press in upon all the Port Gramercians who packed the place and were watching the proceedings with uneasy attention.

Ariel and I had gotten in the night before. We tied up Serio's boat at an old abandoned fishing pier about half a mile from Port Gramercy Docks. He'd set off early in the morning to find a freighter to take him to Cuba. I envied his resolve.

He'd told me he'd join me here, but he hadn't shown yet.

*

The Judge returned to the bench—it was a table, but they called it a bench. Her curly white hair was held back by two clips. A small box-like hat was perched on the back of her head, which other clips seemed to secure. She wore a judicial smock, in an ugly dark green. Behind her was the round FREE WHEEL insignia, very elaborately drawn, the naked figures copulating at the bottom, and the infant at twelve o'clock, the old, bent man with a cane at nine, and youths opposite. It was the largest one I had ever seen, gaudy, polychrome. When everybody was settled again, Serio took his place. And I couldn't see him anymore over the heads in front of me.

I sat there, in the darkness that had been surrounding me for days and days. Then, something started to lap at my heels, follow me in my deepest thoughts, demand attention. For the first time, I saw the edges of it, bright, and wondrous.

Then it grew, and came back and grew more, and then I heard the question:

How would you have lived differently if you knew, you really knew what Lazarus would do in the end? How he would negate his life? Now that you know how he turned out? Now that you know what you know, what would you do? Then my demons came to me—their indigo, their fists. They showed me Lazarus's body swinging, his pitiful orange-pink toes. How could he choose that? Then angels asked, what could I choose now?

"Stand. I call out the names and you stand," the judge said and picked up a long piece of paper. "Aubert, Babineaux, Bascomb, Costello, Cox, Fabio, Gagin, Gert..."

The entire group had been brought in for drunk and disorderly conduct. A strange assortment of every color and shape. She gave them all a lecture about how, every year after the Cycle Fest "we have to crack down—"

Ariel suddenly slipped in next to me and whispered: "She's just behind us. Did you see her?"

I hadn't. When I turned, a shiver went through me. Her hair was up and seemed lighter somehow. Perhaps it was the sun on her through the low window.

"Look at you, what a puppy," he said.

"What?"

"You should see your face—" he grinned.

*

The public drunkenness crowd had been chastised and given suspended sentences after a very long speech full of Free Wheel Philosophy about the "Golden Mean," and the cliché that there is "for everything, a season." And then, another recess.

I followed her out into the crowded vestibule. Why wouldn't she turn and notice me? She had pulled her hair back tightly. She was trying conceal her beauty, and this upset me. I took it personally. I thought the same of the high-necked shirt with its folds and stitching that obscured the line of her figure. In front of me, as I tried to get to her, I felt my sadness over Lazarus like a broad and thick impenetrable blue, a dense pool. But somehow, on the sides of that indigo, bright flashes, the closer I got to her, and I heard a new question.

I touched her shoulder. She turned around. The miracle of her gorgeous, open face.

"You're alive! They lied!" She stopped, took me in, started again. "Careful. My brother-in-law is around. Or one of his crowd. They follow me everywhere." She put her sturdy fingers in the pocket of the apron she had around her waist and came out with a folded piece of paper.

"Lazarus is dead," I said in a whisper—Ariel had said we should tell no one, WELLFI might eventually come around and ask questions. But instinctively, I knew I could tell her. I had to. She had to understand how I was, how I was free.

"I thought they couldn't? Dead?"

I shook my head. She glanced into the crowd, saw something, or someone following, mouthed the expression, *see me, bye bye,* and pointed to the folded paper, which she'd given me, then to the corner of her eye. When she turned, all light went out.

*

"PORT GRAMERCY COURT OF FREE WHEEL JUSTICE IS IN SESSION," the bailiff shouted. The crowd was larger than ever, now. We could hardly squeeze back in our seats. Not far in front of me was Domino's wide head, his short neck. He was in a different costume, a jacket with epaulets.

"Don't you need to get to the pier?" I asked Ariel after we sat down, for he was obviously uncomfortable in his tiny space at the very end of that pew.

"Look, shut up, you need me, I got there early. I'm set. Have a berth.

S'great. Madder Rose, sails after the hurricane warning is lifted—" he said.

"Shhhh," said someone behind us.

"*Serio de Klamath Johnson Kieu, Chef Mentuerian,*" the bailiff called.

I saw him once again, moving in his shackles to the low table opposite the Judge's. He was alone, except for his lawyer, a thin man with a broad nose, a Rouge Gaist, as far as I could tell—they always wore red. He looked bored. Serio's hands were drawn down almost between his legs—he was hobbled, had to throw out his feet to take a step. Where was Klamath? I didn't understand. Ariel touched my shoulder. "It will be okay," he said. "It will, just speak for him, you can do that—"

"His father isn't even here," I whispered.

Serio looked forlorn and cowed. In jail on account of me. I wanted to call out, shout out.

"Calm down," Ariel told me. "They are pretty fair, even lenient, in Free Wheel court. Make up for the hard ass police."

"Shh—shhh." The man behind us again.

"State's Advocate? Read the charges," the judge began. "Read the charges to the prisoner."

A narrow little man with a bow tie—I recognized it was Sy, the one who had won the bet, had warned me about Lou Rae—stood and said, "State's Advocate has been called to the jail. I came here to tell you that he won't be back until this afternoon. He's sorry."

"And what has happened at the jail that is so pressing he can't come here and try this case?"

"Arceneaux brothers are talking, Madam Judge."

Shouts. Movement. Gasps. The whole courtroom, afire with this information—except for my brother and me, who had no idea what it was about. Ariel turned around and asked someone.

"People say they raped a woman with a quadruple P.C. Could have birthed four. They are why this place is full. Waiting for their case," the man behind us said.

"Until two-thirty this afternoon," the judge stated, and then she stood, as if relieved, and banged on her gavel again, removed her stiff collar, and her hat, and walked rather loosely, wiggled, actually, all pomp abandoned, out the side door.

The crowds pressed the exits to leave, again, in a roar of conversation.

"Psst—"

I had tumbled into the vestibule, about to read Camille's note, when someone touched my shoulder. "Psst. Psst. Ear looks good." The voice was familiar.

Serpenthead.

"How are you here? How did you get out of that riot?" I was glad to see him.

"Stowed on one of the yachts. Peet knew the steward." He grinned, his eyes widened. "Quite an evening, say? I saw your brother looking for a freighter to get to Cuba. Steered him in the right direction. He wants you to go with him. You going?"

I felt a jolt of fear, had to reach for breath. "Go to Cuba?" I could. Anything was possible now.

"Never been." He showed me his pink palms, free—empty. "Say it's nice."

"Well should I?" I asked.

He shrugged. Squeezed his temples. "You want me to answer that?" he asked.

"You been following me?" I asked. "Answer that." But I couldn't accuse him. He'd saved me too many times. He looked better, rested. I was glad. This smockshirt was a little shorter than the last and considerably whiter. He leaned slightly against a door, scratched his head. People were crowded all around us, but I felt alone with him.

"Swear that day coming in here was the first time I saw you." That kind open look of his. I would believe anything he said. I'd do what he told me to do, why not? He saw that.

"And the Mo Lion clan? Did you send me north, to them?"

"They had somebody to sew you up, didn't they?"

"Do you believe I'm kin to these...Salamanders?"

"What matters is what you believe," he said. "Far as I know they are made up."

Everything was reversed. I wanted to tell him they were real, Ariel said so. I was willing to believe what I thought most outlandish. Part of me did believe. I trusted what I was supposed to despise. *How would you live if Lazarus was all wrong? All wrong?*

"Answer my question!" I pleaded.

"Malc, it is your question—" He turned and looked off.

"Why won't you help me?" I felt the very ground beneath me disappearing. "You planned it all, everything. You knew from the start."

He put his arms akimbo, as if that were not a proper inquiry into exactly what he was up to. "It will come to you. S'happened to me once or twice. All of a sudden, you see the cause. Of the convergence. Like I said day I met you." He hooked his finger in the air to ask me to crunch down to his level for a secret.

I did it.

He said, "I didn't know. I didn't know. Just what they say, is all I know."

"What do they say?"

"They say you will know when you hear."

"Know what? Know what?"

"I never heard it. Just heard of it," he said, and he turned again. "Gotta go. This guy over there owes me money." Then he stopped and whispered, "And you already know."

"Wait! Wait!" I called after him. I had his knife. He didn't stop. He kept moving, in the thick, loud crowd.

Malcolm. I need to tell you some things. Go behind the Sugarhouse Café, enter by the back screen door, wait—Yours truly, C.

"Yours truly," was enough. I was a new man.

It was a very clear morning—crisp. I'd heard someone say that the air was emptied of everything because there was a "storm out there winding up in the Gulf."

But I saw no sign of it.

I found the cafe where Serio and I had got into trouble. I slid in the small corridor in the back, hoping I wasn't too late or too early. Finally, she appeared—her hair coming undone, slightly out of breath.

I hadn't been alone with her, really alone, in years. I grabbed her and kissed her.

She let me. Then she stiffened and asked about Lazarus.

I gave her details.

"That he would do that. After all he taught you. Promised you. You must be—oh Malc." And she kissed me again, her own kind of sweet kiss. "I am so sorry." She shook her head. "I am so sorry. What happens to you? Who has your Trust? All that?"

"Lydia," I said.

"Lydia?" she asked, backing away a few inches. I was too upset, I hadn't realized how that would sound.

"He put it in her name. But let's not talk about her." I tried to come closer. She stepped to the side, even further away.

"Oh Malc." She looked straight at me. "I thought they killed you. That's what they said, on that boat, shot you dead. That's what I thought.

I'd lost you. Then here you are."

"What?"

"Don't take this the wrong way." She shook her head. "Don't think I'm trying—I just thought you should know is all." She looked down. "I'm not saying this because I want anything. You are headed off, aren't you?"

"What is it? Tell me."

She brought her lips inward. That determined face she could have. "You know why I did that for Ariel and you that night?" she asked. "Why I took the blame, said he was with me?"

I never knew. I said so.

"'Cause I didn't want to break my promise. I knew how it could be with you. Or I thought I knew." She held her two hands, her fingers woven, she stood apart, the same as it was when she would stand in the doorway and not come in my room, and would tell me how she couldn't do this or do that. How dangerous I was. "I knew how it was with you. That we had such a grand way of talking, knowing what each other meant, how we could be. I saw it. And when you touched me, I saw I could fall into it." That web was forming, it always did. It was invisible, but it grew up around us like an eager vine. I wanted another kiss. She pulled her clasped hands up to her chest. She was barring me from her heart. "I didn't want to work at the Towers anymore. I was afraid of what—I wanted with you. First time I saw you—first time I saw the real you. It wasn't to hurt you that I left. It wasn't because I *didn't* want you. Then, just the last few days, they said they'd shot you—"

"You wanted me?"

She nodded quickly with her dimpled chin. "You know I did. I wasn't toying. Greenmore knew it. She didn't like me around you once she saw it. Then, she got your tests back, found out your 'potential.' She got meaner—really turned on me."

For a second, I was certain of something. I said, "Go with me."

"Where?"

"Cuba—Ariel is going." I sipped in a little air, to fortify myself. She saw it.

"You're gonna be an Heir, though. Don't mess with me."

"For us. To live. To get out of here." Saying it widened me, opened me, steadied me.

"I'm flesh," she said, breaking her gaze. "I'm a dier. You know what that means? Really? Yeared and ugly one day. You could go back to what you know." She shook her hair so hard wisps flew out. But she was closer to me. Her hands, unclasped.

"Why would I go back when I want to be with you?"

"Because you were raised for it." There was a slight noise then, her eyes dashed to the left, and down. Someone walking in the kitchen cooler, which was on the other side of the flour sacks. The door slammed, the sound was gone. "We can't be here too much longer, " she said. "The lunch crowd will be in."

"You are doomed if you stay here."

Her expression opened some. I thought I had a chance. But then she said, "What about Greenmore? Lydia? She runs you now."

"What about her?" Though that didn't seem exactly right, to just say, *What about her?*

"When you left, what did you tell her?"

She knew. How did she know?

"You were coming back to her? And now she has your Trust? Your future in her hands?"

I didn't deny it. I just said, "I won't keep to that now—"

She tightened her mouth. "You won't keep to what now? What?"

I didn't say a word. She saw I was hiding.

"Well then how do I know you will keep your promises to me? If you make a promise to me?" she asked. "We keep our promises here. I gave you up for one. To Landry." Her warm breath on my face.

"But you have to leave. Your brother-in-law's—"

"I have a fate." She avoided my gaze entirely for a second.

"You hate him. You'll have his children? Be a second wife?"

Her mouth lost its shape.

"Ariel says we have people in Cuba, we—"

"Well how do you know that's not some story? Hasn't he told a few in his life?"

"Ariel tells the truth. He's always—I found out. He's not a liar."

"Well, that is new." She paused for a second, straightened. She arrived back into her face. She was not slim and tall and regular like all the Heir women. She was true and ample inside her dress. I saw reason for hope. She was imagining it. Imagining us.

"If we did this, it wouldn't be just about our love. It would be about giving up who we are. Giving it up. You understand." She nodded, looked into me.

For a moment, I had a theory of everything—what I was doing, what I was going to do. It was Camille's clarity. She was taking it seriously. She knew more than I did. She knew what I felt and why I felt it. In her gaze, even, I saw Lazarus's actions—and his faith, too, and his loss of faith. It was Lazarus, not something that I, myself, Malcolm, had caused. I saw her as she saw me. She was considering it all, the whole plan, conjuring it in those brown eyes of hers. It became real, there, for the first time. I had to have her thoughtfulness in my life, to guide me. Her love.

"You will do it," I said. "You will. You will come with me."

"If you go talk to her first. Greenmore. Tell her where you are going."

"I'm not going," I said. "I can't be away from you."

"Yes, you are," she said. "You have to talk to her and see if you can say goodbye. See how it feels to go back to—that easy life. It's got no ordinary trouble, that life— "

"The ship leaves after the hurricane warning passes. Ariel told me the name. The Madder Rose. It's in the harbor now."

She shrugged, but I saw her softening. "You are asking a lot of me, and you aren't my kind," she said. "Maybe you are my love but not my kind—"

"I won't leave you." Someone came into the kitchen then. We heard him on the other side of the sacks. He turned on a recording of old rickety jazz.

"Well, then I will leave you—you talk to her, then come back to me," she said.

"Will you come with me?" I asked.

She looked straight at me. It was a very long pause, hovering near *yes*, a single nod. Then she left me there, joyful, bursting behind the flour sacks.

*

As soon as I started climbing up the steep pine stairs to the courthouse at two, I saw Klamath at the landing, waving at me. Throngs were behind him, scurrying down the stairs. I didn't understand. It was time for court to start again. "You are the one I need to see!" he shouted. He was wearing a hooded slicker, the one he wore on his boat.

He was in a terrible hurry. He explained briefly: court had been dismissed. The noon report said the hurricane, Isis, was indeed heading for the Sea of Pontchartrain. Serio's charges had been dropped; because they couldn't secure the jail in a storm, all but the serious felons had been let free. He was being released at this moment. They were headed out to the Pearl River, to the new Exodus lands, so was the entire population still left in Chef Menteur. Lydia was back from her Re-job and very worried about me, and hadn't left even though WELLVAC had recommended it, since a hurricane was in the Gulf. Why hadn't I communicated? I'd disappeared, as far as they were concerned. WELLVAC was coming for her that afternoon. She'd put it off to the last minute because she was waiting for me. "You need to see her. You have to come home. She has news, she says."

"What?" I asked.

"Don't know, be safe," he said, and he smiled at me like a man with a secret. He hugged me and as soon as he let go, I missed him. "Have to get moving," he said.

He meant both of us.

XIII

3:10 PM, October 21, 2121
Wood Palace on the Sea of Pontchartrain
Western Gulf De-Accessioned Territory, U.A. Protectorate

*I*t was a glassy sea, a white sky without any clouds. I pulled Serio's boat up to the dock. Klamath had given me the real keys and told me to put it in the boathouse for protection. When I turned from tying it up, there was Lydia, by the kitchen doors, looking splendid, in high water boots, a new long white storm coat with a shining collar framing her face. It was good to see her, in a way.

"Come in, I've missed you so—oh, what is that? Stitches in your ear? What has happened? You look so different, rough—the elements." That jarring intimacy. She had not forgotten. It seemed a lifetime since I'd last seen her, and also, no time at all. In her unblinking, steady, newly-lensed eyes, I saw. I was not blind now. Not to her desire.

She was larger, newly Treated, just had her Re-job. "Come now, take off your jacket, have you washed these things?"

She led me inside. Everything was the same as when I left, except that the pool in her room was overflowing slightly, so that there was a thin film of water on the floor, and the edges of her sheets and blankets on the square blue mountain in the corner that was her bed, were soaked. Things that might get wet from a surge were stacked up on the highest shelves. Klamath's handiwork. She did not seem to notice the water.

Her eyes were now gold again, her cheeks full, and vibrant. Her new prodermis round and inviting, I had to admit. She resembled herself when I first met her—same ash head job, same blue ivory, even teeth. Same scentless breath. But she had also changed. She was more contemporary. And she was solicitous of me. I didn't see her the way I used to see her at all. She was copy-beautiful—kin to ugly.

But I didn't exactly want to leave.

She said, "Sit beside me." I went over and sank into the bed, recalling the last time I was on it, making her promises. That now, I wasn't going to keep. Or was I? I felt sorry, confused.

"Home from the voyage," she said. "Let me look at you. What waylaid you? All these injuries—"

I began with the lien on my Trust. I was quite vague. Then, the scene in Port Gramercy, in the Sugarhouse. I left out certain characters. Then, jail, then Mississippi—the Sim Verite. I edited, didn't throw Heirs around, or strip them naked in swamps, flay them, or—I told myself I was getting to that scene in the back of the Sugarhouse, by the flour sacks, I was getting to that.

She interrupted. "He was always unstable, radical," when I got to Lazarus. "What did he do? Give yours away?"

I hesitated. Ariel told me not to tell anyone.

"What? What happened?"

I said, "He went the so-long."

Her mouth hung open.

"It is true," I said, and the sadness of it came to me, all over again.

"What a waste, he was an Heir, even if he was an idiot—it just isn't done. It is never done," she said.

I told her yes, I was sure. Made her promise to tell no one, but I was worried.

"Oh, that idiot, that radical idiot, I never liked him." She leaned forward, as if to embrace me.

I pulled back. I didn't fold into her arms. She didn't understand.

"It's all right, the taboo can be broken—only you and I are here—" she said. "Did he ruin your Trust? Please," she said. "Explain."

I shook my head. She thought I was only shy. I was shy, but also—

The back of Lydia's bed was wrought iron, and antique, and looked like a pair of gates. That I was never going to go through. I thought of that, for a moment. All this luxury and ease forsworn, for some beach in Cuba, some legend. For brown eyes.

"What did he do with the Trust?"

"He told WELLFI bank to put it in your name," I said. "Make you the sponsor."

"One thing rational," she snorted.

I nodded. "He had his reasons, he wrote them, he told us the story of his whole life—"

"Before he was an Heir, even?" She combed through my hair with her fingers. I was weary. Exhausted. I had been through so much. The difference between this timeless time with her, this suspension, and the low, noisy world where I'd spent the last twelve days. *You are back with her, you are home, the rest is chaos, she was good to you.*

"Never mind, don't trouble yourself with his reasons, he lost his mind, years ago. Honestly, anyone who would still cling to those old North notions, that everyone, even has a right, or that the world could sustain, or, or—such people would be mad, that is clear." She continued, stroking my rough hair. I wanted her to stop—it was pleasing, and confusing. She went on. "Would you hang yourself over the fact that dogs only live fifteen years? Or cats? Or—someone said something up at Memphis, that I thought was very wise—*Albers made us a new species, and we can't concern ourselves too much with the survivability of the other one.* I thought that very meaningful. I knew I had to take it in. That wisdom. I thought about how I had to give up my investigations. I see my error now. To think that other species have anything to teach—"

"I'm one of that kind," I said.

She looked up, sharply, for I was crossing her. "Not for long," she said. "That's my news. I know a way for you to be Treated sooner. Right after your Boundarytime. So we don't have to wait—I talked to Memphis, I made—"

I was alarmed by what I saw, behind her, in the two windows on either side of the bedstead. There was supposed to be a period of calm, another six hours before Isis approached. But crests of foam were marching forward toward the outside decks. She continued: "For me it was all still in the realm of theory—apparently not with Lazarus—I never doubted the Promise of the Reveal. Now you may think I may have—but my investigations were about *keeping* the Promise—I was looking in the wrong place, however. And you saved me. I am grateful."

"Well, he is gone now," I said and pulled away. She couldn't see what Camille saw, what losing him had meant to me.

"There used to be some saying among the Gramercy Nats—'don't speak ill of the so-longed,' something like that. The ones who worked at the Curing Tower. I guess you would know," she said. "I heard from Klamath about your exploits among the Gramercy girls. There was no way not to hear about that—went to jail with Serio? This girl—was it that fat thumb who used to work at the Curing Towers? Never mind. Of course it doesn't matter. *You know who you are, after all.*"

She stretched out her long, newly plumped and fattened arm. The prodermis was slightly thicker than the one she had before. She explained women were being minted, as it was said in Memphis, slightly thicker these days. She wanted me to notice. She went on. "Lazarus didn't get over that yearning, that Nat thing—that his life should mean something, have a purpose, that gnawing, you think can be satisfied, really satisfied—that's what he failed to overcome." Then she smiled. "It's an absurd proclivity, actually. What broke him? The truth! That it doesn't. That Chotchko thinks she has isolated, chemically—there is a way it might be obliterated. It's a trace of end-consciousness. It comes from having a deep imprint about the end, the foreknowledge there will be an end, when things will have their final meaning—this fallacy. In fact, she's trying something out on me, and I think it works very well. But you never had the problem. Grandiosity. It's a late form of grandiosity. In that you are lucky—except for your promise to me, your life hasn't had that impulse, to see a system, a shape, into which you might fit. You have controlled the impulse, haven't you? Once you told me, *What if its meaning is that it doesn't end?* Well you were right. Indeed, for a Not Yet you have done such a wonderful job of managing mostly all of your impulses, I've never said this before, have I? I think you are going to be a marvelous Heir, very apt, certain to fit in. In this floating world. I was taken in by some hope for a grand theory, but I went too far," she said. "You brought me back. I am so grateful. I mean, why go after the unknowable? Futility. Futility. Nothing is fixed. You kept me on the right path. You broke the strat rules, you knew that all rules can be broken—they are fluid like everything else—" She leaned over to me and kissed me—it wasn't what I'd thought. She was soft and cool, like cotton, that softness. She said, "Thank you. "

I winced. I worried when she saw this. "You aren't going to look for the conduit anymore? You aren't going to try to help the Chronics that way?" I asked. "Chart the territory?" I had to change the subject.

"I think that other purpose—the grandiose purpose—of finding the way out while in the body, is too ambitious. And probably dangerous. Even the mystics back there, the ancient Nat mystics, said most who ascend will come back mad. Look at our Chronics. Lunatics, half of them, certainly without Chotchko's serums. I was going mad. And you saved me. Your love!" Her features crumpled, and flopped, into a sentimental expression I'd never seen on her before. Very awkward, even ugly. She put her hands into my hands, humbling herself, and mouthed, "I love you."

I missed her old hands. These were recast. Hands speak of the person, say things the eyes and the face do not reveal, say things about the person's instrument, the person's interior, her capacity, her sensibility, what means she has been given to get through life, what tactics. Weakness and beauty, technique and roughness, sheer power, rapacious desires—these were things hands could announce. The proclivities of the body, the capacities—an artist's hands, a musician's hands, a mason's hands, a wrestler's hands. Even in Heirs these proclivities could be announced. I thought these things while she made me hold her newly-designed hands. She told me she chose from an array of one hundred and ninety-eight patterns. She explained the new ones were formed with nanotech cartilege fibers, which grew in her own bones like crystals might grow, amazing—this was done to lengthen the tips. Her fingers were so long that the tip past the final joint seemed to have been designed by some ancient, expressionist painter, like the long slender wisps of lily stalks, of iris leaves. But more and more, I missed her emaciated, blue-white body, that we found when we flayed her. Her actual, vulnerable, self. I had cared for her when she was that.

Then, with enormous relief, I thought of Camille's wide, supple hands, fingers thick and each one round as a child's sturdy pencil, all full of strength, and flexibility as well, and ready for rapid-working.

"I thought you might like them," Lydia said and then she showed me her ears. "I got these new at the same time. I was tired of the old ones," she said. "Soon as we leave, we can both go in and be redesigned. You will have to get a new ear, anyhow, up in Memphis. You can't have that scar. We don't have to always be the same lovers—we can change—you can be Hercules, and also Malcolm, and I can be Venus or Mona Lisa or Cinderella, or—we can do it every few decades. The prices are coming down."

She could see I was put off.

"Of course we can remain who we are if that is what you would like—Lydia and Malcolm and Malcolm and Lydia." And she kissed me full and dry on the mouth, again. I did not respond. She did not feel real.

"What is it?" she asked.

"You should go," I said. "Get ready to go—WELLVAC wants you out of here. Klamath said—"

"There's time," she said. "Besides—I don't really, believe in the hurricane, or whatever it is. I have never believed in these storms. These images they have of the past, of the wind, the risings tides, these promises of the doom—they never pan out. It just will not happen—I know this—these calamities they promise never do. Klamath was always claiming the house was going to flood. It never—"

"We shored it up for you two times," I said. "We raised it at least a foot, altogether, so you could stay here—Klamath and Serio and I, we spent months—when you were in retreat."

"Is that what you were doing?" she asked blankly.

"We used jacks, special ones, for fixing pilings underwater—don't you remember?"

"So many things have happened ," she said, with a laugh. "You and the staff, your little escapades—out here in the country. I thought, after I get you back from Memphis, we will go to civilization. Back to the Towers. I would like to return, rework my opus—I don't think the gossips will be that bad. My lover, a Nuovo, that will just be the way it is. We will overcome. They will just have to get used to it." She kissed me again.

"What is wrong?" she asked. "You miss that madman? Things you have seen on your journey? Forget them. Chotchko has wonderful protocols for forgetting. Everything will be so obvious when you are Treated. I've called in all sorts of favors. They will take you within the year. They will. Isn't that wonderful?"

I did not want to disappoint her. It was a small thing, a thread—this not wanting to hurt her—and also, something more, possibly, held me back.

I didn't answer. She said, "Oh darling, don't be so shy. You have always been so shy. Be bold."

But I wasn't bold.

Later we were puttering around in the kitchen—she'd taken up the notion that I needed coffee, and then she had taken up the even stranger notion that she was going to prepare it for me. It was oddly charming, to see her in her elegant gown and her elaborate head job, and her new pin-point thin fingers trying to negotiate around a Nat kitchen, trying to do something for her "lover." To please me. I wondered if she'd seen my face when she'd referred to Camille, called her a fat thumb. Of course Lydia was pitiful at making coffee. While I was watching her, it came to me to tell her—about Ariel and his quest. And the Mo Lion episode in Mississippi. As a way of working around to my subject, the thing I had to tell her that I hadn't been able to tell her yet. Would I be able to? She asked several questions, which seemed to me casual. When she finally put something in front of me in a dark glass cup—something that came from a coffee press, something mixed with half a can of Mexican canned milk, the same thickness and color as river mud, I finished the Ariel story, and briefly outlined the Mo Lion story. I thought of taking out the letter to show her, but then, I remembered I was keeping it, taking it with me—wasn't I?

She was dipping her finger into the mud, taking a taste. She was cheating, of course—brosias only is the rule for the newly returned from the Re-job, any hint of Nat food could hurt the newly worked stomachs. But she was taking the risk, in order to share something.

Her interest reminded me of the days last summer before we had persuaded her to go, when she insisted we sit outside. She would slurp down bits of shrimp and broth out of my bowl. When she wanted things she couldn't have—it was her yearning, that had attracted me, her curiosity, her bravery—for an Heir, she was very brave. I saw.

"Did I show the charm? What Ariel based his belief on?" I asked.

"What charm?" she asked

"I have it," I said. I pulled it from my pocket, as I had done for Mo Lion.

She picked it up and put it right down. As if handling it were a hazard. Her shoulders crunched, moved up toward her new tiny ears, and then she was consciously trying to lower them, trying to push down on the thin cords of her neck, or elongate her spine so they wouldn't show as much.

"What is it?" I asked.

"Now, you say, he went to these Gaists and they had the birth records for the West Florida Federation—including the rebels? The ones that clung to the idea of a new state? Who followed John of Pensacola?"

"You have heard of this?" I asked. "But then, you knew some of them earlier, didn't you?" I remembered her big books with the pictures.

Something complicated was going on behind her eyes. "The John I knew became the radical, John of Pensacola. I knew him in his youth. Didn't I show you his picture?" Some new struggle, a smaller version of the dance in the cords of her neck. It was odd, to see such a reaction in an Heir. Prodermises were like full body masks. "So you know, then? Ariel saw the records of these births?"

"That was the scientist you were with? Yes, I see," I said. But I didn't see.

"So you know, I knew it would be all right, I never bothered, really, once I realized—" she said. "This was ninety-some years ago. It's practically as if the statute of limitations. The ownership, the—then he did things to them, to their genes," she backtracked. "And Ariel has made some connection between these infants born at the West Florida Federation, all during the time the place was under blockade—and these others born earlier— "

"He says we were born from surrogates, who received the frozen embryos. John had lost most of his followers, so he was breeding more. Something like that," I said. "They call them Salamanders, there are myths about them. Apparently they are revered, by those who believe in the West Florida cause, and others—they have gifts, he says—"

She nodded quietly, timidly, almost. "Well then you don't know," she said.

"He says he and I were two more—"

She told me to shush.

"It is true, the history, the embargo, the raids, the torpedo boats, the sham of help from Spain—some of the refugees washed up on Haiti. Others, on Cuba. One small group fled into the Alabama hills. I thought perhaps you'd come from them. There were always rumors there were more than Jude and Neil." She rubbed her plump new cheek with her long spidery hands. As if she were wiping something away. Her face was thick and hard to read.

She took a long time, not speaking. "So do you know? Or not," she said, finally. Then she took a deep breath. "Remember I used to ask you questions, what you thought about a past life? I thought you were second generation somehow, a descendent." Then she looked out the slender window by the kitchen table, to avoid me.

"What?"

"They are called second-born. That was what John named them, when he saw how they developed—"

I looked out there, too. The whitecaps tumbling over each other, as before, perhaps speeding up. As if a film had been put on double-time, now. She looked back, straightening her spine. She smiled her smile that meant love, which made me feel rather sick inside. I didn't like feeling sorry for her. "What is it?" I asked.

She said, "First, my part. I will tell you. You should know. I suppose. It has to do with your root self. I felt I owed him this small thing. He'd been my helpmeet—steadfast. Like you. So like you—always close. For his part, he saw the best in me, which is my intellect. I thought it would be a good thing, to sacrifice. Sacrifice is always a mistake—you know that, don't you? We are better than such impulses, they are based on a false premise—that we are part of something more than ourselves. A false premise, terribly powerful. But I will never believe it again." She shook her decorated head. "And how many perspectives can one woman afford? Even if she is intelligent? But I was under its spell in those days. And then he gave me that drug, which I couldn't stand. It was part of the procedure. I was past forty, still a Nat. I felt for several days as if I were swimming in my own hot milk. Femininity, breeding—there's a terrible side to it. I felt awful things—sadness, remorse, slogging through these mammal feelings, so good when they are gone—you have no idea, and you won't, you are male. None of the things you yearn for ripen so readily into pain."

Yes they do, I thought to myself. For I yearned to leave her, and I felt all the pain of it.

The waves were rising even more now, one broke over the outside pier. I didn't know what she was talking about. Perhaps by then, I did know, but I didn't let myself. I just felt queasy. As if we were on a boat that was rocking.

"Pain in your belly, this sense of something being drawn down and then in, this yearning one has to give everything away—to turn oneself inside out—to want this—can you imagine, wanting this? Never mind. He put me on a table, and in the stirrups like a cow, just like a cow. With a tiny tube, a miniscule straw, sip-sip-sip, ova, ova, and then I was altered. It was illegal. For me, the Procreation Laws had gone into effect, technically, at that point. It was after I'd won the Albers Prize. I was a Not Yet. I couldn't reproduce! 'Prizewinners,' he said, 'high quality,' he said. He flattered me. He took the eggs, and he went in and worked on them. He fertilized them himself. He was younger than me. I was almost forty." Her face came right into mine, not even inches away. "In fact, I saw that the first moment I laid eyes on you, but I didn't want to believe it. It was only later, when I saw how you did on your tests, then when I'd read his old letters, what he said about the malformation of the mouth. Albers had made it clear that genes couldn't work. Not for our extension. Not for our perpetuation. Our descendants, yes, perhaps, but they were not us, so what was the point? And John said that was short sighted, we could change the whole next generation. The whole race, not just the elite. He said he'd found the genes, the ones for aging, the ones that program death—but he hadn't. Evolving. That thing John always believed in, evolving. But honestly, why evolve?" She looked at me as if I understood. As if I already knew. Or perhaps she hoped it, so she wouldn't have to tell me. "When they matured, the children, whom he called the second-borns, it was clear they would age—so he hadn't succeeded as he had expected: instead, they had a certain vision. He said, 'I've not cured them of death. I've cured them of fearing it. It's amazing. It's how they perceive, what they perceive! They don't live only in this time and place. They are immortal in another way—as if in the moment. It's a flaw, how we see time. *They don't have that flaw!*' Whatever that means. He made sure they were protected, kept out of the public eye in Cuba, so they could develop, undisturbed. But then, they attracted people around them. He described to me, particularly, what they said about the experience of being formed, entering the tiny body of a baby—he said they had told him what it was like—a condensation, a pressure—they remembered death, they knew. He said I should be proud, to be their—donor was not the word he used. He wrote in great detail about their descriptions of the 'voyage' over there, on the other side of this, as he put it—quite a geography, as he put it—mystical clap trap, you know, the kind of thing I was under the sway of." She pouted.

"How many are there?" I asked.

"I'm not proud to have brought such sufferers into the world, who don't have the good genes to find a bearable desirable amnesia. Who are starting, for Alber's sake, some kind of movement, cult. It's disgraceful, actually."

"Was this, that John wrote you, was this why you wanted to go find that way, that conduit? That passage? That's why you took up that research?"

"I suppose," she shrugged. "But I certainly didn't want anyone descended from me to feel any pain, to suffer, to know death—or any who are here now."

"So there were others?" I asked. "He harvested eggs from lots of women? This was a program?"

She didn't answer. "So you really *don't* know?"

Then it came to me. Finally, it came to me, consciously. Came at me from behind, like an attack. I was stunned, numb.

"Well, I didn't bear you. I was nearly a hundred when you were born—I was an Heir when you were born. So it doesn't count. But it turns out I'm actually, technically—but it's just an artifact, I thought grandmother, possibly, even great—but of course he froze them, kept them," she said. "An anomalous, irritating fact, which doesn't make a bit of difference." She wagged her head, and backed away, as if something in my gaze had set her back. "It doesn't make any difference to our love, except to seal it," she said. "In fact perhaps it is one of the reasons I consented to your offer. There is a clarity about it, a symmetry, something mysterious, we have met—somehow—if you want that to be romantic, I suppose it is."

She was hugely offended when I laughed. Her long lie to me now exposed, that last thread, burned away in an instant. I was free. My freedom was the name of that laugh. I was free. "How could you not have told me?"

"You are going to enter the Reveal, you are going—once you do you will understand the sense of keeping all that at bay, you will, you won't see the world as you do now. Not at all. We are different. You are my son, but if you stay like this, you will—you still wouldn't be who you are. We are actually formed by what we don't know—why probe? What's the use?"

"You knew? You were my mother? You let me promise—"

"I imagined—" she said. "From the first time I saw you. Then there were your tests. I already said this. Do I have to go over it?"

"From my looks?"

"If you must know," she sighed. "You look a great deal like John. At first, this was unconscious. I couldn't have known, or even imagined. But then I heard more and more about the West Florida remnants, and so I entertained the idea. Oh, this is so unpleasant. You have his height, his build. Really, if you think about it, it's such a fateful, surprising, marvelous—maybe I did know from the beginning—"

Then she was angry because I stood up, and I was walking over toward the French doors, the ones she'd come through that day when she said she wanted some of our dinner. "Well are you going to be some kind of hysteric, with an antique prejudice? You are not a Nat. You've practically been to Memphis. Besides, the Salamanders don't get this vision clearly until they are twenty-six or twenty-seven. We can stop you before—you are so well suited to help me with the research! Who better!"

I saw, then, a large boat anchored at a great distance out the window. A helicopter buzzing overhead, the size of a bumble bee on the horizon but coming our way.

"How could it matter to you? These entanglements don't matter, the things John made me do, they don't matter—we don't *have* to live in consequences. We are going beyond them. We aren't Nats. But what if we were? Look how you cling to that unfortunate event with Lazarus! Look at what grief is! Cast something over it. Forget its face, its contours. Is that not natural? That angel is natural, she comes and gives you forgetting. Is that not the truth? It's something good, that John manipulated it away? What if what John did is the greatest curse? If you see how life really is, when it burns down to black, or when you are squeezed out of it or back into it, some flailing pitiful baby, vulnerable—how could you go on at all?" She touched the place above my lip. "You don't have to remember coming into this body, you don't remember where you were before, you don't—the filter, the philtrum, is natural, and John etched that out. What he's done is wrong. It's against—is that not natural, to want a perimeter between yourself and that pain? That's the whole point. Albers knew—"

I shook my head *no*. No.

"You will have years—years, our therapies are intricate, sublime—"

"I am not getting Treated," I said. "I'm going away." I felt the ground beneath me steadying.

"How could you? Are you mad? Not be Treated?"

"Not be Treated."

She sat down and took it in. "Oh, that Nat prejudice. It doesn't matter! I can't believe you would care!" But she knew I meant it. As if she had expected this all along, she regained her composure. She told me I was being an idiot, romantic, and romanticism was idiotic, as there was no such thing as "ceasing upon the midnight with no pain." She even said, "You are a show off. Hah! So was your father."

Of all the things she told me that day, that was the one I liked the most.

I told her, simply, no. I didn't even ask her, '*How can you take your son for your lover? How do you do that?*'

"Heirs are eternal, we've no low rules, you don't see, you poor boy, you don't—" But, she was, for a moment, defeated, resigned. "You will regret this forever, not coming with me. When you are lying on your bed and saying goodbye, so long, no matter what you see, you will regret it," she said.

I sensed she was a bit cowed by the fact of who I was. Of our relation, exposed. I knew she would have always kept it from me. It didn't serve her purposes for me to know.

The WELLFI copter came in close. It opened its door, lowered a harness. Called for her. It was quite sudden, in a way. Abrupt.

I helped her out onto the deck outside the kitchen. She let me lift her into the stiff, fortified straps. They lowered a helmet. I strapped her in. I didn't think about touching her. With her big gold false eyes she looked up at me, pleadingly. I signaled they could haul her up.

There she was, my mother, dangling in the air, her new hands long claws in her lap. I wasn't used to any of it yet. But it was all very true.

*

And two minutes later, she was settled into her swinging seat, being hoisted up, up into the WELLVAC helicopter. She had yielded, before, but now at the last moment, she was chatting and talking as rapidly, as fondly, as when I first came in. As if there were still a chance for me to change my mind. The odd thing was, she was no longer beside me. I was still standing on the docks outside the kitchen. There was a patch of the watery marsh—ever widening—between us and a good twenty feet of sky. She was swinging in the air and completely ignoring the fact. Two at the top were waiting to receive her, and unstrap her, fly her away to the ship at the horizon, rescue her.

I was waving goodbye. But she wouldn't stop talking.

"You really aren't coming? How crazy are you?" she shouted as she drew closer and closer to the open machine. "How can it matter what we are as Nats? Heirs don't have the categories, mother, son, father, daughter—these are absurd, I can't believe!" She was yelling over the sound of the blades. It was possible I would never see her again. I didn't want that to be true.

The attendants above didn't understand. One screamed down through a megaphone: "We have a place for you—she's your holder? She reserved two seats! We got the authorization to take a non-Heir!"

I shook my head and shouted, "NO!"

She was inside the copter, then, in the doorway, being lifted out of the straps. As it rose, she was getting harder and harder to comprehend, with the sound of the sea and the motor, and the wind of the blades, which took her speech and broke it down into small parts, like the feathers flying off of a bird. She was being shuffled back into her safety, her envelope. She was being cloaked and covered—being swaddled, carried off, nursed and cared for.

Yet, I felt as if I were being born.

She said I was a fool. I yelled back, "Yes, I am a fool!" Oh, I would miss her, her intellect, her curiosity, her bravery. It was my mother's bravery. And I would be brave. I remembered Serpent's knife, opened it, found the wire cutters, and, in a gesture I hoped she could still see, I clipped away my collar, tossed it out into the roiling waves.

"You fool! You will regret forever!" she screamed, but the words fell into little bits, only the feeling, which was a sort of love.

But, then, at the last, as I watched her, and as the helicopter hovered over the gray rough water—something happened I could not have predicted.

First, there was a sort of shudder in the air, as if some kind of depth, or thickness, had been added. At the same time, a form, like a shroud, a veil, came away. It was invisible, nevertheless, I saw it with an inner eye as it peeled back.

And, then, all at once, at least for me, for Malcolm de Lazarus, for that one man, with his limits, his outline, his tale, this: the air, and the sky, merged—the wood of the pier and the crisp fabric of my jacket, the air going in and out of my mouth, my anger at her, and my adoration of her, and the terror and thrill I felt at the future, and the soft face of my Camille and the journey we had dared to imagine—became all one single thing. My life so far, and in the future, collapsed, closed in—all the boundaries were lines that led to this one instant. There was only the moment, which was a passage, an opening. This was not simple, it was not painless. It was almost too much to know.

I saw a single wave that all was a part of, and I was part of it, as well as watching it. It went through me, even as I observed it. This was not a contradiction. The perimeter was porous. The boundary, no boundary, only a winding line, a path, just then—

Her last words to me I could make out: "But you want to live forever. Don't you? Everyone does. Don't lie, you can't lie—"

"Of course I do, of course!" I said with my own voice. "I do."

Then, in my wounded ear, I heard the roar.

Acknowledgements

Thanks to Rodger, first, for his constancy, his love, and his idea of hero.

Thanks to Laura Mullen, Lady of the Resurrection, for a vision of the whole brought to me out of friendship.

And to the editors and agents and fellow authors who helped it along the way:

Ralph Adamo and Chris Chambers of *New Orleans Review*, Anne Gisleson of *Intersections*, Joshua Ellisson of *Habitus*, Valerie Martin, Stuart Dybek, Rosellen Brown, and Ellen Levine.

And to the Louisiana Board of Regents for the ATLAS grant to complete this work.

And to Bill Lavender, for taking this chance.

Also Available from

General Titles

The Neighborhood Story Project

Signed, The President by Kenneth Phillips, 978-1-60801-015-8 (2010)

Houses of Beauty: From Englishtown to the Seventh Ward by Susan Henry, 978-1-60801-014-1 (2010)

Coming Out the Door for the Ninth Ward edited by Rachel Breunlin, 978-0-9706190-9-9 (2006)

Cornerstones: Celebrating the Everyday Monuments & Gathering Places of New Orleans edited by Rachel Breunlin, 978-0-9706190-3-7 (2008)

The Engaged Writes Series

Medea and Her War Machines by Ioan Flora, translated by Adam J. Sorkin, 978-1-60801-067-7 (2011)

Together by Julius Chingono and John Eppel, 978-1-60801-049-3 (2011)

Vegetal Sex (O Sexo Vegetal) by Sergio Medeiros, translated by Raymond L.Bianchi, 978-1-60801-046-2 (2010)

*Wounded Days (Los Días Heridos) by Leticia Luna, translated by Toshiya Kamei, 978-1-60801-042-4 (2010)

When the Water Came: Evacuees of Hurricane Katrina by Cynthia Hogue & Rebecca Ross, 978-1-60801-012-7 (2010)

*A Passenger from the West by Nabile Farès, translated by Peter Thompson, 978-1-60801-008-0 (2010)

*Everybody Knows What Time It Is by Reginald Martin, 978-1-60801-011-0 (2010)

*Green Fields: Crime, Punishment, & a Boyhood Between by Bob Cowser, Jr., 978-1-60801-018-9 (2010)

*Open Correspondence: An Epistolary Dialogue by Abdelkébir Khatibi and Rita El Khayat, translated by Safoi Babana-Hampton, Valérie K. Orlando, Mary Vogl, 978-1-60801-021-9 (2010)

Gravestones (Lápidas) by Antonio Gamoneda, translated by Donald Wellman, 978-1-60801-002-8 (2009)

Hearing Your Story: Songs of History and Life for Sand Roses by Nabile Farès translated by Peter Thompson, 978-0-9728143-7-9 (2008)

The Katrina Papers: A Journal of Trauma and Recovery by Jerry W. Ward, Jr., 978-0-9728143-3-1 (2008)

Contemporary Poetry

California Redemption Values by Kevin Opstedal, 978-1-60801-066-0 (2011)

Atlanta Poets Group Anthology: The Lattice Inside by Atlanta Poets Group, 978-1-60801-064-6 (2011)

Makebelieve by Caitlin Scholl, 978-1-60801-056-1 (2011)

Dear Oxygen: New and Selected Poems by Lewis MacAdams, edited by Kevin Opstedal, 978-1-60801-059-2 (2011)

Only More So by Tony Lopez, 978-1-60801-057-8 (2011)

Enridged by Brian Richards, 978-1-60801-047-9 (2011)

A Gallery of Ghosts by John Gery, 978-0-9728143-4-8 (2008)

The Ezra Pound Center for Literature

The Poets of the Sala Capizucchi (I Poeti della Sala Capizucchi) edited by Caterina Ricciardi and John Gery, 978-1-60801-068-4 (2011)

Trespassing, by Patrizia de Rachewiltz, 978-1-60801-060-8 (2011)

*The Imagist Poem: Modern Poetry in Miniature edited by William Pratt, 978-0-9728143-8-6 (2008)

Contemporary Austrian Studies

Global Austria: Austria's Place in Europe and the World, Günter Bischof, Fritz Plasser (Eds.), Alexander Smith, Guest Editor, 978-1-60801-062-2 (2011)

From Empire to Republic: Post-World-War-I Austria Volume 19 edited by Günter Bischof, Fritz Plasser and Peter Berger, 978-1-60801-025-7 (2010)

The Schüssel Era in Austria Volume 18 edited by Günter Bischof & Fritz Plasser, 978-1-60801-009-7 (2009)

*Also available as E-book